IRRESISTIBLE TEMPTATION

Ellie's nearness was intoxicating enough, without the heady scent of rose water, and although Kale had intended to remain aloof, he found himself drawn closer and closer to her. Cupping her face in his hand, he brought his lips to hers.

And although Ellie had intended to resist, her need was too great. She swayed toward him and he steadied her with a hand to her waist. How easy it would be to give in to his passion—and her own. She had never experienced a need quite as great as the yearning to be in his arms, loving and being loved.

His hand tightened on her waist. "You're hell to resist," he mumbled against her mouth.

Her heart skipped precariously. "Lust is a hard thing to control."

He rested his lips on the top of her head, savoring the silky feel of her curls against his skin. He removed the combs she wore and let her hair fall around his face. "You're right," he whispered. . . .

FIERY ROMANCE

CALIFORNIA CARESS (2771, $3.75)
by Rebecca Sinclair

Hope Bennett was determined to save her brother's life.
And if that meant paying notorious gunslinger Drake Fra-
zier to take his place in a fight, she'd barter her last gold
nugget. But Hope soon discovered she'd have to give the
handsome rattlesnake more than riches if she wanted his
help. His improper demands infuriated her; even as she
luxuriated in the tantalizing heat of his embrace, she
refused to yield to her desires.

ARIZONA CAPTIVE (2718, $3.75)
by Laree Bryant

Logan Powers had always taken his role as a lady-killer
very seriously and no woman was going to change that.
Not even the breathtakingly beautiful Callie Nolan with
her luxuriant black hair and startling blue eyes. Logan
might have considered a lusty romp with her but it was apparent she was a lady, through and through. Hard as he
tried, Logan couldn't resist wanting to take her warm slen-
der body in his arms and hold her close to his heart forever.

DECEPTION'S EMBRACE (2720, $3.75)
by Jeanne Hansen

Terrified heiress Katrina Montgomery fled Memphis with
what little she could carry and headed west, hiding in a
freight car. By the time she reached Kansas City, she was
feeling almost safe . . . until the handsomest man she'd
ever seen entered the car and swept her into his embrace.
She didn't know who he was or why he refused to let her
go, but when she gazed into his eyes, she somehow knew
she could trust him with her life . . . and her heart.

*Available wherever paperbacks are sold, or order direct from the
Publisher. Send cover price plus 50¢ per copy for mailing and
handling to Zebra Books, Dept. 3533, 475 Park Avenue South,
New York, N.Y. 10016. Residents of New York, New Jersey and
Pennsylvania must include sales tax. DO NOT SEND CASH.*

Vivian Vaughan

Sweet Autumn Surrender

ZEBRA BOOKS
KENSINGTON PUBLISHING CORP.

To the Alvin Library Staff
and
To the Alvin Library League

friends, supporters, ALL

ZEBRA BOOKS

are published by

Kensington Publishing Corp.
475 Park Avenue South
New York, NY 10016

First printing: October, 1991

Printed in the United States of America

Prologue

August 1878
Summer Valley, Texas

"Ellie Jarrett! You know better than to use my front door. Get inside this house before someone sees you!"

Ellie allowed Lavender Sealy to drag her inside the opulent foyer, close the rose-etched front door, and pull her down the thick Persian carpet to the back of the Lady Bug Pleasure Emporium.

Skidding past the parlor, she managed a fleeting smile for Daisy and Poppy, who lounged on the red velvet settee with tall glasses of pink lemonade.

To her left, she glimpsed Snake in the gambling room, plinking away at the piano to empty gaming tables and unoccupied barstools.

Two o'clock on Wednesday afternoon was a slow time at the Lady Bug. Wednesday always had been the slowest day of the week, except when a trail drive was passing through town.

Ellie followed her benefactor down the long corridor.

5

Memories of her years spent here with Lavender and the girls brought a rush of poignant emotion. Regardless of what others chose to call her—madam, painted lady, or just plain whore—Lavender Sealy was acknowledged by all as a businesswoman of the first order, managing her finances, her house, and her girls with the acumen of an investment banker. Although she specialized in selling flesh by the hour, she was also a mistress—madam, some preferred to say—at buying respect.

The community of Summer Valley was living proof of that fact. No sooner had she moved to town than the children received a new school building complete with desks and ample sets of *McGuffey's Readers*, the church received new pews and a new bell, and the schoolmaster and pastor were given free services for life at the Lady Bug Pleasure Emporium. The last of these, of course, was not as widely publicized as the others.

Which was the reason Lavender Sealy had chosen a hill on the edge of town on which to erect her three-story pink frame establishment: the path to the back door could not be viewed from town.

"I've told you to use the back entrance." Lavender ushered Ellie into her own lavish quarters at the rear of the mansion. As usual, upon entering these private rooms one was overwhelmed by lavender—both the scent and the color. Every piece of satin, velvet, lace, and voile was some variation of the color; every tabletop held cut-glass dishes filled with potpourri made from the flower. If one asked for a chance to wash one's hands, Ellie knew, the offered soap would be a pale shade of lavender; one's hands would reek with the aroma for days.

Having been part of Lavender's household for most of

her twenty-four years, Ellie rarely noticed, except, as now, when she had been away for a while.

"I wasn't thinking," she explained, dropping to the needlepoint settee—worked in shades of lavender, of course.

"Start thinking, Ellie. You're a married woman. Your reputation—"

"Lavender, I need your help."

Instantly the older woman ceased her tirade. Stooping, she peered into Ellie's face. "Mercy, you look like you've been through a wringer. What is it, baby?"

"Benjamin—" The thought of finally uttering the dreadful words brought a tremble to Ellie's voice. "He's gone."

Lavender straightened as if someone had rammed a poker up her spine. "Gone? That bastard left you? I thought I knew men! Can't you trust any of them? Why, he was old enough to be your father, a kindly gentleman . . ." She sank to her knees before Ellie, clasping Ellie's hands in her own. "God, baby, why did I talk you into marrying him?"

"Lavender, hush. He didn't leave me. I don't know where he is, but something terrible has happened to him. I know it. I—" Again her voice faltered and she felt tears rush to her eyes.

Rising to the occasion, Lavender poured pink lemonade from a silver pitcher into a crystal glass. She handed it to Ellie along with a heavily embroidered linen handkerchief.

"Blow your nose, baby." She set the glass on a lacquered coaster on the marble-topped side table, then seated herself opposite Ellie. She watched silently while Ellie obeyed by blowing her nose into the handkerchief.

7

"Now, drink a big swallow of my special lemonade."

Ellie drank. By *special*, she knew Lavender meant *laced with red wine*; how heavily depended upon in what part of the Lady Bug one found oneself, in whose company, and especially upon who one was. Ellie was privileged around here; she always had been. Lavender considered her the child she never had, and the girls did, too—even those who were younger than Ellie herself and those who had not been with Lavender half as long.

"Now, why do you think something terrible has happened to him?" Before Ellie could answer, Lavender cursed again. "If that sonofabitch has run off and left you, he'll answer to me."

Ellie smiled, comforted somewhat by Lavender's predictable reaction. The dear woman meant every word of her threat, and she could carry it through. Only a fraction of an inch below six feet tall, with bones to fit her size, Lavender Sealy was a force to be reckoned with, and not many men—or women, for that matter—chose to. For Benjamin's sake, Ellie wished he would have to face Lavender's wrath; that would mean he was still alive.

But deep in her heart, she feared the worst. "He didn't run off from me," she protested. "He rode out to the north bedding grounds." She paused to catch a ragged breath. "And he never came back. It's been over a week, now."

"Over a week? Why didn't you come to town earlier? We should have had a posse out looking for him days ago."

"I *have* been looking, Lavender. I've ridden over every part of the ranch, practically inch by inch. There's no sign of him."

Lavender's jaws tightened. "The sonofabitch likely—"

Ellie shook her head, stopping Lavender's words with her tear-filled eyes. "Yesterday morning I found one of his boots on my back doorstep. It was covered with . . . with dried blood."

Tears rolled down her cheeks. This time when Lavender dropped to her knees, she pulled Ellie's head to her own ample bosom, smoothing her hair against the crown of her head with gentle strokes. "There, there, baby."

Ellie drew back and wiped her eyes. "Something *terrible* has happened to him."

"Maybe his horse pitched him off, and a varmint dragged his boot—"

"No. I would have found his body, or the horse would have returned by now."

Lavender nodded in hushed agreement.

"I found no sign of his horse." Her voice rose in frustration. "His horse would have come home. Horses always return to the place where they've been fed. His horse—"

"There, there," Lavender shushed. "I agree. It does look bad. You can't go back to the ranch. You're staying right here until we settle this thing."

"I have to go home," Ellie objected. "There's something else. Several times since Benjamin . . . ah, several times since then, I've seen a fire up on the hill. Late yesterday afternoon I slipped up there and caught them red-handed."

"Caught who?"

"Circle R men. Two of them were camped in one of the rock shelters above the house. They denied it, of course. Said they were hunting strays. But I saw the provisions inside the shelter."

9

"Now, it's certain . . . you are *not* returning to that ranch."

"I must, Lavender. Don't you see? Matt Rainey and his coyote of a brother are just waiting for a chance to take our creek bottom. They could even have moved in while I was in town." She shrugged. "But I had to have supplies."

Lavender ran a hand through her lavender hair, a color she achieved, as Ellie had observed on numerous occasions, by adding bluing to the rinse water. The older Lavender got, the more color her hair took on as her blonde hair turned gray and absorbed more of the blue color.

"Well, you aren't going back out there alone, baby. I'll send Snake with you."

"You need him here."

"Not for a few days." Crossing to the door, Lavender called down the hallway. "Snaaaake." She turned quickly back to Ellie. "Did you bring the wagon?"

Ellie nodded, comforted once more by the familiarity of Lavender's manner: she could have been issuing orders to her girls at receiving time. She was good at issuing orders and at seeing them carried through.

"Snake will drive you to the Bon Ton for supplies," Lavender continued. "While he's filling your order, you run down to the telegraph office and wire the sheriff—"

"In Llano County? He wouldn't drop everything and ride a hundred miles to find a missing man."

"There's no other choice, baby."

"Unless I do what the Raineys have done. I can hire gunfighters, too." Her words were couched in grim tones which seemed to rise from her very heart.

Lavender sighed. "Didn't you tell me Benjamin has a

10

brother in the Texas Rangers?"

"Carson Jarrett. But he—"

"No buts. You telegraph him while Snake picks up your order at the Bon Ton."

"What do I tell him? What if he's busy?"

"Ellie, you need help. And if Benjamin is missing, his family needs to know."

Ellie sighed. "There's a mess of them, his family. Two sisters and five brothers, not counting Benjamin. I suppose they should all be told."

"Yes, they should. If Benjamin Jarrett has met with foul play, his family is entitled to know about it."

In the end Ellie relented, allowing Snake to drive her to the general store. She gave him her grocery list to fill while she sent a telegram—to Carson Jarrett, in care of Ranger Headquarters in Austin. Alerting the entire family would have been admitting to a hopelessness she refused to consider.

Besides, a few members of the Jarrett family would be worse to deal with than the Raineys themselves. One brother, Kale, his name was, was a known gunfighter. And regardless of what she told Lavender, she had no intention of stooping to the level of the Raineys. If Carson couldn't help, she would discover some other way to find Benjamin.

Armando Costello greeted her when she emerged from the telegraph office.

"What's this all about, Ellie? Lavender tells me Benjamin is missing."

She explained in clipped syllables, afraid to tempt tears here on the boardwalk in the presence of her husband's best friend.

"You've searched the entire ranch?"

11

She nodded, ducking her head when she felt her chin quiver. Armando Costello did not miss it, however . . . his gambler's instinct, she thought. A gambler would of necessity possess sharp eyes and a quick wit.

He placed a consoling arm around her shoulders. "Come, come, my dear. You are no longer alone. Together we will find my friend Benjamin. But I must chastise you for not coming to me immediately."

She shrugged, tears brimming. "I thought—"

"No need to explain," he assured her. "We'll move forward from here."

And indeed they did. Armando Costello sent Snake back to the Lady Bug and drove Ellie to the ranch himself.

"If Circle R men are still spying on you, you can bet I won't just send them packing," he exclaimed. "I'll be hard pressed not to plant them six feet under."

"I won't tolerate violence, Armando. You know that. Not even if—"

Her shoulders trembled, and he loosened one hand from the reins to draw her near. "Come now, my girl. There's a simple explanation for all this, and I intend to find it. We'll have Benjamin home before that Texas Ranger even gets your message."

October 1878
Doan's Crossing on the Red River

Kale Jarrett slapped dust off his breeches with the brim of his hat and pushed through the bat-winged doors of the Bee Hive Saloon. The telegram from his brother Carson crackled in his shirt pocket, reminding him of urgent

12

business down south. But Sheriff Yates had said McKenzie wanted a word with him here in the saloon, and he could sure do with a drink to wet the trail dust.

Ordering rye at the bar, he faced the crowded room, searching for Mack McKenzie . . . the usual mixture of buffalo hunters and trail-herd cowboys like himself, he decided, and a couple of soldiers from Fort Griffin.

He tossed back the rye, then saw Mack in the far corner, waving in his direction.

"Kale Jarrett, you ol' leather pounder! Come on over here."

A sudden hush fell over the room when Kale picked up the bottle and headed for Mack's table. He stepped gingerly, as if through a den of rattlers, avoiding stares and outstretched feet as he would have the deadly snakes. He set the bottle down and shook hands with his friend.

"Long time no see."

"Same here, Jarrett," Mack smiled. They sat down. "Where've you been keeping yourself?"

"Just rode in from a drive up the Western. We took old Shanghai's herd clear up to Wyoming." Kale lifted the bottle, took a long pull, and wiped his mouth with his sleeve. "This here rye sure hits the spot after three months of gyp water and belly-wash." Laughter and conversation commenced around them and Kale relaxed, hearing the crowd return to its own business.

Mack leaned across the table toward his friend. "What you got up your sleeve for the winter?"

"I was headed for a line camp on the Spinnin' S, but Yates had this telegram waiting for me." He patted his shirt pocket and took another swig of rye.

"Yeah?"

Kale nodded. "From my brother Carson, the ranger.

Says our older brother Benjamin has turned up missing down in Summer Valley. Left his wife Ellie alone and in some kind of trouble."

"Why don't you let Carson handle that and you throw in with me?"

"No can do," Kale answered. "Carson's off on business in Mexico, and Ellie needs help fast. The telegram's been sitting here going on two months already."

"The trouble's likely settled, then," Mack said. "Sure hate for you to miss out on this deal. My brother-in-law out in Californy has made me a proposition, and I need someone like you to come along."

Kale cocked his head sideways. "Someone like me?"

"Now, don't go gettin' riled. I didn't mean no offense. You know what I'm talking about, someone with horse sense, but who ain't afraid of the devil. Hell, Jarrett, nobody steps on your toes or rides your pet horse."

Kale Jarrett shook his head, grinning self-consciously. "Beats me how I come up with such a hell-raisin' reputation. All I want out of life is to ride free and stay out of folks' way." His eyes rested on the barmaid, Molly Banks. "And maybe to toss a few saloon girls in the hay now and again. What's this proposition?"

"We each throw in what money we can, and—" Mack stopped in mid-sentence, eyeing two young soldiers who approached the table.

Kale came instantly alert, tensed yet steady, like a cat about to spring. The blond-headed soldier's voice pierced the air with its shrillness, stilling the other voices in the room once more.

"So you're the great Kale Jarrett?" he mocked.

14

Kale looked squarely, silently into the young man's eyes.

"Answer me!" the soldier demanded.

"That's my name, son, but I got no business with you." He turned toward Mack. "I've jawed too long. Time to hit the trail."

"You don't look so fast to me," the soldier jeered.

Kale took a swig from the bottle and addressed his friend across the table. "See you—"

Without warning, the soldier slapped the bottle from Kale's hand. "Stand up and face me like a man."

The other soldier had held back. Now he placed a restraining hand on the blond boy's shoulder. "Come on, Doric, that's enough. Let's get out of here."

The one called Doric shook himself free. "Take your hands off me. Can't you see this here gunfighter needs to be taught some manners?"

Kale glanced around the room. The crowd had divided and moved back out of the line of fire. It had happened before, yet it always surprised him. Every time someone recognized him or a friend called his name, there was some still-wet-behind-the-ears kid around who wanted to prove his speed at drawing a pistol from a holster.

"Look at him," the soldier jeered to the crowd. "Look at the great gunfighter!" He spat on the rough plank floor. "I say the only thing he's good at is turnin' tail and runnin'!"

Kale knew any move he made would draw fire. He also knew he was not going to draw on this kid. There had to be another way.

Maybe there was. He caught Mack's attention, winked, and muttered one word.

15

"Mazón!"

Santos Mazón was a mutual friend, a bear-cat of a man known from Texas to California for his love of a bar-room brawl. While most brush-poppers went into a saloon for a little red-eye and rotgut and to catch up on the latest gossip, Santos went to enjoy the relaxation of a good old-fashioned knock-down-drag-out. The very mention of his name brought instant reactions from anyone who knew him, including, Kale was relieved to see, Mack McKenzie.

The two men sprang forward as one, throwing the table into the soldiers.

The towheaded soldier staggered sideways, regained his footing, and reached for his gun.

At that instant Kale struck him, a left to the stomach, followed by a right under the chin. The boy reeled backward, catching himself against the bar.

From the corner of his eye, Kale saw Mack holding the other kid in an arm lock. Kale lunged for Doric—*grab him around the middle, throw him to the floor, pin him down.*

The kid would have learned a cheap lesson, Kale figured. But he was wrong.

As he lunged forward, the boy pivoted suddenly with his right foot. Just before Kale's chin hit the foot rail, Doric's left boot made contact and drove him backward. Kale heard his jaw crack and his tongue tasted salty blood. He fell into the crowd; two fists grabbed his shirt and jerked him forward.

Kale bent his knees, missing a smash to his chin, and struck an undercut to the kid's midsection which sent the soldier tottering.

The soldier was tough. Much better, Kale suspected,

16

with fists than with a gun. He was young, seven or eight years younger than Kale, who was twenty-eight. He was powerfully built, like a farmer or a frontiersman, and he stood an inch or so taller than Kale, who was six-foot even in his stocking feet. Worst of all, he knew how to fight the right way, as if he'd been schooled at it.

No doubt about it, Kale Jarrett had his work cut out for him. And he loved it. A good fight, a real fight . . . not a punch-drunk, Saturday-night brawler, this, but a worthy opponent. Anger never spurred Kale on as did the pure love of a fight.

He lunged after Doric with adrenaline flowing. They clenched a moment, then broke and circled, breathing hard.

Kale stepped in first, punching with his right, catching the boy's jaw. Doric recovered quickly and countered with a left to Kale's belly and a jarring right which caught him above the left eye.

Kale stumbled, got his feet under him again, and came back slugging. His head roared. Streams of blood and sweat blurred his vision. He took another wicked left to the temple and somehow landed a roundhouse blow that sent the boy sprawling, while the roar in his own head built to a great crescendo, cutting out all other sounds, then breaking suddenly, as a wave breaks on the shore. The room spun wildly, knocking his feet out from under him, leaving him suspended on a soft pillow of blackness with only a distant roar in his ears.

When Kale came to, he was lying on a cot in Molly Bank's cabin. Mack's voice reached him as from a great distance.

"Listen to what Molly here has to say, Kale. I'll fetch your horse."

Kale shook his head to clear the fuzziness. Pain shot up his left side, through his temple. Molly's voice sounded urgent, but he couldn't grasp her meaning—something about the soldier . . .

"Did I kill him?" he asked.

Molly shook her head. "A bad cut to the head. He'll likely recover, but that won't be much help to you now."

His mind reeled, searching for something to grab hold of. Molly shook him by the shoulders.

"Listen to me, Kale. You've got to get out of here. That other soldier went after some of their friends. Sheriff Yates says he can't afford trouble from the army. You know how they come down on us if their soldiers get hurt here at the crossing."

Three soft knocks sounded at the door, but before Molly could get to it a large man stepped inside, quickly closing the door behind him.

"Sheriff Yates, what—?" she began.

"I'm not taking him in, Molly." The sheriff turned his attention to Kale, who had risen and stood facing him on unsteady legs.

"My deputy was in the Bee Hive, Jarrett. Saw the whole thing. Says you avoided a shootin' best you could. But I want no trouble with the army, and I understand they're headed this way."

"Is Summer Valley far enough away, Sheriff?"

"Summer Valley? Hell, Jarrett, there ain't nothin' between here and there 'cept lots of prickly pear and maybe a few red Injuns."

Mack came through the back door. "You'd better hit the trail, Kale. I seen dust comin' down the hill from the fort."

Kale nodded. "Let me know how the kid fares."

Molly handed him a sack of food as he went out the back door. "Be careful, Kale. Don't get caught by Injuns. And don't go stealin' your brother's wife."

Kale tried to smile, but the pain was excruciating. "Any woman my brother married would be a lady, and I ain't fit for nothing but—" He coughed to cover his embarrassment over the words he'd almost spoken, then finished in a lame fashion. "A lady would likely cramp my style, honey."

He stowed the sack of food in his saddlebags and mounted up, tossing a leather pouch to Mack.

"Here's two hundred dollars in gold for my stake. What part of California did you say?"

"San Francisco," Mack called after the departing horseman.

Summer Valley lay almost due south of Fort Griffin, but no road ran that way. So Kale headed east, looking for the least likely place to cross the river. That wouldn't stop the soldiers, he knew, but it might slow them down. And he needed all the time he could get.

The Clear Fork of the Brazos River skirted the fort to the west and south. A mile east of town the river cut back north and then shallowed up to about knee deep. Kale waded his horse in, kept north for a hundred yards or so, and came out on a bank that was mostly gravel. He turned sharply south, touched spurs to the bay, and gave him rein. With luck he could reach Hubbard Creek before dark.

Twice he glanced back. Nothing.

They'd find the trail if they were serious about pursuing him. But not until after they searched north

19

toward the Spinnin' S, he hoped, and by that time he'd have a good head start.

Only he knew he'd better hurry if it was to be good enough. He was about two miles from town now, but in this level country his dust could be seen a long ways off. And there was nothing to break the view.

The mid-afternoon sun bore down on his beaten, bruised body. What remained of his shirt was caked with dried blood and sweat. His left arm still had a tingling, almost numb feeling, as if a nerve had been hit. His jaw worked enough that he figured it wasn't broken, and Molly had washed his face, but that cut over his eye kept opening up. He dabbed it with his bandanna and considered this reputation that kept getting him into trouble.

It all started when he was sixteen and shot that carpetbagger for tearing up Ma's rosebush. Thinking back, it sounded like a damned foolish thing to have done. At the time . . .

He sighed. Benjamin had always said his hands were quicker than his brain. But that rosebush was the only thing of beauty in Ma's life. Pa had given it to her, and it was about all she had left to remind her of him, though heaven only knew why she wanted to remember a man who up and left her with six boys and two girls to raise, single-handed. Of course, he said he would be back to get her soon as he'd made his fortune, but she never saw hide nor hair of him again.

Once in a while someone would pass through who had run into him someplace. Last they heard, he'd been seen up in Alaska, shuffling cards in some saloon.

From the time Pa left, Benjamin, the oldest of the brothers, tended the farm and minded the other children, while Ma tended the rosebush, watering it, cultivating the soil, trimming its puny branches. At first it produced right pretty roses, red as a dancehall girl's painted mouth, he still recalled. As the years went by, though, the roses became fewer and more scraggly, and Ma became quieter and more withdrawn, until all she knew was that rosebush—as if she thought by coaxing it to bloom, she could coax her man back into her life.

Then that carpetbagger came to the door saying they would have to pay all they got for this year's crop to make up for last year's taxes.

The scene was carved into Kale's brain as though it had happened yesterday instead of twelve long years ago. Benjamin stood at the edge of the unpainted, weather-worn porch. A gray stone slab served as a step down to the path where the carpetbagger stood. With rolled-up sleeves and black suspenders, he looked more like a bouncer in a saloon than a government agent.

The rosebush grew beside the slab step; the ground around it was tilled and pliable in contrast to the hard-beaten, clean-swept path. The bush bore no roses and few leaves.

Benjamin argued, persuaded, and tried to reason with the man. Carson and Kale came out the front door on their way to rustle up meat for supper. Just as Kale stepped even with Benjamin, the man on the path stooped, and with both hands near the base of the bush he jerked Ma's rosebush from the ground and shook it in Benjamin's face.

"This is what we'll do to your whole crop, Jarrett, if you don't toe the line."

The rifle was fired from pistol position, suddenly, accurately. The bullet would have gone straight through the carpetbagger's heart had the man not leaned to the right to toss the rosebush away. Instead it pierced his side.

Kale Jarrett had shot his first man, and all he could think about at the time was how the thorns must have dug into that carpetbagger's hands. Later, remorse set in—remorse for his family and for the man he had shot; and fear—fear for himself and for the man he had become.

Within an hour of the shooting, Benjamin had sent him packing.

"I understand what took hold of you, Kale, but the fact remains, you shot the man. They'll hang you for it, regardless of whether he lives or dies. This is reconstruction—they're right, we're wrong. There's nothing in between."

One by one the brothers shook hands; Ginny hugged him, and he stooped to kiss little Delta and to hug his ma.

"Stay away from the outlaw trail, Kale," Benjamin admonished. "Work on your temper and your self-control. You have an obligation to your family as well as to yourself. All we have now is our name and what we do with it."

At the end of the lane, Kale had turned around for one last look at the homeplace, a lump in his throat the size of that carpetbagger's fist. Carson and Ginny waved from the porch. Benjamin stood stoically beside Ma, who sat on the step, cradling the rosebush and crying.

Five years passed before he saw any of his family again . . . five years in which he grew to manhood and became more proficient with the handgun strapped to his side.

The day wore on, and so did Kale and the bay. Once he

stopped and poured canteen water into his hat for his horse. While the bay drank, Kale scanned the distant horizon for any sign of movement.

Nothing yet. But he feared they would come. His hope now was that they were acting on impulse and not orders. That way they would be forced to turn around sooner or later to avoid becoming deserters, and Hubbard Creek seemed the logical place for them to turn back.

He was sorry about the fight. Because of him, and because of an idiotic notion some folks had that a man could prove his prowess by facing down a known gun-man, a kid lay near death. This had never made sense to Kale. If those people could see that reputation from behind the eyes of the man who held it, they'd likely understand better: always leery in crowds, always running, not from the law, necessarily, but from every harebrained man who thought he'd found a surefire way to prove his manhood.

The sun began to set in the west. Several times he recalled the telegram in his pocket, but his throbbing head kept him from being able to think about the situation clearly.

He knew however that if Carson said Benjamin and Ellie needed help, they needed help. He also knew he was in no condition to meet up with a fight just now. After he got to the creek and cleaned up some, maybe his head would clear and he could get the swelling down in his right hand. As a gun hand it wasn't worth two bits, swollen this way.

The moon was up when he finally reached the coarse, sandy bank of Hubbard Creek. He stopped long enough to rest the bay and soak his aching body. He hoped he was right, that the soldiers would turn back here. But right or wrong, it would not do for them to catch up with him, so he headed south, picking his way in the moonlight.

A couple of miles off he bedded down in a cedar brake. He didn't know how long he slept, but it was still plenty dark when he awoke. Thoughts of Benjamin kept tugging at his mind.

Years ago, after Pa left, Benjamin stayed on to take care of Ma and the farm. The only time he ever left was to fight in the War Between the States; even then, he hadn't been gone long. He caught a bullet in the leg, and by the time the wound healed, the war was over. He hadn't married; instead, he raised his brothers and sisters, seeing that they tried their wings and left the nest in due time.

Two years back Ma died, and Benjamin sold the farm and went to Texas to be nearer his family. Kale saw him once, just over a year ago. Benjamin hadn't married Ellie then, but he did have the ranch started. Kale and Carson had spent some time helping him get things cleaned up around the place and catching up on family news. A few months after that, Benjamin met and married Ellie Langstrom. "A fine young woman," Carson had written.

Kale saddled up and rode on through the night, clenching and unclenching his right hand. Something told him he was going to need it.

24

Chapter One

Ellie lugged the bucket up the hillside, squinting against the magenta rays of the afternoon sun. All day she had intended to water the rose cutting at the head of Benjamin's grave, but this was the earliest she had been able to make herself come up here. It was her guilty conscience, she knew.

Benjamin Jarrett hadn't deserved to die a brutal death. But try as she had these last two months since she'd found his body, she had not been able to banish her own feelings of guilt. Her life had been a steady stream of catastrophes; why had she believed marriage would be different? Why had she risked bringing her bad luck to a man who had been nothing but kind and good to her?

Benjamin couldn't have treated a daughter with more respect than he'd treated her, a girl raised in a house of prostitution. And now he lay dead—murdered—and she felt so very guilty.

When she stubbed her toe on a limestone outcropping, half the water in her bucket sloshed down the front of her calico skirt. She stopped to tuck the tail into her waistband, taking care not to rip the portion she had mended the night before.

Sewing was definitely not one of her talents. She trudged the rest of the way to the rock-blanketed grave. Not that Lavender hadn't tried to teach her a few homemaking skills . . . but Lavender herself was dreadfully lacking in the day-to-day essentials of running a household—a regular household, that is.

Once she married Benjamin, Ellie diligently mended his socks and patched his breeches and shirts, and even though her stitches were far from uniform, and the results bulky and unsightly, Benjamin never complained. Patiently, he assured her that she would learn in time.

She tossed the remaining water on the rose cutting she had taken from her bush at the front step. Then she sank to the ground beneath the old oak tree, reflecting on her future. The very idea of what lay ahead for her brought tears to her eyes.

The uniformity of her stitches wouldn't matter, not working for Lavender. At least, she now had experience under a man.

And it hadn't been bad, actually . . . certainly not the ordeal she had imagined. From talk around the Lady Bug, she had fancied it a horrid, painful experience, giving in to a man's physical needs night after night until one could hardly walk from the soreness.

Of course the girls spoke of soldiers and cowboys. They especially dreaded the trail herds passing through. Some of those cowboys were as wild as their mounts, to hear the girls talk. And their lack of manners and decorum was a thing to dread. Why, some even refused to remove their boots and spurs. And some demanded privileges and wanton ministrations that brought a burning to Ellie's cheeks even now, thinking on it here in the diminishing light of day.

To be fair, she recalled, now and again a girl would entertain a gentleman, exclaiming afterward, "He can pay me to satisfy him any day of the week and twice on Sunday." From time to time one girl or another had proclaimed a customer the kind to send shivers up a girl's spine.

Ellie plucked a stem of dried mesquite grass and chewed on it, smiling. Lavender's first Poppy—all Lavender's girls were named for flowers; when one girl left, Lavender the businesswoman always named her replacement for the same flower, so as to avoid redecorating the girl's room or buying new costumes— Lavender's first Poppy had actually fallen in love with a client.

Ellie could still hear her giggles, giggles which turned to tears, tears which led to Poppy's eventual disappearance.

"The mere sight of him leaves me weak-kneed and dewy," Poppy had enthused after her first encounter with her prince charming. "His lips light my soul," she had sighed later. "I can't live without him," she cried one night when he hadn't been around in two weeks. The next day she packed up and left, and no one ever heard from her again.

"Silliest thing I ever saw," Lavender had fumed. "Chasing a pair of pants halfway across the country when we have more of those things hanging around in here than snakes in a rattler's den. I know men, and no woman needs one; not on a regular basis, anyhow."

But Lavender had changed her tune when Benjamin Jarrett turned up in Summer Valley. He came to the Lady

Bug not to be entertained by the girls, but to drink a slow toddy, play a single hand of cards, and go home. It had been Lavender's idea for him to meet, then marry Ellie Langstrom.

"You need someone," she had insisted to Ellie. "So does he. He's had a lonely life, but he's a man who knows how to take care of a woman. He isn't demanding. At least, I don't think he'll be. He'll understand your lack of education in the finer arts of homemaking, and he'll go easy on you in the bedchamber. You won't find another man of his caliber."

No, Ellie thought now, Benjamin hadn't been demanding. And if the few minutes she spent beneath his body once or twice a month had given him pleasure, she considered it small payment for the home he provided her in return. Once again, like most times since she'd been orphaned at the age of six, Lavender Sealy had made the right decision for her.

For her, but not for Benjamin. Ellie glanced toward the grave which she had covered with flat limestone rocks in an attempt to keep varmints from desecrating it. Once more her inherent bad luck had surfaced, this time striking a gentle man whose only ambition had been to make a home for the two of them here in the wilderness.

A whirlwind whipped up by the late afternoon breeze tossed a dried tumbleweed in its path. Ellie watched it roll down the hillside, wondering how much longer she could hold out in this place she considered her first and last true home.

Now the best she could hope for was to work for Lavender at the Lady Bug. How she hated the idea of it! Not that she didn't love Lavender, but that work . . . that sordid work!

She rubbed her arms to warm away a sudden outbreak of gooseflesh. What choice did she have? She sighed into the soft autumn air. Of course talking Lavender into letting her work the way the other girls did would be her first hurdle. Lavender had always protected her from such a life.

But then Lavender hadn't anticipated Benjamin's untimely death—or his murder, Ellie corrected herself fiercely. No one had. Now she was left a widow with no means of support, other than this land which evil men were intent on wresting from her.

Why hadn't she heard from Carson, Benjamin's Texas Ranger brother? Since she wired him in care of ranger headquarters, she hadn't expected an immediate reply, but two months was a long time. And she needed help now, badly . . . quickly . . . before Matt Rainey and his brother succeeded in running her off her land.

Only one day after Lavender insisted she contact Benjamin's brothers for help, his body had been left on her back doorstep. Since then the campfire in the rock shelter above the house had become a nightly reminder of her vulnerability. A Texas Ranger would be the very person to instill fear in the hearts of the Raineys; she knew it. But as day after day passed with no sign of Carson, she also came to realize that she could depend on no one but herself. If she were to keep this home Benjamin left her, she would have to do it alone.

Standing, she shook rocks and dust from her skirts, picked up her pail, and started for the house where another cold supper awaited. A cold supper which she would eat alone at her table in her empty house.

Benjamin Jarrett had been good company, a companion. Tears blurred her vision. She missed him. And she would miss this home he provided for her.

Suddenly hoofbeats sounded through the stillness, and she glanced toward the valley in which her house nestled. Two horsemen sprinted away from the barn. Her first thought was that Armando Costello's men had brought more meat; they came almost daily to keep her in a supply of game and an occasional side of beef.

But these horsemen had not come from the town road, nor did they return that way. Instead, they raced away from her barn as fast as their mounts could carry them, crossing Plum Creek and tearing out up the hillside in the direction of the Raineys' Circle R.

Tucking up her skirts, she hurried down the hill. Whatever had they done now? Her stock had been driven off a number of times during the last two months, but never in broad daylight. Today no stock remained in the pen except her milk cow and saddle horse.

Damn them! They'd better not have . . .

By the time she reached the bottom of the hill, smoke billowed from the barn windows. She picked up her pace, fury growing by leaps and bounds inside her.

Kale nooned at Hord's Creek. The country was changing, becoming more broken now. He saw several peaks rising to the south, marking the Colorado River region. From here on he paid extra attention to what lay ahead, recalling the rustlers who had holed up along the Colorado that summer, preying on trail herds.

He crossed the Colorado River at the mouth of Mustang Creek, well to the east of where the painted cliffs rose above the Concho River, a place passing Indians once used for a sort of message center. He had never seen the rock drawings himself but had heard stories about them ever since coming west. Benjamin had been planning a trip there when Kale and Carson visited the ranch.

Mid-afternoon found Kale, hot and tired, approaching Summer Valley. Benjamin's ranch lay south of town, so Kale skirted the village. Across town an imposing pink structure rose from the top of the highest promontory. No doubt what kind of establishment that was, he thought wryly. His mouth watered for a taste of whiskey. He crossed the San Sabá River to the east. No time for such diversions; leastways, not until after he learned the status of things at the ranch.

Chances were good Benjamin had returned from wherever he had gone and Kale could expect a home-cooked meal for supper.

The country was rocky, brushy. Often shinoak grew so thick a man had to ride way around then switch back to get where he was going. In many places rains had washed the limestone bedrock clean of any soil.

He cut across a dry gully, spurred the bay up a hill, and hit a road leading south. Around the next turn he topped out on the hill overlooking Benjamin's ranch.

From where he sat, the road wound down the hill, around boulders, trees, and stumps, then crossed a meadow to where the house lay nestled against the far cliff.

Hills converged on three sides to form this valley. A spring-fed creek started at the foot of the hill behind the house and continued on out of sight, its banks rimmed with cottonwoods, pecan, and a few cypress and black walnut trees.

The barn stood to the right as one approached, but

with one end behind the house. This enabled a person to move from barn to house to creek with less risk of being seen from the surrounding hilltops. It had been built that way years ago to protect the inhabitants against marauding Indians.

Kale nudged the bay, and they began picking their way down the hillside in the early dusk.

It was then he noticed movement outside the barn. Looking closer he watched two horsemen sprint away from the barn and up a gully toward the northeast.

At the same moment flames leapt from the barn window and a figure emerged from the right, running pell-mell down the hill.

The bay jumped forward at the touch of his spurs. They raced toward the house and burning barn.

At the water trough, Kale slid off the bay, picked up an empty bucket, and dipped it into the water.

When he raised up, their eyes met. She was on the other side of the water trough, golden hair tumbling every which way, wet strands clinging to her throat and soot-smeared face. Her hazel eyes sparkled naturally, and when she spoke her voice sounded as if it belonged in a parlor rather than in this smoke-filled dusk.

"What are you staring at, Kale Jarrett? Wipe that silly grin off your face and get to work. We have a fire to put out."

Indeed we do, he thought. *Indeed we do.*

Ellie had been so eager to put out the fire she had not even heard Kale's horse, but when she rose from filling her bucket and stared into his deep blue eyes, she almost threw the water on him.

She knew him instantly. Benjamin had talked about his family so often she felt as though she knew them all.

But she doubted she would have recognized any of them except Kale, the renegade brother, the gunfighter. Kale, who stood six-foot even in his stocking feet, the same as Benjamin. Kale, who had the same unruly brown hair, the same work-strengthened physique as Benjamin, but who was a good twenty years younger. Kale, who unlike any other member of the Jarrett family except younger sister Delta, had eyes the color of the clear West Texas sky. Eight children and only two with blue eyes. And this virile man across the water trough from her was definitely not Delta Jarrett.

Kale, the gunfighter, when she had sent for Carson, the Texas Ranger . . . her body flamed at the thought of such a switch, at the violence this man could bring to her simple life.

Or was it the escalating fire that caused heat to travel up her spine?

Kale took in the situation, evaluated the fire, and went to work, half his brain tumbling with surprise at the kind of woman his brother had chosen to wed. Carson had called her a young woman, "a fine young woman." And nothing could be more true.

Unless it was a description of her womanly charms and vibrant sensuality. He would never have dreamed such of old Benjamin. He surveyed the burning building.

The barn, like the house, was a stone structure with an open lean-to attached on the east end, where the fire had been set. The opposite end held oats and an assortment of saddles, bridles, and other goods.

Fortunately, Kale observed, Benjamin had not changed in other ways: his fastidiousness, for one thing. The barn, both inside and outside under the lean-to, was clean of scattered debris or hay.

"Keep dousing water along here," he called to Ellie, indicating summer-dried grass around the lean-to and clusters of tumbleweeds that were already crackling under the flames.

He stripped the blanket from his bedroll and began attacking the fire inside the barn.

Either the arsonists had been in a hurry to get away or they were just plain careless, because with any effort they could have rounded up enough dried grass and tumbleweeds to start the fire right. Once ignited, it would have flamed straight through the wooden roof, destroying everything inside the barn; it would likely have spread to the house as well.

Holding two corners of the blanket, Kale beat down on the flames with all his strength, trying to smother them before they licked the rafters and caught the roof on fire.

He worked quickly with nothing on his mind now but the task at hand. His bandanna kept him from choking, but smoke still burned his eyes and the insides of his nostrils.

Finally the soreness from his fight with the soldier turned to numbness and then to exhaustion. His arms drooped; he held the blanket motionless in front of him, searching for more sparks.

"Looks like you've about gotten it all."

He turned at the sound of her voice, studying her thoughtfully, nodding. "How about you?"

"It's out. There wasn't much to burn in the lean-to."

"Or in here. Benjamin hasn't changed in one respect—he still keeps a pretty good house."

Her eyes dimmed at the mention of her husband, smothering Kale's hopes as he himself had just smoth-

34

ered the arsonists' flames. Benjamin had not returned. And his own mention of it had brought despair to this beautiful woman, his sister-in-law.

She spoke again.

"Wash up at the well and take care of your horse. You'll find oats at the other end of the barn. I'll get supper."

"What about the stock they drove off? Shouldn't we look for them?"

She shook her head. "I didn't have anything in the pen today except the milk cow and my horse, and they'll come back. They always do."

"Always? This has happened before?"

She nodded, silently measuring the difference in this man. The Lady Bug drew some pretty tough customers, and although Lavender had tried to shield Ellie from them, she had not always been successful. Ellie had seen her share of gunfighters. And Kale Jarrett did not measure up. On the exterior, she reminded herself. He hid his profession better than some.

Kale watched her turn away. Although he knew she must be weary, her step was light when she walked toward the house, ready to prepare his evening meal.

A strange sensation stirred inside him at the sight, an easy, comfortable feeling . . . as if this were the natural way of things, a beautiful, strong woman working beside him, then fixing his meal and sitting across from him to share it.

He slapped the side of his leg to bring some sense back to his being and chided himself.

"Kale Jarrett, you old coot! That woman yonder is your brother's wife."

35

But after he finished up and headed for the house, he wondered how she had known him by sight. She was expecting Carson.

Ellie strode toward the house, her brain reeling with questions. Where was Carson Jarrett? Why had Kale come in his place? Or was Carson close behind?

The slight lift in spirits she felt at this possibility was quickly squashed by a feeling of guilt. Kale had come in the nick of time.

Absurd! She could have put out that piddlin' fire. She wasn't in danger. She never had been.

Yes, she had been in danger and would be again.

Regardless, she didn't need or want a blue-eyed gunfighter around to wreak havoc in her life.

Dusk had gathered quickly inside the house, so she lit a lamp, stoked the fire, and wondered what to fix to go with leftover stew.

Company! What to do?

Not company, she retorted, angry with herself now . . . Armando Costello was company; Kale Jarrett was a gunfighter.

Taking the last half of the loaf of bread she baked three days ago, she cut large slices, then set them aside to beat a couple of eggs with a pinch of salt. Fried bread wasn't a company dish. If she'd had warning . . .

Company!

Kale Jarrett was *not* company. If he wasn't Benjamin's own brother, she wouldn't even allow him to sit at her table.

Certainly not.

No gunfighter was welcome at her table. Why, Kale

Jarrett was no better than the men who murdered Benjamin, no better than the men who were trying to drive her off her land.

She placed the skillet over the coals, and while the grease heated she set the table.

Company! And her dressed in one of Benjamin's faded shirts and a patched skirt . . .

She inched the coffeepot near the fire so it would heat. Herself, she would drink it cold and go to bed, but *company* . . .

The stew bubbled in its pot and she stirred it while anxiety stewed inside her stomach. Company?

Was she so starved for companionship she would welcome a gunfighter to her fire?

No! Armando Costello came almost daily, and any time she wanted she could ride into town for a visit with Lavender and the girls.

The back door squawked on rusted hinges; boots scraped against the threshold.

She stood.

Inside her, anxiety simmered on.

"I drew you some water, ma'am." Kale offered the crude wooden bucket as though it were a basket of wildflowers.

She smoothed a strand of hair back from her face, conscious now of her unkempt appearance—a man's shirt, for heaven's sake, and not much beneath it.

"Over there," she motioned. "On the cabinet. Ah . . . thank you."

Kale had trouble tearing his eyes away from her to set the bucket down. Lordy, Benjamin was full of surprises. Even in that shapeless getup, Ellie Jarrett was all woman. And young . . . much younger than he'd expected, even though Carson had warned him—"a fine young woman."

When he turned toward the cabinet, lamplight caught the ivory handle of one of his revolvers. Ellie cringed.

"You can't wear those guns in this house."

Her voice was sharp, and he jumped as if he'd been shot. "Yes, ma'am," he mumbled. "I'm sorry. It's been some time since I've been around . . . ah, inside a lady's home."

"Well, I don't allow guns indoors."

He frowned, thinking of the difficulty just past. "Not even with trouble about?"

"I will not brook trouble inside my home," she insisted.

While she dished up two bowls of stew and carried them to the table, Kale complied with her wishes, albeit hesitantly. Little the lady knew about trouble, he thought. Did she think it always stopped at the barn? More often than not, trouble came uninvited, when and where it wished.

He surveyed the room: pieced quilts hung in two doorways, separating sleeping rooms from this main one, he recalled. Coarse curtains and a rag rug added warmth to the sturdy limestone building. Dried wildflowers in an earthenware jug sat on the rough-hewn mantel, along with some candles and a fruit jar filled with cartridges which propped up a photograph of Ellie. He studied it— the Sunday-go-to-meetin' gown she wore, the fancy wood-frame house in the background.

"You've sure fixed this place up, ma'am. It's a sight more homey than it was the last time I was here."

She smiled in a curt manner and motioned to one of the two hide-bottomed chairs flanking a small oak table. Kale slung his gun belt over the ladder back of the chair, gun butt at hand, and slid into the seat.

Watching him she grimaced but held her tongue. "I hope you like stew . . ." Her words trailed off when she observed for the first time the bruises on his swollen face, the cut over his eye. He looked like he'd just come from a brawl.

Whatever had she gotten herself into? A gunfighter in the house? Violence begets violence, she recalled hearing. What would Kale Jarrett do when he learned of Benjamin's violent death? Whatever would he do?

"Stew's my favorite, ma'am." He ate silently, thinking she acted a bit starched, but he'd be the first to admit how little he knew about womenfolk—ladies, especially.

"It was Benjamin's—" She bit off her words, wishing she hadn't mentioned her husband's name. The idea of Benjamin's being murdered had never filled her with as much dread as at this moment when she faced telling his brother.

His gunfighter brother . . . how would a man violen† by nature react to such news? Would he jerk out those ivory-handled Colt revolvers and start shooting? Would he hold her responsible? Tears brimmed in her eyes, and she quickly buried her face in her apron.

Startled by this turn of events, Kale stared in helpless panic. He knew he should do something to comfort her, but what? When he opened his mouth to speak, no words came forth. He felt big and awkward in the presence of a lady like herself.

"Don't cry, ma'am," he finally managed. But she kept right on crying, and he didn't blame her very much, what with her husband missing and her barn having been set afire. From what she said earlier, this kind of thing had happened before. He wondered how long it had been going on, and who was behind it. More important, where was Benjamin?

When she quieted down some, Kale spoke softly to her. "I'm here to help, ma'am. We'll find Benjamin."

She glanced up quickly and his steady gaze held hers. She had to tell him. She *had* to . . . but how? She couldn't recall ever being so terrified. If only Lavender were here, or Armando.

The apprehension in her hazel eyes took Kale aback once more, but he held his tongue while she scrutinized him. Under his watchful stare, her apprehension turned to fear. Then, like a bolt out of the blue, he realized what she was seeing: the cut over his eye, the bruises, the swollen jaw and hands.

"Why didn't Carson come?" she asked at length.

Kale bristled. So *that* was it! She was afraid of him . . . his reputation, leastwise. Here she was, a lady who allowed no guns inside her home, entertaining a gunfighter at her table. He would have laughed had the situation not been so grave. She had sent for Carson Jarrett, Texas Ranger, not Kale Jarrett, gunfighter. And it was clear as rainwater she was not satisfied with the switch.

Generally, he didn't tarry long in a place where he was unwelcome, but the situation here was different. His brother was missing, and whether this little lady liked it or not, he was presently the only person in a position to help find him. He answered her question simply, without excuses.

"Carson had business in Mexico, so he asked me to come in his stead."

Ellie cringed at the news. Carson wasn't coming at all. Not tonight, not tomorrow, not ever. She couldn't count on the Texas Rangers.

All she had was a gunfighter! A damned gunfighter. Whatever was she to do?

"You're a strong woman, ma'am," he said, thinking to reassure her. "I saw that by the way you handled yourself during the fire."

Anger flashed through her body, displacing some of her fear. Little *he* knew about strong women. "You sound as if I had a choice."

He took another bite of stew, swallowed it, and ignored her attitude as best he could. "Whenever you feel like it, you can fill me in on what's been happening around here. The sooner we get down to business, the sooner we can find Benjamin." And the sooner you can be shut of me and my guns, he concluded with a silent oath.

Ellie stared down at her plate. She ought to tell him now and get it over with, she argued to herself. She would . . . she would tell him as soon as she fetched more coffee.

Bringing the pot from the hearth, she filled his cup, then hers. His blue eyes softened when he thanked her.

He was good looking, no question about that, she reflected involuntarily. Why, those blue eyes would likely put a bluebonnet to shame, come spring. And his dark hair, tousled like it was, only added to the mystery of the man.

Mystery, my foot, she fumed. There was no mystery about a gunfighter . . . only bad news.

Kale felt his strength return with every bite of stew. This was good, substantial food—meat with potatoes and onions from the garden he had seen out back. And the mustang grape jelly on fried bread filled a craving for sweets that had plagued him constantly on the trail.

"My goodness, ma'am, this meal is mighty good. After the jerked meat and Arbuckle diet I've been on, this here's king's fare."

She grinned a little at that, and his breath caught at the beauty it brought to her formerly dismal expression.

Suddenly she experienced the disquieting notion that he knew she was lying, lying by her silence. "Why are you staring at me?"

"Sorry." He grinned sheepishly. "To be honest with you, ma'am, I haven't sat at a lady's table in so long I'm all thumbs. The only females I've seen in a good long while were . . . well, they were far from ladies, if you know what I mean. Dancehall girls, mostly."

Dancehall girls? The words struck a new and discordant chord within her. Didn't he know about her own past, for heaven's sake? What would he do when he discovered this additional bit of bad news?

"Is that who you expected Benjamin to marry? A dancehall girl?"

He laughed at that. "No, ma'am . . . not Benjamin. I don't rightly know what I expected . . ." His words drifted off. He wondered how he managed to get himself caught in such a conversation in the first place. He couldn't very well tell her that she was far younger and more beautiful than he'd anticipated, that he hadn't figured Benjamin to be in the market for a wife who would set his blood to boiling, as Ellie surely must have done.

"Benjamin said I reminded him of Delta."

"Delta?" He frowned across the table at her. "My little sister?"

She nodded.

"But Delta's only—I mean, you're taller . . . ah, grown up."

Ellie laughed in spite of herself. She had never considered herself tall, but then, she'd been raised around Lavender Sealy, who towered to six feet, well above most men who frequented the Lady Bug.

Her height, of course, was not what bothered Kale Jarrett. She knew that. "Delta's grown up, too."

Kale shook his head. His eyes reflected the dilemma between his memory and the reality across the table from him.

In that moment Ellie saw not a dangerous gunfighter, but a man—a wandering man who'd been a long time away from his family. "How long since you've seen Delta?"

Suddenly self-conscious under her scrutiny, he dropped his head and took a bite of fried bread. "Twelve years, or near enough."

"Twelve years ago Delta would have been twelve years old. I was twelve then too, and probably not any *taller* than Delta was. Benjamin said we're about the same size now." She watched him add things up in his mind. "He also told me that Delta has your blue eyes."

Kale studied her while her words sank in. "That's how you knew me," he glanced toward the barn, ". . . out there at the water trough."

"Benjamin described all of you," she confirmed, "but I probably wouldn't have recognized any of the others straight off. He said only you and Delta have your pa's blue eyes."

"He likely told you more than that. Benjamin always accused me of being like Pa in most ways."

"He said you both have itchy feet and—" She stopped, suddenly realizing what she was about to say.

"And an itchy trigger finger," he finished for her, staring into his empty bowl.

43

After a time she offered him more stew, but he refused. Somehow his appetite had vanished. "Like I said earlier, the sooner you fill me in on the trouble around here, the sooner . . ." He settled back, studying the way the lamplight played on loose strands of her blonde hair.

Again she knew she should tell him about Benjamin's fate. She hedged. "Men from the Circle R started the fire."

"You recognized them?"

"No, but I know that's who they were."

"The Rainey brothers had a hand in Benjamin's disappearance?"

"I don't have proof, but they must have been involved."

Kale waited patiently while she set the plates on the far counter and returned to the table.

"The springs down behind the house are the head-waters of Plum Creek," she explained. "In droughts like the one we're having now, it's the only running water around. Livestock can't survive without water." She refilled his coffee cup. "The Raineys want Plum Creek; it's that simple."

Things are never that simple, Ellie, he thought, wondering where she'd been raised, sheltered as she was. "When I was here before, Benjamin mentioned the Raineys. They're the biggest landowners around Summer Valley, aren't they?"

Ellie nodded; she sat down across from him once more. "Matt was the first settler in these parts; his younger brother Holt followed soon after. Matt is a tough, land-hungry man, and Holt is mean. Together they're capable of taking any piece of land they want. If Matt can't get hold of it by threats, Holt kills for it. They have a few cowboys at the Circle R, but mostly their hands are hired killers."

Kale had listened with interest, but at her inflection on the last word, their eyes locked as if in combat. At least now all her cards were on the table, he thought. When he spoke he ignored her implication. "You think the Raineys are trying to run you and Benjamin off this place for the headwaters of Plum Creek?"

"That isn't farfetched," she replied, defensive more at her inability to make herself tell him about Benjamin than at his question.

"No, ma'am, it isn't." Again he ignored her starched attitude. "What else has happened?"

Her heart fairly stopped at the question. Now was the time to tell him. Now. "All sorts of things," she hedged again. "My garden was trampled, the stock have been run off several times. This was the first time they tried burning me out, though."

"How long has the trouble been going on?"

"The harrassment didn't start until after Benjamin . . . ah, disappeared." She dropped her eyes to the table. "Since then someone has been watching me from the crest of that hill up there." She finished with a curt nod toward the direction the arsonists had taken when they left the barn.

"How do you know?"

"I'm not making it up," she snapped. "Several times when I've been out tending chores, I've seen sunlight glance off something—a gun barrel, I'm sure. And at night, sometimes, I've seen what had to be a campfire.

Pushing back his chair, Kale crossed to the window. A full moon had risen while they ate; it cast a bright white glow over the ground, illuminating the valley and

45

parts of the hillside. He saw no light on the hill. He believed Ellie, he supposed, yet why would anyone use such an obvious position from which to strike at the house? Why not just burn her out and be done with it? Instead of that bungled attempt they made today . . .

"Did Benjamin file on this place?" He glanced back at her. Yes, he decided, Ellie Jarrett was an uncommonly handsome woman. *Your brother's wife,* he reminded himself sharply, bringing his wandering mind—and eyes—back to the situation at hand.

"I don't know. We never discussed business." She glared at Kale, reminding him once again that he was an intruder, an interloper, even here inside his own brother's house. "Whether he filed or not," she said, "I'm not leaving. No one can make me leave my home."

"No, ma'am," he agreed, "not long as I'm here."

His steady gaze bore into hers in a relentless fashion, bringing a rush of heat up her neck, causing her to suddenly, inexplicably, think of talk around the Lady Bug, talk about tingling spines and knees going weak.

She rose quickly and went to the kitchen, where she poured some of the water he brought earlier into a pot, then carried it to the hearth to heat.

Turning away, Kale leaned his palms against the mantel and stared into the smoldering ashes. The ashes weren't all that was smoldering in this room, he thought, knowing he'd best get things settled and quick. Slowly, as though in a trance, he repeated his earlier survey of the cabin, all the while trying to bring his attention back to the puzzle of his brother's disappearance and away from the spitfire of a woman—lady, he corrected mentally—his brother had married.

A shotgun and a falling breechblock Spencer rifle hung

46

on pegs above the front door. Kale recognized both from his childhood, leading him to thoughts of his own wayward youth. Like as not, he would never succeed in finding a woman like Ellie to marry.

That idea filled him with a new and different kind of trepidation—not the idea of Ellie, but of marriage. He was quite sure that word had never entered his mind before in association with himself.

Turning once more to the fireplace, he set his mind to studying Ellie's likeness. She stood in front of a fine three-story house. Something struck him as familiar about it, but then, a lot of houses looked alike.

She was a handsome woman, sure enough, all dressed up in a fancy gown. Benjamin was a lucky man. And to think she fought for this humble home as though it were the best thing she'd ever known.

A piece of tanned leather was stashed behind the fruit jar. When he took it down to examine it further, he found the leather had been torn into two pieces. Held together, they formed a crude map.

"What's this?" he called over his shoulder.

Ellie crossed to the fireplace, where she knelt to test the temperature of her dishwater. The silence had given her time to gather her wits, and she knew she could put off the inevitable no longer. She had to tell Kale the truth about Benjamin. Tonight. Rising to stand beside him, she answered his question in a preoccupied manner.

"A plat to an old Spanish mine."

Her presence did pleasing, yet disconcerting things to his insides. "Is it around here somewhere, the mine?"

"Supposedly." She cleared her throat. "Would you . . . ah, would you come outside with me, Kale?"

Chapter Two

The sound of his name falling from her lips sloshed around in Kale's brain like well-water in a bucket. With a stiff nod, he replaced the plat and followed her to the door. Yes, indeed, his brother had married an uncommonly handsome woman.

Ellie took up her shawl, but when he reached for his gun belt, she stopped him.

He glanced toward the hillside, shrugged, then moved to hold the door for her.

"Do we need a lantern?"

She shook her head. "The moon is bright enough."

The distance across the rock-littered clearing that separated Benjamin's grave from the house couldn't have been more than a hundred yards. They walked it without speaking. For the life of her, Ellie couldn't think what to say now, nor what she would say after they arrived. She had never been the bearer of such news before, but she had been present on occasion when others were told of a loved one's passing, and she knew folks reacted to the news in peculiar, oftentimes volatile ways.

She drew the shawl closer to warm herself against a chill unrelated to the weather. How would a gunfighter react? At least she had managed to get him away from his guns. All he could do now would be to throw a few rocks at her.

About halfway to the gravesite, she sensed that she walked alone. Stopping in the middle of the rocky clearing, she glanced back over her shoulder.

Kale Jarrett stood stock still; he stared past her, straight ahead, and without turning she knew what he focused on. She wouldn't have to tell him after all.

Beneath the light of the pale moon she watched his face take on the stony features of a mask. His Adam's apple bobbed; his hands gripped into tight fists. Whether from the action to clench his fists or not, his arms trembled, the sight of this engulfing Ellie in a wave of sympathy.

Without design she extended her hand and Kale reached to place his inside it. By the time she led him to the grave of his brother, he gripped her hand so tightly she thought he might crush it.

"Watch your step," she cautioned when they drew near. "The ground is muddy where I watered a rose cutting."

Kale turned a stricken face to her. "Rose . . . ?"

"A cutting from the bush by the front porch."

"Roses?" The word rasped from his throat. Suddenly he clasped her to his chest, holding her fast against his throbbing heart. He saw Ma and her rosebush, he saw the carpetbagger, he saw Benjamin. Still clutching Ellie tightly in his arms, he buried his face in her hair and worked hard to hold back the tears.

Ellie felt his chest heave against her own. One of his

50

hands grasped her head; his face nuzzled her hair. She heard despair whisper from his lips as the wind sighed through the liveoak leaves above them. She held him close and felt him tighten his grip on her.

Far removed from what she had expected, Kale's reaction reproved her for her earlier fear of him. His grief brought a return of her own.

For an indeterminable length of time, he held her without uttering a word while the breeze stirred around them and the stars twinkled merrily from the midnight blue sky. When finally he did draw back, it was with an embarrassed apology.

"I'm sorry, ma'am. I didn't mean to—"

"Shhh." As one would a child, she reached to smooth a lock of hair out of his eyes. "He was your brother."

Kale sank to his knees beside the grave and she sat near him.

"Tell me about it," he whispered at length.

"I don't know much. He was gone for over a week, then one morning—the day after I sent the telegram to Carson—I found his body on the back steps. He had been shot. I buried him. That's about all."

He sat with his elbows propped on his knees, holding his face in his hands. "Have you notified the others?"

She shook her head. "I was waiting to hear from Carson."

The mention of Carson brought a reminder of her earlier rejection of him. "We'll have to let them know."

She nodded.

"Benjamin is . . . was . . . like a father to us all after Pa left, and with Ma sick and all."

"I know," she whispered. "My folks died when I was young, too. Sometimes after I married Benjamin

51

I . . ."—she hesitated, then told him the truth—
". . . sometimes I wished I had been Delta."

Kale turned to stare at her distraught face. The
moonlight made her hair look like spun gold. Her mouth
was set in sorrow, her brow creased in an implacable
furrow. She stared off into the hills.

"Delta?" he questioned.

She nodded. "Benjamin must have made a wonderful
father."

They sat in silence a while, then she rose. "I'll go do
the dishes and leave you alone with him."

Before she had taken more than two steps, however, he
called to her.

"Ellie."

She turned and gazed into his mournful face. In the
moonlight his eyes looked black. "Yes, Kale?"

"What happened to your folks?"

She studied him a while before answering. "They were
bushwhacked by a gunfighter who hid out in our corral."

The water was hot, the dishes few, and before she
finished she had had ample time to reflect on her lack of
knowledge about gunfighters. She had judged this man
by a pattern created in the mind of a child, a pattern she
had done nothing to modify since she'd matured.
Perhaps Kale Jarrett was the cold-blooded killer she had
judged him to be from Benjamin's story about the
carpetbagger and the rosebush.

But he was also a human being. Tonight he had lost a
brother—more than that, a father. Tonight he was not a
killer, and tonight he did not need her rejection. She
watched him out the window, sitting where she had left
him, staring still at the grave of his brother. Tonight he
needed a friend.

In her earlier disappointment that he had come instead of Carson, she had lashed out at him. She had deliberately rejected him, and in doing so had undoubtedly caused him to think her rejection mirrored Benjamin's.

Such an idea was neither right nor fair, and she must correct it. Taking up her shawl once more, this time carrying a lantern, she walked to the edge of the porch and looked toward the gravesite. Light from the moon played off his face, but his dark head faded into the blackness of the landscape.

The slamming of the front door alerted Kale, and he looked across the clearing to see Ellie standing on the porch, outlined in the soft moonlight. She looked fragile, almost helpless, although he knew she could not be. Not having survived the loss of her parents, not having grown to womanhood in this wild country. Again he remembered the photograph on the mantel and wondered at the fashionable gown and fancy house. She hadn't always lived in a humble shack beside a disputed creek. But you wouldn't know it by the fierceness with which she defended her home.

Rising, he brushed dirt and gravel off his pants with half a mind. He would take care of her . . . he owed Benjamin that much. He would see she kept her home, even if she did have a mighty low opinion of gunfighters.

Seeing him start down the hill, she hung the lantern on a peg and waited until he reached the porch to speak. "Cooking always heats up the house. Why don't we sit out here, while I tell you what little else I know about the situation?"

Kale squatted on his heels with his back propped against the rock wall of the house. He fished makings from his pocket and began to fumble with a sack of Bull Durham. "Mind if I smoke?"

She shook her head, taking a seat across from him at the edge of the porch, leaning against a post, dangling her feet over the edge. Again she studied Kale's features in the moonlight.

"I'm sorry I didn't welcome you properly," she began.

His gaze held hers. He saw pain etched in the fine lines at the corners of her eyes. The first words she had ever spoken to him leapt to his mind, along with the heat generated by those words and by her lovely figure poised opposite him at the water trough. As far as welcomes went, that one ranked high on his wish list. Leastways, in a different situation it would have. In a different situation her initial welcome would have held a generous amount of promise.

He would like to have teased her about it, but jesting was out of the question—for her and for himself. His brother lay dead in a grave not a hundred yards from this very porch. His brother, her husband . . .

"No need to apologize," he replied. "Let's just figure out how to keep you from losing this place. Why don't you start at the beginning? Maybe between the two of us we can piece this puzzle together."

She turned back to the yard. "Over two months ago Benjamin rode out to the north bedding grounds; he never returned. For a solid week I rode the pastures but found no sign, neither of him nor of his horse. Horses always come back to the place where they've been fed." She looked to Kale for confirmation.

"His horse should have returned," he agreed. "Unless the critter stepped in a varmint hole and broke his leg."

"In which case I'd have found the carcass. Anyway, a

week later one of Benjamin's boots turned up on the back step."

Kale frowned.

"The next morning I rode into Summer Valley. That's when I wired Carson. The day after that, Benjamin's body was left on the back doorstep, the same place I found his boot."

Only by concentrating intensely was Kale able to force emotion out of the way, to compel his brain to work on the problem at hand. "You say trouble with the Raineys didn't start until after he disappeared?"

She nodded.

"Did he have disputes with anyone else?"

"You knew Benjamin."

"Yeah. He could get along with the devil himself. I guess that's the result of raising up five rowdy brothers."

Ellie suppressed a shudder. She knew what Benjamin had meant to his family. Lavender had played much the same role in her own life. Lavender wasn't even blood-kin, yet her rejection would devastate Ellie. "Benjamin was proud of you, Kale."

"Humph!"

"He was."

Fiercely he broke their gazes, turning to look into the tidy, swept yard. "We'll whip that horse later. For now let's work on finding his killers."

After a while the tension eased, and Ellie continued her story. "He'd gone into town a few days before," she mused. "Said he wanted to send some wires."

"Wires? What about? Who to?"

"I don't know. I told you we never discussed business. Benjamin was so much—" She stopped abruptly,

55

searching for the right word, then continued, "He was much more experienced than I, so he handled our affairs."

Kale puzzled over her words. The one she hadn't spoken traveled between them on the soft night air—*older*, she had started to say. Why hadn't she gone on and said it? Benjamin had been more than twenty years older than Ellie.

"He was also a practical man," Kale told her. "He would have known the odds of you outliving him were in your favor—"

"In my favor? What do you mean by that?"

"Nothing," he answered quickly. "I'm sorry. But it's true. And that truth doesn't make sense. Benjamin was always open; he believed in talking a matter through." Kale shrugged. "I can hear him yet, 'Talking about a problem makes it easier to get a handle on, Kale, so open up and let's hear what's eatin' at you.'"

She grinned at him, then looked quickly back toward the town road, while Kale considered the inconsistencies in what he saw and heard here. Something was cockeyed. He recalled the two guns hanging above the door, leaving no empty pegs, no place for the saddle gun Benjamin would have carried with him.

The moment he asked her about it, however, he knew he had stepped into a den of rattlers.

"Benjamin did not carry a gun," she insisted.

Kale held the steady gaze of those penetrating eyes. Instead of smiling, they now accused. "Not even with the Raineys out to take this place?" he quizzed.

"I told you the harrassment didn't start until after Benjamin disappeared."

"You're saying the Raineys waylaid Benjamin without

first trying to get hold of the ranch some other way?" This lady was living in a world of her own making. "I'm sorry to upset your nice little world, Ellie, but if you'll open your eyes and look around, you'll find that things aren't as simple as all that. Folks don't generally resort to kidnapping and murder without trying other means first."

Even as he spoke, Kale knew he could be wrong. Anything was possible; believing that had kept him alive the past twelve years.

"I can see you're going to be a lot of help," she said at last, turning her attention to a large oak tree growing in front of the house.

"I may not be much help at that," he answered. "But for now I'm all you have."

"Armando Costello is helping," she retorted, then bit her tongue.

The sound of the man's name, stranger though he was, flashed through Kale like a gunshot. So the grieving widow was not so grief-stricken after all. He should have known; the pretty ones were always the most fickle. "Who the hell is Armando Costello?"

"A friend." Recognizing the anger in his voice, she quickly added, "Benjamin's friend."

The silence between them deepened. After a while, she sighed and told him the rest. "Armando is a gambler up at the Lady Bug Emporium. Lavender, she's the owner of the Emporium, introduced them when she learned about Armando's interest in the old mission. That plat—the one on the mantel—it's supposed to lead a person to some sort of treasure connected with the mission."

Kale flicked his cigarette to the ground, then quickly ground it out with the toe of his boot and scattered the remaining tobacco into the evening breeze. Lordy, his habits needed sprucing up.

"Don't get the wrong idea about Armando because he's a gambler," Ellie said. "He and Benjamin became fast friends. They spent hours together combing these hills. We even made a trip up to the painted caves on the Concho River."

With her explanation, Kale's anger had subsided, only to be replaced by a sense of confusion. "I'll admit it takes some doing, picturing Benjamin a close friend to a gambler." He drew a lungful of fresh night air. "Fact is, though, he earned any pleasure he could squeeze out of life after the way he stayed home and took care of Ma and us younguns. Even searching for buried treasure, if it pleased his fancy."

"They weren't really searching for treasure," she assured him. "Benjamin said it never existed. He said that was the way the Spanish priests had of getting missions built so they could convert the Indians. They knew the king would never spend money to build missions, so they traveled out here and made maps of gold and silver deposits—some real, most fake. What king could pass up gold and silver?"

"Sounds like a bunch of hogwash to me." Kale immediately regretted his attitude. He was beginning to dislike this situation to a great degree. Not that he had envisioned it being pleasant, but on the other hand, he certainly hadn't expected to find Benjamin dead and buried. Why, he'd been busy finding fault with everything Ellie told him, and now he even questioned her knowledge of history, about which he actually cared very little. She seemed not to notice.

"How else were they going to keep all those poor

heathen souls from going to hell?" She asked the question with such seriousness that he laughed.

"Why, ma'am, I must have been misinformed. I judged lying to be a sin, same as carrying a gun." The words escaped his mouth before he could stop them. He felt the accompanying smile die on his lips as the implication dawned in her eyes.

"I'm serious about that, Kale Jarrett, but I don't expect you to understand." She turned her back to him, and Kale reflected how he'd never seen such a lovely back.

After heaving a sigh, she continued. "I won't stand for violence. I want to see Benjamin's killers punished more than anything in the world, but it must be done without lawlessness and violence."

"Regardless of what you think of me, Ellie, I do understand. I understand about your folks, and now Benjamin, all killed needlessly. I understand your fear of me. I'm a fighting man. I live in a fighting world. But from the very beginning I've fought against lawlessness. And I edge to the far side of violence every time it gives me a chance."

"That's what we have sheriffs and peace officers for," she responded.

"That's why you sent for Carson?"

"Yes."

He exhaled. "Someday we'll have enough peace officers to go around. Right now the few good men we have wearing a badge need the help of ordinary folks who don't mind putting their necks on the line to see justice done."

"Vigilantes are lawless men."

"So are men who waylay a man in his own pasture."

He watched her catch a sharp breath. After a while she answered in a soft whisper. "I know that, but I don't want any unnecessary shooting or killing."

"Neither do I. I know my reputation. I know Benjamin likely told you that I use my gun first and ask questions later. I don't, but in this day and time a man can't always avoid using a gun."

"I understand that, Kale, but I worry."

"Then you'll just have to worry, because I aim to find my brother's killers and to see you keep your home, even if I have to shoot up half the country."

Her shoulders tensed, and he instantly regretted having shocked her, but he knew she was likely in for a good deal more unpleasantness before this shindig was over.

The thunder of hooves announced the approach of three riders along the town road. Reaching for his handguns, Kale found himself unarmed. Without hesitation, he rose and headed for the doorway. "Do you recognize them?"

Jumping to her feet, she watched Kale step to the mantel, where he shook some cartridges from the fruit jar into his palm. She tensed. Trust a gunfighter to know right where to find bullets.

He lifted the shotgun from its peg over the doorway, broke it, and slipped in a couple of shells.

Distraught, she turned back to the road. "The one in the middle looks like Holt Rainey. I'd recognize him in pitch darkness. The others I don't know."

When Kale moved back onto the porch, she placed a restraining hand on his arm. Their eyes met, and she saw the determined glare in his. She felt her hand tremble on his arm.

"Trust me, Ellie," he whispered. Then he stepped to the edge of the porch, shotgun cradled in the crook of his arm.

The riders drew up. Dust swirled around their horses' legs and settled into the evening air. Ellie stifled a cough. Kale stood impassively beside her, his breathing even, his voice clear and calm.

"State your business and be gone. Mrs. Jarrett isn't receiving callers." Kale addressed the group, but his eyes rested on Holt Rainey.

That the man fancied himself a gunfighter was evident in his getup and fancy guns: hat brim concealing his eyes, coattails tucked behind ivory-handled guns. Kale grimaced when the gun butts caught the lantern light. He hoped Ellie wouldn't make the comparison; he knew she would.

Suddenly he saw a dozen or more other men wearing Holt Rainey's hat, their chests panting with shortened breath, their hands poised above tied-down guns. Most of the others were by this time dead and buried.

How long before Holt Rainey followed them? he wondered. The man's insolent voice brought Kale back to the present.

"Who the hell do you think you are?" Rainey started to draw as he spoke, but his hand had barely touched ivory when the silence was punctuated by the cocking of Kale's shotgun. It was aimed at Rainey's heart, and the sight froze the man's hands an inch above the gleaming handles of his Colts.

"Mrs. Jarrett's brother-in-law." Kale's eyes never wavered from Rainey's; his voice was measured and even. "Come to clear up the matter of my brother's killing."

He watched them study him then, all three of them, trying to decide, he knew, whether he was Carson. They were likely unprepared to tackle the Texas Rangers at this meeting. The man on Holt's left spoke.

"Haven't I seen you somewheres before?" He looked Kale up and down contemptuously, then spat tobacco juice off to the side between his teeth and wiped his mouth with the back of his hand.

Kale turned his attention to the speaker, who looked as though he hadn't seen a clean suit of clothing since at least the beginning of the drought.

"I doubt it, Newt," Kale replied in a deceptively casual tone. "I don't hang around with the likes of you and Saint, there." He indicated the man to the other side of Rainey.

Ellie took it all in—Kale's easy manner, his calm way of facing these hard men. It eased her mind somewhat and at the same time chilled her to the bone. She drew the shawl more tightly about her shoulders. How could he have known these killers, unless he had ridden the same trails?

Kale redirected his attention to Rainey. "State your business."

Ellie was sure Holt Rainey would not cringe before the fires of hell. She watched him withdraw a piece of paper from an inside pocket and shake it out, apparently unconcerned by the fact that such a move could have triggered a blast from the shotgun had Kale been the least bit edgy.

She stole a glance at Kale. Her breath caught like a lump in her chest. She had never seen a man further from being edgy. She looked at his arms, remembering how earlier tonight they had trembled at the loss of his brother. No tremors now . . . he radiated calmness and strength.

"This is an eviction notice for Miz Jarrett."

Holt Rainey's words brought her abruptly back to the confrontation before them.

"Eviction?" she demanded. "On what grounds?"

Neither she nor Kale moved to take the document Rainey held toward them.

Rainey shook the paper. "Your husband nested on another man's property."

"You claim this land?" Kale demanded of Holt.

The rancher's mouth tipped ever so slightly at the corners. "Your sister-in-law here has till sunup next Friday to get the hell off. After that the law will move her out." Holt shook the paper again, but still neither of them made a move to take it.

"An' since there ain't no law hereabouts," Holt continued, "we'll come and do the honors ourselves."

Outrage and anger vied with terror inside Ellie. She drew her shawl tighter about her shoulders, unable to tear her eyes away from the savagery in Holt Rainey's glare. Cruelty shot from his pupils, which shone as mere pin dots in the flickering light of the lantern. The image of him drawing on Kale sent shivers up her spine.

Kale motioned with a jerk of the shotgun. "Be gone with you, now . . . and give your brother a message." His eyes narrowed on Holt. "Tell him Kale Jarrett's come looking for his brother's killers, and if either of you had anything to do with his death or with the harrassment of Mrs. Jarrett, you'll answer to me."

After a final insolent nod, Holt whipped his reins against the neck of his horse and the three rode away, the eviction notice falling beneath their horses' hooves. Dust kicked up behind them.

When Ellie slumped against Kale's shoulder, he shifted the shotgun to his other hand and put his arm around her. Recalling how his chin had rested on top of her head up at the grave, he judged her to be about five-foot-six or so. And she couldn't weigh much more than a sack of corn. Wordlessly they watched until the riders were out of sight, then he turned her toward the house.

"They'll be back," she murmured.

"We'll think of something. We have a week." *When we could use at least a month*, he finished to himself.

She hung the lantern on a peg and proceeded to light a lamp on a side table, all the while watching Kale replace the shotgun on its pegs above the door. "Thank you for not firing at them. I feel much better now."

He studied her. Although she appeared calm, her movements fluid and graceful, he knew fear was eating her up inside. That was understandable, what with her folks being bushwhacked by an outlaw, her husband meeting the same fate, her home being threatened by lawless men, and now finding herself with only another violent man to depend on.

After what had happened to her folks, combined with the horrors Benjamin would surely have told her about him, he knew it would be a hard thing, gaining her trust.

"I know what you think about me, Ellie, but I don't go around shooting folks unless there's no other way. I may as well warn you, though, the fight has just begun. We're far from done with this thing, and I can't promise there will be no gunplay ahead."

She replaced the chimney on the lamp, then quickly turned her back to him. He heard her stifle a sob.

"Ellie—?"

"I don't know what's come over me," she interrupted. "I'm not the weepy kind." She dried her eyes on the cloth she held. "Just when I found a home and some peace . . ." She stopped when her voice quivered.

Kale was hard-pressed not to take her in his arms and comfort her. He resisted, however, considering the fact that he hadn't been able to get the feel of her softness off his mind since she left him alone up at the grave. He felt guilty about that, her being Benjamin's widow and a lady to boot. To encourage a closeness between them wouldn't be fair; it would only add to his guilt.

When he spoke, his voice was unintentionally gruff. "Peace isn't a permanent thing, Ellie. Once you've found it, it takes a near-constant fight to hold onto it." He stared at her rigid back across the small table. His voice softened. "But you haven't lost your home. Don't start thinking that way."

After drying her eyes again, she turned to face him. He noticed how light played around stray ringlets of her hair, framing her face as with a halo. Her eyes were sad, about the saddest he could recall ever having seen, and serious.

"Kale, I need to tell you something else. About . . . ah, about how Benjamin and I met. I want you to hear it from me, to believe that I loved him—truly, I did."

"Now, hold on a minute, Ellie. Your word's good enough for me."

"But—"

"Besides, if you start recollecting things, why I might chime in myself. No telling how far you'd run if you were to hear about some of my shenanigans."

She smiled. "Are you Jarretts all alike? Taking everyone you meet at face value?"

65

Kale considered her question before responding. "That's pretty much the way of things, I reckon. Benjamin had a saying he got from a book somewhere, 'Let the dead past bury its dead.' I guess that means we've got troubles enough to keep us busy right now without worrying over something that's long since gone."

Tears sprung to her eyes once again at his gentle tone, at his matter-of-fact philosophy, or perhaps at the fact that tonight at least his calm strength reassured her. Tonight she welcomed his presence.

Tomorrow the outlaw in him could surface; tomorrow she might be sorry he was here, but tonight . . .

Suddenly she clapped her hands to her cheeks. "Excuse me for being so thoughtless. You've had a hard day, and there's nothing more we can do tonight. Why don't you turn in? We'll worry about the Raineys tomorrow."

At the suggestion of sleep, he yawned in spite of himself.

"Take the back room there," she continued. "I'll put out the light after I bring in some wood for morning."

"Let me help." Removing the lantern from its peg, he followed her out the back door.

The woodpile was a good fifteen feet in back of the house. As they approached he held the lantern higher so Ellie could choose the sticks of firewood she wanted.

Suddenly she gasped, her hands flew to her face, and she drew back against his chest. Again he instinctively reached for his guns only to come up short.

Scanning the area, he saw nothing . . . no movement, no unfamiliar shapes or forms. Tentatively, Ellie stepped toward the stack of wood, her arms outstretched, then a soft cry escaped her lips.

His gaze followed and his breath caught at the sight of a work-worn boot.

"It's Benjamin's. His other one." She gathered the boot in her arms and stood frozen.

Again Kale inspected every inch of space within his range of vision, wishing to hell he had a weapon. "Do you see anything else?"

She didn't move a muscle. He doused the light. "Go back inside. I'll be along as soon as I have a look around."

She stared at him, hearing only her own heartbeat. He spoke more firmly.

"Ellie! Go inside. *Now.*"

Obediently she turned and walked toward the house.

A thorough search tonight would be futile, he realized, and foolish, especially unarmed. He would either get himself shot or disturb any tracks the intruder might have left. So after he found no one lurking about the buildings or in the grove of live oaks behind the woodpile, he returned to the house.

Ellie had coffee making on the fire. She sat in a hide-bottomed rocker, holding her body rigid. Her eyes were as cold and hard as the topaz Benjamin had said they found in the hills around here. The boot was nowhere to be seen. When the coffee was made, she poured it with wooden movements.

It burned his throat on the way down and warmed the dull chill in the pit of his stomach. He squatted before the fire, holding the cup in both palms, staring into the blue flames.

His brain whirred with questions, but his first obligation was to Ellie, Benjamin's widow. He was fairly certain he could protect her through this night. Tomorrow—well, tomorrow was another question. The only thing he knew without a doubt was that she had been put to a test a lot of folks would break under. His first job was to make sure she didn't.

"It was meant to scare you, Ellie. If they'd wanted to harm you, they had every opportunity. Actually this is a good sign. It tells us the killer hasn't left the country." Turning toward her, he paused, swallowing the scalding coffee while he studied her face. It was frozen in an impassive expression he couldn't read.

"This means we have a lead," he continued. "Come morning I'll follow their tracks until we find the culprit at the other end."

Ellie stared into the fireplace. Life had never seemed so hopeless to her, at least not in a long, long time. If they were so bold in the presence of a known gunfighter, what would they do next?

"If they were to come around with you here . . . ?" Despondent, she stared into the fireplace. "They won't stop until they've taken this place. I know they won't."

"Now, Ellie, talk like that will get you nowhere but down. We'll catch them, even if it's the Raineys themselves. I promise you that. And no one is going to take this place away from you, not with me here to stop them." He gazed into the leaping flames, hoping to hell he would be able to back up such a bluff.

Ellie stared straight through the back of Kale's head, seeing Benjamin as he had stood here in this very room soon after they were married, hearing his voice, his instructions. "I have to do what Benjamin told me."

Kale jerked his head around, almost spilling his coffee. "What did he tell you?"

"Not to leave this place. To stay here no matter what happened."

"When did he tell you that?"

"Different times. He would say, 'Ellie, don't give this place up. No matter what happens, stay here. You'll be safe in this house.'"

"Safe?" Kale scanned the simple rock cabin. "Safe from who? From what?" That was foolishness. Benjamin would know a lone woman couldn't hold out in a place like this, not indefinitely.

"He said to remember the tunnel," she continued. "If there was trouble, to hide in the tunnel. People used to hide there when the Indians came."

"The tunnel? Where is it? Where does it lead?"

"Probably nowhere." Her voice was listless, as though she didn't really care. "The trap door is under the bed in the spare room. I looked into it once, but it was just a dark hole."

Kale had heard stories of such tunnels where settlers could hide until attacking Indians left, or through which they could escape the area altogether. Likely this one was no more than a root cellar, at best. Although he voiced no such concern to Ellie, he had his doubts that any hole in the ground would be of much help against the likes of Holt and Matt Rainey.

No, the way things were shaping up, it would take more than a tunnel to save this place from the land-grabbing clutches of the Raineys and their hired killers. Tomorrow he would have to find a better way.

Later, after Ellie went to bed, Kale lay down on the bed in the spare room. Tired as he was, however, sleep would not come. His mind jumped around, trying to reason out why Holt and Matt Rainey would use scare tactics in addition to legal means to take Benjamin's ranch—and his life. It didn't add up.

69

Perhaps Benjamin's friend Armando Costello could help. He might know something Ellie didn't. Kale made up his mind to see Costello tomorrow.

He recalled the episode at Fort Griffin and decided he might as well have stayed there and taken his chances with the soldiers, for all the good his coming to Summer Valley had done Benjamin. The only thing he could do for Benjamin now was to save the ranch for Ellie. And that he intended to do.

Drifting off to sleep he recalled Mack McKinney and the stake he had given his friend. He grunted, realizing he didn't even know what enterprise he had invested in. Oh well, Mack would take care of that. At least, he'd better.

Chapter Three

Ellie's eyes flew open. She lay still and tensed, listening for the sound that had awakened her. None came.

Pale light filtering through her shutters alerted her to the rising of the sun. Somewhere a rooster crowed.

She tugged at the light sheet wrapped around her legs, stretched lazily, enjoying a comfortable, soft feeling. She inhaled.

She sat up. Her smile broadened. She hadn't been awakened by a sound, but by a smell. The aroma of coffee drifted through the quilt which hung in the doorway separating her bedchamber from the living area of the small cabin.

Coffee brewing, when she lived alone.

Coffee.

Kale Jarrett, Benjamin's gunfighter brother.

Involuntarily she thought how Kale had best be about the business of living up to his reputation before he ruined it.

Give him time, she retorted. Slipping out of her cotton

nightgown, she fumbled with petticoats and chemise. The day was young, the problems facing them grim.

With her ears attuned to any sound that might come from the living area, she hastened into the second of her two skirts, another calico. This time she paired the skirt with her next-best cotton waist, even though it was a dingy white from repeated washings. Why hadn't she remembered to buy bluing when she was in town? She pinned her hair loosely, pushed aside the quilt, and surveyed an empty room.

Kale Jarrett was nowhere to be seen. No sign of him remained.

Except the smell of brewing coffee.

Surely he hadn't left. She crossed the room; the plank floor felt chilly against her still-bare feet. Granted, she had been less than welcoming last night, but he hadn't indicated he would run out on her.

To the contrary, she argued, standing in front of the fireplace. He had specifically said he would help her, beginning today.

Her heart lurched. Two cups sat on the hearth, one obviously used—coffee dregs still clung to its edge; the other was clean, unused, waiting. She poured it full of coffee, inhaled the damp, sweet fragrance, sipped the hot liquid. It was stronger than what Benjamin made, she observed while studying the quilt that closed off the spare bedroom. Was he in there asleep, having gone back to bed after making coffee?

Or was he already out hunting Benjamin's killers? And if the latter . . .

Hesitantly she approached the hanging quilt. "Kale?" Her voice sounded ragged with her first spoken word of the day. She tried again.

When no answer came, she pushed aside an edge of the quilt. The room was empty except for her own furniture: the bed, its covers neatly made; her trunk, containing the only items she had salvaged from her home so long ago; and the plain oaken dresser Lavender had given her when she married Benjamin.

The room held few signs of its recent occupant. She recalled Kale's observation about Benjamin's tidiness. Benjamin had obviously taught his brother well.

She tiptoed across the room, then wondered at her sanity. Who did she think to disturb?

At the dresser she picked up a leather shaving cup, the residue of lather on the inside still damp; the spicy scent of soap tickled her nose. A bone-handled razor lay beside the cup, and from the mirror frame hung a strop.

Where had he shaved? she wondered, chagrined at her inept hostess skills. She hadn't provided a bowl or pitcher.

Suddenly she caught her frowning reflection in the looking glass. Heavens, she looked a sight! Her fingers fumbled with the pins in her hair in an attempt to tidy it. Catching her eye again, her reflection mocked, her cheeks flushed. She clasped them in her palms. Whatever was she thinking, she, a recent widow?

And he a gunfighter.

Chasing that idea, another raced through her brain. This time when her gaze swept the room it was for the answer to a much different question: Where were his guns?

Those dreadful Colt revolvers were gone.

Dashing to the living room, she studied the back of the chair where he had hung them the evening before.

Gone.

73

He had taken those guns and set out after the killers. The thought of it stirred her blood. Before he even had breakfast, he had set out to kill a man—or men. No telling how many he'd already killed. Headstrong and lawless, that's what he was, like Benjamin had implied. Hadn't she specifically told him how she felt about guns?

Irritation grew inside her. How could she have let her guard down? Why hadn't Carson come?

Why did it matter? she fumed. A man who set out to kill another man before breakfast wasn't her concern.

How could a man arise, fix coffee, then blithely set out to kill a man? *Or to be killed . . .*

With a hand to her breast, she forcibly tried to halt the fluttering that came to her heart at the idea of Kale being shot by the intruder he pursued.

He could at least have waited until after breakfast, she seethed. How could she fix him breakfast if he was gone?

How could she cook him breakfast anyway? He would have used all the water for coffee; she would have to draw more.

Moving around the room in a trance of discontent, she found herself in the kitchen staring into a full pail of water. So he had not gone out to kill a man without drawing fresh water.

What did that prove? Still in a stew, she stomped out the door. Its squawking grated on her nerves, while Kale's six-guns loomed as large as life in her mind's eye.

Taking the trail to the springhouse, she surprised herself by entering the barn, where she stared at Kale's horse, which switched its tail contentedly in its stall. Across the way, his saddle lay spraddled over the top rail of the fence. Her own horse had returned during the night and now strained its neck through an open window

74

at the rear of the barn, sniffing for the oat bin. Behind him she glimpsed the russet hide of Old Gunnysack, her milk cow.

So he hadn't ridden off to kill a man before breakfast. Where had he gone? Outside she paused, chastised by the sudden knowledge of where he must be. She glanced contritely toward the hill, expecting to see him beside his brother's grave. But he wasn't there.

Again she had judged him wrong. She continued on to the springhouse, aggravation once more replacing her contrition. Where had he gone, he and his Colt revolvers? To the outhouse? Did an outlaw carry his six-shooters to the outhouse?

At the springhouse, she sliced several thick steaks from a slab of venison Armando's men had brought her the day before. By the time she prepared breakfast he would likely have returned—six-shooters and all.

As was his custom Kale awakened before sunup. But since it was not his custom to awaken alone in a room inside a house, he found himself momentarily disoriented. Quickly, however, a warm feeling spread over his confusion like honey poured on hot Johnnycakes, a feeling that remained even after he recalled the tragedy that had brought him to this place.

Benjamin was dead at the hands of unknown killers, and now his widow was being threatened. The thought occurred to him that if he could find the killers and help Ellie keep this place, the empty hole left in his life by Benjamin's death would be if not healed certainly mended.

As this idea took form, a plan emerged, filling him with

an urgency to be about the business at hand. While he set the coffee on to boil and drew another bucket of water, he laid out his activities for the day.

The first would be to track the perpetrators who left Benjamin's boot for Ellie to find. That he could do before she awakened.

An hour later, however, he'd learned only one thing: whoever left that boot on the woodpile knew his way around this place.

The hard-packed ground and sun-parched grass surrounding the woodpile could have been trampled as easily by Ellie and himself as by the intruder. The garden, the soft sand around the springhouse—in fact, every place where the earth was soft enough to hold a print—had been carefully avoided.

Finally he pieced together a trail of sorts by aligning crushed blades of grass, a broken pecan limb, and the row of stepping stones which were used to cross the creek below the springhouse.

Then, suddenly, leaping from the last stone to the grassy bank beyond, he found what he was hunting—crushed grass and scattered sand. So the intruder had left tracks after all! He had also been careful to cover them.

When the grassy bank leveled off, Kale found where a horse had been ground-hitched behind a stand of mesquite. Still no boot print, but his worries eased up a mite as he studied the horse's prints: a large-footed horse, a puddin'-foot, some folks called it, with a small crack in the right rear shoe. Likely it would be chipped by this time, given the rocky terrain the horse had to cover during the night.

Yes, Kale decided, his job had suddenly become easier. This was a horse he would recognize without even seeing his tracks again. He'd be large-footed and awkward. And limping, if that shoe hadn't been changed.

Kale studied the direction the horse headed out. Toward the Circle R. He cursed. Matt and Holt Rainey called themselves horsemen! No horseman worth his salt would ride an animal with a cracked shoe. Of course, it could have cracked on the ride over.

Scanning the area, Kale recalled what Ellie had said about a camp on the hilltop. Reluctantly, for walking was definitely against his better instincts, he climbed toward the area she had indicated.

The hillside was covered with rocks and patches of prickly pear and sage, with a few scrubby cedars and mesquite scattered here and there. By the time he came up on the rock shelter, his shirt was soaked with sweat. He bent over, rested his hands on his knees, and breathed deeply, all the while confirming his contention that climbing was for goats.

After catching his breath he investigated the small cave. These hollows in the limestone cliffs were common in the hilly regions of Texas. They looked as if somebody had scooped out portions of the rock and soil with a giant shovel, leaving a place where man or beast could find shelter from the elements. Some of the shelters were hardly big enough for one man, while others could house several families.

Kale stumbled onto a small rock shelter carved out of the hill, with a slight overhang and a ledge in front. The evidence was not hard to read: two men, and the remains of a campfire which had been used more than once, but which was too cold to have been used the night before.

A trail led alongside the shelter to the top of the hill,

where the men had staked their horses beside a live oak thicket. The tracks did not match those of the puddin'-foot, but the horses set out in the same direction, northeast toward the Circle R.

Kale squatted on his heels at the edge of the hill, plucked a stem of dried mesquite grass, and began to chew on it. Somehow this all made sense, but for the life of him, he couldn't figure how.

From where he sat, he looked down on the spring and across it to the house. The leaves were already beginning to show yellow and red, a warning that cooler weather was not far ahead. He noticed the good stand of grass. The creek was running full. No wonder the Raineys wanted this place. Benjamin had chosen well.

And now Benjamin was dead, and except for a puddin'-footed horse and a man bent on covering his tracks, Kale had no leads to the killers.

While he watched the valley, Ellie came up the path from the springhouse. The sun illuminated her face and glistened from her tawny hair, reminding him of the photograph on the mantel. No fancy gown today, no grand house in the background. Studying her he thought again of the difference between the luxury she must have known and the cabin she now fought to keep. Had her folks' death left her so destitute that this was all she could hope for?

At the back door she stood a moment, looked around, then searched the hills. Kale realized she was probably looking for him. She'd been asleep when he left, and he hadn't considered her worrying when she awoke and found him gone.

Standing up, he waved his hat in the air to catch her attention. In answer she waved the towel in her hand above her head a few times, then turned and entered the house. He imagined the squawking of the door. He'd have to fix that for her before he left.

Before he left . . . the idea erased the earlier comfortable feeling he had awakened with, calling forth the one image he had tried in vain to banish from his mind during the past twelve years: the picture of himself sitting on his horse atop the hill the day he shot the carpetbagger; the image of himself leaving home for the last time, the most painful leave-taking he had yet encountered. Would it be as hard to leave this place? The idea, coming unbidden as it had, unsettled him.

An idle mind, he thought, suddenly recalling another of Benjamin's adages: an idle mind will lead a man to trouble. Disgusted with himself, he flicked the blade of grass he had been chewing on toward a horned toad sunning itself on a rock not far away. The toad hopped off, and Kale started downhill, scolding himself as he went.

"Kale Jarrett, you're plumb loco. You'd best get Benjamin's business settled and hightail it out of here, before you find yourself in a mess of trouble. That's not some dancehall floozy down there, it's your brother's widow, and she doesn't set much store by gunfighters."

The house smelled sweet, of freshly baked bread. The door squawked when he opened it, and that, combined with the sight of Ellie standing hands on hips, staring at his hips—at his holsters, he corrected wryly—further irritated him.

"You can't wear those guns—"

"I'm taking them off, Ellie . . . taking them off." He fumbled with the buckle to his gun belt, conscious of her eyes scrutinizing him.

"There's a peg." She nodded to the door beside him. "Take the lantern down and use that peg for your guns while you're here . . ." Her words drifted off and he turned quickly toward the peg, where he removed the lantern and hung his gun belt over it. His hands lingered on the well-oiled leather; his mind lingered on her last statement. While you're here . . . before you leave . . . the disjointed nature of his life suddenly rankled him.

Ellie watched him, while her emotions tossed and tumbled. She hadn't intended to speak so harshly, but after all, it was her house and he should have remembered.

Perhaps he would have, her conscious needled her, if she'd given him time. "Breakfast is ready, if you're hungry." She tried for a conciliatory tone. "You can wash up at the well."

At the well he considered his good fortune at never having found a good woman to wed. Maybe for someone like Benjamin, who hadn't so many faults to correct, a wife was a blessing; for himself, a man with considerable ways that needed mending, a loving wife would soon become a shrew, and living with her a curse.

Drying his face and hands on the towel spread across the top of the well, he happened to glance toward the woodpile. His mind raced back to the night before, to Benjamin's blood-splattered boot, to the violence Ellie had known.

His resentment vanished in a flash, to be replaced by remorse. My dear Ellie, he thought, don't you know we all hate violence?

She served him a breakfast of fried venison, gravy, and sourdough biscuits with more mustang grape jelly, accompanied by a volley of chatter about how Armando Costello's men had brought the venison the day before and how she herself had put up the mustang grape jelly in the springtime. He knew she was apologizing in her own way.

The warmth he had felt earlier returned, and with it his determination to help her through her difficulties. He ate the meal with relish.

"Woman, you're going to have to cut this out," he joked after he finished off a second venison steak. "You'll have me spoiled so's I can't take care of myself."

She laughed. "That's all right. Benjamin worried about you. He thought it was high time you settled down."

He sopped the last biscuit in gravy. His eyes found hers and quite without intending to, he asked, "What do you think, Ellie?"

She held his gaze, willing her brain to steady at the unexpected twist to her innocent observation. Of course he hadn't meant the question the way it sounded. Nevertheless . . .

When she answered, the twinkle in her eyes belied the seriousness of her words. "I'm glad you're here, and I'm sorry about—"

"No need," he interrupted. "You have reason enough for the way you feel. You're a strong woman, though, Ellie. You'll come through this just fine; I'm here to see you do."

While she cleared the table he informed her of his plans to go into Summer Valley. "I need to wire the family, and I want to look up this fellow Costello. Make me a list of supplies you need." Before she could speak, he rushed on, trying to reassure her.

"I've scouted the camp on the hill. It was like you suspected—two men have been camping there, but the camp is deserted now. I don't think they'll be back for a while. The tracks—"

"Kale, don't worry about me. You're as bad as Armando. He's forever trying to convince me to move into town." She shrugged. "He doesn't think I should live way out here all alone. I'm not afraid of the Raineys, but of them taking this place away from me. They've had plenty of chances to harm me," she added, "and they haven't. They won't start now."

He grunted. "They aren't fools. The man who harms a woman in this country is in a peck of trouble and he knows it." He watched her pour water from the bucket she had placed on the hearth, carry it to the kitchen, and begin to wash dishes. The cup towel she had tied around her hips like an apron accented her trim waistline. He imagined how it would feel, resting his hand there at the small of her back. "Their harrassment is enough," he said. "I intend to put a stop to it. I promise you that."

She made the list he'd suggested and said nothing when he took his gun belt from the peg; he didn't buckle it on, however, but carried it in his hand. She followed him to the barn where he saddled the bay and led him into the yard.

"You stick close to the house," he told her. "If I'm not back by mid-afternoon, saddle up and ride into town."

She started to protest.

"Don't argue with me, Ellie."

She watched him sling the gun belt around his hips. Her eyes riveted on the ivory butts, the *worn* ivory butts.

"Benjamin couldn't have foreseen this situation when he told you to stay here," he was saying. "He wouldn't have wanted you hurt or harassed." He studied the top of her bowed head. "Neither do I. So do as I say, understand?"

His gentle tones only heightened her rising sense of panic. Was she to lose everyone to a violent death? Her mother and father? Her husband? And now, her . . .

Her eyes darted to Kale's. *Her what?* She searched his face for an answer, but her brain remained unable to function. She clasped her hands about her own arms in an effort to keep from throwing herself into his—from clinging to him. She wanted desperately to keep him here where he would be safe. Here, with her.

She tried to bite back an outburst, but lost the battle nonetheless. "Don't wear your guns."

He stared long at her, looking deep into her soul, causing her to want to plead with him all the more. "Please."

Slowly he shook his head. "Don't ask me that, Ellie. I can't . . ."

He watched her clamp her lips between her teeth, watched her struggle to contain her words, her fears. The impulse to hold her, to comfort her was overwhelming. He fought it the only way he knew how.

By swinging into the saddle. "I won't kill anyone," he retorted. "I won't even draw the damned things unless—" Jerking the reins around, he cut off his own words.

When he looked back from the top of the hill, Ellie stood in the yard watching him ride away.

She washed the dishes and tossed the dishwater on her garden. Weeds had already sprung up around the late-blooming beans, and their runners needed staking. Soon

83

it would be time to prepare the soil for spring planting. Spring . . . would she be here, come spring?

Glancing at the sky, she drew herself back to the day ahead. Time enough to finish the chores before Kale returned for supper. She would milk, then begin the wash.

After the fire was going under the washpot and the water poured into it, she shaved a good measure of lye soap into the water, then went in search of Kale's clothing. Traveling as he did, he would surely have no more than a change or two . . . certainly not enough to last the week.

As she herself, she thought, flinging her petticoats and calico skirt from yesterday across her arm, along with Benjamin's old shirt, which Kale had caught her wearing when he arrived.

In the spare room, she found Kale's breeches and shirt neatly folded inside his bedroll. Shaking them out she studied the hole in the right leg of the breeches and the tear in the shirt. She was miserable at mending, yet she couldn't very well let him run around the country with torn clothing.

Suddenly she remembered Benjamin's things. Kale and Benjamin were very nearly the same size. She had buried Benjamin in his only broadcloth suit, but Kale didn't strike her as a man who needed a broadcloth suit, anyhow. Only last week she had packed away Benjamin's other garments—shirts and breeches, and even his heavy coat. She would pull them out and offer them to Kale when he returned.

Then she recalled the clothing Benjamin had been wearing when she found his body. Unable to throw them away, she had also been unable to make herself wash them.

Lifting the lid of the trunk, she stared at the blood-splattered boots and beneath them at the equally bloodstained shirt and breeches.

Clothing was hard to come by, she admonished herself at the queasy feeling that tumbled in her stomach. It was wrong not to put good clothing to use. The shirt, of course, would never do; it had been ripped too badly by the gunshots that took Benjamin's life. But the breeches would be fine, if she could remove the stains.

The boots, too, she decided, taking them out one by one before lifting the gray flannel shirt and coarse breeches from the trunk. Perhaps Kale's feet were the same size.

She jumped when something fell from the pocket of the breeches and landed with a clunk on the floor. A rock. So like Benjamin Jarrett.

He rarely rode the ranch without bringing home strange pieces of wood or interesting rocks. She turned this latest acquisition over in her hand. The memories it evoked were not of specimens found here on the ranch, however, but of a place far away.

The piece of limestone was about the size of a hen egg, but flat . . . a porous white on one side, smooth and weathered to a mottled grayish brown on the other. And it was streaked with paint. Angled lines drawn in red and black hinted at a shape she recognized from trips to the painted cliffs.

Confused, she hurried to her own bedchamber, where she took out the box in which Benjamin had kept his treasures. On their two trips to the painted cliffs, he had collected several loose specimens of limestone which had been painted by Indians long forgotten. This piece certainly matched those in the box.

But why had he carried it with him that fateful day? Or had he? Could he have found another area of Indian pictographs closer to home . . . here on the ranch?

The bloodstains in his breeches came out with a good soak in the creek. Afterward she finished the wash and hung Kale's and Benjamin's clothing side by side with her own on the corral fence to dry.

Although from time to time she glanced at the hillside from where the Raineys had watched the valley, she saw no movement. Kale had said he didn't expect them to return anytime soon . . .

Suddenly she laughed out loud, feeling safer and more alive than she had since Benjamin's disappearance. Last night she'd actually slept through the night.

It had taken her a while after marrying Benjamin to grow accustomed to sleeping in a place so far removed from other people. Her life had been spent at the Lady Bug, in the company of a houseful of women. Benjamin's presence had provided security, but in the months since his abduction, she had slept lightly, awakening often and arising weary.

Not so the night just past. What a difference a man in the house made!

A specific man, she corrected, then winced. A gunfighter. She was lucky she hadn't awakened to flying bullets.

While she weeded and watered her garden, her thoughts returned to the piece of limestone in Benjamin's pocket. What did it mean? Where had it come from? She had at first considered the possibility of his finding it here on the ranch. The more she thought about it, however, the more certain she was that the stone couldn't have come from anywhere around here.

She had ridden over practically every inch of this ranch herself, even before her trips to search for Benjamin's body. Pictographs would most likely be found in rock shelters either along the creek or in the surrounding hills, and she had seen none.

The gardening finished, she turned her attention to supper, kneading a loaf of bread she had prepared that morning; greasing it again liberally with bacon drippings, she set it on the hearth to finish rising. While she worked she thought of Kale Jarrett the gunfighter, once more, and of the contradiction he turned out to be. Certainly he was nothing like what she had imagined. Although even gunfighters were human, she supposed.

"Ellie Jarrett!" she swore aloud. "Get this man off your mind. He'll be out of your hair soon enough."

Disgruntled with her inability to keep Kale off her mind, she headed for the creek, where she washed her hair and bathed in a pool sheltered on one side by the barn and the house and on the other by a high cliff. A bend in the creek upstream and a stand of reeds downstream lent the spot the privacy of a bathhouse. To Benjamin's amazement, she actually enjoyed the frigid spring water.

Today it invigorated her. By the time she finished bathing and dressed in fresh underclothing and the same calico skirt and next-best waist she had worn all day, it was mid-afternoon.

Carrying a bucket of water to the rosebush beside the front step, then another to the cutting she had planted on Benjamin's grave, she was suddenly struck by the lightness of her step. The realization of what this meant hit her like a splash of the cold spring water she had just bathed in, and she arrived at the grave filled with guilt.

Contritely she replaced some of the stones which had become dislodged. "Oh, Benjamin, I did love you. I still do. It's just that . . ."

Settling herself beneath the oak tree, she thought back on her year as Benjamin's wife. It was the happiest year she had ever known.

"You knew that, Benjamin. You knew I loved you." Her words were whispered, a plea singing on the breeze like the wistful drone of a honeybee.

He had known it, she assured herself. He must have known it. They had been happy, both of them . . . happy and content. No one had ever been as good to her as Benjamin Jarrett. No one. Not even Lavender. No one ever would be, except . . .

But this was different.

She glanced toward the town road. Somehow this was different. Very, very different. She had sensed that last night at this very spot when Kale held her in his arms and wept for his brother.

The difference had swept through her like a wildfire across the prairie. Benjamin had held her, of course. She had felt safe and secure in his arms.

But she hadn't felt herself aflame. Never had she felt herself so consumed as when in Kale's embrace, engulfed by a flame so intense she knew without questioning exactly what it was.

And what it was was wrong.

Not because she was physically attracted to Benjamin's brother. Now that Benjamin was gone, he would want her taken care of.

Not because her emotions for Kale already ran deeper—stronger—than those she felt for Benjamin. She had loved Benjamin Jarrett with all her heart. No one could deny that.

Not even because her feelings for Kale were different. She closed her eyes and inhaled the comforting aroma of the sweet earth, the pungent muskiness of approaching autumn. Yes, the feelings evoked by Kale Jarrett were different from anything she had ever imagined a person could feel.

Different—and wrong.

Not because he was Benjamin's brother. Not because a bare two months had elapsed since her husband's passing. Benjamin would be the first to understand that.

Wrong because he was Kale Jarrett. Kale Jarrett—wanderer, gunfighter, everything she abhorred, everything she feared.

But the heat of his arms around her would not subside. The tingle of his voice in her mind would not still. The fire in his eyes still singed her spine as it had this morning when he held her gaze across the table, asking, "What do you think, Ellie?"

What do you think? Should he settle down, find a good woman? She clasped her head in her hands. What she thought was her own business. What she thought was wrong.

What she thought would never be known to another person, neither in this life nor in the next.

It wasn't until she was elbow deep in pie dough that the implications of Kale's visit to Summer Valley hit her full force. His words of the night before rang through her senses: *the only females I've known lately were . . . far from ladies . . . dancehall girls . . .*

What would he think now, after he learned where she grew up?

And he *would* learn, she had no doubt about it. He would learn about Lavender—dear Lavender and the Lady Bug Emporium.

What would he think? What would he believe?

What did it matter? she retorted. Slamming the pie dough to the floured board, she slapped the rolling pin against it, then repaired the rips with trembling fingers.

What would he do, once he learned the facts? Would he leave? Leave her to face the Raineys? To face losing this place?

Would he leave her alone?

Alone, to face her own loneliness?

Chapter Four

Kale Jarrett rode into Summer Valley with the noontime sun warming his shoulders. He surveyed the short, wagon-rutted main street: a livery stable and blacksmith shop made up the first block, the Crazy Horse Saloon and the Bon Ton Cafe & General Store the second. Two buildings stood at the far end of the street—the San Sabá Hotel, and a one-story building of native stone which sported a new sign: *Summer Valley Mercantile Bank*.

Nudging his mount toward the livery stable, Kale found his attention drawn to the large pink house high on the hill beyond the bank. Something familiar tugged at his memory. He had seen that house before . . . somewhere . . . recently.

Then he laughed. Of course he had seen it before—the day he arrived, as a matter of fact. This was the front of the house he had seen from the back when skirting Summer Valley on his way to Benjamin's ranch.

He left the bay at the livery and walked to the hotel, where the hostler had said he would find the telegraph

91

office. The street was deserted except for a lone buckboard taking on supplies in front of the general store.

Dinnertime, he recalled, reading the *back-in-an-hour-or-so* sign hanging in the window of the telegraph office. He scanned the street from north to south, finally settling on the Bon Ton Cafe as the most promising place in town to find folks at this hour.

He stepped onto the boardwalk and tipped his hat to a lady who sat patiently on the seat of the wagon being loaded in front of the general store. Ellie's list rustled in his pocket.

A bell jangled when Kale entered the Bon Ton. He closed the door behind him and removed his hat. The savory aroma of baking and frying food mingled and wafted through the room from the kitchen beyond.

"Be with you in a minute," a friendly voice called above the clack and clatter of dishes.

Kale took a seat near the kitchen, at the end of one of two long tables, leaving a space between himself and the other three men at the table. Their animated conversation hushed when he passed, then resumed when he nodded a silent greeting.

He sat with his back to the wall, a habit formed through years of living in a land where trouble could often be avoided if a man saw it coming. He had a good view of the room and of anyone who entered the front door, but gingham curtains at the windows blocked his view of the street.

"What can I do for you?" A robust lady bustled into the room, addressing Kale while she placed steaming dishes of peach cobbler in front of the other men.

"Whatever you're serving for dinner, ma'am," he

ordered, then proceeded to eat the heaping plate of steak and potatoes she brought him, pondering how best to approach Armando Costello, thinking also of the peach cobbler. He hoped the lady saved enough for him.

When the three men left, the proprietress returned to clear the table. Suddenly, in the midst of cutting a bite of steak, he felt her eyes on him.

He glanced up to catch her studying him, one hand perched on an ample hip. "You're a Jarrett," she said at last. "Cousin or brother to Benjamin. Can't hide that fact."

"I'm not trying to, ma'am." He introduced himself.

"Zofie Wiginton," she returned, offering her hand. "Mighty glad to make your acquaintance. Sorry about your brother."

While she was speaking, a wiry man on the far side of forty came through the arched opening between the general store and the cafe. Crossing to the table, he scrutinized Kale much the same way Zofie Wiginton had. At her queries as to whether he recognized their customer, the man considered the situation; then his eyes brightened. Introducing himself as Otto Wiginton, Zofie's husband, he offered his condolences. "Pity about your brother. Benjamin was a fine man."

"You must be here to see after his affairs," Zofie said.

"Something like that," Kale admitted.

"This thing sort of took us by surprise," Otto told him. "We're not as lawless out here as city folks figure. Murder is rare. And intolerable."

"'Specially the murder of a good man like Benjamin Jarrett. He never did nobody no harm," Zofie added.

"I'm not city folk," Kale said, "and murder is intolerable to me, too. Is there any . . . ah, speculation?

93

What're folks saying about it?"

"That it's a cryin' shame," Zofie said.

"Way my sister-in-law figures it," Kale explained, "the killers are after Plum Creek." He finished off his last bite of steak. "That doesn't quite add up for me. Do you know any other reason someone would have had to take my brother's life?"

Both Wigintons looked thoughtful.

"Or to harass his widow?" he questioned.

"What do you mean, harass?" Otto inquired.

Zofie pierced Kale with a stern look. "Don't you go judgin' that girl by her past. Not many folks can stand up to such criticism. And she don't deserve it."

Kale fidgeted, uncertain of what he was being accused. "I'm in no position to judge anyone, ma'am. All I'm after is my brother's killers."

This seemed to satisfy Zofie, so he continued. "I'm in town to see a man named Costello—Armando Costello. My sister-in-law thinks he might be able to shed some light on the situation."

"Harrumph!" Zofie scoffed. "The only thing that man can shed light on is a poker table."

Otto agreed. "That gambler is as useless a man as ever I've run acrost. Why, I'll bet he ain't never done an honest day's work in his life. Sitting there playing cards day and night."

Kale studied Otto Wiginton's work-worn features and simple dress. If Costello fit the bill of other frontier gamblers he'd met—fancy of dress and simple of mind— he'd be an affront to such honesty.

"Where did Costello come from?" he asked.

"New Orleans, he claims," Otto answered. "Said he was headed for San Francisco, but he's been here six months and he ain't got the passage together yet."

Kale had been cussing his own ill feelings toward Costello, a man he'd never met, yet judged by his occupation; now he found that others who'd met Costello held the same view. This was a country where the work ethic was of necessity strongly embedded. One had to work to survive. And a man who shunned work was invariably looked upon with suspicion.

He wondered what the Wigintons would think of him were they to discover how he'd spent his life drifting from job to job. It was different, of course. He had done hard physical labor for everything he ever earned. Yet solid citizens like the Wigintons might consider him shiftless, too. Somehow he hoped they never found out, or leastways, not until after he'd had a chance to prove himself.

"I can't figure Benjamin and Costello being friends in the first place," Kale confided.

Zofie grimaced. "You can blame me for that. I hope he hasn't been too big a pest about that plat."

Kale frowned, recalling the leather plat above Ellie's mantel. "The one Ellie . . . ah, my sister-in-law has?"

"That's the one. My brother—Johnnie, his name was—won it in a faro game down in San Antone," Zofie explained. Beginning her tale, she cleared the table, taking Kale's cleaned plate to the kitchen, calling over her shoulder as she went.

"It's supposed to show the location of that mine Jim Bowie found back before Texas's war with Mexico. When Johnnie went off to fight in the War Between the States, he tore the plat in half. He took half with him and left half with me, figuring if either piece got stolen, the thief couldn't find the mine without the other piece."

Kale watched as Zofie approached the table carrying a heaping bowl of cobbler. "Would anyone want to steal it?" he asked. The idea sounded ludicrous; the cobbler tasted every bit as good as he had imagined it would.

"Johnnie thought so. The man he won it off of had several plats—seems they had been given to his grandfather by the Mexican government for service of some sort. He told my brother hair-raising tales about that plat. Said evil seemed to come to ever'body who touched it, that he was tired of struggling against the mess of bad luck it brought him."

Zofie refilled Kale's cup from a soot-blackened coffee pot. "But to get back to the story, Johnnie'd had enough of looking for that mine and not finding it, so after the war he brought me his half the plat and headed for California. He's out there still, fiddlin' around in them gold fields."

"How did Benjamin get hold of it?" Kale asked.

"Zofie gave it to him, both halves." Otto favored his wife with a knowing grin. "Might say she's superstitious."

"Superstitious about the stories, ma'am?" Kale asked.

Zofie shrugged. "It's not so much superstition, more like doubt. Far as I can see, it's a waste of time to go out digging for buried treasure."

"Is it authentic?" Kale asked. "The plat?"

"You bet your boots it is," Otto responded. "Only that don't mean there's a goldmine underneath your brother's house. According to them Spaniards, every mesquite tree with a hole in it was stuffed full of silver or gold."

"I never figured Benjamin for the kind to be taken in by such things," Kale said.

"Mostly he was interested in its history," Zofie assured him. "Other folks don't care about history . . . it's the riches they want."

Kale considered all he'd heard. He'd come to town for information, and he'd got an earful, but what did it mean? What did any of this have to do with Benjamin's killing? Very little, he supposed.

"How does Armando Costello fit in?"

"That woman up there on the hill, Lavender Sealy, found out I'd given the plat to Benjamin," Zofie said. "She told Costello—introduced the two, if I'm not mistaken."

Kale paid for his meal and picked up his hat from the table beside him. "Thanks for the dinner, ma'am. I'd best be going. Ell . . . ah, she's expecting me home before sundown, and I have a passel of things left to do. Where would I find this Costello character? Over at the Crazy Horse?"

Zofie and Otto exchanged glances.

"No," Otto said. "Likely he'll be up on the hill at the Lady Bug." He and Zofie followed Kale to the boardwalk.

"You let us know if there's anything we can do," Zofie offered.

"Benjamin was a fine man," Otto claimed. "But regardless, we can't have acts of violence like this going on now that folks are beginning to move in and make Summer Valley their home. We need a safe place where a man can raise a family."

A safe place where a man could raise a family . . . Kale glanced up and down the simple, rutted street. A family? Before yesterday he'd never even considered the possibility.

Leaving Ellie's list with Otto, Kale retrieved his horse from the livery and rode the half mile up the hill to the pink frame house which stood like a watchtower atop the highest promontory for miles around. The closer he got to it, the more familiar the place appeared.

Drawing rein, he slid to the ground, thoughtful. He looped the reins . . .

The house in the photograph, that's what it looked like. The Lady Bug Pleasure Emporium resembled in every detail the house in Ellie's photograph.

His mind struggled to assimilate this new idea into something coherent, but to no avail. Finally, he slapped his chaps with the brim of his hat and stomped up the steps of the garish pleasure palace.

Lots of houses looked alike, he argued. What did that prove?

Inside the rose-etched front door, Kale was immediately accosted by a large woman garbed in purple from head to toe—with noticeable exceptions of bare flesh here and there. She reeked of perfume, a minty-sweet fragrance he didn't recognize.

"Well, well, cowboy. I thought the trail herds were over till next spring."

He had but time to observe, *these houses are all alike, and the floozies inside them,* before she began unbuckling his gun belt, which she slung over a coatrack in a corner of the foyer.

"Now, what can we do for you? Or should I ask *who?*" She drew him through an arched doorway into about the gaudiest parlor he'd ever set eyes on. "My name's Lavender. I own this place."

"Costello," he managed. "I came to see a gambler by the name of Armando Costello."

98

"Why, sure, honey. First things first." Leading Kale back across the hallway, she continued, "Only don't you be losing all your money before you sample my wares. Name your favorite flower, and I'll plant her beside you for luck."

Kale cleared his throat. "Thanks, no, this is a personal matter." Then in case she put up a fuss, he added, "I won't take much of his time."

The room was filled with gaming tables, green baize-covered and fancy. Business must be good, he reflected, with a place of this caliber in the middle of nowhere.

"Armando, this cowboy wants a word with you. Personal, he says."

Kale studied the gambler, who was flanked by two other men at the playing table. The floozies weren't all that ran true to form in the Lady Bug Pleasure Emporium, he saw. Armando Costello looked every bit as sleazy as his profession demanded: slicked-down black hair, sharp features which added a touch of the sinister to his hooded black eyes. Although women likely would find him handsome, his dingy white shirt and faded brocade vest gave him the appearance of a man who might be entertaining a run of bad luck.

Kale extended his hand. "Kale Jarrett."

Beside him he felt Lavender's intake of breath.

"Benjamin's brother," she mused. "I should have noticed the resemblance. So you finally saw fit to come to Ellie . . . ah, to Miz Jarrett's aid."

Kale kept his eyes and his attention trained on the gambler. The opinion of the proprietress of the Lady Bug meant nothing to him—nor to Ellie.

Costello dismissed his two companions and Lavender with a nod, then rose and extended a hand. His fingernails were the cleanest thing about him, Kale observed.

"Sit down," Costello invited. "I'll tell you what I know about your brother. A drink?"

It turned out Armando Costello couldn't add much to what Ellie had already related. "Last time I saw him was the day before his disappearance. He came into town to send some wires."

"Who to?"

Costello shrugged his shoulders, dismissing the question. "My men scoured the countryside for any clue as to what became of him. To no avail, I'm afraid."

"Who besides the Raineys would want Benjamin out of the way?"

"No one," Costello answered firmly, adding, "Aren't the Raineys and their hired killers enough?"

"Perhaps." Kale thought of the bloody boot Ellie had found by the woodpile. That boot had probably been delivered about the time Holt Rainey was issuing his eviction notice. Rainey's arrival could have been timed to draw Ellie's attention away from the woodpile, but somehow Kale had trouble buying that. The two didn't go together. Both were lowdown and mean, all right, but one was straightforward, while the other was underhanded, sneaky.

Costello persisted, espousing Ellie's own argument. "The Raineys mean to have Plum Creek, and they don't intend to let a woman stand in their way. That's why I've tried to persuade Ellie to sell the place to me. A man stands a better chance against that kind of opposition than a member of the fairer sex."

Kale studied the down-and-out gambler, while his

distaste for the man's occupation grew into dislike for the man himself. Buy Ellie's ranch? What the hell with?

"Much obliged, Costello." He spoke between clenched teeth. "There'll be no need to sell the ranch. I'm here to take care of things."

"I'd like to help out, Jarrett," Costello insisted. "Tell you what I'll do. You convince Ellie to come to town where she'll be out of harm's way, and I'll take care of the ranch, leaving you free to hunt down the killers."

Kale clamped his jaws over an objection. Costello's use of Ellie's given name rankled him, especially here, inside a house of painted ladies. "Mrs. Jarrett is determined to remain at home."

"Then you must convince her otherwise," Costello returned. "With Benjamin dead, what use is that ranch to her?"

Again Kale forced himself to hold his anger inside. Most men would question a woman's ability to run a ranch; he realized that. But it was Ellie's choice, and by damn, he intended to see she got her wish.

"She'll be safer in town," Costello argued. "In fact, she could likely return to her old job."

At Kale's frown, Costello hurried to apologize.

"I'm sorry, Jarrett. You weren't aware of Ellie's former occupation?" Speaking, Costello scanned the room. His gaze lingered in lewd fashion on the lifelike painting of a voluptuous nude hanging over the bar.

To Kale's way of thinking, the implication bordered on slander. "Hold on a cockeyed minute, Costello. I didn't come here to discuss my sister-in-law—"

"Of course you didn't," Costello agreed. "Regardless of what she was before, Ellie made Benjamin a good wife.

101

I'll vouch for that. But now that he's gone, I'm sure Lavender would be glad to take her back. She was quite popular at the Lady Bug."

Irritation which had lain like a smoldering coal in the pit of Kale's stomach suddenly burst into flame. He kicked back his chair and stood up, glaring down at the gambler. His hands fairly ached to wipe the satisfied smile off that smug face.

"There's nothing wrong with it, Jarrett. We all have to make a living—one way or another."

Kale wheeled and strode from the room, desperate for a breath of fresh air. He reached the porch before Lavender caught up with him.

She offered his gun belt without a word, but her eyes spoke volumes, all of it confused. From force of habit he buckled on his guns, tied them low. What the hell was going on? He inhaled a deep breath and tried to still the rage building inside himself. He knew Costello had deliberately baited him. But why? The man had answered his questions about Benjamin, and what he said was sound, most of it.

"Don't you listen to him, Jarrett," Lavender scolded. "Ellie's a fine girl."

He frowned at her; Costello's words swirled like a whirlwind inside his head.

"Be good to her, you hear?"

Suddenly he felt as if his brain had been blown to pieces. He stumbled backward, down the steps, away from this woman, this floozy, before he struck out in his rage.

"Like all the others?" he hissed.

Turning, he was fairly knocked from his feet by Holt Rainey and the two men who had accompanied him to the

102

ranch the evening before. They shouldered past without a pause and entered the Lady Bug.

Lavender rushed after them, holding the door frame. "You break my rose-etched glass, Holt Rainey, and you'll have the devil to pay."

Gathering his bearings, Kale stared at the horses tied to the hitching rail. He didn't see the horse Holt rode to the ranch last night, but instead a big black stallion which had been ridden like a bat out of hell.

Studying the horse, Kale suddenly realized what he was seeing. Cautiously, he made his way toward the heaving animal. The stallion was big—but not as big as his hooves. Could this be the puddin'-foot?

Anticipation vied with the anger already simmering in Kale's gut. Would he find a cracked shoe on this horse? He rubbed the horse's neck, wiped lather from its flank. The stallion was powerful and deep-bodied. He had been ridden hard and, for what? An orgy in a whorehouse?

Kale lifted the right rear hoof and stared at the cracked shoe which, true to his earlier predictions, now had a chip off the inside edge. What manner of man would ride a horse with a cracked shoe this hard? He had to be nasty-mean—or drunk—or both.

"Adding horse-stealing to your other crimes, Jarrett?" Holt had returned to the porch. He stood on the top step, thumbs tucked loosely in his gun belt. His belligerent tone of voice had not mellowed overnight.

"This your animal?" Kale held Holt's glare with unwavering determination.

"Yeah, so take your goddamn hands off it."

Newt and the man called Saint had followed Rainey out the rose-etched door. Now others emerged, and a crowd began to gather on the porch.

Kale spoke in barely controlled tones. "This horse paid a call on my sister-in-law last night, and the rider left a gift. I didn't get a chance to thank him proper."

Newt and Saint spread out a little to either side of Holt; their stance dared Kale to draw his guns.

Holt sauntered down the steps, screwed up his eyes against the burnished sunlight. "If you're accusing me of something," he taunted, "spit it out plain-like."

"I think you get my meaning. And I suggest you change your horse's shoe. If you want to call yourself a rancher, you'd better learn their ways. No rancher worthy of the name would ride an animal this hard on a cracked shoe."

"You stinking varmint!" Holt lunged at Kale.

Kale, however, was quicker. He turned his shoulders ever so slightly, drew back, and landed a devastating cross to Rainey's head. The man crumpled to the ground, felled by ignorance of his opponent as much as by the blow.

Stepping back, Kale withdrew his right hand from the punch even as his left leveled his revolver on the crowd.

"One of the boots my brother was wearing when he was killed turned up on our woodpile last night. It was caked with dried blood and left for his widow to find. As you can imagine, it caused her considerable pain."

The gasps which followed were what Kale expected. In this country, harassing a woman was an unthinkable crime, second only to rape or murder.

Kale waved his gun muzzle toward the puddin'-foot. "This morning that animal's tracks were all over the place." He glared back at Holt. "Climb on your horse and go home; tell Matt I'm tired of playing games. I came here to find my brother's killers, and I won't let up until I see those responsible behind bars—or hanged."

He watched the men begin to mount. The one called Saint brushed by Kale, spat on the ground, then glanced from beneath his hat brim. "Don't rightly know why I'm telling you this, Jarrett . . . but for what it's worth, that puddin'-foot's been missing for the past week. Turned up just this morning outside the corral."

Kale considered the man and his words without answering.

A few people remained on the porch of the Lady Bug— the bartender and several of Lavender's painted ladies— flowers, she had called them. Armando Costello lounged in the doorway, chewing on a matchstick. Kale held the man's gaze for an instant, an instant filled with mutual dislike.

He wondered at his own feelings. Was it only Costello's comments about Ellie that rankled him? Or was it something deeper? Did he see himself in this gambling man—and dislike what he saw?

The telegraph office was open by the time he rode down the hill. The operator was new, and no records had been kept of the wires Benjamin sent.

With a few discreet questions while he sent his own wires, Kale learned that the former operator left town suddenly, shortly after Benjamin turned up missing. Kale knew this incident might or might not be connected with Benjamin's killing. Many people came west to escape the changelessness of their lives, so out here, when a man took a notion to up and leave a place, no one paid it much mind.

Still, it was a coincidence to be pondered. Together with the other things he had learned this day, it was indeed a puzzle. A nagging feeling in his gut told him he had all the pieces, but how they fit together was still a riddle.

He hoped the wires he sent would clear up a few things. After advising his family about Benjamin's death and requesting information from the State concerning Benjamin's deed, he added one last wire—to Brady Jarrett, a cousin down in New Orleans.

Brady might be able to shed some light on Armando Costello. If Costello was indeed a two-bit gambler from New Orleans, Brady would have run into the man in his hotel and gaming emporium on Bourbon Street. But for now, Kale wondered exactly what it was he suspected Costello of doing.

He had befriended Ellie, and his talk of her was likely more from lack of social graces than from malice. This shortcoming could also explain Costello's untimely offer to buy Benjamin's ranch. Other than that, the man's arguments that the Raineys posed threat enough had to be considered sound.

Kale picked up Ellie's supplies from the general store and packed them in his saddlebags, then he headed for the ranch.

But he didn't ride easy. He tried to take his mind off the things he'd learned in town by studying the countryside. A man never knew when his knowledge of this draw or that cedar brake would save his life.

Prickly pear and bear grass grew in sporadic clusters along the hillsides. In the meadows where he rode, dried stems of shallow-rooted witchgrass crackled beneath the horse's hooves. With a little moisture this whole country would green up real nice.

But Benjamin would not be here to see it. And Ellie . . .

Kale knew he was riled at the way Costello spoke of Ellie, other than the obvious truth in the man's remarks. But true or not, he didn't like her name bandied about in town like that. If Costello was the friend he professed to be . . .

No sense getting himself worked up over the gambler, Kale cautioned. He would in all likelihood have to deal with the man to get Benjamin's affairs straightened out, Costello being a friend and all.

Some friend. He'd come dangerously close to slandering Ellie's name back there in that painted house, even if what he said turned out to be the gospel truth. One thing he knew for sure, however, Armando Costello was not getting his hands on Benjamin's ranch.

Ellie's ranch, he corrected.

Ellie's ranch . . .

Kale found himself sitting his horse, reins held in limp hands, his thoughts on the evening before, on the desperation with which Ellie had professed her determination to hold onto the ranch.

Ellie, the lady he had been fearful of offending with his own coarse ways. Kale kicked the bay.

Ellie, who turned out to be nothing more than a common whore.

That development needled him the rest of the way to the ranch, and in needling, revealed to Kale a surprising fact: he was beginning to care for her himself. Not as a man cared for a sister-in-law, but—

Had been beginning to care for her, he corrected, trying to forget the lilt in her voice when she called him to supper, the concern in her voice when she asked him not to wear his guns into Summer Valley, the fear in her eyes. He tried to forget the comfort she brought him at

107

his brother's grave, the feel of her in his arms. Especially that—the feel of her.

He tried, but didn't succeed. About the only thing he succeeded at was remembering more than he wanted to of the short time he'd spent with her.

His own thoughtless remarks haunted him. He'd left no doubt how he classified women: ladies and floozies. Lordy, he'd never suspected her of falling into the second category.

How had she felt at his coarse references to floozies and dancehall girls? Dancehall girls, when she herself was . . . so much more.

He recalled the photograph on the mantel, how he had taken her for a highfalutin lady. Highfalutin, all right, but lady? Not even the chaste gown she wore in the photograph could change the stripes of the tiger underneath.

Underneath . . . the very word conjured up softness and passion. Kale cringed.

Softness and passion. What had she given Benjamin? Benjamin, of all people. Benjamin had married a common whore.

Nearing the ranch, Kale tried to prepare himself to face Ellie Jarrett, his sister-in-law, rightful heir to Benjamin's property.

He cursed beneath his breath. What the hell did Ellie's previous occupation have to do with her role as Benjamin's wife—or as his widow, for that matter?

But his tortured brain persisted. Her previous life had everything to do with it. She had probably married Benjamin to get away from her sordid life at the Lady Bug and wherever else she'd worked. For a moment he contemplated whether he could have met her before on a visit to some other pleasure palace here or there. What if he had already . . . ?

Abruptly he cut off his thoughts, imploring himself to be fair with her. Fair? Fair with a woman—a whore—who'd married Benjamin for his ranch?

Benjamin . . . who had deserved so much more.

Chapter Five

The pie had been a spur-of-the-moment idea, conceived after she returned from Benjamin's grave. Wrapped in a cup towel to avoid soiling her good skirt, she rolled out the crust, then filled it with wild plums she had put up last spring.

The fact that Kale would learn from strangers the very thing he refused to let her tell him sickened her. Although he professed not to care about her past, his remarks concerning floozies and dancehall girls clearly showed the categories into which he placed women: those who were ladies, and those who were not.

Very likely he would return from town feeling the same way about her that she did about him.

If the previous idea had unnerved her, this one struck a blow she was not expecting: that Kale would hold her past in the same contempt with which she scorned his was unthinkable, yet more than possible. For although she knew the truth about herself, and Lavender and the girls knew it, the fact remained that to most people in Summer Valley and elsewhere, she had been reared in a house of painted ladies, and therefore was one herself.

Wasn't that the reason Lavender had insisted on her marriage to Benjamin? And wasn't it the primary reason she agreed?

But Kale was worldly where his brother had been wise. Kale would see the truth as the world saw it, not the truth as it really was.

Clearly there was no chance for them to meet each other on neutral ground.

The gunfighter and the floozy . . . they were too far apart, one in truth, one in image.

The gunfighter and the floozy.

While she rolled the piecrust, however, she had the hardest time remembering that Kale Jarrett was a gunfighter. No sooner would she remind herself of the fact than a contradictory image would negate it: Kale carrying well water, Kale brewing coffee, Kale dealing with Holt Rainey on the porch the night before—restrained, strong, confident.

After she finished the pie, she recalled Benjamin's boots, which she had decided to offer Kale; she really should clean them first.

Although she had knocked mud off the first one before storing it in the trunk, red clay still clung to the sole of the one they found on the woodpile the night before. She took them both to the front porch, where she had a clear view of the road to town. Cleaning the boots, her thoughts lingered on the man who would wear them.

The gunfighter who would wear them, she reiterated, gazing defensively around the countryside. This was her home, and in spite of everything and anything she intended to keep it. She would not return to the Lady Bug and sell her body. She would work to keep this ranch, and

112

she would have to do it alone. She couldn't depend on a gunfighter to help her. He would only get her so tangled up in his crooked schemes that she would end up losing her home.

Not until she saw him top the hill did she realize she'd been sitting here all this time with one purpose and one purpose only: to await the return of Kale Jarrett.

Quickly removing the towel from around her waist, she took it and the boots inside the house. Within seconds she stepped out the back door to find Kale racing toward the house like a band of wild Indians was after him.

He drew rein and slid from the saddle. "Grab a bucket, Ellie. Grab a bucket!"

The sight she saw swept Kale's alarm through her system like the mass of blowing tumbleweeds which swept a trail of fire down the hillside. Already the first wave had hit the fence.

Kale stripped his saddle blanket from the bay and set about putting out the fire—the second one in as many days.

For an instant when he topped the hill overlooking Benjamin's valley, he had thought a heavy fog hung in the air. His next idea was that he was imagining things, because like the first time he sat his horse atop this hill, the valley was filled with smoke.

This time a mass of tumbleweed had caught fire and was blowing rapidly toward the house. The skeleton-like balls of dried weed spewed and flared in the last rays of the day's sun, rolling with ever-increasing speed ahead of the gusting wind.

Sinking his spurs to the horse, he made short work of getting down the hill. By the time he slid from the saddle,

Ellie had emerged from the back of the house. At the sight of fire, she froze in mid-stride.

He watched terror ignite her eyes, while his own anger flared at the perpetrators of such a vile deed.

On his instructions she moved toward the well. He unbuckled his cinch, jerked his saddle from the bay, and began beating flames with his saddle blanket. Some of the tumbleweeds caught up on the picket fence, others tumbled over it into the yard.

Ellie came running with a bucket of water. Kale yelled to her. "Throw water on the window frames." He turned his attention to the fence. One portion was already gone. He thrashed at the flames until they were quiet on one end, then moved to the opposite side.

Pungent smoke rose up, burning his nose and filling his lungs, but still he labored at the flames. Fortunately the yard was barren and the house made of stone. The only exposed wood was around the eaves and windows and on the porches and doors. Ellie watered down the window frames and the ground around the house.

The fragile tumbleweeds collapsed when they reached the wet earth, finding nothing on which to feed their flames. Ellie carried bucket after bucket of water to douse the sparks still smoldering around the fence.

Kale looked up the hill to where the fire had started. A smoking path about twenty yards wide blackened the earth, beginning on the opposite side of the live oak tree near Benjamin's grave.

"Let's get this." He motioned up the fire's path. "We don't want to wake up tonight in the middle of a grass fire."

Ellie grabbed a saddle blanket from the barn and joined him, thrashing and stomping her way up the hillside.

114

The wind had blown tumbleweeds across the rock-strewn ground at a good clip, leaving little fire in its wake. What grass there was grew in small sprigs around rocks and at the base of prickly pear clusters. The cactus plants were so full of water only their needles would burn, but Kale kicked the fronds aside with his boots to make sure no sparks were hidden beneath them.

Reaching the top of the hill, he slumped against the oak tree. His body was soaked with sweat and covered with soot and dirt. He reached out a hand to Ellie as she staggered the last few steps to the tree.

"With a little more practice, we'll get good at this," he said.

At the tug of his hand, she fell against him. Their heaving chests labored, first his, then hers. His hand spread across the breadth of her back, holding her steady.

She relaxed, supported by the strength of him. "No, thank you," she managed at last. "Two fires are enough for me."

She sounded tired inside and out. He rested his head against the solid trunk of the tree, conscious of her body molded to his own. His shirt was wet through and through from the exertion of putting out the fire, and he felt wetness seep through the back of her shirt too.

He inhaled, feeling a giddy sense of vitality seep back into his body. "If you don't mind, ma'am, I believe I'll soak awhile in the creek before retiring."

She jerked her head up, looking into his face. "Kale Jarrett, don't you even *think* of retiring before you eat the supper I worked all afternoon to prepare for you."

Their gazes held while the meaning of her words registered simultaneously in both their brains. His lips descended quickly then, meeting hers.

115

His hand crept along her back, between her tired shoulder blades, up her neck, finally cupping her head at the nape of her neck, pressing her face closer, guiding her lips.

His moustache felt silky against her skin, his lips soft and slippery, like satin, as they stroked hers, gently yet fervently, igniting a fire in the pit of her stomach to rival the fire they had just extinguished on the hillside.

She responded eagerly, increasing his ardor and hers with her reciprocating passion. Her head swam and she pressed closer to him for support.

His heart pumped against her own. Tentatively her hand moved up his chest, paused over his heart, moved to his face. Her fingers traced the outline of his jaw, and she felt a tremor beneath his skin.

At first Kale only savored the sweetness of her lips, the slight scent of baking on her skin. She didn't immediately open her lips to his quest, as though she didn't grasp the meaning of his tongue against them. When she did so, this movement, too, was tentative, as if she hadn't experienced such before.

That couldn't be, of course, his mind registered. He pushed the thought aside and deepened his kiss, losing himself to the passion rising within him. When her hand crept up his chest and her fingers caressed his neck, then his jaw, it was more than he could take. His muscles quivered with the growing want of her, and he broke the kiss to stare into her innocent eyes.

Innocent? He studied her expression. After what he had learned today, she certainly wasn't an innocent. Yet . . .

Abruptly she knew. As surely as if he had spoken the

116

words, she knew what he was thinking. She withdrew from his embrace, her eyes holding his.

Her heart pounded faster now, not with passion for this man, but with shame. She broke their gaze and turned away. Looking down the hillside, she tried to steady her brain, to keep tears from spilling down her cheeks.

Kale watched her fumble with her skirts. Somehow, he wasn't sure how, she had fastened them up to keep the bottom from dragging the ground. He grinned in spite of it all, seeing a couple of inches of pink calves exposed between the coarse lace of her pantaloons and the tops of her black shoes.

She shook out her skirts and let them fall to the ground. "Go ahead to the creek." She spoke quickly without facing him. "I'll warm supper. You won't be long, the water's too cold. Benjamin couldn't—"

"Ellie." Grabbing her arm, Kale turned her to face him. He caught and held her distraught gaze; the late afternoon sun reflected from the tears brimming in her eyes. Lordy, how he wanted her. Her past had nothing to do with it. Benjamin had known, and it hadn't bothered him enough to keep him from marrying her. Surely it wouldn't stand in the way of a little—

Damning his own wicked mind, Kale let go her arm. "Fine. I'll take a minute to look around first, before the sun's completely gone."

Resolutely she started down the hill, but he called after her. "Tuck those damned skirts back up, Ellie. We don't want them catching a stray spark."

The fire had been set by two men, he discovered, like the fire the day before. They hadn't even bothered to

117

cover their tracks. Kale followed them to the hideout on the hill, knowing before he got there he would find it empty.

By this time dusk had settled over the valley, but he headed for the creek nonetheless, where he stripped and sank into the icy water, letting it ease the tension from his muscles and stir up the blood in his veins.

Somehow Ellie managed to get back to the house without falling flat on her face, although her legs trembled so badly she wasn't sure how she made it down the hill. Stumbling into her familiar kitchen, she leaned against the doorjamb and let the squawking door welcome her back to her own world.

But would that world ever be the same again? The fear which had been growing inside her all day had sprung to life. He knew, and in knowing, he would reject her.

His kiss still sang on her lips with a poignancy that made her heart feel as though it were weeping. She rubbed the back of her neck where his hand had been. The spot still stung with his touch, still ached for it.

She sighed, tried to regain the resolve with which she had conquered other disappointments, and stoked up the fire in the fireplace.

She set the skillet over it and rose to fetch water from the well.

Yes, she had conquered disappointments before, but this one was different. This was one disappointment a determined mind would be hard pressed to drive away. This disappointment would likely haunt her to her dying day.

At the well, she hauled up the rope, filled her bucket, and turned to go back inside. Then she noticed his clothing still hanging on the fence.

118

He had gone to the creek without fresh clothing. What good was a bath, for heaven's sake, without clean clothes?

Inside she set the bucket on the cabinet, surveying her kitchen like one set apart. She moved as through a dream, stirring the stew, testing the bread, setting the table. She looked at the pie in the window and wondered whether he would stay around long enough to even taste it.

Suddenly she felt herself perspiring as though she was still fighting the fire. Lifting her arm to wipe her face on her sleeve, she realized quite by surprise that instead of perspiration, she wiped away tears.

She was crying, for heaven's sake. And her clothes smelled of smoke. Sadness like a heavy weight settled inside her, and she imagined herself smothering from the smoke in her dress.

She ran to the bedroom and began peeling off her clothing, desperate to breathe, to be free of the stifling smell of smoke.

He would leave now, she knew. He would leave before . . .

Her body dewy with the heated emotions swelling inside her, she threw open her wardrobe and stared at the bare interior.

He would leave, and she didn't know what to do to stop him. What would Lavender do? Or the girls? She thought of Poppy—the first Poppy—and her lost love.

Her hand touched silk.

He would leave before . . .

The green silk kimono was embroidered in lavish shades of orange and red. Lavender had given it to her for her wedding night, but she had never had the courage to put it on her body.

119

He would leave.

No! He couldn't. Not now. Not before . . .

Slipping into the silky garment, she belted it at the waist and rushed out the door barefoot. At the fence she grabbed up his clothes, and without pausing to consider what she would do next, she raced to the creek.

Dusk had enclosed the area in a dim circle of hazy light. Fireflies flitted to and fro like revelers at a celebration. Crickets chirped; a bullfrog karoomped from somewhere in the black water.

She skirted the stand of reeds and came to a halt beside the big old cottonwood tree. When her eyes adjusted to the dim light in the glade, she saw Kale, his back to her, lounging in the cool water, savoring it, the same way she had.

Suddenly she was very sorry she'd come out here this way. Awkwardly she knelt and set his clothing on the limestone slab where she often sat on warm days to dry in the sun before dressing after a bath.

"Ellie?" Turning, Kale squinted at her.

"I . . . ah, I washed today. I brought you some fresh clothing. And a towel to dry off with."

"Thanks," he mumbled, still squinting at her. Whatever it was she was wearing was bright green and glowed in the fading light of day. He watched her rise to her feet, then just stand there, looking down at him. The cold water rippled across his chest.

Still as death she stood, her arms limp at her sides. When she felt tears roll down her cheeks, she lifted a hand to wipe them away, but instead, her fingers found the sash and quite without thinking, she untied it and let the kimono fall open.

"Ellie?" Alarm rose inside Kale, echoed in his voice.

He found his footing on the rocky bottom of the creekbed.

Seeing him move, she panicked. Quickly, before she could stop herself, she shrugged the kimono from her shoulders and let it fall to the ground around her feet.

"Ellie, my God! Put that back on!" While his mouth went dry and his brain riveted on the vision before him, he felt himself react to the situation at hand. Whatever had come over her? He leapt from the icy waters, reaching for her kimono.

"I know what you heard in town," her voice rasped in a half-whisper.

He stood, kimono in hand, water running in rivulets from his body. Her words only half registered in his bewildered brain; his gaze took in her loveliness, all of it—her creamy skin, her firm, full breasts, her rounded hips and flat belly . . .

"I know what you're thinking . . ." She left the words to hang between them in the stillness.

His eyes darted to hers. Their gazes held. He saw tears streaming down her face. His breath came in short, sharp gasps.

"Lordy, Ellie, you don't have the faintest notion what I'm thinking."

Reaching, he cupped her face, his thumb stemming the flow of tears. She covered his hand with hers.

At her touch he jumped as though she had scorched him with a hot coal. In that instant he realized that he stood before her stark naked, and if he hadn't told her in words what he was thinking, the reaction of his body illustrated the point all too clearly.

Embarrassed, he thrust the kimono into her hands. "Get dressed."

Turning away, he struggled into the breeches she'd placed on the rock. He called to her over his shoulder. "Go on back to the house, Ellie."

She crumpled the green silk into a ball and rubbed her eyes with it. Why couldn't she stop crying? "Are you . . . leaving?"

"Leaving?" He turned, buttoning the flap of his breeches as he did so.

His eyes searched hers; hers implored him. But what were they asking? He felt himself becoming more confused by the minute.

"Leaving?" He stared at her as she stood, still clutching the kimono in her fists, holding it to her breast now.

He approached her with hesitant steps. Slowly he reached out, took the kimono, and slipped it around her shoulders. Methodically he worked to get her arms through the openings, then he crossed the front panels over her breasts and tied the kimono securely in place with the sash.

Only then did he allow his trembling arms to pull her to his chest. He held her tightly against him, feeling the rigid tips of her nipples work into the mat of hair on his bare chest through the single layer of green silk. He heard her heartbeat in his ears, along with his own.

God, how he wanted this woman!

After a moment during which he could make no sense of the situation, he held her back and looked into her troubled eyes. At least she had stopped crying.

But when she spoke, her chin trembled. "Will you come to the house first?" Instead of tears falling from her eyes, her voice now cried, like a sad and lonesome wind sighing through the trees, loosening the last summer leaves from the branches, taking all the life, leaving it barren—barren as his soul felt looking into Ellie's eyes, hearing the lonesome cry in her voice.

He swallowed the lump in his throat. *Leaving?* Where had she gotten such a cockeyed notion? Turning her toward the path, he nudged her in the direction of the house.

"I'm right behind you, Ellie . . . right behind you."

She walked before him up the path. Her body swayed sensuously beneath the green silk, causing him to wonder what demon had taken hold of his senses.

She'd offered him her body, same as she must've done to many others before him. And he had all but refused. Why? He had thought of little else but taking this woman to bed since he'd first looked into her hazel eyes across the water trough. Now, given the chance, he'd reacted like a skittish virgin.

Ellie picked up her pace when they neared the house, and he found her still robed in the silk kimono, stretched the length of his bed. Her look of pure innocence added to his confusion.

The same way she must have affected countless others, he reminded himself once more. Desperately he tried to bring this encounter down to the level of the other nameless, faceless painted ladies he'd enjoyed in the past.

But the fact that she was his sister-in-law made a grave difference. He studied her closer, his heart beating out a rhythm at once ancient and new. What he saw on the bed before him was not a painted lady, however, nor even his own sister-in-law.

What he saw was Ellie, a woman who set his body ablaze. Nothing else had anything to do with anything. Not now, not at this moment, with her lips, soft and sensual, beckoning him. Not with that thin layer of green silk covering a soft woman's flesh, flesh he had but glimpsed, yet burned to feel against his own.

Without removing his breeches he eased onto the bed beside her, stretching himself to his full length, supporting himself on one arm. He stared long into her face, and she into his.

All the way to the house Ellie chastised herself for the fool. What had she done this time? What was she about to do? By the time she reached the porch she had decided to go straight to her room and stay there until he left.

But then she heard his footsteps behind her. When she stepped inside the kitchen, she felt him take hold of the door. Crossing the room, she heard it squawk closed. His words rang in her ears: *I'm right behind you, Ellie.*

Quickly she slid onto his bed—to keep from crumpling to the floor, she assured herself. Her legs had never felt so useless. She held her body rigid and still, trying to quell its tremors.

She wasn't at all sure what to expect. Yes, she had slept with Benjamin, but she knew beyond a doubt that what she wanted, what she craved at this moment, what she saw smoldering in Kale Jarrett's eyes, what she felt inside her own body was different, vastly different. She thought of the girls at the Lady Bug and wished she'd asked them more questions. Especially the first Poppy, who had fallen so in love with . . .

Ellie's mouth fell open at the idea.

Love? She had loved Benjamin. But what she felt at this moment was different from anything she'd ever felt before. She stared at Kale through the shadows. Although she could see little, she could practically feel his desire, the heat boiling inside him, and this intimidated her, frightened her.

She felt herself on the precipice of one of the volcanoes she had read about, and as Kale approached the bed, she thought how the boiling lava was drawing ever nearer.

When he stretched beside her, her flesh tingled. Then he stared into her eyes, and she knew she was helpless to save herself.

With one hand he cupped her chin and drew her mouth to his. Their lips touched gently, the kiss began slowly, increasing in intensity with the increasingly fervent beat of her heart. She felt his tongue, hot and wet against her lips, and when she opened her mouth to him, she knew if she hadn't been lying down she'd have swooned, so powerful was her reaction to his slow, seductive exploration.

His fingers left her face, traveled down her neck, and dipped inside the neckline of her kimono. Where his hand touched, her skin burned, and where it did not, her pores begged mercilessly for him.

Slipping the garment over one shoulder, he freed her breast, then covered it with his lips.

She clutched his head in her hands, pressing him to her, knowing this was what she had craved, satisfied . . . for a moment. Then, like a chain reaction, she felt the begging begin again, intensify to escalating heights, but lower now, much lower, deep inside her loins.

She nuzzled against him, trying to bring him nearer and nearer. Was this what Poppy had meant when she'd spoken of her lover's lips lighting her soul?

Poppy. Ellie's mind plummeted back to earth. She knew what Kale had heard; she knew what he believed about her.

She bent her face toward his ear. The sweet torment of his lips tugging at her breast brought tears to her eyes. "I never worked for Lavender," she whispered.

His lips paused; he kissed her breast, then looked into her face. He could barely see her in the near-dark room. "I never asked."

His gentle words brought her tears to the verge of spilling. She squenched her lids. "Only because you thought you already knew."

Falling back on the bed, he pulled her halfway on top of him and held her close. His lips touched her cheek, moved to kiss her lips softly.

"She wouldn't let me," Ellie explained. "She took me in when I was very young, treated me like a daughter. I wanted to work for her, but—"

"You *wanted* to?"

"To pay my way."

Her innocent nature brought a bittersweet smile to his lips. He rubbed her back through the kimono, then began to nudge the fabric up and up until his hand stroked the length of her bare, very soft back. He remembered the delicate, creamy color of her skin. Her innocence combined with her womanly body fired his passion as though another stick of wood had been thrown into an already blazing fire.

Her innocence—or her innocent nature?

Ellie could hardly breathe, what with the feelings he aroused inside her with every stroke of his hand, with his furry chest cushioning her aching breasts.

Tugging and pulling, he finally managed to free her of

the silky garment and toss it aside. She snuggled to him, feeling the softness of his skin, the rough fabric of his breeches. Her hand traced his shoulder, his chest, his ribs, resting at last on the band of his pants.

"I didn't want you to think I worked that way."

"Shh, Ellie." He kissed her lips, then her face, from cheek to cheek. "Don't talk." Suddenly sealing her lips with his, he wriggled his body away from hers, unbuttoned the placket, and removed his breeches, quickly clasping her to him again. Their bare skin fairly fused together, dislodging their lips.

"But—" she began.

"If you have to talk about it," his breath came in gasps; he cupped her buttocks, pressing her to the center of his overwhelming need, "wait till later." His hand traveled around her hips, over her taut belly. "Right now you're filling up my senses. I can't hear anything, I want you so bad."

With these words his fingers slipped inside her, taking her breath away . . . and with it all need to talk vanished, burned away, as it were, by an all-consuming fire, by a throbbing, desperate yearning almost violent in force.

His lips found hers again, and he kissed her until she felt numb with the insistent wanting of him. She felt as if her entire body must surely glow in the darkened room.

Trailing his lips down her neck and across her chest he tasted the familiar mixture of baking bread and wood smoke, a combination of scents that took him back to his youth, to hearth and home. A heady sense of happiness and joy suddenly overwhelmed him, and when he shifted her to her back and thrust deeply inside her, he had the strange sensation of creating something . . . something good, something right.

In merging their two bodies, he had made them one, one in power and passion. In perfect harmony their bodies moved together as one, and the whole was more powerful, more passionate than anything he had ever experienced.

And when at last they reached the pinnacle, it was as to the crashing of lightning and clapping of thunder, and her cry in his ear was like the explosion of a thousand lonely nights.

He clasped her to him, rolled them over, and clung to her. And it was good. So good, and so right.

She felt as though she'd been caught up in a tornado, but one made of fire instead of air. The fiercely swirling flames lifted her higher and higher until she could bear it no longer. Her lips felt parched when she called his name. The sound of her voice came from deep in the pit of her stomach, and, leaving her body, burst into a light like the sun and became him, and he settled over her, soothing, protecting, loving.

Drawing her head back, she stared into his shadowed face. She didn't need light to see him; already he belonged to her heart. "I never knew such feelings existed."

Sighing against her, he cradled her head in his shoulder, and they slept.

Chapter Six

She awoke at first cock's crow, pulled the cover over her shoulders, then realized she was nude.

The aroma of brewing coffee filled her nostrils, a sweet smell that stirred pleasant memories. She stretched her arms along the narrow bed. The air was cool with the promise of fall; the anticipation of it filled her with satisfaction.

Then she remembered. Sitting up in the spare-room bed, she listened for sounds from the other room.

When none came, she slipped on the kimono, sashed it, and stepped barefoot into the hall. The front door stood open, and through it she saw Kale, bare to the waist, sitting on the porch. Forearms on thighs, he cradled a cup of coffee in his hands and stared toward the town road.

Lowering herself to the step beside him, she lay her head against his shoulder and half-expected him to put his arm around her. But he didn't.

After a while she began to feel awkward and started to rise. "You must be starved. We forgot about supper."

"Ellie."

His voice called her back, and she settled down again, their shoulders touching. Still he stared at the road.

"Yes?"

"What did you mean when you said that you sometimes wished you were Delta?"

His question surprised her. Yet instantly she knew it shouldn't have. It was the answer she had been seeking herself only yesterday. Without thinking, she mimicked his position, resting her elbows on her knees, letting the bottom of the kimono fall loosely, forgotten, around her legs.

"If you had asked me that question before last night, I wouldn't have known the answer."

She spoke quietly, following his line of vision toward the road. She felt him look at her then, and with his gaze came a renewal of the heat she had felt last night. Now, however, her pleasure was diffused by a growing concern.

She didn't continue, so he questioned again. "What is the answer, Ellie?"

Meeting his eyes, she was disconcerted by the troubled look she saw, by the questions reflected on his face. Her concern grew to distress. What had happened to the happiness they'd shared? What had happened in his mind while she slept and dreamed sweet dreams?

She sighed. "I loved your brother, Kale Jarrett, and don't you go thinking I didn't."

"The thought did occur to me," he admitted. "After the way you reacted last night."

She jumped to her feet. "Are you saying last night was a test?" Tears sprang to her eyes, forced there by shame. Utter shame. Shame at her behavior . . . shame at her feelings . . . . shame at having assumed he felt the same things she did.

"A test," she repeated, "to judge whether I loved Benjamin?"

His face was solemn, and she turned quickly away.

"No, of course not," he hurried to say. "But you'll have to admit . . . I mean, it's only been a couple of months, and—"

"And what?" she demanded, swirling, hands on hips. The cool fall air penetrated her thin layer of silk, chilling flushed skin.

He shrugged. "Well, the way you responded to me last night, I don't see how you could have loved my brother like a wife—"

"You bastard! What would *you* know about how a wife loves a husband? First you accuse me of selling my body—"

"I never accused you of such."

"You thought it. And now you accuse me of not . . ." Pausing, she wondered exactly what he did mean. "I made Benjamin a good wife, Kale. You can ask anyone in town. He was happy. We—" Tears brimming, she turned away from him again.

Rising, he caught her shoulders. "I didn't mean that, Ellie. And I know what folks in town say. I already heard it. They said you were . . . ah, that you made Benjamin a real good wife."

"Then what are you accusing me of?" The quiver in her voice stabbed at his guilt. Damn it, he wasn't used to sparring with words. All he knew how to do was use his fists—and those damned guns.

What the hell difference did it make anyway whether she married Benjamin for this ranch? If she'd made him

131

happy . . . he suppressed an unfamiliar pang of jealousy. If she'd given Benjamin half the pleasure she'd given him in one night, she deserved the ranch—and more.

"Nothing," he finally managed to admit.

He squeezed her shoulders. The silk beneath his palms was the same that had enticed him the night before; the flesh beneath the silk the same that had captured him, made him feel happiness and joy, made him feel whole for the first time since he was a kid, since before he knew the world for what it was.

"Nothing," he repeated. "But if I'm going to save this ranch for you, I'll have to hang around, at least until some of the family comes. And I don't want you falling in love with me."

He felt her tense beneath his hands. "You were right about me, Ellie."

She tried to turn, but he held her in place.

"I came here ahead of the army. Those bruises you noticed that first night, they were from a fight with a soldier up at Fort Griffin. If he dies, they'll . . ."

When his words trailed off, she forced herself from his grasp and turned to face him, concern written all over her face. "They'll what?"

He looked away. "Prison, if he dies, or—"

"If he doesn't?" Her words escaped in a ragged breath. She studied his face, his strong features, remembered his strength and his gentleness. She wanted to stroke his face so badly her fingers twitched. "If he doesn't die, Kale," she implored, "what will they do to you?"

At the plea in her voice he turned back. Their gazes held. "Probably nothing."

"Then—?"

"But I'm not staying here. I'm going to California. I

132

have a stake in a—"

Her heart felt suddenly lodged in her throat, and she spoke with difficulty. "I never asked you to stay."

Your voice asked me, he thought, *and your eyes.* Recalling last night he suppressed a shudder. *And your body—your wonderful, passionate body begged me to stay.*

"I don't want you to be hurt all over again," he pleaded.

Ellie knew how inexperienced she was. The only women she had ever known were what he would call whores. And the men—Snake at the Lady Bug, who had treated her like a daughter until she grew up, whereupon he ignored her, probably on Lavender's orders; Armando Costello, her friend, but a man who she knew instinctively would lie and steal and cheat if it served his purposes; and Benjamin Jarrett, her husband.

She'd been a good wife to Benjamin, giving him all he wanted and more. And he'd been a good husband. Until last night she hadn't known, and she strongly suspected Benjamin never knew, that passions between a man and a woman could run so fast and carry two people so far. Yes, she had loved Benjamin, but never in the same way she could learn to love his brother.

Kale knew that too, she decided, and it scared him to death. She could see it in his eyes. He was like a skittish colt who'd never known the halter, yet who shied away from it anyhow, determined to hold onto his freedom.

But the fire from last night was still there as well. She could see that in his eyes, too. The fire and the gentleness. And the only thing that frightened her now was her own inexperience. What if she didn't learn how to play the game in time to win it?

But what if she won the game and later regretted it? As

133

a warning, she recalled his admission that he was indeed a man at odds with the law. Yes, she'd been right about that; but she was right about the other, too—about the fire and the passion and the need.

Seized by this new understanding, prodded by a desperation to save what had been offered her, Ellie straightened her shoulders, tightened the sash on her kimono, and looked him squarely in the eye, trying with all her wits to sound worldly.

"Don't you think you're rushing things a bit?" She brushed by him, taking the bottom step. As she did so, her kimono fell open, revealing a bare thigh to the cool fall air—and to Kale Jarrett. She turned to smile at him, striving to calm her racing heart.

"Since you fixed coffee, I'll fix breakfast."

His fingers caught a strand of her hair. When he spoke, his voice was low. "Why is everything so complicated?"

With the slightest movement, she turned back, then went naturally into his open arms. "Everything isn't complicated," she lied softly. Her lips moved toward his. "This isn't."

He kissed her with a hunger that had nothing to do with missed suppers or late breakfasts, and she returned his assault, passion for passion. He could almost feel a noose slipping lower and lower about his neck. He would wriggle out of it later, he argued . . . he would stay until some of the family came; surely she couldn't fall in love with him that quickly, especially not after the way he had just added to her concern about him being an outlaw.

He would stay until some of the family came; he would secure the ranch for her, then he would hightail it to California.

But as his kisses deepened and he slipped his arms

beneath her kimono and felt again his passion grow by leaps and bounds, he knew the family had better come soon.

"This most of all," he whispered into the moist folds of her lips.

And she knew he was right.

Armando Costello arrived in time for supper two days later. By that time tension ran so high between Ellie and Kale that she was sure one of them would soon snap, like a twig after the first blue norther.

"You'd better go put some clothes on," Kale had finally managed to tell her on the porch that morning. "This silky thing will go up in smoke at the first ember from the fireplace."

Already her heart was beating out of control. She had completely forgotten her offer to fix breakfast until he reminded her, and even then she was reluctant to leave his arms. She tugged at his lips with her own, felt his hands roam her back. She ached for him.

His voice cracked beneath the extent of his own passion. "I'm not very good at putting out a fire."

She grinned, feeling her flesh flame. "You do know how to start one, though."

After that he had sent her into the house to fix breakfast while he milked the cow and then turned the calf in with her.

They had spent the rest of the day apart, Ellie doing chores around the house, Kale riding the pastures, inspecting Benjamin's herd, looking for sign of foul play.

"No," he had answered when she suggested riding with him. "You stay here. You must have things that need doing, and I don't need distractions."

He had grinned when he said it, and she laughed with him. But she knew what he meant: he needed to get away from her, to put some distance between them. And she knew he was wise to try.

That evening after supper they sat on the porch. Discussing the day's activities, they steered clear of anything personal—physical contact, eye contact, intimate conversation. She ached to touch him, and she could tell by the determination with which he avoided her that he knew it.

Kale studied the rosebush beside the step, thinking instead of that other rosebush, the one long ago, the one the carpetbagger had pulled from the ground and gotten himself shot over. What would his own life have been like, he wondered now, if that had never happened? Would he still live in Tennessee? Would he have settled down with a place of his own and a wife and a passel of kids? Or would he have ended up a drifter anyway? Was it in his blood, a thing over which he had no control?

"Where'd all this red dirt come from?" The sprinkling of red clay on the ground around the rosebush provided him a topic of conversation he hoped would ease the tension.

"Off Benjamin's boots," she answered. She had given him the boots and Benjamin's clothing that morning. He had thanked her kindly, taken them to the spare room, and worn his old clothes. She didn't mind. It was a gesture she needed to make.

But she cringed at the thought of him not wanting to wear Benjamin's clothes. Her mind had run in circles all day, and she had come to regret their night together. What must he think about her now, since, as he said,

Benjamin had only been gone a couple of months and here she was throwing her body at another man?

If he had an aversion to wearing his brother's clothing, how had he felt making love to his brother's wife—widow? The difference between the two words had done little to reassure her of her own lack of guilt in the matter. She felt ashamed. Her skin fairly prickled with it, with the shame and with the want. Must she live in this vicious circle of torment until he left?

"Where's any red clay around here?" he asked. "I rode all over this place today, and all I saw was black loam—and lots of rocks."

"There isn't any red clay on the ranch." Desperately she tried to concentrate on his conversation. Red clay was a much safer topic than the direction her own mind seemed bent on taking, safer and dreadfully boring.

"Then how did it come to be on Benjamin's boots?" he queried.

She frowned. "I don't know. I didn't think about that when I cleaned them." Her thoughts were elsewhere. Even then, before they had lain together, her thoughts had been full of nothing but Kale Jarrett. Since that first moment when she'd stared at him across the water trough, her mind had been filled with him.

"So," he prompted, "where did it come from?"

"I don't know. The only red clay I've ever seen is up at the painted cliffs."

"Along the Concho? That's a good day's ride from here."

"More. We went up there a couple of times. Benjamin and I, once; Armando went with us another time. Each of the trips took us two full days on the trail."

He considered this new development. It might be the

lead they needed—in addition to providing a different direction for his pitiful mind. He'd thought of little else today but her. And that, he chided, he must put a stop to . . . pronto.

The moon had risen over the treetops now, and darkness had fallen all around. Nighttime had come. Bedtime. With a sigh that turned into a yawn, Kale rose and stretched.

"Why don't you run along to bed?" he suggested without looking back at Ellie. "I think I'll ride up to the rock shelter, see what kind of varmint I can bag tonight."

"I'll come—"

"No." He spoke too quickly, he knew, to cover his charade. "I won't be long. You go ahead, turn in. See you in the morning."

So that was the way it was done, she thought. Fortunately, one of them had enough experience in the way of things to keep them both out of trouble.

But even that didn't help as much as it should have, she reflected later when she lay in bed wide awake, wanting him to return, wanting him to come to her, knowing he would not.

She couldn't go to him, not again. She had thrown herself at him twice. It was his turn. And he had already proved himself stronger than she was.

Stronger—or less affected.

By high noon the next day they'd had a really big fight and Kale had stomped off. From the back door she watched him saddle up and ride into the pasture without so much as a howdy-do.

It started quite innocently when she asked him to tell her about the fight at Fort Griffin. They had just sat down to a bowl of stew and a platter of corn fritters. Kale had praised her cooking, saying again how she was going to spoil him for camp fare, and she had suddenly recalled his contention that she shouldn't fall in love with him because he was an outlaw.

Kale Jarrett was not an outlaw—no matter what he had done in his past, no matter how hard he might try to convince her.

"Tell me about the fight at Fort Griffin," she had requested.

And he had, not remembering until too late to correct himself. This time he forgot to make himself out the villain.

"You weren't at fault," she said. "You avoided killing the soldier. You had no choice but to fight him."

He stared at her face, alive with this discovery; her lovely face so full of love.

"Don't you understand, Ellie? I *wanted* to fight him; I *enjoyed* fighting him."

"But you didn't want to kill him," she answered. "You said yourself you avoided a gun battle. You said yourself he was determined to cause trouble, that you tried to talk him out of it, but—"

"I didn't try hard enough," he argued.

"You aren't to blame, Kale, whether you admit it or not. You did everything you could to avoid that fight."

"Not everything. I could have walked away."

She stared at him while their previous argument came back to her full force. "Oh, I forgot," her voice dripped with derision, "that's your speciality, walking away. Like you intend to walk away from me."

They stared at each other, dumbstruck at the words she'd blurted out.

She clamped her lips between her teeth, wishing to

God she could take back what she never intended to say, knowing without even having to think about it that she'd done more to drive him away with that one sentence than she could have done with a million other words. She might as well have told him she loved him, for heaven's sake!

"I warned you not to fall in love with me," he hissed through clenched teeth. Rising from the table, he started to take his plate to the kitchen.

She grabbed it from his hand, furious with herself and with him. "Love you?" she spat. "How could I fall in love with you in three days' time? I couldn't fall in love with you in three years!" Quite suddenly one of Lavender's favorite sayings came to her rescue: *Men confuse love with lust—that's why my business is so good.* "As much as you've been around, Kale Jarrett, you certainly should know the difference between love and lust!"

She shocked him, all right. His head jerked up; he stared at her with a look akin to horror. Then his emotions gave way to anger, and as she watched, his anger grew to a rage that brought a tremble to his arms.

Later, she thought how that must surely prove she had nothing to fear from this man; if he was ever going to strike her, it would have happened now. She half expected it. But after an indeterminable length of time during which he glared at her without moving a muscle, she saw his jaw twitch. When he stomped away, all she heard was the squawking of the back door.

The encounter took the life out of her. For the rest of the afternoon she was good for almost nothing. While she swept and mopped the floors, tended her garden, and carried water to Benjamin's rosebush, she reflected on how she'd run him off for good.

Vaguely she wondered what she would do about the Raineys, how she would hold onto her land.

The land didn't really matter anymore. The fight was gone from her, or the reason to fight. Benjamin was dead; no amount of avenging would bring him back.

And Kale was gone. He hadn't taken his belongings, of course. But then, he didn't have all that much to take. Certainly nothing that could be of much value, she wouldn't think.

Suppertime neared, but she didn't even stoke the fire.

Then Armando Costello appeared, bearing a side of antelope, a broad smile, and a bright countenance which set her nerves on edge even more.

Kale stormed out of the house, cursing the squawking door. *Lust!* So that's the way she had him pegged.

He saddled the bay and rode to the north pasture where Benjamin's land bordered the Circle R. On the way his anger grew. If she thought all he did was lust after her body, he should have thrown her down and shown her the meaning of the word right then and there.

If that's all she thought of him, he should have taken her the morning before on the porch when she was dressed in that flimsy silk piece of nothing.

Lust? Not on your life, honey! he fumed. That wasn't lust shining from her eyes. That wasn't lust in the lilt in her step.

It wasn't lust she felt for him, it was something more like quicksand. And by damn, he wasn't getting himself caught in it.

For the next few hours he crisscrossed the country looking for red clay. But he found nothing except the usual limestone, covered in places by a thin layer of black topsoil. Riding around shin oak thickets and cedar brakes, he forced his mind to the task at hand. The sooner he found Benjamin's killers—or connected the Raineys to the deed—the sooner he could head for California.

And it wouldn't be near soon enough to suit him.

The sun traveled across the sky, warming him against the early fall chill. Deep red sumac berries and soft blue cedar berries brightened the otherwise dull countryside. He'd never seen so many rocks in all his born days.

Toward sundown he made his way back to the rock shelter but found no one around. Had the Raineys taken his warning to heart?

If they had, they were the only ones who had paid any attention to his advice, he worried. The ride had done him good, cooled him down. His anger had settled into a general disgruntlement at the prospect of having to hurt Ellie. After all, she was his brother's widow, the very person he'd come to help.

But by *damn* if females weren't the most predictable species the Man Upstairs had ever created. Give her a man and she wanted to put him in a house; give her a house and she was determined to put a man in it.

Well, this man wouldn't be so easily caught. This man had no intention of being locked inside any woman's house.

Nudging the bay down the hillside, he studied the yellow glow of candlelight coming through the windows of the house. The sweet scents of baking bread and wood smoke mingled in his imagination, suffusing him with an easy feeling. By the time he approached the barn, his disgruntlement had been properly replaced with a good measure of concern for Ellie.

A man in her house—that's what she needed. Before he left for California, he would find her one.

Smoke curled from the chimney, and when he finished in the barn and started toward the back door, he saw his other set of clothes hanging over the fence rail.

He ran a hand through his hair, then unconsciously across his stubbled chin. He couldn't sit at Ellie's table with trail dust clinging to him like moss on a river rock.

The creek water felt good, and after he dressed in clean clothing and shaved at the well, he felt like a new man.

It was the decision about Ellie, he knew. What a relief to have that little problem settled. A man, that's what she needed.

The first thing he noticed when he reached the yard was an unfamiliar horse hitched at the rail.

He was met at the door by the delicious aroma of Ellie's supper and her cheerful voice.

So she had regained her good humor as well. He smiled, inhaling the sweet smells of the meal she had fixed for him. Then her words registered.

"Kale, look who's come to dinner. Armando Costello."

Costello stood across the room in front of the fireplace. He wore a black broadcloth suit and a fancy white shirt, and here in the lamplight he didn't look the least bit sleazy. At Ellie's call, he replaced the plat he had been studying, turned, and bowed from the waist.

"Jarrett and I had the pleasure of meeting at the Lady Bug." His fingers skimmed over his brocade vest, calling attention to his city attire.

"Howdy." Kale extended his hand without a great deal of enthusiasm. He had no desire to welcome the man to this house, not after the things he had said about Ellie in the Lady Bug.

143

Costello's honey-coated greeting rankled Kale even further. He'd be the first to acknowledge his own plainness. In fact, he was sure he was about as ugly as homemade soap, but he didn't need some fancy gambler to show him up. He'd never trusted folks who had to put on the dog. If a hand couldn't be played straight out, something was wrong.

Involuntarily his plans to find Ellie a man surfaced with a jolt. Not this man. Certainly not this man.

Costello tugged at his cuffs before returning the offered hand, and Kale felt his own wrist bones protrude from well below his faded shirt sleeves. He'd always had trouble with his sleeves being too short. Not that it bothered him. He rarely worried over his dress, except when in the presence of a handsome man and a woman he greatly admired.

As he turned to look at Ellie, his startled expression echoed the confusion on her face. *Greatly admired?* All right, greatly admired . . . what did it prove? He had greatly admired his mother, too, but that hadn't kept him in Tennessee. No, that was wrong, he countered, his mind suddenly reeling . . . he hadn't greatly admired his mother, he had pitied her. He greatly admired . . .

"You two sit down and get better acquainted while I put supper on the table." Ellie scurried around, bringing a plate of biscuits, a large bowl of cream gravy, and a heaping platter of fried meat.

"Armando brought a side of antelope," she explained.

A pang of guilt stirred Kale's conscience.

Costello acknowledged the fact with a nod. "My men like to hunt, so we keep Ellie in fresh meat." While he spoke in matter-of-fact tones, Costello held Ellie's chair, then seated himself at her left hand.

Glaring at the gambler, Kale took the seat to Ellie's right. He started to say that he could damn well provide meat for this table himself, but held his tongue. One insufferable man was enough.

Another pang of guilt reared its ugly head. Whatever else Costello was, he had taken care of Ellie the past couple of months. But listening to the smooth-talking man from New Orleans, Kale began to get riled all over again. It suddenly struck him what game Costello was playing—the bastard was courting Ellie.

"Are you interested in horses, Jarrett?" Costello was asking.

"Horses?" What kind of fool question was that? In these parts, if a man wasn't interested in horses, he had no way of getting from here to there. "You mean the fancy kind like's tied up outside?"

"The Morgan, yes," Costello agreed. "I won that animal last week in a game of chance."

Kale took a bite of antelope and nearly choked before he got it swallowed. "Mostly, I stick to mustangs. Texas prairie, born and bred." Drowning a biscuit in gravy, he took a bite, washed it down with a swallow of coffee, and complimented Ellie.

"I could make a meal on your gravy and biscuits, no need for anything else."

Ellie studied him. His gruff replies to Armando had embarrassed her. Now, while Armando launched a sermon on the virtues of the Morgan, she watched Kale eat the gravy and biscuits with relish new even to him, ignoring the fresh meat their guest had brought to her table.

It was all she could do to keep from laughing. Kale Jarrett was jealous. And he wasn't doing a very good job concealing it.

"If I'd known how much company would raise your spirits," she told him, "I'd have invited Armando to supper earlier."

He glanced up, prepared to object, then saw the smile on her lips.

Costello paused in his discourse. "Did I miss something?"

Kale glared at the gambler, but when Ellie apologized, saying, "Please continue, Armando" in a syrupy voice she'd never used with him, Kale broke in.

"Actually, Costello, we have more important things to discuss than Morgan horses. Have you come up with any new leads to our problem?"

Costello's black eyes flashed at Kale. Clearly he did not intend to relinquish command of the conversation. "My thoughts have not changed since we last spoke, Jarrett. In fact, they are greatly reinforced by this latest fire. Ellie cannot remain here another day. I shall be out first thing in the morning to take her to town."

"Hold your horses—" Kale began.

"Wait a minute," Ellie broke in. "Don't I have anything to say about this?"

Kale gripped his fork, forcibly keeping both fist and eating utensil on the table . . . otherwise, he knew, he'd be in danger of striking the man on the spot. And Ellie already thought him nothing but a ruffian.

Costello was smiling at Ellie. "I thought we settled everything."

"Armando has repeated his offer to buy the ranch," she told Kale.

Expelling a deep breath before he allowed himself to speak, Kale strove to remain calm. "My brothers will arrive in a few days. We'll consider your offer then."

"I meant no offense," Costello replied tersely. "I don't know your reasons for keeping Ellie out here, but I did know my friend. Benjamin Jarrett wouldn't have wanted his wife to remain in a place where her life was in peril—from whatever source."

Kale scraped his chair back, cautioning himself to act with restraint. He gripped his hands into fists, rested them on the table, and felt Ellie cover one with her hand.

He looked down into her worried eyes. He spoke in measured tones, diverting his attention to the gambler. "You forget yourself, Costello. As Benjamin's brother and Ellie's brother-in-law, no one could feel more responsibility for her welfare than I do. Like I told you before, she has her heart set on remaining at home, and I aim to do my damnedest to see that she gets to."

If he had thought to intimidate Armando Costello, he had judged the man wrong, Kale now saw. The gambler jumped to his feet, paced toward the fireplace, then turned—at a safe distance, Kale noted—his black eyes ablaze with hatred. "Brother-in-law or not, you, a known criminal, have no right to come in here and endanger the life of this dear lady."

Ellie rushed between them, intercepting Kale as he crossed the floor. She stopped him with her palms flattened against his chest, and her eyes implored him to back off. As soon as he had stopped, she turned away, flattening her back against his chest, whether to shield him or to hold him back, Kale wasn't sure.

"Hush up, both of you," she commanded. "I intend to stay right here, and I'll not hear another word about it."

At that instant a commotion erupted in the front yard; they heard hooves beating a path away from the house.

"Someone's stealing my horse!" Costello rushed through the door.

The idea crossed Kale's mind that he wouldn't have to worry about the gambler after all. In this country, a man that reckless wouldn't live long.

By the time he and Ellie reached the front window, the riders were already out of sight. Taking the shotgun from above the door, he checked the load, then stepped cautiously onto the porch.

"No one stole your Morgan, Costello. He's still tied to the rail. But we'd better search the area and see what they were really up to."

"I'll take this side." Costello rushed around the corner of the house toward the barn.

"Careful," Kale whispered after him, but it was too late. Cautiously he checked the other side of the house and the thicket out front.

Ellie came onto the porch, carrying a lantern.

"Looks like they've gone," Kale called to her. Then he noticed the second horse tied to the hitching rail behind Costello's Morgan. When the gambler came around the side of the house, Kale called him over.

"Looks like they brought you another horse, Costello. All saddled and ready to ride."

"Good God!" the gambler muttered.

Without listening to Kale's admonitions to stay back, Ellie rushed toward the hitching rail. Suddenly she dropped the lantern and screamed.

"That's Benjamin's horse!"

Kale righted the lantern just as she came into his arms. The hairs along the back of his neck prickled, but he couldn't let her go; holding her close, his eyes searched warily in all directions. "You're sure?"

148

She nodded against him, then struggled free, approaching the horse with tentative steps. "This is the sorrel Benjamin was riding when he rode away that last morning."

Kale brought the lantern closer. He inspected the horse, the saddle. This animal had not been running free for two months. It was curried and well fed, and the saddle had been kept inside, out of the weather. But where? What was the point of it all?

Again Kale had the feeling the Raineys would not trifle with such tactics; they were men of action. Not that they were incapable of intimidation. Kale didn't doubt that either brother was capable of anything the situation called for. But why bother? They planned to take legal possession of the ranch in four more days.

Kale herded them back to the house. Inside he fetched his Winchester from the spare room, filled his pockets with shells, and cautioned Ellie.

"Keep the doors bolted and the lantern low, and stay away from the windows." His eyes fastened on Costello; briefly he considered the man. This was no time for personal vendettas. "Stay here with Ellie until I get back."

"I'm coming with you," the gambler replied.

"What are you going to do?" Ellie's eyes, wide and expressive, held Kale's. "It's too dark to see anyone. Besides, they're gone by now."

"Maybe so," Kale conceded. "But if not, we can give them a good scare, perhaps pop a varmint out of the brush."

To save time Kale rode Benjamin's horse.

"Go south," he instructed Costello. "Cut behind that cedar brake and check the thicket down by the spring. I'll

149

take the opposite direction. We'll meet at that lightning-split cedar at the crest. Do you know it?"

Costello nodded and swung into the saddle of his prized Morgan.

"And Costello," Kale added, "ride wary. We've no notion what we're up against, but they've shown themselves to be savages. None of that hero stuff you pulled back yonder, running around the house without looking first."

After checking the barn, he headed for the north hill, retracing the path the riders had taken. It was his idea to follow the trail for a while, then cut around, ground-hitch his mount, and climb to the rock shelter on the hill.

Ellie was likely right: it stood to reason that the riders would light a shuck once they left the horse. They hadn't tarried the other times, not when they left Benjamin's boots, nor when they returned his body.

But what if they had intentionally caused all that commotion tonight, knowing they would be followed? Suppose they were waiting at the rock shelter? If he could come in from behind and take them by surprise . . .

He rode alert, his eyes scanning every thicket and any bush large enough to conceal a man, his ears attuned to any sound foreign to the night.

The moon which had come up so brightly an hour ago was now covered by a veil of clouds, making black shadows of the bushes that dotted the hillside.

When he approached the foot of the hill a hundred yards or so below the rock shelter, he dismounted and made his way on foot. The trail he chose was almost straight up and down, the path he figured the intruders would least expect him to take.

Earlier he'd noticed a good-sized mesquite tree

growing near the mouth of the rock shelter. His plan was to come up behind that tree. If anyone was inside the cave, he could work his way around the cedar and take them while they watched the other side. At least, that's how he hoped it would work.

It took him a good twenty minutes to reach the mesquite tree. For another few minutes he crouched behind it, waiting to hear an indication that someone was inside the shelter. None came.

The cave lay directly between him and the lightning-split cedar where he was to meet Costello. Anyone watching the cave would likely wait in the brush on the opposite side. If they moved in, he and Costello could catch the intruders between them.

As he stood up slowly and moved two steps to the right, lead glanced off mesquite at about ear level. In one movement Kale rolled behind a small oak to his right and fired in the direction of the shot. Instantly he dashed to the next cover, a protruding mass of limestone.

A second shot ricocheted off the rock, grazed his cheek, and showered him with limestone fragments. He shot back three times in rapid fire, then moved on up the hill. Another shot hit the tree where he was headed.

The night was as dark as all get-out, and Kale knew he didn't offer much of a target. But whoever fired those shots seemed to know exactly where he would be.

Maybe they already had Costello. That pilgrim! Surely he hadn't gone out and gotten himself caught. He really should stick to gambling halls. Kale made up his mind right then and there to talk to him about it.

Another shot hit the trunk of the oak, not two inches above his head. Then he heard scrambling and horses' hooves beating away from the cliff. Kale swore to himself, turned abruptly, and literally slid straight down the hill. He came up running ten yards in front of Benjamin's horse. Jumping astride it, he retraced his path and took the trail to the top of the hill.

With his bandanna he dabbed his cheek where the bullet grazed him. It was only a flesh wound, and he knew he was lucky. He couldn't tell whether any of his shots had scored.

Ellie had been right: it was too dark to man hunt, although that wasn't exactly how she put it, he recalled. What was she thinking with all this firing going on?

At the crest of the hill he found Costello, and they headed toward the house.

Come morning he would start fresh, track those horses, scout the area where the shots were fired, and then head over to the Circle R. The Rainey brothers had a lot of explaining to do.

At the road to town he bid the gambler farewell, all too conscious that "good-bye" was the most pleasant word he'd spoken to the man all evening.

He stabled Benjamin's horse in the stall next to the bay and headed for the house. Here, within the protection of the two buildings, the night was pitch black. He heard the familiar squawk of the door before he could make out her form in the doorway.

"What was the firing about?" She strove to control the quiver in her voice.

"Not much, Ellie," he called, dabbing at the side of his face to staunch the blood before she could see it.

She held the door until he took it, then preceded him into the main room of the house, trying to steady her trembling limbs. Although she'd kept the lantern low, like he told her, she had managed to clean the dishes and put away leftover food before he returned. Now she went to the fire and poured him a cup of coffee. "That isn't much of an answer, either. Tell me what happened."

He turned up the lamp, then immediately wished he hadn't, for when she handed him the coffee she noticed the blood on his cheek.

"It's nothing," he protested.

But she insisted on cleaning the wound. "For one as accustomed to gunshot wounds as you," she said lightly, "I suppose this is *nothing*. To the rest of the world—"

He cocked his head, wriggling away when she dabbed the wound with tincture of iodine. "Ow!"

"Be still."

"I didn't say it was a gunshot wound," he argued in a light tone. "What if I told you I fell down the hill?"

Finished, she leaned back to scrutinize her handiwork. Her eyes flitted to his; their gazes held. She felt her heart skip a beat and hoped it didn't show. "I wouldn't believe you, of course. A gunfighter like yourself, it wouldn't be fitting."

Before he could stop himself his lips had found hers. He cupped her face gently in one hand, stroked her lips lightly, wanting, desperately wanting to do so much more.

Lust? he wondered.

Definitely.

Drawing back, he held his hand on her face. "I did a lot of thinking today, Ellie. I don't intend to leave you here all alone. Before I go, I'll find you a man."

The shock rocked her back on her heels. "You'll what?"

Dislodged, his hand slipped to her hair. He splayed his

153

fingers about the side of her head. "I'll find you a man. But it won't be that bastard who was here tonight."

"Costello?" she mumbled, not even aware of what she was saying, wondering what kind of fool he took her for.

"No, it won't be Costello. I'm not sure I can ever let that bastard inside this house again."

The numbness of his pronouncement spread over her senses. "You'll find me a man?"

He nodded gravely. "I won't leave you alone."

All thought of the earlier commotion vanished in her rising fury. She shook loose from his hand and stumbled backward. She had intended to pry from him the details of his chase up the hillside, to learn what he had seen, who was doing the shooting, who'd shot him. Now she didn't care. She didn't care if he went outside and shot up the whole country.

"You certainly have a low opinion of my charms, Kale Jarrett. I'll have you know I can find my own man—*if* I ever want one again. Right now that possibility seems most doubtful."

After this she stomped off to bed, leaving him to bank the fire and consider his way with women from the lonely vantage of the bed in the spare room.

When finally he sank into the feather mattress and drifted off to sleep, it was to dream of quicksand.

Chapter Seven

Ellie slept fitfully. Time and again she awakened thinking herself in Kale's arms, only to be reminded of his decision to find her a man—some other man. Finally, while it was still dark outside, she arose, put coffee on to boil, and considered what to fix for breakfast.

Starting out the back door to fetch a slab of bacon from the smokehouse, she stopped short on the step. Suddenly she recalled the commotion of the night before: Benjamin's horse mysteriously returned, Kale shot on the dark hillside.

She glanced around nervously. *Would that this matter were settled* . . . Kale believed the Raineys were acting out of character, furtively harassing her while at the same time taking open measures to remove her from the land. She had to agree, it made no sense.

But that was the only thing she agreed with him on. *A man*, of all things! If he thought he could run her life, she had a surprise for him! She didn't need anyone to find her a man. She could live quite well without ever seeing another man.

Glancing toward Benjamin's grave, she was overwhelmed by a feeling of being all alone and very lonely. She needed someone to talk to, and she certainly couldn't talk to Kale Jarrett. All he wanted to do was—

Striking out for Benjamin's grave, she clutched her shawl about her thin batiste shirtwaist. The fall air was cold this early in the morning.

Lust? She had blurted out the word without thinking. But had she been right? Was that all she felt for Kale? She didn't know. She truly didn't know.

Walking east she studied the sky; its growing colors began to soothe her spirits. She watched a gilt edge form on the deep purple horizon, promising a golden day. Ever since she'd moved to the ranch, morning had been her favorite time of day, rarely failing to fill her with expectancy. Today, however, her expectations were not at all bright.

She sank to her knees at the grave, focusing on the mound of rocks. "Oh, Benjamin," she whispered, "I need your help. You were right about him. He *is* headstrong and footloose, he won't ever be any other way. But why didn't you tell me the rest? That he was a wandering man who would steal my heart and leave me all alone . . ."

She talked to him as she imagined she'd have spoken to a father, confiding her deepest wishes and greatest fears. She always had, though before, her deepest wishes and greatest fears had not involved . . .

Lust. The fact that Kale was Benjamin's brother did not concern her. She hadn't resisted a physical love with Benjamin, she realized, she had let him lead her, and this new trail of passion—and lust—was one he had not

156

found . . . for what reasons, she did not know.

She suspected, however, that the trail she and Kale plummeted down every time they looked into each other's eyes was a trail less traveled than most. Surely the average person didn't walk around with the top layer of his skin aflame, a permanent yearning in his heart, and a deep, demanding ache in his loins.

This, she knew, must be lust. What role could love play in such a physical ailment? Love was gentle, while this feeling bordered on being violent; love was peaceful, but her feelings for Kale Jarrett were turbulent—they left her perpetually tormented and angry; love was supposed to be an antidote to life's problems, while whatever possessed her now made her physically ill.

Except when she was in Kale's arms.

She wished he would leave now, while she could still recover from this illness. Before his family arrived. She wished his family wouldn't even come. Were they all like him, disagreeable and demanding?

Was Benjamin the only kind and gentle person among them? At that idea she cringed. She couldn't deal with a houseful of headstrong people.

"I'm going to have to build a fence around here."

Kale's voice, soft as it was, shattered her senses. Turning, she stared into his solemn face.

"Don't worry about it," she answered. "I'll take care of it—later."

He knelt beside the grave at right angles to her, his back to the rising sun. "Ellie . . . ah, I'm sorry about last night, the things I said."

"Don't be."

"Well, I am."

157

She tensed at the defensiveness in his voice. Why hadn't she accepted his apology and let it go? "No need." She started to rise.

He grasped her arm. "Look at me, Ellie. I didn't mean to sound like I'm out to take charge of your life."

His palm warmed her through the thin shawl. She wished he would leave. Now. She wished he'd never come.

"I can take care of myself, Kale. And I intend to. You have no obligation to me."

He released her with a sigh. "Benjamin was my brother. Regardless of what you think, we Jarretts are a close family. We take care of our own."

"I'm not one of your own. In fact, if it weren't for your relationship to Benjamin, I'd insist you leave right now." Feeling herself breathless, she paused to steady her emotions. "I suppose you have a right to stay and settle his murder, if you think you must."

Lifting her chin in a quest for resolve, she turned determined eyes on him. "But that's all. You're not here to take care of me. I can take care of myself. I don't need you, Kale Jarrett."

He heard the hurt in her voice, saw it in her eyes; but he didn't blame her for closing him out this way. He felt about as helpless as a man could feel.

He'd proved himself incapable of running his own life. How could he have thought to run hers? And why? "Have it your way," he retorted. "But while I'm here I intend to see you set up to take care of yourself."

The concern in his voice began to soothe the ragged edges of her nerves. "If that's what you want," she whispered. Deep inside, relief seeped into her turmoil, stirring up a mass of confusion between what she knew was right and what she wanted to be true. Knowing she'd be better off with him gone was a far different thing from wanting him to leave. She wanted him to stay, however short the time, on whatever terms necessary.

When he sighed, clapped his thighs, and rose, extending her a hand, she accepted against her better judgment. The heat of his touch raced up her arm, as she had known it would, to her neck, singeing all the way to her ears, bringing joy and agony—blissful, unrequited agony.

"But I'll still refuse to let you marry that damned gambler."

His tone was playful, and she followed him down the hill with a lightened step. Perhaps his stay wouldn't be so unpleasant after all, she argued to herself. If he cooperated in keeping that wicked word *lust* out of their relationship, he would be pleasant company.

Neither of them spoke again until they reached the bottom of the hill, then he said, "After we got off on the wrong foot up there, I forgot what I came up the hill to tell you."

She looked at him, wary.

"I found the track of the puddin'-foot."

"Where?"

"At the hitching rail where they left Benjamin's horse."

While he helped her prepare breakfast, he surprised her again. "On my way up the hill a while ago, I noticed a fire in the rock shelter."

"Now we can catch them."

"I'll take care of it, Ellie. I've already made plans."

She frowned but listened. She could at least hear him out before making demands.

"I'll ride off like I'm headed for town," he told her. "A couple of miles from the house, I'll switch back, cut around behind the brush, and surprise our fellers in the rock shelter. This time I figure to give them an earful to take back to the Raineys."

When he finished, she uttered one word: "We."

"No, Ellie," he objected.

"I'm coming, too. You might as well know now—if you stay, I intend to help you solve this problem." She shrugged. "You shouldn't object. It'll mean you can be on your way to California sooner."

"All right, Ellie . . . all right."

While she washed up in the kitchen, he saddled their horses, and they made a show of leaving by the town road.

He led the way to a thicket not far from where he had met Costello the previous night. At his signal, Ellie dismounted, and they hitched their mounts, proceeding the rest of the way on foot.

She had changed clothes before they left the house, donning one of Benjamin's old shirts and a pair of his breeches, which she belted with an old leather strap.

Kale watched her now, thinking he'd never seen a woman who could make even the sloppiest, most shapeless garments look feminine. He wished he could buy her something nice, really nice, and pretty.

He admired the way she came quietly, stepping carefully around fallen leaves and an old rotted log. She'd probably be able to make it out here by herself, just as she figured on doing.

When they gained the lip of the rock shelter, he motioned her to stand back while he slipped into the cave, his six-shooter drawn. His ruse worked; the two Circle R cowpokes were taken completely off guard.

They had obviously been so confident Kale and Ellie had ridden into town that they were sitting by the campfire preparing a large breakfast and swapping yarns.

"Sorry, fellers," Kale told them. "Your stomachs will have to wait. You're going on a little trip."

Ellie watched with held breath. When Kale drew his gun, it was all she could do to keep from reaching to stop him. His voice, when he spoke, sounded light and carefree, as if he charged men with a gun every morning of his life.

"What're you talking about? We ain't done nothin' wrong," the men protested in turn.

"How 'bout trespassing?" Kale questioned. "You're camping on my sister-in-law's property."

When he mentioned her, Ellie stepped into the opening, showing herself. "If you're hungry, you can come to the house and ask for food," she said. "Otherwise, you're not welcome here."

The men looked from Kale to Ellie and back again. "I know you," one of them told Kale. "You're that outlaw brother of Benjamin Jarrett's."

"Call it any way you like," Kale responded. "But the lady says you aren't welcome, and this is her land. Get your gear together and hightail it."

"You won't get away with this. Matt Rainey'll eat you alive."

"I'm sending you on a little mission." Kale ignored their threat. "You're to take a message to the Raineys.

161

Tell them that before Friday every Jarrett from the Atlantic Ocean to the Pacific will arrive here to bid Benjamin farewell. The Raineys may think I'm the outlaw of the clan, but wait till they meet my kin. Tell them we'll make a call on the Circle R, and in the meantime to keep their men and horses off Jarrett property. And tell them I'm glad to see they shoed the puddin'-foot, but to keep him off Jarrett land anyhow."

The news didn't set well with either man, Ellie could see that. But when Kale ushered them to their horses, she marveled at his command over the situation. His gun was drawn, yes. But she sensed it wasn't really necessary.

When he returned to the rock shelter his six-gun was holstered, the thong snapped, and he was in a jolly mood.

"What did you learn from them?" she asked.

"Their names. Actually, not even their complete names," he corrected. "Ira and Till was all they said."

"And their reasons for spying on me?"

He shook his head. "Not a word. My idea from looking them over is that they're average cowhands, not hired guns, stationed as lookouts, ordered to keep an eye on things."

"Why?"

"That's the question I intend to put to Matt Rainey today. We'll get this thing straightened out once and for all."

Once and for all . . . the words settled like stones in her heart.

Kale crossed to the fire, where he tested the skillet for heat, then picked it up gingerly. "Ira and Till ride for the brand. They're doing the job the boss gave them, and from the looks of things, they'd prefer to be punching cows. That's my idea, anyhow."

He pierced a piece of bacon with a knife. "How 'bout something to eat?"

She shook her head, laughing. "We just finished breakfast, remember? You must have a bottomless pit for a stomach."

He grinned sheepishly, but nevertheless bit off a hunk of bacon. "I've never been one to let food go to waste."

When she stepped back onto the ledge he followed and squatted on a rock, still holding the skillet and eating from it.

She had never seen a man so ready to eat, nor one who enjoyed his food more. "Talk about me needing a man," she said, joking easily now, "I think you need a woman."

He cocked his head. "Me? What for?"

She hesitated only slightly while seating herself on the ledge and catching her knees up with her arms. "To cook for you. I don't see how you get anything done by yourself; you must spend all your time cooking."

He laughed. "Starving is more like it."

She stared out over the valley. The sun had risen, warming the morning, warming her, helping her relax. She studied her house, thinking how much it meant to her. It was the only house she'd ever been able to call her own. Even though it had been built years before by people she'd never met, and even though it was now badly in need of repairs, it was still hers.

"You could use someone to mend your clothing, too," she added. "Or learn to do it yourself."

"Me?"

"A man with only two good pairs of pants, one of them full of holes, ought to learn to use a needle."

He took another bite, talked around it. "I'll swap talents with you. You teach me to use a needle, I'll teach you to punch cows."

She started to tell him that the only thing she knew how to do with a needle was to thread it, but decided not to. "You don't think I know how to punch cows?"

He shook his head. "It's doubtful."

She laughed at his honesty. "Yes, very doubtful. Benjamin never—"

"Benjamin, rest his soul, didn't know how to punch cattle either."

"He did too."

Kale studied her. "Now don't go getting riled, Ellie. I meant no disrespect. But Benjamin spent most his life farming." He looked back to the valley.

"Don't know why he decided to raise cattle, anyhow. Riding the pasture the last couple of days, I noticed things you're going to have to learn—and change—if you want to hold on to this place."

He was right, of course: she couldn't run a ranch without knowing the slightest thing about it. "You'll teach me?"

"Sure, that's my business. Granted, I've spent most of my life working for others, but once I get to California, that'll change."

The statement took her aback. She'd never even wondered why he was going to California. Truth be known, she suspected he'd invented the trip, an excuse to leave. "Why are you going to California? Or should I ask *to whom?*"

"Whom?" His lips lingered on the final consonant.

She grinned, but resisted the urge to look at him,

continuing instead to stare out at the valley. "Whom?" She kept her tone playful. "Perhaps I worried too soon about you needing someone to cook and mend."

"The *whom* is a *he*. His name is Mack McKenzie, and he isn't any better at using a needle or cooking than I am, I'm afraid. He's an old friend. Before I left Fort Griffin, I gave him a stake to put into some venture he's cooking up out San Francisco way."

"What kind of venture?" she probed.

He shrugged.

"You don't know?"

"Does it matter?"

"I suppose not. Depends on how much money you gave him."

"Everything I had," he answered.

"Everything?"

"A puncher like myself doesn't pile up a whole hell of a lot of money—"

"Certainly not if you give it to every friend who comes along to invest in whatever venture he chooses. Don't you worry about the future?"

He turned to look at her. She felt it. She heard his heavy sigh. "The future, Ellie, is for men with . . ."

His words drifted off. This woman wouldn't let up, would she? He had to admit, though, the conversation had been pleasant enough up till now. "Men with responsibilities need to consider the future, not a man like myself, who's—"

"Hardheaded and footloose," she supplied, knowing she was annoying him, determined now to turn the conversation back to a more neutral topic.

Resting her head against the rock wall of the shelter,

she inhaled a lungful of pungent fall air. A peaceful feeling diffused to some extent the anxiety that had eaten at her continually for the past few days. She closed her eyes, letting the sun warm her body.

She heard him set the pan aside, heard grass rustle. When she opened her eyes, he had pulled a handful of bear grass and was cleaning the skillet. Afterwards, he took it back inside the cave, then returned and sat on the ledge like before. The mouth of the cave separated them.

"How many do you think will come?" she asked.

"How many what?"

"The family . . . how many do you expect?"

"Hard to say . . . all who can. Not much besides death and illness will keep them away."

Her eyes opened. "A houseful?"

He shrugged.

"Then we'll have to get food and figure out where everyone will sleep—"

"Ellie, don't carry on so. They're used to doing for themselves."

"Not when they're guests in my home."

"They're not coming for a party," he objected.

"I know, but they'll have to eat."

"You're right. I'm sorry—"

"And if they all eat as much as you do, we're going to be in trouble," she added, hurrying to cut off whatever it was he intended to apologize for. His apologies usually turned into a quarrel of some sort, and she didn't want to quarrel. Not now that she was feeling comfortable.

"Guess that means I'll have to go hunting."

She felt his eyes on her again and turned to catch his smile. They worked well together, she thought quite

166

without intending to. Quickly she stopped such fanciful thoughts.

But they must have showed, she decided, for the instant she realized what she was thinking, her smile froze in place and she turned away. The innocence of the moment was lost. How hard it was to keep things simple around him.

He moved first, bouncing to his feet, reaching to give her a hand. "Come on. That old sun's almost half a day old, and here we sit like we didn't have better things to do."

"What will you do with the rest of the day?" she asked when they rode up to the house.

"First I'm going to pay a call on Matt Rainey. Then, if there's time, I want another look around this place. That red clay on Benjamin's boots had to come from somewhere."

Her eyes widened. In one movement she slid from the saddle, tossed her reins over the hitching rail, and ran for the house.

"Where's the fire, Ellie?" he called, taking time to properly hitch both their mounts before he hurried after her.

They collided when she ran back out the front door. Grabbing his sleeve, she fairly dragged him to the edge of the porch. "Look at this." She held a piece of limestone toward him.

Taking the rock from her palm, he turned it over, studying the markings, what there was of them. He looked at her with a grin. "My talent is punchin' cows, honey, not . . ."

She blinked at the appellation, then looked down

quickly. He hadn't meant it like that, she chided. Lots of men called women "honey." Why, she'd heard it a million times at the Lady Bug, dropped from lips that never knew the meaning of the word *love*.

Kale cleared his throat. "I'm no mindreader," he finished.

With the greatest of efforts she regained her composure. "I know." Taking the rock again, she ignored the warmth of his fingers when her own touched them. She sat on the porch and motioned him to follow. "This rock is important, Kale."

"I'm listening." He sat beside her but made no attempt to touch the rock again.

"I found it in Benjamin's pocket, the pocket of the pants he was wearing when they returned his body."

Now he was listening. "Where did it come from?"

"The painted cliffs."

He frowned. "But they're—"

"Two days away, like the red clay. I don't know why I didn't put the two together before." Except that half her mind had been taken up with other things, she thought, anxious now that she might have let an important clue slip by.

"No place on the ranch has Indian drawings?"

She shook her head. "We'd have found them. Benjamin, Armando, and I've gone over every square mile, or near enough, looking for artifacts."

"I don't understand what this has to do with Benjamin's death," Kale mused.

"Neither do I, but it must fit. He collected these fragments, but he wouldn't have carried one in his pocket that day. He had no reason to."

"Unless it was already in his pocket."

She shook her head. "I'd have found it when I washed."

He agreed.

"The answer must be at the painted cliffs," she said.

"Why would he have gone up there without telling you?"

She shrugged. "I don't know. But I won't be satisfied until I see for myself."

Kale sighed. "Two days away?"

She nodded.

"We can't leave the place unprotected, Ellie. Certainly not before Friday, when we see what the Raineys are up to. As soon as the family comes to keep an eye on things, we'll ride up there. Unless . . ."

He stood, absently brushing the seat of his pants.

"Unless what?" She rose to stand beside him.

"Unless I can settle things with Matt Rainey before we leave." He clamped his hat on his head. "I'll be back in time for supper."

"I'm coming—"

"Not this time."

She sighed. "At least wait until you've had some dinner."

He grinned. "Don't you think I've eaten enough to hold me till supper?"

She laughed at that.

"And Ellie, that shotgun over the door is loaded. Use it if you have to."

"Okay."

"Promise me?"

She nodded.

Before he took time to think, he bent forward, stopping himself before he'd gotten farther than her forehead, where he planted a quick kiss. "See you at supper," he mumbled.

She stood deathly still, not daring to move lest she betray her feelings.

When he reached his horse, she stepped onto the porch, hugging her arms around one of the support posts. "Be careful," she called.

After he left, she fairly danced through the house. Her heart sang with the idea that what she suspected might indeed be true. Two slips in such a short time must surely mean something. *Surely* . . .

With her lack of experience in the matter, she hesitated to make judgments, lest she be disappointed to discover her error. Her brain spun with dizzying speed—surely all men did not resist falling in love as stalwartly as did Kale Jarrett.

Never mind. Now that she knew—or thought she knew, she cautioned—she'd figure out some way to help him over the hurdle. First, of course, she must not let him know she suspected.

"And you must not let him know how you feel," Lavender Sealy cautioned, sipping a glass of lemonade on the porch. She had arrived mid-afternoon to see what Armando Costello's fuss was all about. "Keep him guessing until he's fallen into the snare and can't get out."

Ellie had finished a layer cake for supper and was putting the remaining antelope roast into a Dutch oven with carrots, potatoes, and onions from her garden when Lavender and Snake drove up in the surrey.

Snake carried Lavender's packages, and Lavender rushed forward, talking as she came. "I had to see for myself what Armando meant about this brother-in-law of yours being the most dastardly thing to hit town since the last hurricane."

"We don't have hurricanes this far north, Lavender," Ellie laughed, hugging the woman. How glad she was to have a woman's company. And not just any woman. She could talk to Lavender. Lavender would understand and counsel, and Lord knew how she needed counseling.

"I know, baby, but a jealous man can be as dangerous as a hurricane; two of them might be worse." She scrutinized Ellie, turning up her nose at Ellie's attire. "Jealousy, however, comes in handy in a pinch. It can be downright healthy for a man from time to time. How're you holding up?"

"Fine." Ellie bit her bottom lip. So much to tell—where to begin? "Let me fix you something to eat."

Lavender shook her head. "We ate before we left. Fix us some lemonade while I show you what I brought."

Ellie complied. "But . . ."

"Now Ellie, I won't take no for an answer. When you married Benjamin I tried to give you some nice things, but you said I'd done enough—"

"You had . . . have."

"And I'm fixin' to do some more." Speaking all the while, Lavender tore into the packages. "Of course, I ought to get to know the man in question before I encourage this thing."

"What thing?" Ellie teased, knowing full well what Lavender meant, feeling giddy and happy and in the mood to tease nonetheless.

171

Lavender eyed her with cocked head. "Love, Ellie. Love and marriage." At Ellie's grin, she paused. "Oh, pshaw, you know well enough. Where is he?"

"He rode over to see the Raineys. Wants to hear from them why they've been harassing me."

"Good."

"Good that he's gone to the Raineys? Or good that they're harassing me?"

"Good that he's out of our hair for a while. He'll take care of anyone who's after you, if I read him right that day. His absence gives us time to do something about your appearance."

Ellie sucked in her breath at sight of the first gown Lavender withdrew from the brown wrapping paper. Truth be known, she had dreaded to see what Lavender brought. She certainly didn't want Kale to come home to a dancehall girl. But she had worried needlessly.

"I bought these things from Zofie Wiginton over at the Bon Ton. She ordered them a while back for that little wife of the preacher, you know, the one who took a week's look at Summer Valley and ran home to Mobile."

"It's beautiful." Ellie set the pitcher of lemonade on the table and fingered the fine cotton fabric striped in yellow and white; the yellow stripes were figured with tiny white flowers.

Lavender held it against Ellie's sloppy shirt and breeches. The waist dipped to a vee; the bodice was attached to a rounded yoke and topped by a crisp white linen collar.

Ellie held her breath. "Do you think it'll fit?"

"I know it will," Lavender chided, pulling petticoats and pantaloons and two corsets and shoes and stockings from various bags.

"So many things!" Ellie clapped her hands to her face. Her words stopped when Lavender proceeded to unwrap two more gowns—one a brown-and-white check, the other made of a rich russet material.

"Too much," she corrected.

"Not enough, if your wardrobe is to be judged by the outlandish garb you're wearing at the moment. He didn't see you in that, I hope."

Ellie cringed, but her face brightened again at the sight of a chestnut-colored riding suit of fine wool with matching velvet collar and cuffs. The next item was a pair of boots to match.

"Whatever will I do with such fine clothes?" she wailed.

"Seduce him, of course. Isn't that what you want to do?"

Ellie blushed in spite of herself.

Lavender pushed aside the unopened packages. "The rest can wait until later. Right now we have to get you into something presentable. Which will it be?"

"If I have anything new, shouldn't it be black?"

Lavender shook her head. "Black is for old widows. Young ones don't have the time for it."

"But what will he think when he comes back and sees me in all this finery? He'll know what we're doing."

"All he will see is you, baby, the way you were meant to be seen, not looking like some old ragamuffin."

"You don't know him—or the problem."

"Then fill me in while we get you dressed." Lavender carried the bags into Ellie's bedroom, stopping in the door to scrutinize the bed.

Ellie blushed in spite of herself. Then she quickly regained her composure. "He sleeps in the spare room,

Lavender," she chastised.

Lavender frowned. "Oh, well, that'll change in time. Which gown? I think the yellow?"

Ellie nodded. "He's sure to wonder why I've started wearing fancy clothes all of a sudden," she called after Lavender, who had taken the water pitcher into the kitchen, where Ellie heard her fill it from the bucket.

"We'll say you were having a few things made up and I brought them out when they were finished."

Taking the cloth Lavender wrung out in rose-scented water, Ellie began to bathe off, worrying all the while. "That's a lie."

"A small one. We women are called upon to supply fictional information from time to time. I can't see it will do much harm in the afterlife, seeing how it's certain to improve both your situations here and now."

"That's definitely a matter of opinion. And not his." She sucked in her breath while Lavender tightened the laces on the corset, then slipped a delicately embroidered corset cover over it. Ellie wished she had time to admire one garment at a time, they were all so beautiful.

"What is his problem?" Lavender demanded, handing Ellie one of the three petticoats she had shaken out.

"He's afraid I'm falling in love with him."

Lavender's eyes found Ellie's. "Is that bad?"

"He's determined not to settle down. He wants to go to California and . . . oh, Lavender, what difference does it make? He's a wandering man, footloose. I have no business falling in love with a man like that."

"Have you?"

Ellie chewed her bottom lip, nodding quite without thinking.

"And how does he feel about you?" Lavender began to

174

button the myriad of tiny buttons that ran up the back of the bodice.

"He's resisting with all his might." Ellie stopped abruptly, trying to catch her breath in the too-tight corset. She rarely wore one anymore, and now she knew why. Suddenly an additional worry surfaced. "Lavender, stop. I'll never be able to unbutton this gown by myself!"

Finished, Lavender gave her a pat on the bustle and turned her by the waist, inspecting as she went. "What's the use having a man in the house, baby, if not to help out?"

"Lavender!"

"Time's wasting. I'll hang the rest of these things in the wardrobe while you do something with your hair. Where are those lovely silver combs that belonged to Benjamin's . . . ah, and Kale's mother?"

Chapter Eight

"He'll take one look at me and ride straight out of here," Ellie predicted. Once she had dressed, she and Lavender carried ladder-back chairs from the house onto the porch, where they now sat enjoying the soft air of a late-fall afternoon. Since it was nippy out, Ellie covered her yellow gown with a knitted wool shawl, a white one she had saved from her mother's things.

"No man ever left a woman because she looked too pretty," Lavender objected.

"He'll know why you brought these clothes."

Lavender scowled. "And why did I bring them? Because you needed your spirits lifted, and because Mrs. Wiginton needed the money she was out for that preacher's wife, and since the clothes were just your size—"

Ellie laughed nervously. Her stomach felt tied in knots, as much as its girded state would allow, that is. "Why are you trying to catch a gunfighter for me, Lavender? You don't even know him."

"That man's no gunfighter. Benjamin always said his

177

brother Kale had been a sweet, sensitive child, and that the scrapes he got himself into were because he was taking up for an underdog somewhere. Besides, I saw for myself how he acted when he came to my place."

"How's that?" Ellie demanded.

"Concerned. About you, about Benjamin. And angered over what he took to be Armando's derisions."

"Armando's what?"

Ignoring the question Lavender nodded toward the road where it meandered down the hillside. "Here comes your Prince Charming."

"Lavender!" Rising quickly, Ellie hugged her guest. "Thank you for the clothes . . . I hope. You'd best be getting back to town now."

The horse and rider came closer. Passing in front of the house on his way to the barn, Kale tipped his hat. From the way he craned his neck, Ellie knew he was trying to figure out who their company was.

Snake came around the side of the porch. "The team's hitched, Lavender."

"Good." Ellie nudged Lavender toward the steps.

"We'll be staying for supper, Snake," Lavender replied. "Ellie's been good enough to invite us—"

"That was before—"

"And from the smell of that delicious roast, I wouldn't miss it for the world. Venison, you said? From the side of antelope Armando brought yesterday?"

"Lavender," Ellie pleaded. "Please."

Lavender turned cheery eyes on Ellie. "Don't worry, baby. I promise to be quiet as a mouse. I just want to check out this gunfighter of yours once more; perhaps I made too hasty a judgment."

"You!" Ellie sighed. "I know what you're up to, and

178

you'd better not run him off!"

Lavender hugged Ellie. "I'm a good judge of men, baby, and I'll tell you this: if a pretty dress or an old geezer like me can run a man off, you're better off without him. Come on, I'll help you get the table set."

Inside Ellie took down the dishes while Lavender went about doing all sorts of unnecessary things . . . things that made Ellie even more nervous, like lighting every lamp in the room and the candles on the mantel.

"Lavender, you'll burn the place down," Ellie objected, knowing this too was something different, a romantic touch that Kale would be sure to notice and wonder at.

"After all the trouble I went to to fetch that dress, and you to wear it, we don't want him to miss a single detail."

By the time she heard the back door squawk, Ellie was fit to be tied, what with anticipating Kale's reaction to her new gown and worrying over what Lavender would say at supper.

She didn't have long to wait for Kale's reaction, for when the door squawked, she was in the process of lifting the Dutch oven from the fireplace to carry to the table. At the sound she automatically glanced toward the door in time to see the startled look on his face.

"Howdy," he blurted out, just before his words were cut off by an intense perusal of her from head to foot. He didn't miss a thread of her gown, nor a strand of her hair, most of which was pinned on top of her head, held in place by the silver combs. Then his eyes found hers, and she knew Lavender had been right. The gown pleased him.

When he opened his mouth to speak again, not much came out. He cleared his throat, turning to hang his gun

179

belt on the peg inside the back door.

Ellie struggled to still her jitters. She wished Lavender had gone back to town, and suddenly for more reasons than one.

She set the Dutch oven on a couple of folded towels, striving for presence of mind. "Kale, this is Lavender Sealy. I believe you met her in town."

"Howdy, Miz Sealy." Kale nodded a greeting to Lavender, who stood beside the fireplace studying the old plat. He squinted against the bright lights, feeling like a latecomer to a party. "What's the celebration?"

"Nothing," Ellie hurried to assure him, only to have Lavender contradict her words.

"Good evening, Mr. Jarrett. We're having a party to celebrate Ellie's new gowns. What do you think—?"

"Kale," Ellie interrupted. "Why don't you bring the chairs from the porch? And call Snake. We're ready to eat."

Kale headed for the porch. He wasn't sure what he had walked into, but it was beginning to resemble a den of rattlers. If he hadn't been so hungry, he assured himself, he would saddle up and ride into town.

Once they were seated at the table, Ellie guided the conversation toward safe harbors. The tension eased somewhat when she asked Kale about his trip to the Circle R.

He finished his bite of roast, bit off a hunk of lightbread, and heaved a sigh. She knew he was as uneasy about the situation developing in this room as she was herself.

"Didn't learn much," he answered. "Neither of the Raineys was home. I left word that if they tried to take possession of this place on Friday, they'd be met by a contingent of rangers."

Ellie's mouth fell open.

Kale shrugged. "Figured you'd take to a little white lie quicker'n you would to a full-fledged shootout."

She dropped her eyes to her plate.

"Anyhow," he continued, "some of the family should arrive by then. The Raineys likely wouldn't be able to tell one body of horsemen from another, unless they got close enough to see the badge."

Ellie picked at her food. She wondered whether he had really considered her feelings as he professed, or if he had merely related the story that way. A little voice inside her heart told her it didn't matter when he thought about her feelings; the fact was, he had.

"Funny thing at the Circle R, though," he went on. "That puddin'-foot alleged to belong to Holt was in the pen. Newt stuck by his story that the animal had been missing off and on the past two months. He claimed the horse turned up at the pens this morning after Holt had already left."

Ellie frowned. "Why would that matter? It doesn't make sense."

Kale agreed. "Unless they want us to believe the perpetrator is setting Holt up, using his horse to harass you."

"Benjamin's horse had been well cared for," Ellie said. "If it wasn't by the Raineys, then by whom?"

Kale was in the process of taking another helping of roast when she spoke the last word. He looked up and caught her eye, and for a moment they were alone with only the memory of another conversation between them.

Ellie swallowed, even though she didn't have anything in her mouth at the time.

Grinning self-consciously, Kale finished heaping his plate. He took his time cutting a perfect bite of meat, then worked it onto the tines of his fork before answering. "I don't know. Nothing about the setup makes sense."

"It's the treasure," Snake put in. It was his first contribution to the conversation, and after making it, he preened from Ellie to Kale to Lavender.

"What treasure?" Kale demanded.

Snake nodded toward the plat. "The treasure that's supposed to be buried on this place."

"Not Holt or Matt Rainey," Kale objected. "They're not after treasure."

"I agree," Lavender said. "Ranchmen don't give a hoot or a holler about buried treasure. Besides, if there was treasure here, someone would have found it by now. Those old stories don't hold a thimbleful of truth."

"Costello says they do," Snake persisted. "He says the treasure is here somewhere."

Ellie laughed. "He and Benjamin looked over every part of this ranch. Like Lavender said, if there were treasure on this place, they'd have found it."

Lavender cut a piece of meat, speared it with her fork, and held it toward Kale. She directed her words to Ellie, however. "This antelope is the best I've tasted in years. I assume it's more of Armando Costello's doings." She turned eyes on Kale. "Ellie's told you what good care he takes of her?"

Ellie glared at Lavender. But from the corner of her eye she saw Kale dislodge the meat from his fork and spear a piece of potato instead.

"By the way, Ellie," Lavender continued, "Armando said to tell you he'll be out tomorrow. He wanted to come today, but I convinced him to stay behind since you and I

182

had some . . . ah, some things to take care of."

Furious, Ellie scraped her chair back and stood up. "I'll serve dessert now, Lavender, so you and Snake can be on your way. You're sure to be needed at the Lady Bug." But when she turned toward the kitchen, Kale's reply almost stopped her in her tracks.

"You can tell Costello to save his energy. I bagged a couple of wild turkeys this afternoon."

Without turning around, Ellie could visualize the satisfaction on Lavender's face. She had goaded Kale into a response. What was it she'd said earlier? Jealousy was good for a man. Well, it wasn't good for a woman. Perspiration dampened her armpits, and this her new dress.

As if privy to her thoughts, Lavender continued behind her, her voice lowered to conspiratorial tones.

"Doesn't Ellie look divine in that gown, Mr. Jarrett? I'm sure you agree, but I haven't heard you say so. Take it from one who knows, a woman needs a compliment from time to time."

Ellie turned so swiftly the layer cake almost slipped off the plate in its pool of wild plum sauce. "That is quite enough, Lavender. For your information, Kale compliments me—"

She stopped, realizing what she was saying. Kale's wide-eyed expression echoed her own.

"I mean . . . ah, my cooking." She set the cake in the center of the table and proceeded to cut a huge slice which she transferred to Kale's plate. "My cooking," she reiterated. "Why, he eats more than any man I ever saw."

"I only meant—" Lavender began.

"I didn't wear this gown to draw compliments,

Lavender." She stared at her guest's own attire. "I couldn't very well let you feel uncomfortable, decked out in your finery the way you are."

Lavender behaved after that—not because she had been chastised, Ellie knew, but for the simple reason that she had gained as much ground as she intended to for the night. Ellie cringed at the days ahead. Lavender Sealy was still miles ahead of her in experience with men; she always would be . . . a dismal fact of which Ellie was reminded yet again when Lavender sent Snake to harness the team, then shooed Kale along with him on the pretext that she needed a private word with Ellie. While Ellie cleared the table, however, Lavender disappeared.

Glancing out the back door, Ellie saw her benefactor in conversation with Kale. What now? She had half a mind to charge out there and set Lavender straight. But she knew that would be impossible. She would only end up embarrassing herself and Kale even worse than they were already embarrassed! She searched her mind for some way to explain the situation to Kale in order not to run him off immediately.

Kale Jarrett was the first to admit his inexperience with women. The fact that he'd never tangled with them left him unprepared for the assault Lavender Sealy waged on his intentions. When she sashayed around the corner of the house, beckoning him with the crook of her finger, he considered not going. He ended up listening to her, however.

"A word of warning," Lavender began. "That girl in there is like a daughter to me. You likely have your ideas of what I'm like, but Ellie's not one of us. She's a lady, and don't you let anyone—especially not Armando Costello, who has set his cap for her, by the way—

184

convince you different."

"I know that," Kale replied.

"Figured as much. What I'm not sure you know, though, is how to treat a lady. If I ever hear that you've mistreated her, Jarrett, you'd better have found that damned tunnel that's supposed to be underneath this house. You'll need it to hide in, because I'll come after you. That's a promise."

"You don't need to worry, Miz Sealy. In case you forgot, Ellie's my sister-in-law. I intend to see her well taken care of."

Lavender studied Kale through the pale moonlight. He wondered what she was thinking, what she would say next.

"It's *Miss* Sealy, Jarrett. Miss. I, for one, don't need a man to take care of me." She turned her attention to the darkened shape of the house. "Ellie does."

He didn't tell Ellie the things Lavender had said, not even when she asked him. He knew it would rile her, and he didn't want to do that.

She'd come out to the porch to wave good-bye to Lavender and Snake, and they remained standing there together, watching the surrey take the hill. The moonlight did magical things to her hair, as the candlelight had done inside the cabin. He'd been hard-pressed not to stare, but with Lavender carrying on, he'd managed to restrain himself. Now he let his eyes roam over her hair, her face.

When she stopped waving at the departing surrey, she turned, a frown on her forehead.

"I'm really sorry about Lavender," she said. "You and she are of like mind, it seems."

Kale smiled, hearing not her words so much as the

softness of her voice, seductively low and tempting. Against his better judgment, he reached to stroke a strand of hair back from her face. "What's that?" he questioned.

"She thinks I need a man."

Kale paused at her frankness, then recalled Lavender's talk at dinner. "We definitely disagree on who that man should be," he said.

His seriousness called to mind Lavender's theory about jealousy. "Eligible men are scarce around Summer Valley," she teased. "If you intend to find me someone before you leave for California—saying I agreed with the two of you that I need a man, which I don't—but saying I did, Armando would be the obvious choice."

"Can't see how you figure that."

"He's willing," she argued her point, "and he was Benjamin's very best friend."

Her nearness was intoxicating enough, without the heady scents of baking and rosewater, and although he had intended to remain aloof, he found himself drawn closer and closer to her. Cupping her face in his hand, he brought it to his.

And although Ellie had intended to resist, her need was too great. Her heart beat inside the confines of the corset Lavender had laced a bit too tightly, and when his lips brushed hers, tingles streaked like lightning down to her toes. She swayed toward him and he steadied her with a hand to her waist.

He didn't pull her closer, he dared not; and his senses were still under his control to the extent that he could at least resist. Or could he? he countered, feeling her eager response.

Before she knew it, Ellie's hands had crept up his

chest. She felt his beating heart beneath her palm. Her lips opened to his tender assault. Her hands moved.

She stopped them. How easy it would be to give in to his passion—and her own. Hadn't she dreamed of doing so, both awake and asleep, ever since their first magical night together? She had never experienced a need quite so great as that of lying in his arms, loving and being loved, reliving that moment of total fulfillment.

But her fear was greater. If she satisfied him now, he would have no reason to remain once his family arrived. If she held him off, perhaps he would stay. Not for good, she didn't expect that . . . but for a while longer. She wasn't ready to lose him. Not just yet.

With a heavy sigh, she pulled her lips from his. They remained inches apart; the urgency to fall into his arms seemed unbearable.

His hand tightened on her waist, but he didn't pursue the kiss. "You're hell to resist," he mumbled against her mouth.

Her heart skipped precariously. "Lust is a hard thing to control." Turning, she clasped her arms tightly about a support post, wishing instead they were wrapped around Kale's neck.

Even though his brain admonished him to bid her goodnight and walk away, he was powerless to leave. Studying her from behind, he saw her shape in silhouette: the delicate curve of her neck beneath her upswept hairdo, the tight bodice of her gown, the nipped waist. It was the first time he had seen her in a gown that did her justice, other than that bewitching green silk kimono. With two steps he stood behind her, forcibly restraining himself from taking her in his arms.

He trailed his fingers lightly across her shoulders. He

felt her tense. "Lavender was right about one thing," he said, his voice husky, mesmerizing. "Your gown is lovely. And you're . . . beautiful."

Moving closer, he rested his lips on the top of her head, savoring the silky feel of her curls against his skin. Without thinking, he removed the combs and let her hair fall around his face. "And you're right, too. Lust is a powerful thing."

His touch, his voice burned into her senses. Absently she lifted her hand to receive the combs when he took them from her hair. Desperate for some way to break this encounter short of ending up in his arms, or in his bed, she beseeched her brain to function. She felt the combs lying hard and cold in her hand.

She held them up to the moonlight. "Do you recognize these?"

As though he had been waiting for an invitation, his arms came around her. He cradled her hands in his, studying the combs, absorbing the essence of this woman. "They look familiar."

"They belonged to your mother. Benjamin said your father gave them to her just before he left; that she never wore them. She saved them to wear when he returned." As she related the story, his arms stiffened against hers. Then he dropped them, retaining the combs in his hands.

Moving to lean against another post, he stared hard at the combs. "My father—"

"I'm sorry, Kale. I shouldn't have worn them."

"That bastard!" he continued, unhearing. "He never returned."

"I'm sorry I wore them. I shouldn't—"

"No," he insisted. "It isn't that. I want you to have them, to wear them. It's . . . me."

188

He squeezed the combs in his hands so tightly she listened to hear them crack. When he lifted his eyes to hers, she felt a sharp physical pain at the anguish she saw there. "I don't want to be like him, Ellie. But I am."

Her mouth went dry; she couldn't tear her eyes away from his. The hurt in his voice brought a sob to her throat.

"I'm going to California."

"Of course you are," she managed. "After this mess is cleaned up, after you get me settled with the man of your choice—"

"Ellie—"

With great effort, she smiled. "There's nothing wrong with you going to California. You aren't like your father. He left a wife and a houseful of children, but you're free, Kale—free."

She watched his jaw twitch. Finally he broke their gaze and stared out into the growing darkness. Dropping to the floor, she sat on the edge of the porch and swung her legs over and thought how she'd never be able to make such a speech again.

"What did you start to tell me up at the shelter that day? About what you intend to do with the money from your friend Mack's venture?"

He stared into the darkness, wondering why he didn't turn and go to bed. It wasn't right for him to catch Ellie up in something beyond her power to control.

She patted the floor beside her. "Come on. Tell me. I'm interested. I've never heard much about California."

With a shrug, he dropped to the porch beside her. If he didn't touch her or look at her, perhaps it would be all right, he justified. As long as she thought what she felt was only lust, perhaps they were safe.

189

"Some of the richest, most fertile land on the whole continent is in the northern valleys of California," he told her. "Figured I'd take my share and buy me a place, raise some cattle. The Spanish Californians—*Californios*, they call themselves—are big cattle raisers."

His words brought tears brimming to her eyes. She didn't dare look at him; she scarcely dared draw a breath. Kale Jarrett had just committed himself to settling down, and he apparently didn't even realize it. Far be it from her to challenge him on this.

"What a splendid idea, Kale. Tell me more about this wonderful land."

In the following days Ellie held Kale's confession in her heart, considering, quite without wanting to, what it might mean to her future, to their future. She had a mind to tell him that if he wanted to settle down, he didn't need to go all the way to California to find a fertile valley where he could raise cattle; that he was already in a fertile valley, and it would be far less trouble to stay here than to travel halfway across the continent.

She didn't. She figured that would likely run him off faster than Lavender's interference could do. But more, if by some miracle he decided to stay, it must be because he wanted to.

Because it was his idea to stay, his dream. He could only stay because he wanted to live here—with her. She wouldn't have him any other way. And right now all he wanted was her body. He was incapable of hiding the fact.

It was evident in everything he did and said—in the way he went to extremes to avoid touching her or making eye contact; in the casual, offhanded manner he tried to effect, to the end that his words were often clipped, his sentences left dangling.

She recognized it because she saw her own actions reflected in his, her own stress and short temper, her own desperate longing. When by chance their eyes did meet, his wanting for her shone clear, as clearly as her own must surely be to him.

Lust . . . a powerful adversary.

Armando Costello did not come out the next day, and Ellie was glad for it. She knew she had Lavender to thank for his staying away, and she felt a pang of guilt at her relief. Although he had been helpful during her crisis, and had provided her with welcome companionship as well, she was glad not to have to deal with the added tension his visit would create between herself and Kale.

The day after Lavender's visit, Kale's family began converging on the ranch; by Friday three of them had arrived. Ellie recalled Kale's message to the Raineys. She wondered whether Ira and Till had carried word to the Circle R, and if so, whether they described Kale's brothers as rangers.

Rubal and Jubal, twins two years younger than Kale, and Baylor, an uncle the same age as the twins, rode in together. They certainly looked like rangers to her. Tall, dark-headed, and broad-shouldered, like Kale, they would have intimidated her just walking across the clearing shoulder to shoulder, or setting out on horseback, riding abreast—formidable foes, indeed.

But she was close enough to hear their laughter and a few of their light-hearted jokes; she saw the smiles on their faces and the compassion in their eyes.

Their eyes weren't blue, of course. And although they treated her with the deference and concern due the widow of their oldest brother, they didn't cause her heart to flutter; they didn't set her soul aflame. Only one of them, her blue-eyed Kale, did that . . . and more.

When, a couple of days later, a wagon lumbered down the hill, its canvas billowing over its frame like an overstuffed snowbird, all hands stopped work. Ellie rushed from the kitchen; Kale caught up with her, coming from the barn. Others came from the creek bottom, from the opposite hillside.

"It's Ginny and Hollis," Kale said.

"And Delta." Ellie's heart beat against her chest. She felt as if it was her birthday, or as if she was awaiting a sister, a sister whom she knew but hadn't seen for ever so long.

"Now we'll see how—" Kale began.

"How *tall* she is," Ellie teased.

Hollis Myrick, Ginny's husband, drove. He was a stout man—a newspaper man, Benjamin had said. He looked almost square-shaped next to the lanky Jarretts.

Ginny sat beside him. Hair wisped from beneath her bonnet. She wasn't lanky, Ellie noticed, but then, she had borne four children.

Suddenly a delighted squeal erupted from the wagon itself and a calico-clad figure jumped from the back and ran toward them even before Hollis set the brake.

Ellie caught her breath. Dark hair flew around Delta's lovely face, from which shone the bluest eyes she'd ever seen—besides Kale's.

Delta threw herself into Kale's startled arms. Ellie watched patches of color blossom on his cheeks. Awkwardly he returned Delta's embrace, then reached to tousle her hair.

His eyes found Ellie's; she shrugged and laughed. He

held Delta back and looked her up and down, wonderment glowing from his face. When he turned to Ellie, she saw moisture glisten in his beloved blue eyes.

"This is Ellie, Delta," he said. "She told me you were all grown up, but I guess . . . hell, I guess I didn't believe her."

Then, at week's end the brother whose arrival all had anticipated rode up to the hitching rail and stepped down: Zachariah Jarrett, now the eldest, and as such, the family spokesman.

By this time Ellie was too busy to worry over family politics, however, what with so many mouths to feed and so many bodies to find beds for.

Ginny and Delta pitched right in, and Ellie soon felt as if she had known them forever. Of course, Benjamin had related the family history in great detail, and more than once. It had been a favorite topic for both of them: Benjamin because he was lonesome for his family; Ellie because she had never known a family.

Kale helped her, taking charge of everything from procuring meat to seeing that enough wood was chopped, that the cow was milked, the eggs gathered. At times she felt as if she had a maid.

One afternoon when she and Delta were hanging clothes to dry on the fence rail, he arrived with a dozen quail and two deer.

"We'll have the quail for supper," he told Ellie. "I sent the twins and Uncle Baylor down to the creek bottom to kill one of those wild hogs. We'll grind the pork and venison together to make sausage. I found an old grinder in the barn."

Ellie laughed. "Lucky you've had experience feeding a crowd. I'd never figure it all out on my own. Thanks."

He shook his head. "No need for that, they're my family . . . ah, *our* family. I told you it wouldn't be a problem."

"You also said they weren't coming for a party, but so far everyone seems to be enjoying himself in spite of the reason for being here."

"That'll change as soon as Zachariah comes," he told her. "Since he's head of the family now, we have to await his approval before we lay down the law to the Raineys."

As he walked away, Ellie noticed Delta staring after him.

"He certainly turned into a handsome man," Delta sighed. "Funny, how I remember him."

"How's that?" Ellie asked.

"He was my favorite brother, I suppose because he played with me, roughhoused, Benjamin called it."

"Do you want to know how he remembered you?" Ellie asked.

At Delta's nod, she commenced to relate her conversation with Kale the night he arrived at the ranch. "He had trouble believing you and I were the same age. In his mind you were still twelve years old."

Ginny had come to help them finish the wash. She, too, stared after their wandering brother. "Benjamin would've been pleased with the way he turned out."

Ellie sighed. "I wish you'd tell him that. He worries that he's like your pa. Calls himself a wandering man."

Ginny stared after Kale until he disappeared into the house, carrying two buckets of water. Then she turned amused eyes on Ellie. "Appears to me his wandering days may be fast coming to an end."

Zachariah arrived at the end of the week. He resembled Benjamin in so many ways it gave Ellie a start, from his height and lanky build down to the sprinkling of gray hair at his temples and the solid white streak across the top of his head.

That evening after supper they sat on the porch, spilling out into the yard, talking, laughing, catching each other up on their doings since last they met. They spoke of Carson who, as far as anyone knew, was still down in Mexico chasing bandits, and of Zavala, a cousin up in Wyoming at a place Ellie had never heard of, Jackson Hole, and of Aunt Tizzy, whose rheumatism prevented her from making the trip to see her oldest nephew interred properly.

Uncle Baylor brought out his fiddle and played some of the old songs, "Turkey in the Straw" and "She'll Be Coming 'Round the Mountain," and one that appeared to be Kale's favorite, "My Darlin' Clementine."

He sat across from her, resting his back against the trunk of the oak tree. Ellie watched him through the flickering lantern light, his face all smiles, his slightly off-key but nevertheless robust baritone raised above the others'.

When it was over, Delta requested "Down in the Valley," and Ellie found herself joining in, her earlier inhibitions conquered by the acceptance of the group. She studied each member in turn, recalling the things Benjamin had told her about them.

Their spontaneity invigorated her, and she laughed and sang and listened, taking it all in. Absently she crossed her arms, clasping her hands about them to ward off the slight evening chill, enjoying to the fullest this sense of camaraderie and more, a sense of family, of belonging to a family.

"You're cold." Kale's whispered voice took her

195

unawares, for until he spoke she hadn't known he'd come to sit beside her. When he lifted her shawl up over her shoulders, his fingers lingered a moment on her back before he withdrew his hand.

The fire he kindled inside her remained, though, heightened by his presence, and by the fact that he had gone to her side here in the midst of his family.

When the song ended, Rubal burst into a rowdy rendition of a song Ellie had never heard, something about a woman named Anne Bonny, obviously a pirate, and her lover, a pirate called Calico Jack. Jubal joined his twin, and soon the others had chimed in, all except Kale.

"Cut it out," he called above the raucous chorus. "We don't want Ellie to think we're uncivilized."

"Aw, Kale, don't be a stick-in-the-mud. Anne Bonny was our great-grandmother."

"Ellie's one of us. She might as well get used to family lore."

"No offense, Ellie," Rubal offered. "I figured since you're one of the family—"

"Thank you," Ellie told him. "I'm grateful to be considered part of the family. And I'm enjoying the song. Please don't stop."

But Kale persisted. "It's getting late. If we're going to settle this thing with the Raineys tomorrow, we'd better hit the sack."

To Ellie's surprise, they dispersed with little grumbling, the men to the barn, the three women to the house. Ellie had banked the fire and just blown out the wick in the kitchen lamp when the familiar squawk of the back door drew her attention.

Kale held two buckets sloshing water. "With all the revelry, I forgot about water for coffee in the morning."

"Thanks." A shaft of moonlight shone through the open door, illuminating the sun-streaks in his hair, outlining him in the doorway.

He set the buckets on the cabinet, hesitant to leave, she could tell.

"They can be a rowdy bunch sometimes," he offered. "Thanks for putting up with them."

She thought about the rowdy crowd she'd been raised with. She started to mention it, but Kale knew it as well as she. "There's no need to thank me," she said. "I'm enjoying them, each and every one. They're like family to me, too. I love them."

And one most of all, she sighed later, trying to fall asleep, hoping to dream. In her dreams he never went to California.

Kale knew the minute he stepped into the barn something was amiss. It didn't take him long to find out what.

Zachariah did the talking. "You've convinced us of Benjamin's killing, Kale. Tomorrow we'll see what the lot of us can do to settle it."

"Fine." Kale shook out his bedroll, sat down, and started to remove his boots. That's when he noticed that the others were still dressed. They sat in a semicircle, staring at him.

"Tonight we have another matter to resolve."

Zachariah's somber voice reflected the atmosphere Kale felt permeating the room. He looked from one to the other of the men, curiosity beginning to stir. "Okay, boys. Have at it."

"It concerns Benjamin's place here, and Ellie,"

197

Zachariah told him.

Alarm sounded in Kale's brain. "It's Ellie's place now."

"We can't leave her here by herself," Rubal said.

"We owe it to Benjamin to see her taken care of," Jubal added.

"She can't run a ranch, anyhow," Rubal continued his own argument. "I say we sell the stock and try to find a buyer for the place."

"Hold on." Kale jumped up to face the group. "This is her place, her home. You can't just—"

"Benjamin was like a father to us," Zachariah continued. "We owe it to him to take care of his affairs, meaning his ranch and his widow."

"You damned well won't be taking care of her by selling off her land," Kale fumed. His gaze pinned first one brother, then another. He paused at length on Uncle Baylor and Ginny's husband, Hollis Myrick. "Don't you two have an opinion?" he barked.

"It's best left to the brothers," Hollis said.

"The way Benjamin hung on words from the Good Book," Uncle Baylor added, "I figure he'd want only brothers involved, seeing how there's enough of you heathens."

"Five's enough to make it fair," Zachariah agreed.

"Make what fair? What the hell are you talking about?" Kale's anger escalated quickly.

"The Good Book states clearly that when a man dies, his brother steps in and marries his widow. That is, if he's unwed. In this case—"

"Hold everything," Kale cautioned. "That's already taken care of. I intend to find Ellie a husband before I leave. You don't think I'd run out on her, do you?"

"Nope," Zachariah replied. "But it ain't your decision, Kale. Together we'll decide which one of us would make the best husband for Ellie, while disrupting our own lives as little as possible."

"You sound like she has the plague or something," Kale hissed.

Zachariah shook his head. "She's a comely lass, much to the relief of us all. And agreeable, or seems to be."

"Then if we're not going to sell the ranch," Jubal continued as though speaking his thoughts aloud, "whoever agrees to marry her will have to move here and run things."

"That pretty much leaves Zach out, since he's committed to the stage station over on the Trace," Rubal added.

"No, I'll take my chances," Zachariah told them. "It's my obligation to Benjamin. He was Pa to us all, me included."

"Obligation!" Kale stared around the room, his mouth ajar.

"What about Carson?" Jubal asked, ignoring Kale as if he wasn't even present.

"Carson ain't exempt neither," Zachariah told them. "He never planned to stay in the ranger service for life. He'd be a good one."

"Hold on!" Kale yelled above them. "This is a woman's life you're talking about—"

"And a man's," Uncle Baylor laughed. "One of you heathens is about to bite the dust."

"I told you I have it all worked out," Kale repeated.

"No," Zachariah answered. "It wouldn't be fittin', an outsider taking over our obligation. Besides, Benjamin confided in me about her upbringin' and we can't be sure

199

another man'd treat her with respect, considerin' how she was raised up with a bunch of painted ladies."

"She wasn't one of them!" Kale struggled to believe what his ears heard.

"Even so, we can't let her go back to that cathouse," Jubal said. "Not after the way Benjamin took care of us."

"We know how you feel about things, Kale." Zachariah's voice was placating, or so it sounded to Kale. The room began to reel with words which had no meaning. When Zachariah continued, Kale felt as if a whirlwind had swept through, mingling everyone's thoughts and words until nothing made any sense.

"We're going to let you out of it, Kale," Zachariah was saying. "Don't reckon your wanderin' ways would lend themselves to settling down much."

"It's obvious you're fond of her," Rubal added.

"But Benjamin cut you loose once, and it wouldn't be fittin' for us to shackle you now."

"Let me out of what, for God's sake? What the hell are you planning, Zach?"

"A drawing," Zachariah informed him. "We aim to draw straws to see which one of us marries Ellie."

Chapter Nine

When Ellie awoke the next morning, Delta was curled up on the far side of the bed, sleeping soundly. Snuggling beneath the quilts, she absorbed the warmth and coziness she felt, knowing it came as much from the family gathered around her as from the bedcovers.

She had lain awake long into the night pondering the events that had taken place since Kale's brothers and sisters arrived. They'd accepted her as though they'd known her all their lives.

Only Delta had mentioned the age difference between her and Benjamin, and even she took it to be the normal way of things. After Ellie came to bed the evening before, she and Delta had talked about it.

"What was it like, being married to a man old enough to have been your father?" Delta had asked.

"It was good," Ellie answered. "Benjamin was a kind and generous man. He taught me things I didn't have a chance to learn at the Lady Bug. I grew up without a father, too, so I . . ." She paused, recalling how she had told Kale that she sometimes wished she had been raised in Delta's place. That seemed to have bothered Kale; perhaps it would Delta, too.

Ellie redirected the conversation. "Benjamin talked about all of you so much I felt like I knew you even before you arrived."

Delta laughed. "I heard Kale tell Ginny how you recognized him by his blue eyes."

"You and Kale are the only ones I would have known on sight," Ellie admitted. "But you're all Jarretts, no doubt about that."

"Tell me about the Lady Bug," Delta encouraged. "I've always wondered what one of those places was like."

Not in the least put off by Delta's directness, Ellie complied by launching into a discussion of her life at the Lady Bug. Delta asked question after question, until the back door squawked and they heard boots cross the parlor and enter the spare room.

"That's Hollis coming to bed," Ellie said. "We'd better get some sleep, too."

For an hour or more afterward she heard voices coming from the spare room where Ginny and Hollis had taken over Kale's bed. The next morning Ginny joined her in the kitchen and together they began preparing the enormous amount of food it took to feed the assembled family.

"Do you expect any more relatives to arrive?" Ellie sliced a side of bacon she had retrieved from the smokehouse.

"Doubtful." Ginny stirred batter for biscuits, then dropped the dough by spoonfuls into a Dutch oven to be placed in the coals in the fireplace. "I sent word to Cameron, a cousin over on the Missouri, but I doubt he'll be able to make it. Kale said he wired Brady, another cousin who lives down in New Orleans."

"Are any of them pirates?" Ellie asked.

"Pirates?"

"Like in Rubal's ballad. Benjamin never mentioned Anne Bonny."

"Oh, her," Ginny laughed. "No, we have no other pirates in the family."

"I don't know why Kale thought I would be offended," Ellie mused. "Tell me about Anne Bonny."

"The facts are sketchy," Ginny replied. "We aren't sure whether what we've been told is truth or legend."

"Tell me anyway."

"Let's see," Ginny complied. "She was a pirate, like the song says, and she was in love with another pirate, Calico Jack. There were a number of women pirates in those days, and if caught, their fate was the same as the men, death by hanging. Unless, that is, the woman was with child. According to the tales, Anne Bonny was carrying Calico Jack's child when she was arrested. Her baby, a girl, was born while she was in prison. She grew up to be our pa's grandmother."

"What happened to Anne Bonny?" Ellie began breaking eggs into a wooden bowl.

"After the baby came, she was hanged."

"How dreadful! Did Calico Jack raise the baby?"

"No. Far as we know, he never even saw the child. He was later hanged, too. Likely that's why Benjamin didn't talk about them. Ma always claimed that's where Pa got his wandering ways."

Ellie gripped the wooden bowl with both hands. "And Kale," she whispered.

Ginny shoved the Dutch oven down in the ashes.

Using a poker, she raked coals over the lid to ensure the biscuits would brown all around. "And Kale," she agreed. "Leastways, that's how Kale was made out to be. Don't know whether it was his ancestors that marked him or the way folks thought of him. He and Delta both have Pa's blue eyes, you know."

"The color of a person's eyes doesn't determine whether he roams the world or settles down," Ellie insisted.

"I agree. That's why I took Delta and have tried not to let her think she's going to turn out like Pa, irresponsible-like."

"Kale isn't irresponsible," Ellie objected. "He thinks he is, but he isn't."

"No, not from what I've seen since we've been here. He acts like the whole show is his responsibility. But that could be because he knows it won't last forever. Ellie, I don't know what's between you two." She shrugged. "Something special, for sure. But I don't want you to go setting your hopes—"

The squawking door interrupted her. Ellie turned self-consciously to see Kale standing in the doorway. A sick feeling took hold of her at the thought that he might have overheard their conversation. One look at his face, however, told her it wouldn't have mattered if he had. Ladies' talk was far from his mind.

Kale Jarrett was mad as a hornet.

"Get your things together," he barked at her. "We're going."

"Going where?" she asked.

"To the painted cliffs. I told you we'd ride up there as soon as the family came to look after the place."

"But—"

"Time's wasting, Ellie. We need to get on the road."

Pulling a deerskin riding skirt, cotton shirt, and heavy jacket from among the items Lavender had brought, Ellie recalled his promise. As soon as the family came, he said. Well, the family had been here a week, and this was the first he'd mentioned going to the painted cliffs.

Ginny's voice filtered through the hanging quilt. "You can't run off without breakfast."

Whatever bee Kale had in his bonnet, it wasn't letting go. "No time," Ellie heard him say. She wondered at his gruffness. "We'll need some food for the trail, though."

Ellie stuffed a change of clothing into a cotton sack. Back in the kitchen she found Kale busy packing a bag with loaves of bread and several slices of her applesauce cake. "I took some sausages and jerked meat from the smokehouse," he told her, swinging the sack over his shoulder.

He turned at the door. "Ginny, tell Zachariah to keep a watch on that cave and to stay alert for grass fires and such. Oh, and send someone into town tomorrow to see if the answers to my wires have come."

"Tomorrow?" Ginny questioned.

"It'll take us a good three days up and back." He nodded at Ellie. "Let's get going."

"You can't drag her out of here like this, Kale," Ginny called after them. "The poor girl hasn't had time for more than a cup of coffee. Besides, she didn't say she wanted to go with you."

Kale looked so startled Ellie almost laughed.

His hand nudged her back, guiding her out the squawking door, sending tingles up her spine.

"She does," he barked over his shoulder.

It occurred to her then that she hadn't questioned him

beyond what it took to grasp his meaning. She hadn't hesitated to go with him, to comply with his demands.

This was a new side of Kale Jarrett, commanding—demanding. Was he showing his true colors? His moody temperament persisted throughout the morning, and she began to admonish herself for falling in love with a man without first getting to know him. A moody man would likely make as poor a companion as a gunfighter.

Since he didn't speak, she didn't bother to either until he started across Celery Creek about five miles from the house.

"If you're in such an all-fired hurry," she called, "we ought to take this shortcut."

He drew rein, scanning the dim stock trail toward which she pointed. "You know the way?"

She nodded. "The stage road circles way around. It'll take an extra day's travel. Unless we've had enough rain for Celery Creek to be up, this is the shortest route."

"Suits me." He pulled rein, turned the bay, and headed toward the trail. Ellie kicked her horse to lead the way, but he stopped her.

"Let me go first. Scare any bears out of the woods."

"Fine. But there are no bears where we're going."

She followed him along the narrow trail, which forced them to ride single file. What difference did it make? she wondered. He wasn't talking today anyway.

After his confrontation with his brothers the evening before, Kale soaked in the creek to cool off, then sat on the limestone slab, considering the situation that confronted him. Where was the problem?

Hadn't he intended to find Ellie a husband? Wasn't

206

Zachariah right? One of his brothers would be the best choice. One by one he considered them, imagined each in turn married to Ellie.

Anyone else he chose would be a stranger, and a man couldn't tell about strangers these days. Besides, with Ellie fitting into the family the way she did, likely the girls would include her in family affairs from now on. Since she was Benjamin's widow, Zachariah would probably include her and her husband in family business forever.

Forever. That was a damned long time, he thought. A long time to be married to someone chosen for you by others, no matter how high-minded those others happened to be. A long time to be married to someone you didn't love.

The word came uneasily to his mind, settling over it like curdled milk. But it wouldn't go away.

Love.

Damn it, Ellie deserved to marry someone she could love. Not the way she'd loved Benjamin, but the way she loved—

He hung his head, clutched it firmly in both hands, attempting to dispel the word and all its images from his wretched brain.

Love . . . the very word was enough to give a grown man the heebie-jeebies. Love was a woman's word, a lady's word.

But wasn't Zachariah right? Didn't they owe it to Benjamin? Ellie had made him a good wife; now she deserved to marry a man she could love the rest of her life.

The rest of her life. Damn it. He stared up at the stars glimmering through the barren branches of the cotton-wood tree. Nearby he heard a bullfrog karoomp and crickets chirp, and saw a few brave fireflies glitter in the evening chill.

Ellie deserved to marry a man she could love forever. And that was a long time.

He exhaled until his lungs felt empty, held his breath until they begged, then inhaled deeply, filling his body with the fresh, cool, sweet breath of life.

Forever . . . too damned long to live without the woman you loved, seeing her married to another—to a brother—knowing you could have had her but were too ignorant or scared to take the chance.

Forever . . . a damned long time to live with a wandering man. Time enough for that love to wither and die. Time enough for a woman to wither and die along with it.

While he sat on the slab pondering the uncertainty webbing around him, the moon faded and the sun began to rise. Finally, still far from certain what he was about, he pulled himself up off the slab and headed for the barn, where he saddled two horses. Then he rinsed his face at the well and went to the house to fetch Ellie.

All he knew for certain was that he had to get away from here. He had to get Ellie away before Zachariah held that stupid drawing. What would a woman like Ellie think, to see grown men drawing straws for her?

Following Celery Creek they entered a ravine and wound around the base of the hills. Here and there rock slides or patches of dense brush forced them to ride in the middle of the creek, which was rocky and at this time of year, shallow.

From behind, Ellie watched Kale glance periodically

toward the hilltops rising above them on either side. She realized he was wondering if she really knew the way. Well, let him wonder . . . if he got curious enough, perhaps he'd ask. Even a question about the trail would be conversation.

The sun was already high overhead, glinting down in the middle of the stream, when her stomach began to growl. It reminded her of their missed breakfast. She sighed, her aggravation at his sulkiness growing with her hunger. What sense did it make to ride all day without food, just to outlast a temperamental man?

"Would you hand me a piece of that jerky from your saddlebags?" she called ahead.

He turned to stare at her blankly. When he understood her question, he drew rein. "We should water the horses anyway."

After drinking from the creek, Ellie looked into the sack Kale brought from the house. "How about some sausage and bread?" she asked.

"Dole it out sparingly," he cautioned. "We don't want to run out of food before we get home."

She eyed his saddle gun. "You could kill something."

He shrugged, remounting. "Could."

They followed the afternoon sun toward the western horizon. At times it was obscured by hills and brush; other times it broke through in great streams of light that dazzled their eyes and sparkled like gemstones on the water of the creek.

Finally the draw they followed turned north and still they rode in silence. The sun had begun to sink below the hills when she recognized the place where she had camped before with Benjamin and Armando. Briefly she debated whether to point it out, then she plunged ahead.

"There's a good campsite in that thicket over there," she called forward, "with grass enough for the horses."

Never having seen Kale in such a mood, she wasn't sure he would even answer. After her words registered, though, he did.

"Fine." Without a backward glance, he headed for the thicket she had indicated.

Contemplating that one word, she nudged her horse to follow his. His voice hadn't sounded as sharp as in the kitchen this morning, but of course it was hard to tell, since he'd spoken only one word in the last three or more hours. Whatever was eating at him hadn't let up, she was certain of that.

When they dismounted, she immediately set to untying the pack behind her saddle. "I'll begin supper while you water and picket the horses," she suggested.

With a nod Kale handed her the sack of food and his saddlebags. "You'll find everything you need in here."

Everything except a congenial dining partner, she thought. But at least he seemed agreeable to her suggestions. After locating a skillet, plates, eating utensils, and even a bucket for carrying water, she gathered wood and began a fire in a spot where she and many before her had made campfires through the years. She recalled being here with Benjamin and Armando— the jovial nature of their conversations, the excitement of being on the trail of treasure, as Armando referred to their treks to the cliffs.

By the time Kale returned, she had water boiling for coffee and sausage frying in the skillet.

He tossed their bedrolls toward the back of the small clearing. "I would've hauled the water, Ellie."

Her heart felt heavier than the iron skillet she held in

her hands, as heavy as his own tone of voice. "I thought it best to get started." She forced a pathetic laugh. "If you're as hungry as I am, you're half starved to death."

"I'm sorry I didn't let you eat breakfast."

She stared across the fire to where he stood fidgeting with the toe of his boot in the hard earth. "I've gone hungry before and it never hurt me," she said.

When he didn't move or even look at her, she suggested, "Drag us up a log to sit on; supper'll be ready in no time."

While the sausage fried, she sliced bread. When she glanced up again, he stood in the same spot, held the same position. She squinted through the smoke of the campfire, beginning to worry. He looked up then, and the gravity of his expression alarmed her.

"Marry me, Ellie."

His abruptness startled her; the words he spoke didn't make sense. "What?"

"Marry me."

She stared at him, saw his somber expression. His arms were trembling. "Why?" she demanded.

Her response appeared to snap him out of whatever trance had held him mesmerized. "*Why?* What kind of answer is that?"

"It isn't an answer. It's a question. Why would you ask me such a thing?" Tears formed in her eyes, and she turned quickly, lest he see. If he'd stabbed her with the knife she'd just sliced the bread with, he couldn't have hurt her any more. Her own arms trembled as if in imitation of his, as if the two of them were engaged in some sort of sadistic, mutual bloodletting. She clasped her arms across her chest so he wouldn't notice.

Marry him? Didn't he know she wanted nothing in the

211

world more than to be his wife, to spend the rest of her life beside him?

"Why?" His voice echoed her words, her confusion.

She squeezed her eyelids, trying to keep the tears from overflowing. Didn't he know how she felt? Did he expect her to agree to marry him when she knew how badly he wanted to remain free?

"I know you want to, Ellie." His voice was low, almost weak, as if it had been diluted with pain. But his words were no less dangerous for it. What was he trying to do, get her to admit her love for him?

Was he so vain he needed to hear it, even if the saying of it would destroy her?

Destroy? No. No, he wouldn't do that.

Determination flushed her with anger, and she whirled to face him.

"And I know why you asked," she replied. "Because I'm your brother's wife and you feel obligated."

"No," he protested. "That isn't true. I need—"

"I also know what you *need*, Kale Jarrett, and any girl at Lavender's can sell it to you. For that matter, I can go to Lavender's myself." Her voice rose, stimulated by growing anguish. "I am not dependent on your charity. Your offer is humiliating."

Moving more swiftly than he had all day, he grabbed her arms, stopping her words in her throat. "Damn it, Ellie, don't make it so hard. I'm not good at this. I may not know the words to express my needs, my feelings . . ."

His declaration startled her. She raised her eyes to meet his. The determination she saw there matched her own, weakening both her hurt and her will to resist.

". . . but I've never felt these things before." He

shrugged while his eyes pleaded with her. "Whatever it is, it's different, what I feel for you. It isn't always pleasant, but somehow it's special, and . . . I guess I love you."

Her mouth fell open the same moment her heart stopped beating. "You guess?" she managed.

"Hell, Ellie, how would I know? I never even *thought* that word before I met you."

Her brain held nothing now, she was sure, except a muddled mixture of mush. Her puzzlement over his day-long indifference combined with her hurt over his initial proposal of marriage left her as weak as a newborn lamb. If he hadn't been holding her arms, she knew she'd have fallen flat on her face.

But despite it all, a strange sort of joy began to bubble inside her, and she wanted to keep it from growing.

Feeling her relax, he drew her to his chest, an effort to regain his own strength as much as to comfort her.

Her arms clasped about him, bringing warmth and feeling back to his body, which had been numb for hours now, ever since his damned brothers had come up with that cockeyed notion to draw straws for her.

Strands of her hair whispered about his face; he felt her nuzzle against his neck, showering him with fiery traces of desire. Her heart beat steadily against his own, reassuring his worried mind, regenerating his dormant passion.

Slowly he drew her head back and kissed her. They were the same sweet lips he remembered from his dreams. His hands slipped inside her jacket and stroked the length of her back. In his mind he saw her in that green slippery garment. The image of her satin skin roused the need for her that grew continually inside him.

Finally she moved her lips. "We'd better eat."

"Hmm," he moaned, lips touching lips. "I'm not hungry . . . except for you."

She smiled, willing her own passion to subside for a time. They still had that astonishing proposal to deal with. "We have all night."

Acknowledgment lit his eyes, so she repeated her initial request.

"Why don't you drag us up a log to sit on?"

She pan-fried the bread she had sliced earlier, using grease from the sausage. When he returned, she handed him a plate of food. He took it, seated himself on the log, and began to eat.

She filled her own plate and sat beside him, eating, thinking, wondering what in the world had precipitated such an outlandish proposal of marriage.

"You've worried over this all day," she mused between bites of sausage and fried bread.

"Well, hell, Ellie, it's a damned hard decision."

"Yes," she agreed. "It's a very hard decision. How did you come to it?"

He glanced at her, then looked back at his plate, recalling in gruesome detail the encounter with his brothers, the evening spent by the creek. He dared not tell her of the scheme his brothers had hatched. He might not know a whole lot about women, but he did know enough to be certain Ellie would be offended. It still made him mad as hell, thinking back on it.

Finally he heaved a heavy sigh. "I just did."

"By yourself? No prompting?"

He frowned, wondering whether she already knew. "Prompting by *whom*, Ellie?" They exchanged grins at that, then he returned to the business that troubled her.

"Where'd you get such a notion?"

She recalled Ginny saying just this morning how it was obvious she and Kale had something special between them. Had the others noticed it, too? "You told me you Jarretts take care of your own. I thought perhaps your brothers might have urged you to stay and take care of me."

"You don't need taking care of, Ellie." He said it because he knew it was what she wanted to hear; he certainly didn't believe it himself. He said it, too, because she was coming dangerously close to the truth of things. Then he followed it with the truth. "But I want to take care of you, anyhow."

"What about California?"

He wiped his plate clean with the last bite of bread, stuffed it in his mouth and washed it down with a swallow of coffee. "I've been trying to picture myself in California." His eyes were soft when they caressed her face. "Fact is, Ellie, I can't see me there without you."

She tried to smile, but her lips quivered. His words left her body limp, her brain numb. All day she had watched him struggle with a demon, wondering what troubled him. Now she knew. And it was a surprise to beat all surprises.

"Don't ever say you don't know the right words," she whispered.

While she cleaned their plates and the skillet, using the rest of the water in the bucket, he spread their bedrolls beneath the shelter of the thicket.

Afterward he came to stand in back of her, encircling her from behind, pulling her against his chest. "Ellie, Ellie, this has been a tormenting day."

Turning in his embrace, she put her arms around his

215

neck. "Good," she whispered. "I wouldn't want you to propose to me without giving it considerable thought."

She felt his chest heave, heard a moan escape his lips. When she looked, he was grinning. "Why don't you crawl under the covers where it's warm and change your clothes? When I finish banking the fire, you can answer my question."

At her astonished look, he frowned. "What's the matter?"

"I didn't bring any nightclothes."

"You left that slinky green thing at home?"

She laughed. "I don't sleep in that. The only time I ever put it on was . . ." Suddenly self-conscious, she ducked her head.

Tipping her chin, he kissed her lips. "Don't worry, honey, I'll be there to keep you warm."

True to his promise, he returned in record time, crawling into the bed he had made for them, pulling the covers over them both.

When they came together, she felt the cool outer layer of his skin kindle against her own, becoming hot and satiny to her touch.

"It's just as well you left that little piece of silk at home," he mumbled. "It would have gotten in our way."

She snuggled against him, her breasts swelling into his furry chest. "You feel so good."

Ignited by the flames lit with their first encounter, strengthened by their subsequent efforts to deny that passion, fueled now by the difficulties they faced, they loved with an urgency they had not felt the first time.

Now that she knew how glorious the outcome could be, she strove to attain it. And now that he knew the heights to which he could take her, he resolved to settle for nothing less.

The blankets smelled of him, and when he held her close, filling her with deep, sensuous kisses, she tasted the essence of this man who had confessed his love in such a strange manner that it was tempting to believe him.

"This is much better," she sighed.

"What, honey?" he mumbled, trailing his tongue across her chin, down her neck.

"Your tactics," she answered, thinking of his moodiness during the day.

His fingers traced her hips, her belly, burrowing deep to the core of her. "This?" he whispered. Capturing one taut nipple in his mouth, he mumbled, "Or this?"

"No."

"No?" He raised his face to hers, even though they could see nothing within the confines of the blankets. His nose brushed hers; his fingers continued their devastating attack. "What could be better?"

"Oh, Kale," she expelled his name on pent-up breath, ". . . nothing." She wriggled against him. "*Hurry.*"

Without further talk, he complied, filling her with himself, covering her mouth with his kisses, driving away the torment they both felt with the force of their mutual needs.

Lust, he heard her call it. At this moment, yes . . . lust. What then was love? That complicated word which still stuck in his gullet every time he so much as thought it.

Afterward she clung to him. Instead of feeling secure since his proposal, she felt threatened, terrified now that she'd had more time to know him, to care for him. After their last night of lovemaking, he'd rejected her, saying he didn't want her to fall in love with him. Now he professed to love her.

How could he have changed his mind so soon? What had happened to change it for him?

"I'm sorry it was so quick," he whispered against her temple. "Was it . . . ?"

"Perfect," she responded. "It was perfect, and we have plenty of time. We have—"

"Forever," he prompted. "That is, if you . . . are you ready to answer my question?"

"Kale, you aren't supposed to rush a girl." Quickly, more to cover her own fears than his, she suspected, she kissed him. "Give me till morning."

They fell asleep after that, exhausted, what with his sleepless vigil the night before and all the worrying he had done this day, and she struggling to decide what his new sullenness had meant. Kale slept soundly until morning light.

But Ellie awakened sometime during the night, shivering from doubts aroused by her dream.

She had dreamed of a pet squirrel Benjamin found under the cottonwood tree. His leg had been broken, and she mended it. They kept him inside the house, where he learned to be content, bringing joy to them both. Then one day she had propped the door open while mopping the kitchen, and he saw the outdoors for the first time since his accident.

She had closed the door quickly enough to keep him inside, but afterward he had never been content in the house again. He became frantic, dashing to the door, jumping at the windows. Finally they had to set him free.

"It's the wild in him, Ellie," Benjamin had told her.

She had loved that little squirrel, and she missed him dreadfully. "It's the wild," Benjamin said. "You can't ever tame the wild out of them."

You can't ever tame the wild out of them . . . you can't ever tame the wild out of them . . .

Over breakfast she gave Kale her answer.

"What do you mean, you won't answer me until I get back from California? I told you, I'm not going."

She traced his cheek with her finger. The cool morning air left his skin dry and chilled. She lay her palm there a minute, recalling the past night, how her skin had warmed his, and his, hers. "I want you to be sure."

He studied her, wondering why he'd ever believed the men who called women the weaker sex. This woman was strong as nails, and she could see right through him. At times it was a comfort; right now it was a trial.

"I told you what a desperate day I had, deciding. That included a sleepless night, too, if you want to know. I sat on that damned slab down by the creek all night pondering this thing, Ellie. I'm sure."

"When you come back from California, you'll be even more sure." *If you come back . . .* Quickly, she put the dreadful possibility out of her mind.

Taking his plate, she set it with hers in the skillet and returned to him. She kissed his lips. "You're wild, Kale Jarrett . . . wild and free. You've been that way so long you might not be able to change."

"Now, Ellie—"

She kissed him again, and he pulled her to him and held her close. "You know how I feel about the ranch," she said. "It's my home. I can't run around the world, not even for you." Looking at him, she implored him to understand. "Not even as much as I love you."

219

"Love?" he whispered.

She nodded, holding her bottom lip between her teeth. Finally, she grinned. "Lust, too."

She watched his Adam's apple bob. "I feel both, too, Ellie. I'll change."

Fiercely she buried her face in the crook of his shoulder and hugged herself to him. "I don't want you to change. Please don't think that. Don't you understand how much I love you? I couldn't bear to see you cooped up on that little ranch when the whole wide world is beckoning."

Chapter Ten

He didn't like it, she could tell. But she also detected a feeling of relief in him when he held her and caressed her back with long, gentle strokes. And that would have worried her, except that she knew she was right. She could not cage him up on the ranch; neither could she let him cage himself out of a sense of duty.

At least she wouldn't have to endure another day of his morose silence, she discovered after they packed the horses and headed up the trail.

Soon after they left camp, the draw opened into a canyon which was wide enough to allow them to ride side by side. The country itself became more rocky, traveling more difficult.

Kale studied the trail ahead of them. Centuries of runoff water had washed away any semblance of dirt, leaving for a trail, if indeed it could be called that, nothing more than a jumble of rocks separating two walls of limestone. Several varieties of cactus grew here and there; the base of each hill on both sides was thick with oak and cedar.

"How'd you ever find this route?" he questioned. "Surely it would be easier to travel the stage road, even if it is longer."

She shrugged. "Benjamin and Armando located it. I just followed them."

He winked at her. "All duty and patience."

She laughed. "Not entirely, so don't go getting any notions about the future."

After a couple of hours they came to a fork in the canyon. Drawing rein, Kale removed his hat and wiped his forehead with his arm. "Which way, guide?"

She pointed to the left, where directly ahead of them a sheer limestone cliff rose a hundred feet straight up. Cottonwood trees grew close to the cliff and towered upward to its height. The trees were matted with a covering of wild mustang grapevines, their silvery green leaves glimmering in the sunlight. A small spring gurgled through the rocks and fell into a clear pool. Approaching it, he saw bugs skittering on the surface of the inviting water.

He held Ellie's reins while she lay on the ground, sipping water from her hand to prevent getting a mouthful of waterbugs. When she finished, he did the same, after which he slackened his hold on the reins so both horses could drink.

It was mid-morning by the sun, and the day was warming up nicely. The cold water tasted sweet and felt cool as the wind dried it from his lips. He had experienced these things a thousand times before, but his senses seemed heightened today, alerted, as if he were on the run with pursuers after him.

Ellie stood near, craning her neck to scan the area around them. "The cottonwood branches reach almost to

222

the tops of the cliff," she mused. "Only birds can reach those grapes."

Her melodic voice blended with the singing of a bird high up in the treetops, calling him, singing to his soul.

"What a relief," he sighed. "Here I was fearing you would send me up that tree to fetch grapes for your jelly."

When she turned her laughing face to him, their eyes held, transmitting a deep and sensual happiness from one to the other.

Reaching an arm, he drew her around, found her lips, and felt his senses sway at the touch of her.

Around them the world continued. The horses blew and snorted into the water, slurping it up with such gusto that the burbling of the spring was drowned out—just as his senses seemed drowned in the very essence of this woman.

Ever since her startling answer to his proposal this morning he had vacillated between a state of euphoria and one of utter confusion. She had set him free. *Free.*

His lips stroked hers, savoring, feasting on, consuming her lovely passion, passion she gave freely without reserve, without demands, a gift he held even more dear since her decision to set him free.

Free . . . when he wasn't at all sure that's what he wanted to be.

Anxious to reach their destination before nightfall, they ate in the saddle and by mid-afternoon found their way out of the canyon and into a ravine surrounded by a shin oak thicket. Ahead of them hills rolled forward in waves of dusty green and gold.

At a small creek which Ellie said flowed from the Concho River farther north, they watered the horses, then continued across the grassy banks and now-red soil. In the distance he saw a dark line which could have been either trees along the Concho River or the cliffs themselves.

"The cliffs," Ellie told him. "They're on the north bank of the river." They looked to be five or so miles off.

They came upon the river where it made a wide curve. On the opposite side a fractured wall of rock rose some fifty feet above the riverbed. Kale removed his hat, wiped his brow, and stared.

It looked like an uneven stack of flapjacks, some thick, some thin—some with a reddish tint, others the gray and white of weathered limestone. He could see markings, but from this distance he couldn't make out what they were, except for some that were obviously stars. Cactus grew from hollows which had been weathered in the sedimentary stone.

"There's a good crossing upriver." Ellie pulled her mount to the west and Kale followed.

"What now?" he called from behind her.

"I don't know," she confessed. "There are a number of caves in the cliff." She shrugged. "I thought we could look around, see what we find. I brought that piece of limestone from Benjamin's pocket."

He followed her, considering her innocence. Even though she had been raised in what folks called a house of sin, apparently it had not touched her . . . much to Lavender Sealy's credit, he knew. Lavender had been set on making a lady out of her.

Which was why she had insisted that Ellie marry Benjamin Jarrett. A wise choice. Were she not his brother's widow, he would never have met her. And had she married Benjamin for any other reason, she wouldn't have fallen in love with him.

In love with him . . . exactly the thing he had feared. Somehow it now gave him pleasure to think on it. He prayed he could learn to corral his own wandering instincts. He couldn't stand to hurt her.

By the time they had found the crossing, picketed the horses, and started their investigation of the cliffs, Kale began to suspect the futility of their trip—except for his own desperate reason for bringing her here: to get her away from the ranch before his brothers pulled their dreadful stunt.

And to give himself a chance to come to terms with what he now suspected had been stewing inside him all along, since the first time he and Ellie loved, the night she'd come to him in that silky green thing.

"Ellie," he began. "I know you have your heart set on matching the drawings on that piece of limestone, but, hell, honey, I don't see how it'll be possible. Look around. There're hundreds of drawings that chip could have come from. Look at them—stars, buffalo, turkeys."

"I know," she called over her shoulder. "Aren't they a wonder to behold?"

He agreed, and when she paused on one of the wider ledges, he leaned beside her against the cliff wall and caught up her hand, lifting it to his lips, inhaling a deep draft of the delicate, tantalizing scent of this woman. "A wonder to behold."

Scanning the river and across it the stand of trees they had passed earlier, he realized the sun was fast sinking in the west. "We'd better go. We can make camp over there in those trees."

"No. There's one more place I want to look. Only one. It's the cave where we always camped. We can camp there tonight."

After they fetched their bedrolls and saddlebags and slung the whole lot over their backs, Ellie showed him where to start climbing to reach the cave.

"Up there?" Even glancing up made him dizzy.

She nodded. "It isn't far."

"And I'm no goat."

"Oh, Kale, come on . . . you can do it. We climbed it several times—Benjamin, Armando, and myself."

The mention of Armando Costello steeled his determination and he glanced up the side of the cliff again.

She began tugging at her boots. "You should remove your boots, too. It's easier to get a foothold with bare feet."

He stared at her feet, now clad only in black stockings, and thought of them bare, clasped around his . . .

"There's only two things I remove my boots for, honey, and the side of a cliff isn't a good place for either one."

The way she rolled her eyes, he knew she understood. "The side of a cliff isn't a good place to incite lust, either," she admonished cheerfully.

He watched her climb, her buckskin-clad figure definitely inciting lust as she searched for and found one toehold after another. Drawing his mind back to the task at hand, he followed, telling himself that if that damned gambler could climb this cliff, so could he.

By the time they reached the ledge in front of the cave, both were out of breath. Ellie dropped her backpack inside the lip of the shelter, then immediately began to rummage through it for a lantern and some matches.

"The scenes inside this cave are the most fascinating of all," she told Kale.

He crouched beside her and struck a match on the sole of his boot. Taking the lantern from her hands, he proceeded to light it. "Now, aren't you glad I wore my boots?"

She grinned. "You aren't interested in seeing the artifacts?"

He studied her through the dim light with an intensity that set her heart to skipping. Pecking her quickly on the lips, he turned up the wick on the lantern. "I'm interested in what comes after we see the artifacts."

His innuendoes dimmed her own inclination to pursue what she knew to be a hopelessly dim chance of finding anything to shed light on Benjamin's murder. However, she proceeded to show Kale around the room. Soon her enthusiasm for these drawings returned.

"This is an account of the Comanche and Apache slaughter of the monks and soldiers at the mission outside Summer Valley; it happened over a hundred years ago."

Kale rested his hand on her back, massaging her shoulders and neck in a sensual gesture that set her heart pumping at a rapid clip. "I suppose that gambler figured all this out."

She laughed. "No, Armando did not figure all this out. Mrs. Wiginton told me these stories." Slipping her free arm around his waist, she drew him to the other side of the cave. His jealousy of Armando Costello must surely be a good sign, she thought. Surely.

"This drawing shows the Indian attack near Mason when they abducted a little girl named Alice Todd."

Kale traced the drawing with his forefinger. Then he nodded toward a series of lines; they resembled tally

227

marks. "Wonder what they were counting? Scalps?"

"It's sad, isn't it?"

"Hmm," he agreed. "For both sides. The Indians were fighting a war for survival."

"Look at all the handprints," she said. "What do you suppose they mean?"

"Costello didn't know?" he quipped.

"He doesn't know any more than you do about these things," she responded. "He's just . . . ah, more interested."

"More interested?" Catching her palm, he placed it inside one of the painted outlines of an ancient hand. Painstakingly, he adjusted the angle of her fingers, one by one, to fit inside the outline.

A bittersweet sense of longing arose inside her at the disparity between the rough texture of the stones and the tenderness of his hand on hers. Suddenly she wanted him to kiss her, wanted desperately to feel his lips on hers, warming the chill that swept over her without warning.

As if privy to her thoughts, he bent and covered her lips with his own.

Oh, Kale, don't leave me . . . please don't leave me, she cried . . . but only in the silence of her heart.

Lifting his lips a degree, he searched her imploring eyes. "What's he more interested in than I am, Ellie?"

She curled her lips together, pressing them against her teeth. She stared at him.

"Certainly not in you," he whispered. "That isn't possible."

"I know," she admitted. Turning then, she began searching the walls for a broken place to match the chip she found in Benjamin's pocket. Kale followed, holding the lantern.

228

"It's like looking for that needle in the haystack folks are always talking about," he told her.

She nodded.

"What's it going to prove?"

"That Benjamin was here before he was killed," she responded. "Then we can look for other signs of him, piece together a trail like you did with the puddin'-foot."

They made their way around the room, Kale holding the lantern, Ellie searching with both her hands and her eyes for a chip in the ancient mural on the walls of the cave. When the orb of light dipped toward the floor, she reached for the lantern.

Kale had squatted on his heels. An object made of silver glinted from his palm. He turned it over in his hands. "Look at this," he called up to her. "Someone lost a belt buckle." He started to tease her with Armando Costello's name again, but without warning she sank to her knees beside him, snatched the buckle from his hand, and emitted a sound somewhere between a whimper and a death keening.

"*It's Benjamin's,*" she whispered.

Kale stared at her. "You're sure?"

Nodding mutely, she held the buckle closer to the light.

Kale frowned. "I never knew Benjamin to wear fancy—"

"I'm sure," she repeated. "I bought this buckle myself, from a drummer who came through Summer Valley with trinkets and things from Mexico. It was for Benjamin's birthday, and he always wore it." She closed her fist around the buckle, hiding it from view. "I don't know why I didn't miss it among his clothing."

When her voice quivered, Kale pulled her to his chest.

229

He soothed her head, his own still ringing from the impact of their discovery. Benjamin had come here . . . to this cave . . . just as she'd thought. He had come here, then he had been killed.

With gentle hands he held Ellie back. "Why don't you go out on ledge there, get some air? Let me look around."

She shook her head. "I'm all right. You might miss something."

There was truth in what she said, of course. He'd have dismissed the buckle had Ellie not been along.

They searched until dusk began to fall, but to little avail. As diligently as they inspected every nook and cranny, even sifting the ashes in the firepit in the center of the cave, they found nothing conclusive. A dark stain on a piece of firewood could have been blood, and if so, it could have been Benjamin's. Then again, it could as easily have been the blood of an animal, or not even blood at all.

"There's nothing else here, Ellie."

"Except this." She had spent the last half hour painstakingly comparing the chipped fragment of limestone to every inch of the walls she could reach. "Come look."

Kale's stomach churned with misgivings. He turned to see her holding her hand against the wall, as though merely resting it. As he watched, she withdrew her hand and part of the drawing fell away, etched as it was on the chip she had taken from Benjamin's pocket.

"He was here, all right," Kale admitted. "His buckle proves it; matching this chip confirms it."

"And he was in trouble when he was here," Ellie added.

"Now we have to figure out why . . . and how . . . and who."

"The who should be obvious," she stated.

"You mean the Raineys?" he questioned.

"Who else?"

"I don't know, Ellie. I've seen a lot of land-hungry men in my day. Men like the Raineys, who'd take a man's land at the drop of a hat, killing whoever stood in their way. But frankly, I've never known a one of them to go to so much trouble to hide it. Mostly, they come right out in the open, knowing there's no one to stand in judgment."

"Except Carson," she argued. "And you."

He grunted. "The ranger and the gunfighter?"

She had no answer for him. They began to climb down the hillside and recrossed the river, pitching camp beneath the trees, as Kale had previously suggested. The first thing they had agreed on after Ellie matched the fragment of limestone was not to spend the night in the cave. Neither could bear the idea of sleeping in the place where Benjamin might have been murdered.

Later, they sat side by side, having finished a supper of sausage and fried bread, like the night before. But unlike the night before, their passions were aroused not for each other, but at the cold-blooded killers who had robbed them both of a man they had loved and admired and depended upon.

She leaned her head against his shoulder. "You're no gunfighter, Kale. I know that now. But the Raineys don't. They could fear your wrath as much as they do Carson's badge."

Kale tossed a twig he had been chewing into the fire. "They'd better. Benjamin Jarrett was the best man I ever knew, and he didn't deserve to die."

"No, he didn't," she agreed, keeping to herself the newfound knowledge that the Jarrett family had produced more than one good man.

They arrived back at the ranch near dusk the following day. Little had happened during their absence, but Kale was disappointed not to have received replies to his wires.

"We did hear from Carson, though," Ginny told him. "He's still in Mexico."

"Don't reckon we'll see hide nor hair of him anytime soon," Zachariah added. "He's up in the Sierra Madres, place called Real de Catorce, chasing silver bandits with that hell-raising friend of yours, Santos Mazón. Said he hopes we can handle things down here."

Kale told them, then, what he and Ellie had discovered at the painted cliffs, and as he had predicted on the trail, the brothers did not take well to the findings.

"Saddle up," Rubal demanded. "We'll ride over there tonight and see what the Raineys have to say for themselves. They can't fight us all and win."

"Tomorrow," Zachariah told the group. "Come morning we'll ride to the Circle R. Tonight we have a duty that's been too long neglected."

He meant a family service at Benjamin's grave, where Ellie discovered much to her astonishment the brothers had built a picket fence while she and Kale were away.

Zachariah conducted the service, reading first from the Book of Genesis, a passage which Ellie had never heard, but which surprised her with its violence: "The voice of thy brother's blood crieth unto me from the ground."

Afterwards the group sang "Rock of Ages," and Ellie

232

was glad Benjamin had taught her to sing it.

Zachariah spoke a few words then in remembrance of their brother.

"Benjamin was more father to us than brother," he began. His eyes rested on Ellie, and she noticed the deep sadness within them, a sadness reflected in the eyes and faces and carved into the hearts of everyone there.

"Father and husband," Zachariah corrected himself.

Ellie stood between Ginny and Delta, and at Zachariah's next words she looked up to find Kale studying her from across the grave. She felt her face flush.

"Although Benjamin left no children of his own seed," Zachariah intoned, "we are his children. We will carry on his good name and keep to his high ideals."

Again Ellie felt Zachariah's eyes on her. She stared hard at the ground, thinking her expression would surely give away her thoughts. "To this end, we pledge ourselves, each in the manner appointed, to see after his widow, Ellie."

Zachariah's words gave pause to Ellie. She wasn't sure she grasped his meaning; she didn't think she would like it if she had.

Forcibly she pushed aside the memory of Kale's strange proposal. The group sang about crossing the River Jordan, and again she was glad Benjamin had taught her so well. Obviously, he had taught the others the same things.

When the service ended, she thanked Zachariah and the brothers for building the fence.

"It was Kale's idea," Rubal told her.

"Kale's *orders*," Jubal corrected.

But when she turned to Kale, he stared across the

233

valley. "I see our friends are back." He nodded toward the rock shelter, where Ellie saw the flicker of a campfire.

"Don't worry yourselves," Zachariah told them. "They've been there ever since you two struck out for the cliffs. The boys and I visited with them; they claim they have a right to be there."

"They don't," Ellie seethed.

"Certainly not when they use it as a base to spy on Ellie, or to burn her out," Kale informed his brother.

"Regardless," Zachariah continued, "they say the Raineys claim land to the edge of the crest there. Said Matt Rainey himself holds the deed."

"That's a lie," Ellie said.

Kale laid a hand on her back, gently squeezing her neck muscles. "Don't worry about it tonight. We'll get everything straightened out come morning."

The sun barely showed promise of rising when Kale called to Ellie from behind the quilt hanging in her doorway.

She rubbed sleep from her eyes and sat up. Hearing his voice again, she rushed to the quilt and threw it back, expecting something dreadful to have happened.

He stood casually, his arm propped on the door facing. The look in his eyes sent alarm of a different kind spiraling down her body.

"Morning." With a wicked grin, he perused her flannel gown. "No green silk?"

"Kale!" She twirled back to the bed to see if Delta had heard, then sighed, seeing the girl was still sound asleep. But there were Ginny and Hollis only a wall away. Quickly draping the quilt around her body, she left exposed only her face, which frowned at him. "What do you want?"

"This." Bending, he kissed her lips, leaving her quivering and hot and wanting him desperately. "We'll be riding out soon, and I knew you wouldn't let me do this in front of the family."

A scuffling from the other room interrupted his second kiss and sent Ellie scurrying to throw on some clothes.

Kale had brought a ham with him from the smokehouse, and while he started coffee, Ellie began slicing it. Ginny came in and made biscuits, and Delta arrived in time to scramble the eggs.

The brothers drifted in, they ate, and they left. Soon, Kale had said. The sun wasn't even fully up by the time they rode off leaving the women standing in the yard, waving to their dust.

The day was filled with milking and baking and weeding the garden. After the chores were finished, Ginny and Delta accompanied Ellie up the hill, where they watered the rosebush at Benjamin's grave. They sat awhile beneath the oak tree, enjoying the balmy fall weather.

"What did Kale say when he saw the rosebush?" Ginny asked.

"It surprised him," Ellie admitted. "Brought back memories—regrets. I'm afraid I wasn't much help that night. I had sent for Carson, and when Kale showed up . . . Well, I wasn't very welcoming."

"Don't blame yourself. Kale acquired that reputation of his all by his lonesome."

"It wasn't deserved," Ellie protested. "Besides, he had just lost his brother, and I should have been more supportive. Instead, I was . . ." She paused to tell them about her parents. "I was afraid of him, as silly as that sounds."

"Well, you aren't afraid of him anymore." Delta's statement was issued with such vigor that Ginny laughed and Ellie stared at her, mouth ajar.

"No," she finally managed. "No, I guess I'm not."

"I think you're in love with him," Delta continued. "You may not know it yet, but—"

Ginny interrupted her. "Delta! Hush up. You've been raised not to meddle in other folks' affairs."

"Oh, Ginny, everyone can see it. Kale's in love with Ellie, too. And I think it's grand. It'll surely play hell with Zachariah's plan, though."

Ellie recovered from the shock of Delta's first pronouncements in time to question this last statement. "Zachariah's plans?"

"Delta!" Ginny stood and shook dirt and leaves from her skirts. "You run along and wash up. It's time to begin supper. The men should return soon."

Delta sighed.

"Run along," Ginny repeated. "Fetch some buttermilk from the springhouse."

Delta complied, but her eyes still shone like stars on a dark night. "I'm right, though, Ginny, and you know it. I think it's grand. Kale has needed a good woman to settle him down. You said so yourself, many a time."

Delta flew down the hill, helped along, Ellie was convinced, by the exasperated breath Ginny exhaled behind her.

"What is Zachariah's plan?" she questioned Ginny.

"To see you taken care of."

"By whom?"

236

Ginny shrugged, and when she spoke, it was to address a difficulty she had mentioned before. "Kale's wild, Ellie. He won't ever settle down."

Ellie sighed, hugging her knees with her arms. "I know."

"You've lost one husband, dear. I don't want to see you hurt again. Don't set your cap for him."

"Don't worry about me, Ginny. I'll be all right."

Ginny smiled wistfully. "I've seen that look in your eyes when he's around, Ellie. I've seen the way he treats you. You're sincere, but Kale is—"

"He asked me to marry him."

Ginny squinted through the afternoon haze as though she surely must have misunderstood. "He did?"

Ellie nodded.

"He proposed marriage? My brother Kale?"

Ellie laughed. "Yes."

"Well, when's the wedding?"

"I didn't accept. I guess I did, but with the provision that he go ahead to California, like he'd planned. After he's been out there, if he decides he wants to come back, I'll be waiting. Not forever, of course. But long enough to give him a chance to be sure that this . . . that *I* . . . am what he wants . . . *who* he wants."

Ginny studied her at length, then enfolded her in a hearty embrace. "Here I've been worrying about you, and I see there was no need. Delta was right, I'm afraid."

"About what?" Ellie asked.

Ginny laughed. "About everything."

Leaving the Circle R the brothers remained silent until they were out of earshot of the Rainey house, then began

237

to argue over the outcome of their meeting with Matt and Holt.

"They're guilty as hell," Rubal proclaimed.

"Maybe so," Zachariah agreed.

"I don't think so," Kale argued. "At least, not of killing Benjamin. Matt's hard-edged, all right; the struggle to survive out here leaves hard edges on folks. If Benjamin holds a deed to that ranch, either of the Raineys would likely have killed him for it. But they would've made certain first."

"Who else, then?" Jubal questioned.

"If I knew that, I'd have the sonofabitch locked up, Jube."

"No need to get testy," Jubal retorted.

They stopped at Mustang Creek to water the horses. After loosening their cinches, the brothers handed Kale their reins one after the other and went to sit in the shade of a cottonwood. Rubal pulled out his knife and started whittling on a stick.

The argument continued.

"Why are you so set against it being the Raineys who killed Benjamin?" Zachariah questioned Kale.

"Things don't add up. I've never seen a cattleman go to such lengths to cover his tracks. They usually don't give a damn who they ride roughshod over, or who knows it."

"They didn't cover the tracks of that puddin'-foot," Jubal reminded him.

"And that's odd, too . . . why would they leave such obvious tracks?"

"You're talking in circles," Zachariah said. "But I take your meaning. It don't add up for them to sneak around harassing on the one hand, then leave the puddin'-foot

238

tracks for all to see. Not to mention those men in the cave."

"That's right," Kale told him. "I think we're looking for a crazy man."

"You don't call Holt Rainey crazy?" Jubal asked.

"Holt Rainey's mean, Jube. He may have a hair-trigger temper, but who ever killed Benjamin is calculating and obviously willing to sit tight and wait for his under-handed methods to run Ellie off the ranch. Holt Rainey wouldn't sit still five minutes when he could use his gun instead. Haven't you learned the difference between mean and crazy? Or do I have to teach you?"

"Sure, Kale, teach me. You're the one itchin' for a fight."

"Lay off him, Jube," Rubal advised. "Can't you tell he's doe-eyed? I've seen it eatin' at him ever since we hatched that scheme to draw straws for Ellie."

"You won't be drawing straws, not for Ellie," Kale told them.

Zachariah looked at him. "How's that? We agreed—"

"I asked her to marry me."

The brothers turned disbelieving eyes on Kale.

"You?" Rubal asked.

"You ain't the marryin' kind," Jubal quipped.

"We can't let you do it," Zachariah said.

"You can't stop me," Kale replied. "I asked her on the way to the cliffs."

"And what did the little widow woman say?" Jubal quizzed.

Kale glared at him. For some reason his yen to fight had vanished since he'd blurted out his proposal. Now he didn't care whether they believed him or not. "She'll

239

come around. But I'm afraid I'm going to have to ask you fellers to leave. I'll have a better chance to win her over without half the family breathing down my neck."

"You better be sure of yourself, Kale. You can't go a-runnin' out on her," Zachariah warned.

"There's no chance of that, Zach."

The air cleared after that, and Kale rode easier. He'd expected an argument about Ellie; he'd been surprised the brothers had given in as easily as they had. Now all he had to worry about was convincing Ellie not to send him off to California.

And about not wanting to go, himself.

"On your way out tomorrow," he told Zachariah when they topped the hill leading down to the house, "I want you to check on a man for me."

After explaining Armando Costello's connection with Benjamin, Kale continued, "I wired Brady down at New Orleans for information on the man. In the meantime, I'd like you to look in on him. See if you've ever run into him."

"You suspect him of something?" Rubal asked.

Kale shrugged. "Not really, but . . . well, I can't put my finger on it. No evidence, just instinct." He laughed. "Could be jealousy on my part. The man's fancy, sort of handsome, I suppose the ladies would say, and he's set his cap for Ellie. That much is clear."

By the time they rode up to the barn, even Zachariah was ribbing Kale about his sudden visit from the green-eyed monster.

"It'll keep you in line," Rubal told him.

"And cause you to act like the crazy one yourself," Jubal added.

Kale eyed his brothers one by one. It was good to see

240

them, to travel with them, to eat with them, to joke and argue with them. But he had work that he had to do alone.

"You'll be heading out in the morning?" he questioned, after they stabled, groomed, and fed their horses and headed for the house.

The back door squawked, and Kale stared at Ellie standing in the halo of light.

"Yep," Zachariah said.

"You'll come back for the wedding?" Kale asked.

"If there is one," Jubal gibed.

Chapter Eleven

"What do you mean, you're leaving today?" Ellie demanded over breakfast after Zachariah had instructed the others to be ready to travel as soon as they finished eating.

"Things to do," Zachariah told her.

"But . . ."

"We prayed over Benjamin's grave, now we'll leave the rest to Kale here."

"I thought we were staying a month or so," Delta objected, obviously the only one in the room besides Ellie herself who had not heard the news.

"I have to get back to the newspaper," Hollis told her. "Some other editor's likely set up shop already."

Delta glanced at Ellie. "I think I'll stay on, if you don't mind."

"Of course—" Ellie began.

"I need you to look after the children, Delta." Ginny's tone was firm. "Mama Rachael will have had enough of them by the time we return, and I'll be busy helping Hollis get caught up down at the office. Why, the circus comes to town next week—we'll have to get a special edition of the *Sun* out for that—and the new theater opens soon."

"Perhaps you can come back when things settle down," Ellie suggested to Delta. "I'd love to have your company."

"She'll be back," Ginny assured her.

"We all will." Zachariah frowned at Kale. "You think around Christmas time?"

Kale favored Ellie with a curious sort of grin. "Maybe so," he mumbled.

After the meal the men saddled the horses while the women packed food for the trail. When Ellie returned from the smokehouse where she had fetched two hams to send along, Delta seemed to have adjusted to the sudden travel plans.

"I can't wait to come back, Ellie," she enthused. "Christmas will be a perfect time for a—"

"Delta, run these hams out to Hollis to put in his saddlebags," Ginny interrupted.

"Now, Ellie," she continued after Delta complied, "I won't hear of you sending along all this bread."

"I can bake more. What else do I have to do after you're all gone?"

Ginny hugged her good-bye. "You'll find something, dear. Of that I'm sure."

Leaving the house, Ellie saw Kale surrounded by his brothers, each in turn slapping him on the back, offering advice, or so it seemed.

"I'll wire you as soon as we settle the difficulties," he told Zachariah. He and Ellie stood at the gate, watching the others mount and prepare to ride away.

Rubal pierced Kale with a mocking grin. "Keep us

posted on that other matter, too."

"If you need any help, send for us," Jubal added, and the twins guffawed. Ellie watched a blush creep up Kale's neck.

Then the family moved on out, leaving her with a hollow feeling in the pit of her stomach. Kale draped an arm about her shoulders, and they stood waving and watching until the riders crested the hill and rode out of view.

For a moment longer they stood. His hand gripped her shoulder so tightly she knew something was wrong. Turning, then they started for the house, but Kale stopped at the porch.

"I think I'll sit out here a while," was all he said. Inside she started to wash the dishes, then stopped. Through the open door, she saw Kale sitting, elbows propped on knees, staring at the hillside where his family had disappeared.

Leaving the dishes, she filled two cups with coffee and went to sit beside him.

"You know, Ellie . . ." He spoke without taking his eyes off the hilltop; his voice was husky. "This is the first time I've ever been the one left behind. Watching them go, it's like Ma was sitting here beside me, cradling that rosebush. Now I know what it was like, her sitting there with that faraway look in her eyes. She was searching for Pa—and for me."

Ellie slipped an arm through his, laid her cheek against his shoulder. "They'll be back; they said so." The words spoken brought their meaning to life. Zachariah said the family would return for Christmas, but that was less than two months away. Kale would be in California by then. Suddenly she recalled his curious expression at the table, the glance he'd given her when he'd agreed with Zachariah about Christmas.

"Why did they leave today?"

"I told them to."

"You?" She questioned him, aghast. "But you loved having them here."

When he looked at her, it was for the first time since his family had left, and the softness in his eyes washed her with tenderness. Then he grinned that sheepish grin she had seen so many times before. "I told them I'd asked you to marry me, and that I would have a better chance at winning you over if they left."

Her mouth fell open. When he finished speaking, she asked, "Did you mention my requirement? That you go to California first, to be sure?"

Reaching out, he smoothed a strand of hair back from her eyes. "I told them."

"You intend to solve Benjamin's murder, go to California, and return by Christmas?"

"I'm not going to California."

"Now, Kale—"

"Listen to me, Ellie. I'm through with all this leaving. I'm through leaving places, through leaving people . . ." Lowering his lips, he kissed her gently. "Especially those I love."

Her senses reeled. She returned his kiss, grateful, happy—and doubtful. "I think you should go to California."

His face inches from hers, he whispered against her skin. "*Not without you.*"

"You'll be content to stay in one place, confined to—?"

"Confined to you. I love you, Ellie."

"You guess?"

He shook his head. "I know. Those words are filling me up and running over. It's like I have a big smile plastered across my face for all the world to see. And I don't care; I want them to see. I want the whole world to know I love you." Jumping to his feet, he scooped her in his arms and swung her around the swept yard. His eyes held hers, rapt, laughing, happy. "I love you, Ellie. I want to marry you as soon as it's proper, and I want you to have my children."

He stood her on her feet, held her tight, so tight her lungs felt constricted. Or was that her own sense of joy? Then his hands began to caress her back, her hair. He strewed pins, unfastened buttons.

"Kale—"

"And right now I want—"

"Kale?"

". . . you. I want you right now, even before it's proper."

"Kale. The breakfast dishes are still on the table."

"They'll keep." He worked her dress off her shoulders.

"Your family—they might return."

Holding her face in his palms, he kissed her lips, then each troubled eye in turn. "They wouldn't dare." Again he scooped her in his arms; this time he carried her indoors and straight to the spare bedroom.

"They wouldn't dare," he repeated. "Not when I haven't slept in a good bed with you but once in my whole life."

By the time he'd undressed them both, her heart was pumping to beat the band, and with her hand against his chest she felt his thumping at the same rapid clip.

Picking her up again, he lowered her to the bed and

followed her, burrowing against her, leaning on one elbow to study her smiling face.

"And for the record, I don't intend to sleep anywhere the rest of my life without you by my side."

His commitment, coming so unexpectedly, as it had, and at such a rapid pace, left her head spinning a web of pure joy. She felt like singing and dancing and laughing. She felt like loving this man.

Reaching her lips toward him, she winked. "I'm not sleepy."

"Neither am I, honey. Neither am I."

While his hands set fire to her body, his words ignited her soul: *I love you, I love you, I'm through with leaving.*

And while his lips traced wet and tantalizing circles over her skin, his commitment to stay with her brought her senses to life, senses which from the time he first entered her life had felt benumbed with the prospect of loving him and losing him.

His commitment, coming as suddenly as a blue norther to a spring sky, set her free. Free to love, to live, to laugh and cry. His commitment, freely given, had set her free to belong to him, to hold to him, to depend on him.

And when his body filled her own, his love suffused her being, bringing a wholeness she had never known nor ever expected to know.

Afterward they lay in each other's arms, he tracing circles on her back with lazy fingers, she running her own fingers across his strong jaw, struggling to contain the joy that burbled within her like a brook singing in springtime.

"I don't remember being this happy since I was a child."

He nipped kisses across her face, drawing a wayward

strand of hair through his lips. "I feel it too, honey, like I could dance all the way to town without my boots on."

She laughed. "And to think how we started out: me thinking you a gunfighter, you thinking me a floozy."

He laughed with her, thankful they could now smile over such things. "Want to know a secret?"

She nodded, delighted.

"You're the first woman I ever slept with who didn't charge for her favors."

His honesty caught her off guard; for a moment she didn't know quite how to respond.

"Not that they all charged *me*," he corrected with a wicked grin.

She kissed him sweetly, striving to keep a grin from her face. "Laugh now, Kale Jarrett, because later you may decide that I charged more than all the rest taken together."

He nipped her lips. "How do you figure that?"

"I cost you your freedom."

Suddenly the mood turned serious. Their gazes locked, delving, pledging, recording. Finally, he shook his head, wonderment reflected in his eyes.

"No, honey, you set me free—free to love you like you deserve to be loved every day of our lives."

The following days were idyllic for Ellie. She and Kale spent much of their time on horseback, riding the pastures where Kale inspected the livestock and made plans for their future.

"By next spring we should be able to make a drive," he said one night after supper when they sat side by side on the front porch step.

"To Kansas City?"

"Or Dodge."

"How long would you be gone?"

"*We*," he corrected.

She looked askance. "You'll take me along?"

Slipping his hands down her shoulders, he tickled her rib cage. "I wouldn't consider leaving you at home. Don't you remember what I said? I'm never going to sleep without you beside me again."

"Then let's go to bed," she whispered.

The Circle R men appeared less frequently at the rock shelter now, and things generally quieted down.

"How will we ever settle Benjamin's murder?" she asked one morning.

Kale sighed. "We need help," he admitted. "Carson will contact us when he returns from Mexico. Maybe he can figure out what to do next."

A week after the family left, Lavender Sealy came calling.

"I've been trying to get out here ever since those brothers of yours paid a visit to the Lady Bug, Kale, but we've been busy as a mama sow at feeding time."

Immediately upon entering the house, Lavender had visually inspected everything, including Ellie's bedroom, the spare room, and Ellie herself from head to foot.

"You doing okay, baby?" she asked while Ellie busied herself fixing a pitcher of lemonade and Kale went to the barn to help Snake water and stable the mare.

"I'm . . . ah, fine," Ellie answered, hesitating, discarding the word *wonderful*. If she showed too much enthusiasm, Lavender could be counted on to pry into the most intimate details, and Ellie had no intention of sharing her blissful new relationship with anyone.

"He's treating you all right?"

"Of course he is."

Lavender peered again into the front bedroom.

"Lavender," Ellie chided, carrying a tray with four glasses and the pitcher of lemonade. "You're too nosy."

"I'm worried about you, that's all."

"Don't be." She smiled, a smile that turned suddenly into a conspiratorial grin. "He asked me to marry him."

Lavender perched her fists on rounded hips. "He did, did he?"

Ellie set the tray on a stump Kale had sawed for them to use as a table on the porch. "That's what you wanted, wasn't it?" she asked. "Wasn't that the reason for all these new clothes?" She fluffed the sleeves on her brown gingham dress.

"Maybe I changed my mind."

Ellie laughed. "Well, it's too late. We've already made up our minds. And Lavender, I've never . . . *never* . . . been so happy. I never even *imagined* a person could be so happy."

"Humph!"

"What does that mean?"

Bootsteps coming around the side of the house alerted them. Kale, followed by Snake, stepped onto the porch.

"Howdy, Lavender. How's business?"

"What do you care?"

"Lavender?" Ellie scolded.

"I hear you intend to marry Ellie," Lavender probed.

"That's right." Kale took the glass Ellie held toward him. He watched her offer another glass to Snake, then sit down on the top step. He squatted on his heels beside her, possessively rubbing her shoulders with his free hand.

251

"Soon as it's proper," he added.

Lavender glanced toward the interior of the house, then glowered at Kale. "You call *this* proper?"

Ellie's mouth fell open. She watched Kale's jaws tighten. Color rose along his neck.

"That's quite enough," she admonished. "Stop playing mother hen and tell us what's been happening in town."

Lavender studied Kale, then turned her attention to Ellie. After a moment her gaze softened, and she relented. Fishing into her reticule, she withdrew a couple of envelopes and handed them to Kale.

"Gabe over at the telegraph office asked me to bring you these wires. Said they've been sitting there going on a week now. Don't know why you haven't been into town to pick them up."

Kale tore open the first envelope and scanned the contents, leaving Lavender to Ellie.

"We've been busy," Ellie told her.

"So it seems."

Ellie sighed. "I'll go fix supper." But when she started to rise, Kale caught her hand.

"Wait a minute, honey." His eyes darted to Lavender's at his slip of the tongue; their gazes held. He wondered what bee she had in her bonnet.

"One of these wires is from Sheriff Yates up at Fort Griffin," he told Ellie. "That soldier's still hanging on."

"Wonderful," Ellie sighed.

"And the other one's from the State of Texas," he continued. "Benjamin filed on this place just like I figured. Matt Rainey's bluffing."

Ellie squeezed his hand. "Good. Now we know who our enemies are." She glanced toward Lavender with an exasperated grin. "All of them."

"Don't look at me," Lavender objected. "I'm on your side, baby. I don't like you being gossiped about, that's all."

"Who's gossiping?" Kale demanded.

"Word gets around," Lavender told him. "Folks talk."

"I'm her brother-in-law."

"And you're young and randy, with a reputation to match. Staying out here alone since your kinfolk left, well, it's raised some eyebrows."

Ellie squeezed Kale's hand. "I don't care."

"I do." He lifted her fingers to his lips. "I won't have them talking about you. We'll get married right away."

"It's mostly Costello," Lavender admitted. "And most of that's likely jealousy. Still—"

"That sonofabitch," Kale hissed. "I'll have his hide."

"No," Ellie soothed. "He isn't worth a fight. Words can't hurt us."

When he objected further, she closed the topic. "You two find something else to talk about while I run to the smokehouse for one of those turkey breasts for supper."

Later, she recalled those words, wondering how such an innocent suggestion could have turned into so devastating a nightmare. But it did.

At the smokehouse she selected a plump turkey breast that had been smoking going on a week. It should be just right by now. Returning to the house, her heart fairly sang. What did she care what folks in town said. She was happy; Kale was happy. They would marry in time, that was assured.

Assured . . . until she approached the house to the clamor of a heated argument between Lavender and Kale.

"Costello's a damned liar!" Kale raged.

"The words came from your own brothers, not from Costello. I had heard you were bad news, but knowing Benjamin, I didn't put much stock in it. Now you've involved Ellie in this disgusting arrangement—"

"It isn't like that, Lavender. I can explain—"

"What's there to explain? That telegram confirms the motive. The wandering brother now has a ranch of his own."

"Damn it, Lavender, you're wrong. Dead wrong."

"I wouldn't have believed Benjamin Jarrett could have come from such heathen stock," Lavender hissed. "Drawing straws for her like she was no more than a horse at auction."

"Drawing straws for Ellie was Zach's idea."

"And you won, then sent the others packing so you could have free rein with her. Over my dead body—"

"My brothers didn't say that. It's not—"

"Yes, they did. They told Costello all the gruesome details. Drawing straws for Ellie," she repeated, "like she was no better'n a horse—or a slave."

Drawing straws for Ellie . . . Dear God in heaven!

Time screeched to a halt for Ellie in that one sickening moment. The world stood as still as if forever had come to pass right here in her dusty yard. She watched her life flash in front of her eyes: her parents' murders, being tossed from one uncaring relative to another, finding Lavender, finding Benjamin, finding Kale. The reel of disasters rolled on endlessly, as in the mind of one facing death.

And wasn't that what she faced . . . the death of her dreams? Of love and happiness and, yes, even the death

254

of her livelihood.

If Lavender was right—and who could dispute Kale's own brothers? If Kale's motive for deceiving her was to take the ranch, she doubted not that he could do it. What judge would award a ranch to a widow when the deceased's brother stood by to claim it?

As suddenly as time had stopped it began to spin again, threatening now to explode inside her brain. How could she ever look him in the face again? She must get away. Away.

If she were to lose this ranch as she had just lost Kale, she couldn't bear to stand by and watch it happen.

Dropping the turkey breast to the swept yard, she retraced her steps, stopping at the barn. Struggle though she did, coherent thoughts could not break through the swirling mass of confusion and despair that crowded into her brain, filling her head to the point of exploding.

Blinded by tears, she saddled her horse, giving no thought to where she would go. Then the idea of Kale following her loomed as a specter in her tormented mind.

Quickly she led the other horses from the barn, even Lavender's carriage mare. Turning them loose toward the creek, she slapped each rump in turn to set them on their way.

Then she climbed into the saddle and raced out of the barn, kicking the horse's flanks with her soft-soled shoes. Past the house, she rode, headed for she knew not where. She simply had to get away. The wind tossed her hair. Passing the porch, she heard voices above the clatter of her horse's hooves. Shouting voices, calling, pelting her as with stones with the sound of her name, the sound of Kale's voice, of Lavender's.

Satisfaction over getting away, over leaving them

afoot, filled her muddled brain for a time. She gloated on it, seeing Lavender race about, ordering Snake to catch up the mare, seeing Kale—seeing Kale.

The image of him set her heart to pounding even faster than it already did. Kale, his sky-blue eyes melting her soul. Kale, helping around the house even after his family came and there were women to do chores. Kale, his husky voice calling her name, "I'm coming, Ellie," or "How's this, Ellie?" She'd had her way with him.

That she had. How agreeable he had been, cooperating, helping, loving. She'd had her way with him, and she had taken it as a sign of his commitment.

She felt his hand on her shoulders, caressing her, filling her with fire and desire. Lust, she had called it.

Lust, he had agreed.

Lust and love, they decided.

Except now there was no love. Now she knew, had heard from his own lips, that there never had been any love.

She rode with abandon. Feeling the wind wet against her face, she realized she was crying. Angrily she swiped at the tears with the back of one hand, a futile gesture that served no purpose except to dry her cheeks for more tears.

Heedless of her destination, she approached a creek and was surprised to find herself well on the way to town.

Town. The Lady Bug. When her horse splashed into Pecan Creek, Ellie felt the cold water splash against her legs where her wadded-up skirts had left them bare. The chill somehow settled her mind a bit, as though it had been splashed on her face, recalling the icy waters of her own creek where she loved to bathe.

Suddenly she drew rein and dismounted in the middle

of the stream. While her horse watered, she splashed the icy water on her head and felt it swirl around her legs. It filled her shoes and tugged at the bottom of her skirts until they became waterlogged and heavy. She wrung them out and tucked them inside the band of her pantaloons before remounting.

The water had invigorated her. Combined with the chilly autumn wind, it helped clear her mind. The Lady Bug . . . of course. Where else did she have to go? What else did she have to do with her life? Nothing.

By the time she reached the fancy pink house, her anger had settled like a stone, leaving her with an encompassing sense of doom. She chided herself for playing the fool. Why had she entertained such highfalutin notions?

Love, for heaven's sake! What did someone like herself know about love? Very likely, she decided, climbing the stairs and entering through the front door Lavender had forbidden her to use, very likely no such thing existed.

The ache in her empty heart was from the loss of companionship, that was all. The loss of companionship, and perhaps a lingering of lust.

Off-key notes came from the piano in the parlor. Daisy's thin-voiced soprano warbled a bawdy tune which called forth poignant memories: the camaraderie of the family seated around her porch, Kale's objection to the pirate ballad, Kale's robust baritone voice, Kale's tenderness.

When she slammed the rose-etched front door behind her, Lavender's chimes rang out, bringing her sharply back to reality, back to the only thing she need recall about Kale Jarrett: his deception.

The chaos inside the pink walls lightened her mood

with its familiarity. The Lady Bug, after all, was home. At the sound of the chimes, Poppy rushed into the entrance hall.

"Ellie, what're you doing here? Lavender went out to see you, and she's awful late getting back. We need Snake in the gaming room, and we need—"

"Don't worry," Ellie told the distraught girl. "Lavender's right behind me. You can handle things until she returns."

But the idea of Lavender returning set Ellie's pulse to racing. Kale, too, would come. Her skin flushed. What then? What then, indeed?

"Ellie, are you all right?" Poppy's eyes traveled her tumbled-up length, took in her wet clothing, her red, tear-filled eyes.

"I just need to change clothes."

"Oh, sure. Use my room." She glanced into the parlor, then back at Ellie. "Things are a little slow at the moment. Look inside my wardrobe, you'll find some everyday things; I'll bring a pitcher of hot water. Would you like some tea?"

Ellie shook her head. "Brandy."

She hadn't intended to do such an outrageous thing. But rummaging through Poppy's wardrobe, her hands touched silk, reminding her instantly of the last time her hands touched silk, green silk. As though someone had struck her heart with a hot poker, she felt suddenly wounded to the core. What little life remained inside her cried out, demanding to be heard, sweeping her with a wave of defiance so powerful she knew that if anything could smother her hurt, this would.

When Poppy returned with the pitcher of warm water, she almost dropped it on the floor. "Ellie! Get out of that gown. Lavender'll have my hide!"

Ellie preened in front of the looking glass. "It *is* wicked, isn't it?" She smoothed her palms over the boned red silk bodice, what there was of it. Turning sideways, she lifted her hair atop her head and studied the way her breasts fairly ballooned from the scanty strapless garment. The red silk stopped on a line even with her uplifted nipples, leaving only a stiff ruffle of black lace to fan over the upper swell of her breasts. "I've never worn a strapless gown before," she said. "Do you think it will stay up?"

Poppy rolled her eyes. "It'll stay up, Ellie, but it isn't you. You were raised to walk beside a man, not to flounder beneath him."

The words hit her recently restored composure dead on, bringing a flood of tears. Quickly she twirled away from Poppy. The calf-length red skirt swirled over black petticoats, exposing black fishnet stockings and red silk slippers.

Poppy grasped her by the shoulders and turned her around. "Baby, what is it? What's happened?"

By forcibly concentrating, Ellie was able to bring her tears under control. "Nothing. At least, nothing earth shattering. I just learned what you and the others have known all along—men are no damned good."

Poppy sighed. "That isn't one hundred percent true." She shrugged. "You've had a run of bad luck, that's all. Now, let's get you out of this thing before Lavender comes."

Ellie danced away from her, kicked out a fishnet-clad leg, and pointed a red slippered toe toward the ceiling. "Help me fix my hair."

"No! Absolutely not."

Ellie gulped a big swallow of brandy, coughed at the burning sensation, then sat down at Poppy's dressing table. She rummaged through Poppy's hair ornaments. "If you won't help, I'll do it myself."

"Lavender would fire me, Ellie; you know that. In fact, if you're not out of that dress by the time she returns, we'll both be in more trouble than old man Peters—" Poppy stopped short, clamping a hand over her mouth.

"No, we won't." Ellie lifted her hair to the top of her head again, shaping it, sticking pins here and there. "I'll tell her I slipped into your room while you were working, that you couldn't see me for the portly customer on top of you."

Her eyes caught Poppy's startled expression in the looking glass. "And that you couldn't hear me above his loud—what kind of noises do fat men make, Poppy?"

Poppy held Ellie's amused gaze, finally sighing in resignation. Ellie sat quietly then, while the girl began jerking pins from her hair and repinning it. When Poppy finished, the top of her head looked like a confection, complete with red silk poppy and a black feather that dipped low enough to tickle her bare shoulder.

"Stunning, don't you think?" Ellie complimented.

Poppy wrinkled her nose. "It isn't you."

"I know." For a moment melancholy threatened to claim her resolve, then she gritted her teeth and squared her shoulders. "It is now."

For the fifth or sixth time since Ellie had begun dressing, the front door chimes sounded. Every time anxiety had raced through her blood. Was that Lavender?

Was it Kale?

"You'd better go," she told Poppy. "Business seems to

260

be picking up."

Walking from Poppy's room to the parlor in this getup ranked high among the hardest things Ellie had ever done. Although she and Poppy were virtually the same size, she kept thinking the bodice of her dress was about to fall down.

Several times she glanced down to make sure, and each time she was appalled to see her breasts swelling above the dress. How ever did the girls keep these things on? Then she grimaced. They didn't, not for long.

With every step fresh air rushed up the short skirt, reminding her of her unclothed state from the bottom up. Not only were her ankles exposed, but a good three inches of skin above them. And the silk rustled so loudly that she might as well have had a town crier preceding her, announcing her arrival to the gentlemen callers, or whatever in hell one called paying customers.

On top of it all, she expected Kale to materialize in front of her at each and every step.

By the time she reached the gaming room, she practically fell around the corner, blindly taking a stool at the bar, where Daisy had stationed herself to serve drinks in Snake's absence.

"Ellie!" she hissed. "What are you doing in Poppy's—"

"A whiskey," Ellie breathed, leaning both trembling arms on the bar for support. "Give me a whiskey, a big one, and quick."

"Does Lavender know about this?"

"Yes," Ellie lied. "Give me something to drink."

The whiskey burned down the same path the brandy had taken. But it also steadied her trembling body. Or was it that the burning sensation took her mind off it? She wasn't sure which, but when a customer approached the bar and drew out a stool to sit beside her, she could at least focus on him.

A stranger. Thank God for strangers.

"May I buy you another drink?" he asked.

Ellie stared at the empty glass she held with a death grip. She'd already finished the whole thing? Oh, well, it was a small one. "Yes, thank you."

"No," Daisy said.

"Yes, please," Ellie insisted. "Make this a large one."

"No."

This time the voice was masculine and familiar, and Ellie turned to see Armando Costello looming behind her, a bemused smile on his lips.

"Yes," Ellie repeated. She felt herself drowning in the confusion inside her brain. The room spun like a child's top. "Please."

Daisy complied with a sigh, but she had no more than set the glass on the bar when Armando took it from her hand. With his other hand, he gripped Ellie's very bare arm and pulled her from the stool.

"The lady is with me," he told the stranger. "Put it on my tab, Daisy. And bring us the bottle."

Before Ellie could so much as wonder what reaction to expect from Armando Costello, he had dragged her to a table at the far corner, where he seated her and then sat beside her, dismissing his two men with a curt nod. He handed her the drink and watched her gulp it down. She squinted against the burning sensation.

"I was expecting you, Ellie. I knew you'd come. After all, you belong in this place. It's your home."

Chapter Twelve

Matt Rainey expected results. Ira Wilson pondered this while he sat in front of the rock shelter overlooking the Jarrett ranch house. What was left of the late-afternoon sun sank below the horizon at his back. Till Metz squatted down beside him, offering a swig from their remaining store of whiskey.

"If somethin' don't give soon, we'll run out of belly wash," he grumbled.

"And patience," Ira added.

Well before sunup two days back Matt Rainey had come charging into the bunkhouse, sending them back to their hideout above the Jarrett house. He gave them strict instructions not to leave their post until they had the news he awaited—that the Jarrett place was abandoned.

Ira and Till entertained doubts that it was likely to happen in their lifetime. They were cowboys, accustomed to spending long hours in the saddle taking care of Circle R cattle. If this detective job kept up much longer, they figured they would die of boredom, and neither of them would get a chance to loop a rope on an ol' mossy horn again.

"Anything happen while I napped?" Till asked.

Ira shook his head. "That whore's still down there."

"Never figured I'd live to see the day, Ira . . . ," Till wiped his moustache with two fingers, ". . . but I'm gettin' mighty tired of looking at women. First the Jarrett woman, now the whore . . . I'm about ready to trade 'em both in for a good cow pony and a herd of steers."

"Know what you mean. For my money, it's Newt and Saint should be here. Free us to tend to ranch business. Half the Circle R cattle've likely strayed or gotten theirselves bogged and died by this time. Why, we ain't made a gather in six months."

Till agreed. "Time was the Circle R was the outfit to ride for. Right now I'd quit, if there was anybody to take care of things."

"Same here. I keep hoping Matt'll get shut of this crazy notion and go back to ranchin'."

"He'll have to clean house first. Get rid of them killers—including that brother of his. Hire some cowboys. Hell, we're about the only old-timers left."

Loyalty was important to Ira and Till. They rode for the brand, and they planned to continue that way as long as there were Circle R cattle left—and no longer.

Ira started to rise, then paused in a squatting position. "Hold on a cotton-pickin' minute. We've got some action."

Below them Ellie Jarrett raced past the ranchhouse and up the town road. Kale, Snake, and Lavender rushed into the yard, calling after her, or so it appeared.

"Wonder who lit a fire under her?" Ira mused.

"Lookee there." Till pointed to the opposite side of the

barn, where the horses Ellie had released ran toward the creek. "She's done set 'em afoot."

"A spunky lady, that."

While the evening shadows lengthened and the valley became shrouded in darkness, Ira and Till watched Kale and Snake catch up the horses and harness Lavender's mare. The three set out after Ellie.

"Maybe we're fixin' to be relieved of this dirty work after all," Till said. "Matt wants the ranch abandoned. From the looks of it, that just happened."

Ira sighed. "Reckon we'd best wait till morning to make certain."

After her second whiskey, Ellie felt the room begin to sway. Lights from the chandeliers glowed in fuzzy halos, as if she were seeing them through dense fog. The volume of noise heightened, and she suddenly recalled that she had been about to prepare supper when her world had fallen apart. Her stomach felt hollow, empty, but not from lack of food. A tremor racked her body. She had to find out what Armando Costello knew.

"This is where you belong, Ellie," he was saying. "Not out on that lonely ranch, but here . . . ," he swept the room with his beady gaze, resting once more on her eyes, ". . . here among the bright lights . . . ," with an index finger he traced the outline of her bare shoulder, then ran a thin line down her arm, eliciting a shudder, ". . . and warm bodies."

Warm bodies . . . Kale Jarrett had a warm body. A warm body . . .

And a cold, lying heart.

"Tell me what his brothers said," she demanded.

Costello cast her a knowing look. "By *his*, I assume you mean that gunfighter?"

She started to protest, but her ability to concentrate was ebbing, and she knew she'd best stick to the problem at hand. She nodded.

"Not much to it," Costello answered. "They wanted to see you taken care of—by a member of the family, you understand, because of the ranch and all."

"They said that?"

He nodded, sipped his drink, and wiped his lips with the back of his hand, not vigorously, as Kale would have done, but in a persnickety manner, like a gambler, she thought. Like city folk.

"In so many words," he added.

"*What* words?"

"What words?" he echoed.

"Tell me what they said exactly, word for word."

He downed a shot of whiskey and poured another. "You can't expect me to recall their exact words."

She inhaled a deep, quivering breath, then quickly glanced down to see if her bosom was still in place. When she looked up, Costello winked. He touched her glass with his own. "Welcome home, my dear."

Ellie gritted her teeth. "Tell me about the drawing."

"Oh, you mean when the brothers drew straws to see who'd have to marry you?"

"*Have to?*" Kale hadn't said *have to;* neither had Lavender. Those two words added immeasurably to her distress.

Costello shook his head quickly. "Poor choice of words, my dear. Forgive my—"

"Your words or theirs?"

He sighed. His eyes remained fixed on the baize-covered table. "Now that you mention it, I don't recall. No matter, you're a comely lass. Any one of them would have been fortunate to win you."

Anger stirred within the tight ball of despair knotting in her stomach. She stared at the empty whiskey glass; absently she began to tap it on the table.

"Another drink?"

She glared at Armando Costello. "No. No, I don't want another drink. I want . . . I want . . ." Desperately she threw her head down on the table, cradled it in her arms. What did she want? She knew.

God, how well she knew! Why had she started wanting things in the first place? For years she had lived oblivious to the world and the multitude of wonders it possessed. If only she still did . . .

If only she were still ignorant of the blissfulness of being free, still ignorant of the wonders of sharing— sharing a laugh, a tear, hurts and pleasures, sharing her bed, her life.

Not sharing, she rebuked . . . what she had experienced with Kale had not been sharing, but the illusion of sharing. Like the reflection of a smile in a looking glass: the smile was real, the reflection of it an illusion.

The love had been hers; Kale had merely reflected her love, and the reflection had been a lie.

The front door chimes sang out, a backdrop now to the laughter and talk in the parlor and gaming room. It no longer startled her; she had grown used to it. Or had the whiskey merely dulled her senses?

Suddenly the door banged open, slamming against the foyer wall with a force that shook the chandeliers. The sound brought Ellie and everyone else in the gaming room to attention. Before she had time to collect her wits, Lavender's voice screamed through the melee.

"Break my rose-etched door, Kale Jarrett, and you'll pay for it."

"There are things in life money can't buy, Lavender," Kale's angry voice boomed back, "but I wouldn't expect you to know about them."

His last words were spoken straight into Ellie's wide-eyed face, for he had turned the corner of the gaming room without breaking stride and now confronted her across the crowded room. The patrons separated as though expecting an exchange of gunfire.

Ellie's eyes went to Kale's hips, where she saw his six-guns belted low and strapped around his thighs. Immediately her vision was drawn back to his eyes.

"You can't wear those guns in here," Lavender called from behind him.

"Don't worry yourself," Kale barked, without taking his eyes from Ellie, who had by now risen and stood defiantly beside Armando Costello. "I won't be here long enough to start a gun battle."

In three strides he crossed the room. "Get yourself out of that goddamn fancy getup." He screeched to a halt across the table from Ellie, stopped by her defiant stance. "Put your clothes back on. We're going home."

Home. She swallowed. How wonderful that word sounded falling from his lips! Angry though he was, she knew she could walk out of here with him and calm him down and everything would be all right, same as always.

Except that now she knew the truth, and the truth changed everything. What she considered the same as always had not been real, but an illusion. She didn't want things to be the same as always.

268

She squared her shoulders. Slowly, deliberately, she lifted her chin, then ran her hands down the sides of her boned bodice, feeling the silk, recalling how he loved the feel of her green silk kimono. With measured slowness she raised a knee, rested a red-silk-clad toe on the seat of a chair, and rustled her black petticoats.

When the ruffled edge of her skirts fell seductively over her thigh, Kale bolted around the table and grabbed her arm.

Armando Costello caught her by the shoulder—a bare shoulder, Kale saw—and tugged her toward him. "To my mind, Miss Ellie is gowned most appropriately for this establishment, Jarrett. Seeing's how this is her first night back—"

Kale dug in his heels. "Turn her loose, Costello. I'll deal with you later." Facing Ellie, his voice beseeched her. "Come on, honey, we have a lot to talk about. I'll take you home."

At the sound of that word falling again from his lips, combined with the tender appellation, her resolve weakened; she fought to retain it. Appealing to her anger, she forced herself to recall the truth. Her empty stomach filled with anguish, bitter and cold. But her eyes remained mercifully dry.

Jerking her shoulder from Costello's unwelcome grip, she charged around the table, then pulled free from a startled Kale Jarrett as well. Before he knew what had happened, she had taken him by the hand.

"You want to take me home, Kale? Come. I'll show you my home. But it will cost you a fifty-dollar gold piece."

She couldn't have struck a more devastating blow had she used her fists; she saw that immediately. When he spoke, his voice was hushed.

"Ellie, please . . . give me a chance to explain." He glanced at their wide-eyed audience, first left, then right. "Not here. In private."

"There's nothing to explain. I understand the situation all too well."

"No, you don't—" Kale began.

Costello interrupted him. "Let her be, Jarrett. She doesn't need the likes of a disreputable fellow like yourself. She's happy here. Or she will be, after a few customers have hardened—"

"Shut your mouth while you still have some teeth in it, Costello," Kale shot back. "I've done some checking on you, and when I get that wire back from New Orleans, we'll see who's the disreputable one." He turned back to Ellie. "Show me your ro . . ." His lips closed over the word, as if not to speak it would deny its existence. "Where can we talk?"

"Use my room," Lavender said. "Go on, Ellie. We've got to get back to business around here."

Leading Kale down the hallway, Ellie tried to dislodge her hand from his grip, but he held on so tightly that by the time they reached Lavender's room the pain in her hand had helped take her mind off the conversation looming before them.

Inside she closed the door and watched Kale look around the lavender room in astonishment. "What's that smell?"

She almost laughed. She came so close to it that not to do so only reminded her of the gravity of the situation. She felt as though some giant hand had squeezed every bit of joy and happiness from her body.

"Lavender," she answered. "It's a flower." Releasing

her grip, she pulled free and crossed the room, putting some distance between them. Now that they were alone she didn't dare linger near him.

Not now, when she wanted so desperately to be in his arms.

"Where're your clothes?" he asked.

Steeling herself, she turned to glare at him. She swished her skirts, strutting a bit more than she had earlier in the gaming room. "I have them on."

"That isn't yours."

"No, but I thought you'd like it." She ran her hands up and down the boned bodice as before, toying with black laces which drew the fabric together in front. She lifted her chin, flounced her skirts. "It's such a wicked gown, I was sure you'd like it."

"I do," he answered, but his voice was hoarse, the words whispered from his throat. "In here where no one else can see."

The tension in his voice brought their emotions to a halt; at the invitation implicit in his words, their tormented gazes locked. She tried to swallow the lump in her throat and prayed for the strength to resist him.

Strength to resist, when all she wanted was to throw herself in his arms and hear him say it wasn't true.

"In this house, men do more than look. You're entitled to—"

"Stop this nonsense, Ellie. Stop it right now. Listen to me." With each sentence his voice had lowered, until the last was uttered as a whispered plea.

"Listen to what? Lies?"

"I haven't lied to you."

"Maybe not about going to California, but certainly about everything else."

271

"No, I haven't. I love you, Ellie."

The fervor with which he uttered those words came very near to dissolving her anger. Swiftly, she turned away, clasping the bedpost with both hands, hugging herself to it, striving with all her might not to cry.

When he touched her bare shoulders, she flinched. "I love you, Ellie."

"It will cost you fifty dollars to touch me," she hissed.

"If it would change the last few hours, I'd pay it, and more." His hands fell away and the dejection in his voice pierced her shell of anger and fear. She turned to see that he had retreated a few paces.

"How?" she whispered. "You gave all your money to that friend in California."

At her softened voice he looked up, and their eyes bore into each other's. "I'd find a way," he answered. "But first I have to convince you that I didn't draw straws for you. Nobody did."

The reminder of the drawing brought a bitter return of both her anger and her pain. "I heard otherwise, Kale. The words came from your own lips. I heard you tell Lavender. And Armando told me your brothers told him the same."

"He's lying."

She shook her head.

"Damn it, Ellie. Why would you take his word against mine?"

"It wasn't just Armando's word," she repeated. "Your lips spoke them first. On the porch of our . . . of my . . . of *your home!*" Her thoughts tumbled headlong toward the disastrous conclusion: Everything that had once been hers now belonged to him: her heart, her body,

272

even her home. When he started to object, she recovered. "But that isn't all. I have more to go on than your words. Ginny told me, and Delta."

He frowned, disbelieving. "What did they say?"

"That Zachariah had a plan. That if you . . . if you fell in love with me, it would ruin Zachariah's plan."

"It was Zachariah's plan," he admitted. Seeing her, his brain struggled to accept that this lady in the fancy garb was his sweet Ellie. Not that she wasn't beautiful and desirable, all gussied up. But the only thing he recognized as Ellie's was her voice, so full of hurt and anger. And her skin—her creamy, satin skin. "And they were right, I ruined it. I wouldn't go along with him. I couldn't let them do such a thing to you." His eyes beseeched her. "That's why I sat up all night, studying on it. That's why I asked you to marry me the next day."

Her mouth fell open. "Why? Why did you ask me to marry you?"

He stared at her, wondering how many ways he would have to say it to convince her he meant it. "To keep you from having to marry one of my goddamn brothers!"

"Oh," she intoned. "I must have been mistaken. I was sure you said it was because you loved me."

"I do, Ellie. Don't go twisting things. I *do* love you."

"Somehow you were more convincing before I learned all the details."

She watched him step toward her, felt his nearness, inhaled the welcome scent of him—natural and musky—combined with the sickly sweet smell of lavender that permeated the room.

She felt him touch her, his hands spanning her waist, his thumbs rubbing absently against the silk, creating

273

spots of heated flesh beneath them. Mesmerized by the needs he aroused, she couldn't tear her eyes away from his.

Ever so slowly he slipped his hands up her bodice, molding her rib cage, at length cupping her breasts in his palms. Unable to move, scarcely able to breathe, she felt his fingers, hot and tender, stroke the upper flesh of her breasts through the stiff black lace, then work their way beneath it.

She had heard men talk about how lightning played on the horns of steers they were driving to market. They said it danced around like fairies, leaving brilliantly colored trails and curlicues of electricity in the air.

That's what happened when his fingers played against her skin. She wondered if it was the same thing. She wished she could ask him. At this moment she wasn't sure she would believe him, not even on so neutral a topic.

"I love you more every day, Ellie." His voice was low and so convincing. Or was she letting herself be convinced, opening herself up to yet another betrayal?

His lips lowered slowly and she felt her own pucker in response. She was unable to resist his handling or his husky, seductive voice. "Right now," he continued, "I love you more than ever."

Just before his lips touched hers, she regained enough gumption to jerk her face away. "That's lust, Kale, not love. And it will cost you fifty dollars."

His reaction called to mind a child's toy that had been wound up, then set loose. She read it in his eyes: understanding dawned first, then disbelief, and at the last disgust.

Disgust that wiped away all traces of passion from his

eyes, all compassion from his voice. His hands dropped to his sides, and he stepped back. "Have it your way. But you're still coming home with me. I'll be back for you after I take care of Costello." His eyes swept her trussed-up body. Disgust turned to repulsion. "Get yourself dressed before I return."

Then he was gone. She watched him leave, heard him bark instructions to Lavender on his way down the hall.

"Get her into some decent clothes," he commanded. "Keep her away from the customers."

"Especially Costello?" Lavender inquired.

"All of them!"

"Where're you going?"

"After Costello."

"He left. And I'd advise you to do the same."

Ellie listened through the door with her face pressed to the cool wood, hot tears streaming from her eyes. Filled with bitter despair, her sobs escalated. She cried for all she had given up, for all that had been taken from her.

And for all she'd never had. He said he hadn't won her by drawing straws, and for some reason she believed him. But what difference did it make? He didn't really love her, not the way she loved him. And he had lied about it.

"Alone," Lavender's voice boomed through the door.

"Alone?" Kale inquired. "You mean without Ellie? You're damned crazy if you think I'd leave her *here*."

"Where do you think she spent most of her life? Wise up, Jarrett. And if I may say so, you're not one to call the kettle black."

"I'm not calling anybody anything," he objected. "I just don't want Ellie to . . . I mean, I don't want to leave her, not anywhere."

Her tears flowed in steady streams then, at the plaintive tone of his voice when he uttered that last commitment. Using her petticoat, she dried her eyes.

"It's best," Lavender was saying. "She's had quite a shock. She needs time to recover."

"But I—"

"No, Jarrett. I know women, so you listen to me. You run along to the ranch. Come back in a few days, maybe she'll go home with you."

"I guess you're right," Kale said.

"I know I'm right. Go on now, get out of here."

"If I leave her, will you try to convince her of the truth?"

"From what I heard through the door," Lavender confessed unabashedly, "she already believes everything except that you love her. You'll have to convince her of that yourself."

"She knows it," he replied. "At least she will when she comes to her senses."

Ellie ran smack dab into Lavender when she tried to rush from the room. "Let me go," she cried. "I'm going home with him."

"No, no, not tonight, baby." Lavender pushed Ellie back into the room, holding her by the shoulders. "Not tonight. Give this thing a little time. I take it you believed him."

"Yes." She inhaled. "I know he loves me. It was the drawing—the shock of hearing about it. I couldn't bear the idea that he would marry me because he had to, or because he wanted the ranch, or because he was Benjamin's brother and he'd drawn the shortest straw . . ." She struggled against Lavender's hold.

". . . or the longest. Let me go, Lavender. I want

276

to go home with him."

Lavender's grip tightened. She pushed Ellie toward the bed, where she forced her to sit, then sat down beside her, taking Ellie's hands in her own. "Don't rush after him, baby. That's no way to hold onto a man. A night apart now and then will do him good."

"But he said—" Drawing her hands from Lavender's, Ellie clasped them to her cheeks. She caught her words before they tumbled out. Her face flushed, recalling Kale's vow that they would never sleep apart again. She struggled to rise. "I must go, Lavender."

"Trust me, Ellie. It's best that you don't. I know men. They're jittery as June bugs when faced with the prospect of committing themselves to a lifetime with one woman. If you show him you don't need him right from the start, he'll be more apt to want to stick around."

Ellie didn't believe it. But she didn't argue further. Kale was already gone. A few days, Lavender had told him. Well, she wasn't about to wait a few days. If he didn't come by mid-morning tomorrow, she'd go to him, Lavender's philosophies be damned.

Suddenly she felt rejuvenated. Jumping to her feet, she began to plan for the future, for tomorrow, for tomorrow night . . . with Kale.

She twirled in Poppy's dress. "I think I'll buy this dress from Poppy. Kale would love it—at the ranch." She felt again his fingers on her skin and knew that the morrow could not arrive soon enough.

"And I think," Lavender cut into her reveries, "I think we had best look for a preacher before you go back to that ranch with Kale Jarrett."

By the time Kale stepped into the saddle and rode away

277

from the Lady Bug, his anger had subsided to an aching sense of failure and loneliness.

He'd failed Ellie miserably. Damn it, how was he to know his brothers would come to town talking? He would have expected Costello to use any means available to turn Ellie against him, but he hadn't counted on furnishing him the ammunition himself. That the gambler had twisted his brothers' comments into lies was certain.

Far less certain was how he could convince Ellie of Costello's conniving ways. He didn't know much about women. In fact, he suspected only one person in Summer Valley knew as little as he did about the weaker sex, and that was Lavender Sealy. Once this trouble was settled, he intended to have a talk with Lavender. If he and Ellie were to live this close to that woman, he had to put a stop to her meddling.

The moon rose high overhead, and Kale rode toward the ranch, his heart barely in it. From time to time he had wondered whether his love for Ellie was strong enough to cure the itchin' feet he'd inherited from his pa.

Now, at least, he knew the answer to that. The fear he experienced when he saw her race hell-bent-for-leather away from the ranch rode with him still, a nagging residue which sickened and weakened him yet with the knowledge that he could have lost her, and the despair he would have lived with forever, had he done so.

He loved Ellie Jarrett beyond his wildest dreams. Seeing her in that fancy house, gowned in that fancy dress, set his soul on fire. He could still feel it, the desire that washed over him when he walked in there and saw her.

It wasn't the dress that angered him, and she'd known it instantly. It wasn't the provocative way she tossed her chin, strutted herself, or swished her skirts above her thighs. Lordy, remembering it set him to wanting her worse than ever.

It wasn't Ellie; it was where she was. It was the men around them, ogling her, wanting her—her body, her satiny smooth body; it was Costello, that damnable gambler, with his hand on Ellie's bare shoulder. It was Costello, his insinuations about Ellie.

He could kill the man for it. He should. But Ellie wouldn't have it. His guns rode against hips, heavy now. For the first time in his life, they felt alien, evil.

As soon as he got to the ranch, he would hang them up for good—a gift to Ellie. She'd like that. He had no more use for guns, anyhow, now that they knew the Raineys didn't own Plum Creek. He'd leave Benjamin's killing to Carson. Keeping the peace was Carson's business, after all, not his own.

As for himself, he didn't need guns, he had Ellie.

Or he would have her in the morning. He wouldn't wait a few days, like Lavender said. He would go after her tomorrow . . . tomorrow morning.

The full moon cast its pale light over him. The stars, bright and close to earth, surrounded him with a sense of serenity, almost gaiety. He wished Ellie were here to enjoy them with him.

How he wished she were here. The whole time they'd argued inside that fancy room of Lavender's, he'd been struck by the futility of it all. He had hurt her, he knew that well enough, and he hurt for it.

He understood her fears. Hadn't she lost just about everything she'd ever had that mattered? She was angry and scared, and he understood that.

He had been hard put to resist taking her in his arms

279

and smothering her with reassurances and love.

Love. And she had called it lust.

He had left the stage road, striking out across country in an attempt to get back to the house sooner. Now he sat at the cliff, the stage road well to his left, the house below him, a dark shadow illuminated by the white light of the moon.

Lordy, how he had wanted her tonight. She had called it lust, and it was . . . lust so powerful he felt its pains even yet. But it was also love.

And the combination of the two rendered him practically useless for anything besides loving Ellie.

Tomorrow be damned. He was going back tonight. Lavender Sealy had meddled enough. He gathered up the reins.

He might have hell getting into that house after they'd closed it up, but he would do it. Even if he had to break down Lavender's precious glass door he would get inside the Lady Bug and find Ellie.

He eased the bay around. Hadn't he promised Ellie they would never spend another night apart?

A sudden thunder of horses' hooves shattered his musings just as he was about to sink spurs to the bay. He drew up cautiously, watching two men approach at a rapid clip. His hands went to his holsters, poised there while he let the men draw rein.

Then he recognized them—Costello's two men. "What the hell—?"

"Jarrett, come quick . . . Miss Ellie's taken sick. Costello sent us to fetch you."

Kale's heart stopped in that one second. "What happened?" He struggled for breath. "What the hell happened?"

"Don't know," one of the two men answered. While Kale sat dumbstruck, they had fanned out to either side.

"Let's get going." The man in front flicked his reins. Kale glanced to the right. The other man was now a couple of paces or so behind him.

Something didn't feel right. Suddenly wary, Kale pulled up on the reins and let the lead horse proceed another pace in front.

The man behind him spoke. "Get along, Jarrett. Figured you'd be hot to get inside those satin pants."

Kale froze—not at the words, hateful as they were, but at the sight in front of him.

The front rider turned, glaring at his compadre in the rear. "Shut your trap, Abe. Come on, Jarrett. Time's wastin'."

Suddenly, through his haze of anger and fear, Kale realized what was amiss. The moon shone as brightly as before; it glistened from dark leaves, from the horses's manes and swishing tails. And directly in front of him paced a big black stallion—the puddin'-foot.

That was the trouble with two-bit outlaws, he reflected—they oftentimes got careless, and this was definitely a case in point. Had they figured their news would so alarm him that he wouldn't notice their mounts? Or had they thought the night too dark for the puddin'-foot to be recognized? He shrugged, at once eliminating choices and ruminating on his own stupidity.

He'd recognized the horse, all right, but not in time to do himself much good. They had closed around him quickly, penned him in neat fashion. The man to his rear would have a gun on him by now, so if he drew on the one in front, he would take a slug from behind before his Colt cleared leather.

"Hold up a minute," he called. "My cinch is loose." It was a weak excuse, he knew, but the only one that came to mind. While he spoke, he jerked back on the reins. The bay reared a bit, then stopped short. He pulled the horse sharply to the right and drew on the men.

According to plan, his sudden stop jolted the rider behind him enough to throw off his aim. The first shot missed, but they were ready for trouble.

The last thing Kale heard was the report of a gun as the tearing impact of a bullet hit his skull and knocked him from his horse.

"Is he dead?"

"Hell, I reckon. Wouldn't you be? That was close range."

"We'd better make sure."

Together the two men picked up Kale's body and, swinging it back and forth a couple of times for momentum, heaved it over the side of the hill.

"That oughta do it."

"Yep. Costello said to make sure it was done proper. This should fill the bill."

Slapping dust and blood from their hands, the men remounted and rode for town.

Chapter Thirteen

No one at the Lady Bug paid any mind when Armando Costello arrived early the following morning and seated himself at his usual table in the otherwise vacant gaming room. Costello had patiently led Lavender Sealy to accept this behavior as part of his eccentric but otherwise harmless routine.

She served him coffee, which he drank without speaking. Armando Costello was a silent man, a patient man. At least that was how he saw himself. Take the treasure—he had searched ten years for this treasure, *his* treasure. He'd watched his legacy dwindle, once two dozen plats to mines and caches of buried treasure, now just this one remaining plat. And he had never given up, never wavered from his quest to find the fortune that would one day be his.

The plats had originally been given to his grandfather by the Mexican government for services rendered to his country. When his grandfather died, his grandmother gave the plats—a trunkful of them—to another grandson and helped smuggle the boy and the precious trunk out of Mexico.

But Armando Costello would not be put off so easily. Not only were those plats his legacy, but they meant the difference between a life of luxury and one of groveling for a meager existence. He had determined to follow his cousin to the very ends of the earth, if need be, to claim what rightfully belonged to him.

Now, with his dreams so close to being realized, Costello was filled with an almost overwhelming sense of urgency. But he knew he must keep himself under control for the next few days. It would not be easy, for his worst enemies—how well he knew it!—were his own temper and rashness.

Twice before he had come close to the treasure, and each time his hotheaded ways had gotten him into trouble, forcing him to begin his search all over again.

The first time was up in the Indian Nations, where his cousin was teaching school. He had attempted to steal the plats, but his cousin had caught him at it. They'd fought, and Costello was thrown in jail. By the time he got out, his cousin and the plats were gone.

Costello next traced his cousin to Fort McKavett, east of Summer Valley. While biding his time, waiting to make just the right move, he whiled away the hours gambling in a cantina in Scabtown. One night he got drunk and killed a soldier who accused him of cheating at faro. That cost Costello two years in the penitentiary down in Huntsville, miserable years. But he was lucky— the soldiers had prepared to hang him when civil authorities intervened.

By the time he got out of prison and made his way back to Fort McKavett, his cousin had left that part of the country. He did learn, however, that one of the plats had been won in a faro game by a man who lived in Summer Valley.

Costello's first trip to Summer Valley didn't amount to anything because the man he was after had gone off to fight in the Civil War. So Costello continued his search for his cousin, whom he finally located in a pauper's grave in Galveston. The plats had disappeared, and even Armando Costello was realistic enough to understand that the seaport town of Galveston opened onto a wide, wide world. The two dozen plats could be anywhere.

Costello spent much time along the waterfront, drinking, gambling, and listening. But he never learned a thing about his cousin's death, nor about the lost plats.

By then the war had been long over, and Costello, despondent from his loss but not defeated, headed back to Summer Valley. One plat would be better than none.

In Summer Valley he found his luck running true to form: the man had returned from the war and left again, this time for the gold fields in California.

But here Costello's fortune took a turn for the better. The man left the plat with his sister, Zofie Wiginton. And she in turn had given it—*given*, as though it were no more than a worthless relic—to a stranger, a newcomer to the region, Benjamin Jarrett.

At last Costello was able to see an end to his life of wandering. At last he dared envision himself living the life of wealth and luxury that was his birthright, the kind of life that would be his revenge on a world which had so long denied him his due.

Benjamin Jarrett posed no threat to Costello's plans . . . at least, not at first. The man was absurdly trusting. Costello himself was not woodsman enough to

285

have located the treasure. But Benjamin had found it, and now Costello knew where it was. Of course Benjamin had found it, he reassured himself.

Why else had the man become so possessive of the land surrounding his house and creek? Why else had he suddenly become suspicious of his friend Armando Costello? Why else had Benjamin sent those telegrams, if he had not suspected Costello of being after the treasure?

When the time came to get rid of Jarrett, Costello did it without qualms. It would have come to that eventually, anyhow. Costello had no intention of sharing this last treasure—not with anyone.

Costello grinned into the steam of the third cup of coffee Lavender set before him. Matt and Holt Rainey had unwittingly played right into his hands. Their determination to gain control of Plum Creek gave Costello the foil he needed to cover his own actions. Anything that happened to Benjamin and Ellie Jarrett could be blamed on Rainey.

But even the Raineys would not go so far as to murder a woman. No, this matter had to be handled delicately.

Costello had thought to run her off, had tried every way he knew how. But that woman was a tough one. Even without her brother-in-law's interference, Costello doubted he could have budged her.

Kale Jarrett was one development Costello had not counted on. Jarrett was a persistent cuss, and he appeared to see right through Costello's lies. But the man's own brothers had fixed that by dropping the harmless remark about drawing for Ellie's hand in marriage.

What luck that he overheard their conversation! With little effort he'd altered the information to fit his own purposes. He hadn't been born a fool—only a poor, maltreated relation to a stupid grandmother.

But none of that mattered anymore, Costello reminded himself. By now his men, Abe and Martin, would have killed Kale Jarrett, and only the woman remained.

Armando Costello himself would take care of Ellie. This part of his plan must be implemented with care, her being a woman and all. And afterward he would return to kill Abe and Martin. No one must survive to connect him with the murders.

Only then would he take the treasure and hightail it to Mexico City, where he would live like a king.

Armando Costello knew not what the treasure was, but neither did he care. If it turned out to be a mine, he would find a way to get the ore out of the ground. If it was buried treasure, as he hoped, he would take enough along to set himself up. Then he could return as necessary for a supply of riches that would last a lifetime.

"We have to talk, Armando."

Ellie's voice shattered his concentration—his vision of servants in an imaginary villa bringing him tequila and exquisite foods, of women clamoring for his affection, beautiful, full-bosomed women dressed in lace and silk and smelling of fine perfume.

Ellie's dress was rumpled and dirty. Hadn't she admitted to standing in the middle of the creek, the idiot? Her hair wanted attention; her hands were red and callused from ranch work. He swallowed his disgust at such baseness.

"Why did you lie to me about Kale?" She crossed the otherwise empty gaming room to sit beside him.

He stared at her vacantly, struggling to clear the web of luscious beauties from his brain. He had work to do

287

before he could bask in the loveliness of one of them . . . or two of them . . . or three . . . however many his fancy and his body demanded.

"You mean about the drawing?" He held himself in check admirably, he thought. Didn't he refrain from gloating over the fate of her lover?

"You know they didn't draw straws for me. Kale's brothers wouldn't have told you such a thing."

He shrugged, returning his attention to the cup of coffee. "Perhaps I heard wrong."

"Indeed you did," she accused. "Now you've caused all sorts of problems. From now on, Armando, I want you to . . ." She paused, considering how best to tell a man his romantic overtures were unwelcome. ". . . ah, Kale and I are going to be married," she finished. "As soon as it's proper."

His eyes danced with a wicked gleam. "Proper, Ellie? Now's a fine time to be thinking about what's proper. From the looks of it, the cow's already out of the barn; no sense locking the gate at this late date."

Forcing back a curt response, she stood. "Just don't interfere."

"Me? Don't you worry about that, my dear. I want only what's best for you. If you want—"

At that moment the front door opened and Abe and Martin came in. They stopped short at the sight of Ellie, as though they had seen a ghost, she thought, smoothing loose strands of hair back from her face. She must get herself together before she went home. Kale would think he had seen a witch.

"We need to talk," Abe told Costello.

Alarm rose inside Armando Costello. He jumped to his feet. "What went wrong?"

288

"No need to panic," the man called Martin soothed. "It went smooth as a whore's silk pantaloons." The last words were uttered in lewd tones, while Martin leered at Ellie. She fled the room, her face aflame.

"Pull out a chair, boys," Costello welcomed. "Sit down. Tell me all about it."

Intent on seeing Kale at the earliest possible moment, Ellie rushed back to Lavender's room, where she pinned her hair more securely upon her head. She scrutinized her mussed dress in the looking glass, then sighed.

To hell with finery! Kale would welcome her just as she was; she knew that. Snatching up the package that held the red dress Poppy had loaned her, she hurried to the hallway only to be intercepted by a solemn-faced Lavender.

"Come with me, baby—I'm afraid Costello has learned of a desperate development. It's best you hear it from him."

Indeed, Ellie thought later, Armando Costello's news was desperate, as desperate as any she'd ever received.

"How do they know?" she demanded at length. "How could your men know what the Circle R cowboys have been up to?"

"I explained, Ellie," Armando replied, "when Abe and Martin were in the Crazy Horse Saloon down the hill, they overheard the Rainey men—I wouldn't call paid assassins cowboys—bragging about how they kidnapped Kale Jarrett."

"Kidnapped?" Ellie questioned, as though she hadn't heard him correctly the first time. "Where did they take him? And why?"

Armando's arm had replaced Lavender's around Ellie's shoulders. Now he squeezed her in a supportive manner. "Like I told you, they claim to have taken him to the painted cliffs."

Ellie eyed Costello. Her mind refused to accept such an eventuality. "Why the painted cliffs? And how did they get back so soon?"

Armando cleared his throat. "Well, as to that," he shrugged, "I asked the same question, my dear. The very same question."

"Well?"

"It seems the men in the saloon were cronies of the men who kidnapped Jarrett. The men in the bar helped intercept him on his way back to the ranch last evening, then they came to town, while two of their number made the trip."

As he spoke, he became more fluent, his mind creating a new but equally valid scenario. When Ellie first questioned him, Armando had felt himself grow physically sick. Had he set his plans back yet again by acting in a rash manner? Forcibly, however, he took command of his senses and of the situation, and he now felt confident he had covered his mistake.

"Initially, according to the men in the saloon, they felt the need for a small army of men, Jarrett being a known gunman. After he was apprehended and subdued, however, they considered two men equal to the task of transporting him to the cliffs."

Apprehended and subdued . . . the words tolled an ominous knell in Ellie's mind. "Did they . . . harm him?"

"I'd say murder is about as harmful to a man's life as

you can get," Armando quipped, then immediately bit his tongue.

Ellie grasped the arm of the settee for support. Her head spun, causing her body to sway. "They've already . . . ah, killed him?"

"No. No, I don't believe they have. I think they intend to perform the . . . ah, the foul deed after they arrive at the cliffs. Whether they roughed him up, shot him, or what . . . ?" He shrugged, feeling pleased with his story.

"He wouldn't have given up without a fight. He wouldn't let them take him—" Ellie buried her face in her hands, too stunned to cry. Kale kidnapped, possibly shot or otherwise injured . . . Kale, on the way to his death even now.

She jumped to her feet. "I'm going after them."

"You can't do that," Lavender said. "You'd only put your own life in danger."

"My own life?" Her fears raced unbridled. "I must go to him."

"My plan," Costello slipped smoothly into the conversation. His only problem now was to sound dejected. Dejected! When his plan was working so well. This stupid woman believed every word; she reacted just as he'd known she would. "Charging hell with a bucket of water," they said out here in the West of men unafraid of danger. They should have said it about women, too, or this woman, anyhow. This foolish woman would not be armed with so much as a bucket of water when he fell upon her.

"My plan," Costello repeated, drawing himself back to the intense situation before him, "is already laid. I'll go myself. I'll bring him home, my dear . . . or his body. I'm sure you'll want to bury him proper, beside his brother."

Ellie burst into tears. Lavender pulled her to her bosom, glaring at Costello over Ellie's head. "How dare you speak of this tragedy in such a glib manner."

Costello managed an apology. "A shame. A sordid shame. Two husbands—well, just about—killed in the same manner and in the same place, by the same evil men."

"What do you mean, in the same place?" Lavender demanded. "How do you know where Benjamin Jarrett was murdered?"

Again Armando Costello could have bitten his tongue off. "The men told it, the men in the saloon. Said they took Benjamin to the painted cliffs to murder him so his brothers couldn't connect them with the crime. You know how his family sticks together . . . they'd certainly come out of the woodwork with two brothers killed by the same folks."

"It's true," Ellie told Lavender, "that much, anyway. Kale and I were there. We found Benjamin's silver buckle in one of the caves. The fragment of pictograph I found in his pocket matched a chip in the wall in the same cave . . ." Her voice cracked; her heart was a heavy lead weight inside a gossamer body. "We also found some dark stains that could have been blood."

The last words were barely audible above her sobs.

"I'll bring him back, Ellie. One way or—"

"No!" she fairly screamed. "*I* am going. If you want to accompany me, all right. But I'm going after him myself. And I hope I run into those Rainey bastards on the way."

Lavender objected, of course, but Costello argued that Ellie would be in safe hands; he even promised to have Abe and Martin accompany them, then made a mental note to see that the men left town the same time he and Ellie did. The promise of treasure should encourage them.

"I still don't like it, baby," Lavender worried.

Ellie sighed. "I'm sorry, Lavender, truly I am. But I must go. Don't you understand? I *must*."

Lavender nodded. "I suppose, but—"

"I promise to see after her," Costello interrupted, anxious now to be on his way. "I won't let her ride into harm, even if I have to hog-tie her, as you say out here, when we come upon the Raineys."

Lavender acquiesced after that, since, as she told Ellie, she knew she didn't have much say in the matter. She led Ellie to the back of the Lady Bug to fetch a bedroll and put together supplies for the trip.

After the women left him alone in the parlor, Armando Costello patted his chest where he had secreted the plat his men took from the mantel in Ellie's house after they killed Kale Jarrett.

It felt rough and strangely warm against his body, as though it possessed energy from ages past to quiet his racing heart and to warm the chill of fear which settled over him . . . fear of not succeeding in this one last attempt to find a treasure that was rightfully his.

But this time it would work, he promised himself. Crossing to the gaming room, he stepped behind the bar and took a bottle of whiskey from Lavender's ample store. This time he would do everything right . . . even to not returning to Summer Valley. It would take awhile for Lavender to become worried enough about Ellie to set out after them. By that time he'd have found the treasure and would be on his way to Mexico City.

He had even planned for the outside chance that Kale

293

Jarrett escaped death. If that had happened, which Abe and Martin assured him was not the case, but if it had, he certainly didn't want the gunman on his back trail. With his plan, however, Jarrett would not be able to stop him, neither dead nor alive.

Not now. He was on his way. Like a stone rolling down a hillside gathering momentum, nothing could stop him now. Nothing.

From the moment he regained consciousness Kale knew he was in trouble. Blood covered his shirt; he felt it caked on his face and neck. Every movement brought intense pain to all parts of his body.

He tried to raise a hand to the wound on his head, but his arm moved only a few inches before it fell back to his side, shooting pain up and down his body. Then a great wave of weakness engulfed him and he passed out.

When he came to, the first rays of the day's sun were glinting off the caliche-colored rocks. This time his head was clear. He recalled being overtaken by Costello's men. Looking up, he saw the top of the cliff fifty feet above him. That was likely where he had fallen from or been dropped. He couldn't remember anything past drawing his Colt.

His entire body, from his head down to the tops of his boots, ached like he'd been stuck with hundreds of needles. Gradually he became aware of the reason: he was lying on his back, smack-dab in the middle of a bed of prickly pear.

The more he thought about it, the madder he got. Here he was, weak from loss of blood and a gunshot wound to the head that was serious at best, but he was damned if he was going to die lying on his back in a bed of cactus.

He took a deep breath, gritted his teeth, and pitched himself out of the pear patch.

He landed on his feet, a bit wobbly, but standing up. A few steps, however, told him he would never be able to make it to the house in these clothes, riddled with cactus needles as they were.

He took off his shirt, then his pants. Strapping his gun belt over his longjohns, he was glad the thong had been secured over one Colt. The other gun had likely fallen from his hand up there on the cliff when he was shot.

Kale struck out for the creek in his boots and longjohns; if anyone didn't like it, they could turn the other way.

Actually, the only person to see him wouldn't have mattered, except she wasn't here, and damned if that fact didn't hurt almost as bad as his shot-up head.

The walk cleared his brain, and with clarity came a new fear, one that worried him more than Ellie's absence—which he intended to remedy as soon as he pulled enough thorns out of his behind to be able to sit a horse. What bedeviled him now was that damned gambler.

Since the man obviously believed him dead, what did it mean for Ellie? What the hell was the man up to?

By the time Kale reached the creek, his head wound had opened and started to bleed again, and he was becoming nauseated and weak from loss of blood.

He picked from his body all the thorns he could see or feel, then settled himself in the icy waters. The pain in his head had eased somewhat, and he gingerly washed dried blood away from the wound. With his fingers he traced where the bullet had plowed a furrow along the outside of his skull from near his left eye backward. It didn't seem

295

to have done a great deal of damage, though, beyond the loss of blood.

Even a slight wound to the head bled mighty bad, which was probably what had saved his life. Costello's men had likely taken the splattering of so much blood to mean he was hit bad. Crawling out of the water, he sat on the slab in the light of the rising sun and forced himself to think about Armando Costello instead of Ellie.

Not much in the way of substance formed in his brain, however, so at length he made his way to the house, stopping by the springhouse to collect a jar of buttermilk and then by the corral fence to dress in the clean pair of pants and shirt which he found hanging over the top rail. They smelled of Ellie and her clean homemade soap and left him weak with more than loss of blood.

He wanted her home, he wanted their problems solved. Inside, the house felt empty, lonely. He wondered how Ellie had ever lived alone; he knew she never could again. Like he could never live alone again. He couldn't live anyplace now without Ellie beside him.

Taking a hunk of her bread from the larder, he ate it and drank the buttermilk, feeling his loneliness for her grow by leaps and bounds, until at last he chastised himself. Damn it, Jarrett, quit your bellyaching, catch up a horse, and go after her. If he started chasing down every rabbit hole he came across, he would never get the fox.

And now he had no doubt . . . Armando Costello was the fox.

Nagged by something he couldn't name, Kale wandered from room to room. Something was amiss . . . but what?

Stopping in front of the fireplace he studied her photograph—held it a moment, smiled at it. Replacing it, he noticed the plat was missing, the one Ellie kept above the mantel. He shrugged . . . she'd probably taken it down herself.

Taking another hunk of bread from the kitchen, he paced the main room of the small house, his eyes alert, or as alert as his condition would allow. At every step he was pricked by another needle in another place.

And his head throbbed to beat the band. But through it all, Armando Costello's menacing face glowered at him. What did he know about the man?

He had been Benjamin's friend. They had hunted treasure and traveled to the painted cliffs together.

Benjamin was likely murdered at those same cliffs.

What did that prove?

Costello was, if not in love with Ellie, certainly infatuated with her. He paid her a great deal of attention; he was determined that she move to town.

Even though Kale didn't like the way the man talked about her, like she was one of Lavender's "flowers," that didn't mean anything.

Or did it? Would a man in love with a woman declare her a whore for all the world to hear? But hadn't Costello claimed that very thing—to Ellie's face, no less—just last night?

And he lied about the drawing. He'd made up a bald-faced lie. No one in Kale's family would ever have told such a tale, certainly not that Kale had won her by drawing straws when in fact he'd prevented the drawing. It didn't add up.

And Costello's man had been riding the puddin'-foot last night. Now *that* damned sure added up to something—but what?

What was he missing? Wandering out to the porch,

Kale sat on the step, held his head in his hands, and tried to picture Costello in the house, tried to hear his voice, his words.

But the only vision that would come to mind was of the man standing at the mantel, holding that plat in his hands.

And of Kale, eaten up with jealousy and not even knowing it.

Jealous and thinking Costello a rival, when in fact . . .

Costello's words came slowly to mind. First, last night at the Lady Bug. Gradually, then, Kale recalled words Costello had spoken at other times, in other places. But always the vision was the same: Costello standing there looking so damned smug, holding that plat in his lily-white hands.

Holding that plat and talking about treasure.

Treasure.

Under Ellie's house?

Kale jumped to his feet, then immediately regretted it; the blood rushed to his wound, leaving him dizzy and in pain. The pain came from all directions at once, from the thousand and one prickly pear needles riddling his skin.

But it was physical, the pain, and it did nothing to deter his mind from functioning, now that it had begun to work.

Suddenly he knew all the answers—all the sickening answers. And he felt like retching right here on Ellie's porch.

Costello didn't want Ellie to move to town, he wanted her away from the ranch. He didn't want Ellie, he wanted the treasure that was under her house—or that he believed was under her house. And he had used everyone and everything to help him. The puddin'-foot had been used in attempts to harass Ellie in order to draw attention to the Raineys and away from himself; Costello's man was riding it last night.

And the lie about the drawing. Costello sent Lavender out here to tell it—unwittingly, of course. Lavender loved Ellie like a daughter, so much so that she would not stand by and let her marry a man who was deceiving her.

It all fit. Costello had known Ellie would leave when she heard the tale, he had known Kale would follow her, and he had set his men on Kale, intending to kill him.

Kale's blood raced. What was the man's next move? Was he on his way here even now?

Kale reached for his Colt, unsnapped the thong, and checked the loads. Reholstering it, he entered the house. Thinking . . . thinking.

Ellie had talked about a tunnel beneath the house, a tunnel where settlers had hidden during Indian raids. Benjamin had told her never to leave her house, that she would be safe here.

Kale froze in mid-step: Benjamin had known.

He found the trapdoor exactly where Ellie had said it was—under the spare room bed—their bed, the bed on which they had loved.

And would love again, he swore, hauling aside the iron bedstead. As fast as his aching head would allow, he tugged at a tarp that covered the floor beneath the bed. A nagging feeling told him he was right. He had to be.

Ellie had said this was a tunnel to the creek. Otto Wiginton and later Costello had scoffed at the idea of there being a gold mine under Benjamin's house. The plat itself had a yellow half-moon in a place Ellie said was near here. A yellow moon, as any old prospector could tell a man, meant treasure—*gold*.

Uncovered, the trapdoor was about three feet square. Kale pried up one corner with the blade of his Bowie knife, then set the door aside.

The tunnel had obviously not been used in some time. He tore away cobwebs which formed a screen over the entrance and peered into the dark hole. Nothing but blackness. Even after he lighted a lantern and held it down into the tunnel, he could see only a few feet ahead. Slight indentations in the packed earth indicated footholds along one side. A musty odor rose up and threatened to choke him.

He prepared to enter the tunnel by tying one end of his rope around a trunkful of books which he wedged behind the iron bedstead; he then tied the other end of the rope around his waist. All the while he recalled having told Ellie on more than one occasion that he wasn't a goat. Well, he wasn't a mole, either, but he was damned sure going down in this black hole to find out what in hell a gambler named Armando Costello was up to—a gambler who, as things now stood, was very likely involved in Benjamin's death. There was no guessing about the man's role in his own difficulty last night.

Taking up the lantern, he lowered his throbbing body into the tunnel. The passageway led toward the creek, all right, but about ten yards from the house it forked, with one path leading out at a right angle from the other.

Kale examined the area carefully. The passage that led away from the creek had been completely filled with large rocks which were then covered with a thick layer of mud, evidently to create a natural-looking wall. Through the years, however, the mud had dried and shrunk away in places, crumbling from the rocks.

Sometime in the past someone had closed off this

section of the tunnel. But why? Care had been taken to conceal their efforts. What lay behind that wall of rock and mud?

Things were beginning to shape up: the plat could be genuine. But no matter what treasure was back there, it couldn't be worth the price that had already been paid for it—Benjamin's life and no telling how many lives before his. If treasure was there, it would have to keep a while longer, Kale vowed. First, he was going after Ellie.

Upstairs he replaced the trap door, pulled the tarp, then put the bed back in place.

Benjamin had known, all right. He'd known, and that knowledge could well have been what got him killed.

Kale found the bay horse waiting patiently at the barn. After giving him a quick rubdown and an extra bait of corn, he resaddled him and started for town. First things first. And first in his mind and heart was Ellie. First he would see to her safety, then he would discover what role Armando Costello played in all this.

He no longer worried over the Raineys' false claims of ownership. The telegram from the State proving Benjamin had filed on the ranch rode with him in his saddlebags. When everything else settled down, he figured to ride over to the Circle R and confront the Rainey brothers with proof of their own lies.

Anxious to be shut of their surveillance duty, Ira and Till were up early the following morning. Taking their breakfast of coffee and bacon wrapped in stale bread to the ledge, they squatted side by side and peered out over the valley. During the night they had been aroused by gunshots, but nothing ever came of them.

"Was that two shots you heard last night or three?"
Ira quizzed.

"I heard three."

"Same here."

"Nothin's stirring down below."

Ira nodded. "Peaceful as a sleepin' baby."

Till refilled their coffee cups; they sat staring at the quiet valley and a short time later were rewarded by the sight of a saddled, riderless horse wandering up to the corral.

"Ain't that Jarrett's horse?"

"Same bay he rode away from here last night." Ira built a smoke. Till bit a chew off the plug of tobacco he carried in his shirt pocket.

The sun was rising rapidly now, bathing the valley in clear, golden daylight.

Suddenly Till let out a low whistle. "Lookee yonder what I see!" He pointed to the hillside east of them. "Ain't that Jarrett hisself wearing nothin' but his Sunday suit and boots?"

Ira studied the hillside. "And his Colt," he added. "Looks like the feller run into a mite of trouble on the way home."

Till glanced at his Winchester. "I could take him from here. The woman's gone, and with him out of the way we'd be free to get back to cowboyin'."

Ira responded in a matter-of-fact tone. "No, you couldn't. Newt or Saint could and would. But not you. And not me, neither. We don't draw wages to shoot a man in the back."

Later that morning the sight Ira and Till saw sent them hoofing it back to headquarters.

Their news was what Matt Rainey had been waiting to

302

hear. Combined with Newt's and Saint's report from Summer Valley, he could be sure everyone had left the Jarrett place. The last to go was Kale Jarrett, who'd left this morning with his head bandaged.

Rainey wasn't surprised. He'd known that sooner or later Costello would get Ellie Jarrett. He didn't let himself think about the gambler's motives or what might happen to the woman. Those things didn't concern him. The means to an end had been set in motion, and he didn't question it.

Kale Jarrett would have to be taken care of before he could return and cause them any more trouble, of course; Rainey would see to that. The important thing now was that his plan had worked. He never doubted it would.

"Head 'em up, boys," he bellowed. "We're movin' to our new range."

303

Chapter Fourteen

Ellie followed behind Armando Costello down the trail where she had once followed Kale. As the day wore on, this trip began to resemble that other one, at least in the disposition of her traveling companion.

Armando hadn't spoken a word since they left Summer Valley, not that she felt like talking. Kale's fate consumed all her emotions and as much of her attention as riding down this winding, rocky trail allowed.

By the time Lavender had helped them pack provisions and Armando's men returned with a packhorse, the sun was already midway in the morning sky . . . time wasted, as far as Ellie was concerned. Only Lavender's firm intervention kept her from riding ahead alone.

Armando seemed to be in as much a hurry as she. After only a brief pause to water the horses in Celery Creek, he bid his two men farewell and studied the darkening sky.

Although she wondered at the men's abrupt departure—for points north, was all they said—she wasn't in the least disappointed to see them go. Even as Costello was assuring Lavender that Abe and Martin would accompany them on the trip, Ellie had found herself wishing the men would stay behind. They considered her one of Lavender's "flowers," she was sure of that, and she had dreaded riding with them day and night.

Before the men were out of sight Costello urged her up the trail. There was no time for a noon meal. He didn't say as much—in fact, he hadn't spoken directly to her since they left Summer Valley—but she knew he feared getting caught along Celery Creek in a rainstorm. So did she, but more than that, she didn't want to tarry over a meal when Kale's life could well depend on their arriving in time to save him.

Now and again she noticed Costello glancing furtively at the surrounding hilltops. When she asked him whether he thought the Circle R men might have taken Kale somewhere besides the painted cliffs, he barked a negative response.

Her fear for Kale's life grew by the hour, engulfing her at times, shutting out everything else. The fact that she had sent him away in a childish fit of anger, that she mocked his love for her in front of the entire clientele of the Lady Bug haunted her. She loved him . . . how she loved him.

He must be safe . . . he *must* be.

Thinking on the past would serve no purpose, though, she scolded. Whatever had happened was done. With Armando's help, she would find Kale and bring him home. If he were injured, she would nurse him back to health.

The moon rose to a shroud of clouds. As tired as she was, she hoped Armando would not stop to make camp. But reality overruled emotion, and she knew if they were to save Kale, they must not wear out their horses. Making camp would slow them down, but it could well determine whether they got to Kale at all.

Facing harsh realities was not new to Ellie Langstrom Jarrett. Orphaned when she was barely three years old, she spent the next three years being carted around Galveston from one relative to another, none of whom wanted an extra mouth to feed.

Then, not long after her sixth birthday, the husband of her mother's cousin took matters into his own hands. On the pretext that his wife was down with the ague, he left little Ellie Langstrom with the proprietress of the Lady Bug, an establishment he frequented so regularly that his business was indispensable.

"A day or two at the most," he had assured Lavender Sealy, whereupon he moved his entire family—minus little Ellie—away from Galveston, never to be heard from again.

By the time Lavender discovered the ruse, the precocious orphan-child had worked her way into the hardened madam's heart.

Ellie was sixteen when an official delegation invited Lavender to leave Galveston. She considered the expulsion an opportunity. The location of an establishment such as the Lady Bug, dependent as it was upon the whims of the city fathers as dictated by the city mothers, was never permanent, she explained to her "flowers." Their ouster from Galveston allowed them to follow the westward call to Austin and thence to Summer Valley.

She was sure of success in Summer Valley, because, she argued, the settlement sat in the middle of the Western Trail to Kansas and was bounded by two frontier forts. It might be a rough, uncut land, but they would find growing room there, same as schools and churches.

Life was rosy inside the pink house Lavender built on the hilltop in Summer Valley—except for one thing, Ellie was to learn later.

Through the years Lavender had valiantly protected her charge from the seamier side of her business, raising her as she would have raised a daughter of her own blood. But the true test of Lavender's success still lay ahead. The one thing she was determined Ellie would have, a proper husband, proved the most difficult to provide.

Then Benjamin Jarrett had moved to town. And within six months Lavender had all she ever wanted—or so she told Ellie—a proper husband for her baby.

The night wore on. Lost in exhaustion and in her own reveries, Ellie was surprised when Costello suddenly decided to stop. The place he chose, however, did not surprise her: their usual camping ground, the place where Kale had proposed marriage to her in his strange and wonderful way.

Here she had learned the reason behind his fretful day in the saddle. She wished she knew the source of Armando's disgruntlement.

"We camp here." He tossed bedrolls and cooking utensils off the packhorse. "Fix some food." He led the horses to water.

Mechanically Ellie followed his instructions. Soon she had a fire going and bacon in the pan, all the while admonishing herself to be patient with Armando. He had been dependable and steady since Benjamin's murder, and now he had come through for her again. He'd gone out of his way to accompany her on this journey, a journey fraught with danger.

He returned in no time. "Hear that thunder?" he asked. "It'll rain soon, wash out any tracks."

She stared at him, thinking she'd misunderstood. "Are we following tracks? I thought you said the Circle R men had taken Kale straight to the painted cliffs."

He stared hard at her. The campfire glanced off his high cheekbones but didn't reach the dark depths of his hooded eyes. His face, seen thus, gave off an aura of mystery. No wonder he was a noted gambler, she thought.

"Our tracks," he barked. "Rain will wash out our tracks."

She frowned, wondering at the strange conversation. What did she care about their tracks? All she cared about was finding Kale in time to save his life.

She handed Costello a plate of food, thick slices of bacon and some spoonbread Lavender had packed, which he carried to the log and proceeded to eat, not with the fork she provided, but by scooping and spearing each bite with his razor-sharp Bowie knife.

Scanning the area, she was filled with a poignancy that brought tears to her eyes. This place where Kale had proposed marriage to her would always be special and much too intimate to share with another man, even if that man was helping her save Kale's life.

Thunder rolled and lightning flashed. Tears welled up in her eyes. Her throat tightened as if someone were strangling her. She fought to control her emotions. Once she let go, she greatly feared she would not be able to regain control. And Kale was in trouble. If he needed her, she must be ready to help him.

Pouring herself a cup of coffee she sat on the ground across the campfire from her sullen companion. She watched the firelight dance in the night. It glanced off Armando's steel-bladed knife and flickered around his hooded eyes as he sat on the log Kale had dragged up for the two of them to share.

"What plans do you have for when we come upon them?" she asked.

Costello turned his vacant eyes to her.

"I mean . . . these are desperate men. Perhaps we should—"

"Leave that to me," he barked. His eyes bore into hers with such intensity she diverted her gaze.

Although Armando's ego had always been large, tonight it seemed especially fragile. To hell with it, she thought . . . he would need her help to save Kale from the Circle R killers, so he might as well start getting used to the idea.

"I asked because I intend to help you when the time comes," she said. "You can't be expected—"

"Silence, woman. I'm listening for thunder."

Ellie shivered at the chill in his voice. Did he actually fear getting caught here in a rainstorm? After a while she spoke again, thinking to reassure him.

"This site will protect us from the rain."

Costello stared into the fire again with a fixed gaze. His previous anger seemed to have flared and died. "And from those who follow."

Ellie shivered at his second reference to being followed, then immediately chastized herself. Armando had always been a trifle dramatic . . . hadn't she once commented to Benjamin how he'd have made a good thespian? But when she asked Armando who he thought was following them, he peered desperately into the night. At his reply the skin along her spine prickled.

310

"Those who always prevent me from finding my treasure."

"We aren't being followed," she tried to assure him. Or was it her own fears she sought to allay?

"They're out there," he persisted. "They always follow me and try to steal my treasure. This time I'll fool them."

"After we find Kale—" He cut her off.

"Kale!" He snarled the name, then laughed cruelly. "He's no better off than his brother. Benjamin thought he could trick me, but I showed him. Then Kale Jarrett came along, thinking he had things figured out. Now neither of them can stop me."

"What things?" she cried. "Where is Kale? You said he was at the cliffs, a prisoner of the Raineys. What—?"

A sudden clap of thunder silenced her words. The wind gusted, causing the campfire to sputter. Strange shadows from the thicket skipped like stick-figure marionettes. Another bolt of lightning cracked so close they both jumped as if it had been a gunshot.

Costello shouted above the noise. "Put out that fire, woman!"

She obeyed, throwing their bucket of water on the flames, though her arms trembled so badly by now that she wondered at her ability to lift the heavy bucket, much less to hit the campfire with the water from it.

"Get in your bedroll and stay there."

Quickly she chose one of the bedrolls, and somehow convinced her weakened arms and trembling limbs to drag it to the opposite side of the fire from his. She crawled into it, Armando's words reverberating in her brain: *I showed Benjamin . . . Kale's no better off . . . neither of them can stop me . . .*

311

Large drops of rain began to splatter the ground. First a few, then more, until they fell in a deluge. The thicket offered some protection, but she could feel rain pelting her bedroll, as Armando's menacing babble pelted her imagination.

Her back and shoulders ached from the day's jarring ride. Yet tired as she was, fear plagued her, bringing memories of her trip to the cliffs with Kale, the cliffs where they'd found Benjamin's buckle, the cliffs where Armando was now taking her.

Treasure, he had said . . . treasure. The only treasure she wanted was to find Kale, alive and unharmed.

She shivered beneath the still fierce grip of her fear. Alive and unharmed . . . somewhere out there he needed her, and here she was huddled like a frightened child in her blankets. Yes, she was afraid.

And she should be. For him. Perhaps that was it, she thought, feeling her muscles relax at the notion. Her fear for Kale magnified Armando's ramblings. In the morning she would pry the source of his own fears from Armando Costello.

Feeling no more raindrops on her bedroll, she peered from beneath the blankets. Armando sat across the campsite. Suddenly she realized that rather than having prepared for bed, he had rekindled the fire. Now he sat before it, studying a document . . . or . . .

The fire leapt in the shifting winds. Light played on the parchment in his hands. Her mouth went dry. The plat from her mantel?

For a moment her heart stopped. Just in time she clasped a hand over her mouth to stifle a scream. The plat! He held the plat from her mantel in one hand and that dreadful Bowie knife in the other. The plat from her mantel. How had he taken it? When had he taken it? And why?

Armando Costello sat in front of the campfire all night, studying the plat while raindrops pelted his head and shoulders.

The rain had not amounted to much. Costello hoped it had been enough to wipe out their tracks. More than that, he hoped Kale Jarrett was dead. He had certainly paid enough to get the job done right—one hundred dollars in gold. But Armando Costello knew better than to trust anyone except himself. He had yet to meet the man who couldn't be bought if the price was right.

Take Benjamin Jarrett . . . now *there* was a man he'd thought he could trust. He'd gone along with Jarrett for several months, believing he was being led to the treasure, when actually, Jarrett had been deceiving him, leading him away from the treasure.

Benjamin Jarrett paid for his folly with his life, and Costello vowed that trusting Benjamin would be his last mistake.

Sitting with the plat, he began to formulate his plans. They were simple: with Kale and Ellie out of the way, he could return to the house and take his treasure.

Of course there were the Raineys to contend with, but he had a plan for them, too. They didn't want the Jarrett ranchhouse. He would return under the pretext of taking Ellie Jarrett's household goods to her. He congratulated himself on that plan. It was perfect, foolproof.

Armando Costello's large hands trembled with anticipation. Tomorrow, or the next day at the latest, he would have in his possession enough riches to buy the entire

City of Mexico if he so desired. And one thing was certain, he assured himself, he intended to possess everything and everyone his heart desired.

One last job remained: to do away with Ellie Jarrett. He'd have done it long ago, but people around here looked unfavorably upon men who harmed women.

He scoffed at that. Given the chance, a woman could be more vicious than a man. Hadn't it been his grandmother who'd given his own birthright to his cousin, condemning him, Armando, to a life of wandering?

He had tried to run Ellie off. All he needed was time to retrieve the treasure unobserved. After that the house was of no use to him.

But Ellie Jarrett would not budge. He ought to have known as much; women were like that. Once they latched onto something they wanted, an explosion from the fires of hell couldn't shake them loose.

The rain stopped. The stars came out, then faded before the light of day. Still Costello sat before the dead coals, contemplating his plat, his trusted weapon, his future. Sleep had been impossible in his agitated state. Blood coursed through his veins; his body throbbed with the excitement of this moment, his moment.

He looked across the charred coals at the sleeping woman. If only he could kill her here and now. Angrily he rebuked his impatience. He must wait, get her completely out of the country—to the painted cliffs—kill her there, where he had killed Benjamin. That way he would be free. No one would be left to destroy his dream.

It was high noon by the time Kale discovered where Ellie and Costello had camped. That it was the same

314

place he and Ellie had shared both angered and comforted him. At least Costello was keeping to the known route.

But that did little to assuage his fears, fears which had escalated by the minute since he'd burst into the Lady Bug to be greeted by a surprised Lavender Sealy. She told him of Costello's ruse while she outfitted him with provisions for the trip, provisions which rode as heavily behind him in his saddlebags as his one remaining Colt rode his hip.

He had worried about the rain the previous night. But it had been light at the juncture of the town road and the trail along Celery Creek. The tracks were plain as day: three horses—Ellie's, the packhorse Lavender reported, and Costello's Morgan. Either the man did not care if they were followed, or he was so sure his men had done their work that he made only cursory attempts to hide his trail.

At the campsite Kale entertained the same notion, a fact which again reminded him of his own intended fate, and Ellie's.

Some effort had been made to conceal the camp, but not nearly enough. With a little work Kale uncovered the tracks where Costello led the horses to water. He found the impressions of one bedroll and the log he himself had dragged up on that miserable, wonderful night he spent here with Ellie.

Signs showed where Costello had sat on the log all night. Removing the top layer of dirt from the campfire, Kale felt the coals and judged it to have been out only a few hours. If he hurried, he could make up the time.

Then, in his haste, he almost missed the trail. Closer examination showed where Costello had led the horses out over the soft, wet grass and up the creek a good hundred yards. There the trail suddenly played out.

It took Kale an hour of hard work to pick up the trail again, and by this time his patience was wearing thin. A murder could be committed in this rugged country, and the body not found for years—if ever.

Yet he dared not strike out straightaway for the painted cliffs. That might have been Costello's diversion. He must not underestimate the man. Ellie's life depended on his own sound judgment.

Travel was slow and annoying. Kale had never been much of a follower anyway. Tracking Costello, knowing he intended to harm Ellie, waiting for an opportunity to rescue her—that definitely was not his style. Yet he couldn't be certain of their destination.

A couple of things he did know for sure: Ellie loved him . . . and he loved her.

Strange, how things turned out. He hadn't had the foggiest notion of settling down when he'd come to this territory in search of his brother. Not that he intended to remain a drifter all his life, but until Ellie, he wouldn't have given two cents for his chances of ever finding a good woman to love, one who would love him back.

And now that he'd found her, he wasn't about to let some madman carry her up a rocky draw and do her harm.

As he rode through the maze of boulders and ancient slabs of rock which at some time in the distant past had fallen from the cliffs above, Kale knew he had sensed Costello's guilt all along. But the man's motives had been vague, and Kale had not been ready to accept Benjamin's death at the hand of a friend.

Benjamin was a good man whose path should never

have crossed that of a man like Armando Costello. Perhaps Zofie Wiginton had something in thinking that evil forces followed that plat around. But Kale didn't for a minute believe that. Evil men were found everywhere, in every corner of life, waiting to take advantage of unsuspecting men like Benjamin.

People cringed at violence, and Ellie with them. Yet out here where the law had not settled in, a man had to take matters into his own hands to protect himself and his loved ones. And also to protect society.

Someday, Kale knew, there would be courts and laws to take care of varmints like Armando Costello, but right now it was up to him to get to the man who had surely killed his brother. And he must do that before Costello killed again. If not, Kale would have two graves to grieve over.

The three riders dismounted at the mouth of the canyon. They rested their horses and gave them one last drink before entering the no-man's-land which lay ahead.

Holt Rainey drained his whiskey bottle and tossed it away, and it shattered against the trunk of a gnarled oak. He rummaged through the saddlebags on Newt's horse, then angrily turned to the man.

"Where's that damned whiskey I told you to pack for me?"

"Matt took it." Newt spat tobacco between his rotted front teeth and knelt beside the creek for a drink.

Holt turned to Saint. "You bring some?"

"Nope."

The sun was already hot for this time of year. Holt Rainey looked up the trail, thought about the rough ride he faced, then exploded at his companions.

"This ain't no goddamned picnic! How's a man to get through Satan-country such as this without a drink?"

Both men ignored him. Rainey grabbed his horse's reins.

"I'm heading back to town to wait for Jarrett."

"Do that," Newt told him. "We're damned tired of your bellyachin' anyhow."

Holt glared at Newt, his hand going for his gun.

When Saint spoke, his Colt already covered his boss's brother. "Go ahead and draw. We'll drop your body down between a couple of these here boulders an' nobody'll find you till your bones are gone to dust."

Holt eased his hand back. "Relax, boys. I was only testin' you. Anyhow, I gotta come along. Nobody's gonna get Jarrett but me. I'm due a notch."

The two men glanced at each other, shrugged, and mounted up.

They rode warily up the broken trail.

Newt and Saint were hired killers, professionals to whom emotion was a forbidden thing. They had stayed alive up to now by keeping cool heads and taking their jobs seriously. Neither of them liked riding with a trigger-happy man they had to call boss.

They'd heard plenty about Kale Jarrett, and they respected his ability with a gun and his methods of fighting. If this make-believe gunfighter stepped out of line, he could get them all killed.

"You two remember," Holt demanded, "Jarrett's mine."

"We'll take him as we can get him," Newt responded, "an' hope he don't get a chance at us first."

"I ain't impressed with reputations," Holt scoffed.

"Since you ain't impressed, you'd best leave him to us. We're getting paid for it," Saint said.

"Besides," Newt added, "this ain't no quick-draw contest. First one gets an accurate shot off wins. And the first one of us to get a chance at such a shot takes it."

Holt started to protest.

"Our orders is to kill 'em all, and if you don't toe the line, we might just extend them orders to include you," Saint mused.

"Now, move on up there in front," Newt ordered. "That itchy trigger finger of yours is makin' the hairs along the back of my neck commence to crawl."

Chapter Fifteen

Ellie followed Costello away from camp the next morning as if through a dense fog. She had slept little, dozing off and on, each time awakening with fright. Whether asleep or awake she saw the same image: Armando Costello studying the plat he'd taken from her mantel . . . Armando, the plat, and his razor-sharp blade.

His earlier words plagued her—words about treasure and how he had "showed" Benjamin, how Kale had "figured things out."

What things? she wanted desperately to know. What things? Things relating to Benjamin's death? To Kale's disappearance?

To this trip they were making to the painted cliffs?

Had this friend gone mad? Or had he been mad all along?

As the night wore on, she watched Costello from beneath a raised corner of her blankets, and she became more convinced of the man's madness. He sat the night away staring alternately at the plat, into the flames, and then out into the blackness. Ellie's fears had escalated.

Where before she had been frightened for Kale, now her fears centered on herself . . . the instinct for survival, she supposed.

If Armando had killed Kale, she could see him punished only if she survived. She became determined to escape before his madness claimed her life.

The thought of living without Kale now that she had known and loved him brought tears to her eyes over and over again. The idea that this vital, caring man might well be dead, like his brother before him, at the hands of a madman who hunted some elusive treasure enraged her.

Fear and anger combined to create an almost unbearable combination of doom and urgency within her. Never had she felt so alone in her life. Never had she found herself in such desperate straits with no one on whom she could depend.

Her life lay in her own hands, and she must not give up hope. Perhaps Kale was not dead . . . perhaps he had not even been abducted. In her wildest imaginings she could not see Armando Costello killing Kale Jarrett. The gambler could never have pulled off such a feat.

That thought renewed her hope, and with hope her resolve returned. She would escape before morning. She would watch Armando's every move and she would get away somehow.

He couldn't sit on that log all night. He would have to relieve himself. A madman he might be, inhuman in every aspect—except the physical. He'd have to get up at some point, and when he did she'd escape.

She laid her plans. She wouldn't take time to saddle her horse, rather she would carry the halter along to put on later. She would take Armando's horse, too, leaving him afoot.

Perhaps she could take even his rifle. Perhaps he would leave it propped against the log when he went back into the thicket to relieve himself. If so, she would take that too.

But her chance never came. Never once did he move from his seat on the log. Not once until near dawn, when he called to her sharply to be up and on the trail, there was no time for breakfast.

When he relieved himself, he did so in her presence, eliminating his body waste into the sputtering campfire. She had to turn her back to keep from seeing his nudity. Tears swam in her eyes.

Tears of anguish, of frustration, of fear.

But somewhere deep inside, a flicker of resolve remained, and through the morning, as she followed where he led—for Costello now pulled her horse by the reins—this flicker flamed into a raging firestorm.

She would escape.

If Armando had killed Benjamin and Kale, she would see he paid for the crimes.

The image of his razor-sharp Bowie knife fixed itself in her mind. Perhaps she would even do the deed herself.

Kale pushed his hat back on his head and ran a sleeve across his forehead. Sweat stung not only his eyes but every prickly pear wound in his body. His head throbbed and his left arm was getting stiff. After two hours of stumbling over boulders and fallen slabs of limestone, he had come to the fork in the canyon.

Directly ahead rose the sheer limestone cliff, a hundred feet straight up. Cottonwood trees grew close to the cliff and towered upward to its height.The silvery

323

green leaves of the wild mustang grapevines matted the trees, calling to mind his and Ellie's visit to this spot.

He had teased her about expecting him to climb that cottonwood to pick grapes for her jelly. Her laughter echoed through his brain.

He dismounted to drink and water the bay at the spring, and even those simple activities reminded him of Ellie. But the icy-cold water cleared his mind, and after drinking he filled his hat and poured water over his head. The cold water relieved his headache somewhat, an ache which had intensified with the tedious climb up the canyon. He would be playing old Billy hell for sure, if he came upon Costello with anything but a clear head and a loaded gun.

Despondently Kale thought for the hundredth time about Ellie's fear of violence and a desperate need for haste spread through him.

Costello's tracks were everywhere, as were Ellie's. No attempt had been made to conceal their movements, or so it seemed. Was Costello so sure he was alone? If so, the danger to Ellie was magnified tenfold. With no fear of being followed, Costello could kill her anytime he chose.

Kale studied the cliff carefully. An old game trail led down to the spring. If he could manage to climb the hill, perhaps he could spot them. Then he might be able to circle around and meet them at the mouth of the canyon.

The bay could do with a rest, anyhow. Quickly he stripped the saddle from his horse and rubbed its back with a few handfuls of summer-dried grass which sprouted around the cottonwoods. Then he staked the animal in the shade.

Taking his field glasses and rifle and slinging a coiled rope over his shoulder, he lit out up the trail. He figured it must have been made by mountain goats, but somehow he managed to keep his footing.

Fifteen minutes later the icy spring below was but a memory. Sweat again trickled down his face and smarted in his eyes and in the wound on his head.

Slightly below the crest, a slab of limestone lay where it had fallen from the face of the cliff years before, scotched in its journey down the hillside by a couple of close-growing cedar bushes. A large agave plant grew from a crack in the slab.

Kale slid down behind this rock, his tan clothing blending into the landscape. He settled an elbow on top of the slab to steady his field glasses.

The hillsides were aglow with green, yellow, and gold as the afternoon sun glanced off the tops of trees clothed in autumn finery.

Silence filled the air. Heat waves danced with an intoxicating rhythm from the mass of jumbled boulders in the canyon below. The sun touching his shoulders contributed to a lazy feeling. What he really needed right now was to stretch out in the shade of the boulder and take a good, old-fashioned siesta.

Instead he began a systematic search of the country ahead of him. His field of vision was not nearly so good as he'd hoped. The draw up which Costello disappeared wound around far below. A couple of miles from the spring it curved back to the left and possibly connected with the other arm of the canyon behind this very hill where he sat.

He rose and started for the top in order to get a better view. He had no intention of climbing down the other side and leaving his horse over here unless he was pretty sure of intercepting Costello and Ellie.

At his first step bullets ripped through the agave plant, ricocheted off the boulder, and sent pieces of limestone flying in all directions.

Kale dropped behind the boulder an instant before the report of rifle fire shattered the stillness in the canyon.

Another second passed before Kale realized the shots had come from across the draw to his right. Someone was shooting at him from behind, not from the trail ahead.

Had Costello circled the hill and doubled back? Kale decided that was unlikely, because he was sure he heard the reports of at least two separate guns, possibly three. But if not Costello, who?

Touching the wound on his head, he thought of the gambler's killers. Had they learned that he lived through their attack and followed him to finish the job? If Costello paid them to kill him, as he was sure to have done, then their own lives would be worthless if they failed.

Kale crawled further under cover and assessed his position. From this pinnacle no one could get to him without making an awful lot of racket, and there was no place except directly overhead from which a man could fire into his hiding place. If he stuck his head up, though, he would be as good as a turkey at a turkey shoot for any rifleman sitting on that opposite hill.

Working his way behind the branches of the cedar bushes, he eased himself up enough to scan the opposite hillside with his field glasses. Nothing moved, but several places within rifle range offered good cover.

Kale considered the situation and found himself literally between a rock and a hard place. His horse was undercover directly below, but he would be twice the fool not to expect them to have his campsite covered. If he could come in from behind and get his horse, he might have a chance of escaping, but at present, the only way down appeared to be the way he came up—in full view of the riflemen across the way.

He could wait until dark, which was still a couple of hours off, but it was unlikely that anyone who had tracked him this far would give him a chance to escape, come nightfall.

Burrowing himself further into the cedar, he tried to visualize the layout of the hill as he had scanned it from below. The sun was dropping behind him to his right, which put him on the north side of the bluff. The trail he had taken wound from east to north, so these cedars must be on the brink of that sheer cliff he had approached below.

Edging a bit closer to make sure he wasn't turning his back on an easy trail to safety, he was left with no doubts. A rock gave way beneath his hands and plunged to the ground. He fell forward, his head and forearms draped over the precipice.

Bullets hit all around, pelting his face with fragments of rock. He quickly pulled himself back to his refuge behind the boulder.

It was hot, very hot for this time of year. The pungent smell of cedar, which could be pleasant enough in small wafts, stung his throat and caused his eyes to water.

He wiped his face with his sleeve and considered how to get down off this mountain.

Peering cautiously around the boulder, he studied the trail, his umbilical cord, his lifeline. Devoid of obstructions, it slanted straight down for about fifty feet, then turned at a sharp right angle around the opposite side of a small boulder.

Could he make it to that boulder? The trail was steep, mostly rocks. He was amazed he had made it up. Going down would stir up a ruckus a blind man couldn't miss. But did he have a choice?

Not with Ellie in trouble and needing him, he didn't. He had no choice except to find a way down from this mountain, and in one piece. He would do her no good shot up like one of Buffalo Bill's clay pigeons.

A diversion . . . that's what he needed. If he could fool them—somehow make them think he was going down the opposite side of the cliff, perhaps . . .

Quickly he began cutting branches off the cedar bushes. They scratched his hands and arms even through his shirt sleeves, and the vapor started his nose to itching.

When he had a good-sized pile of branches, he took off his belt and tied them together around the middle. Then he threaded his rope through the bundle, tied one end of the rope to the tree trunk, and threw the free end over the side of the cliff, giving it an extra jiggle to be sure it could be seen from the opposite hill. After a moment he jiggled the rope again, then checked the trail behind him one last time.

Very carefully he slid the bundle to the edge of the precipice. He had tightened the belt enough that the bundle should slide slowly down the length of dangling rope.

At least, that was what he banked on. He had no illusions that a bundle of cedar branches belted around the middle would resemble a man except from a distance, but since this side of the cliff was already in shadow, it might fool them momentarily.

After all, they were looking for him to try to escape,

and a man often could be tricked into believing something he wanted to believe. All Kale needed was enough time to get to that boulder . . . fifty feet.

Slinging the rifle across his back, he tightened the belt and gave the bundle a shove. Then he plunged around the slab and hit the trail with both heels dug into the ground to keep from tumbling headlong over the face of the cliff.

A barrage of shots rang out, but as nothing flew apart near him, he trusted they'd taken the bait.

Thick white dust swirled in his face, choking him with its chalky substance. He flung out his arms wildly to keep his balance but failed, and his hands hit the rocks, losing skin and stinging as dirt ground into raw flesh. He skidded the last ten feet on his rear and careened bodily into the boulder as pieces of limestone flew under another volley of bullets.

The boulder behind which he protected himself was actually two vertical limestone outcroppings. He wiped the blood off his scraped palms with dried grass, slid his rifle into position, and took aim at the far hill.

After a few minutes a bullet hit the hill above his head, and Kale shot at a fiery Spanish oak. A form darted to the right, and he fired directly in front of the man, who immediately dived for cover.

The trouble with Kale's situation as he saw it was that the men shooting at him had the cover of a wooded hillside, while he was on a practically barren cliff, where gully-washers in the past had taken their toll of vegetation and topsoil.

Kale cursed himself for playing the tenderfoot and getting himself caught in such a situation. He had been a fool not to realize those men would come after him.

Ellie's life hung on his mistakes.

He studied the trail as it curled around the right side of the outcropping and then headed straight down. There was hardly enough cover to conceal a rattler from here on down.

To his right all was barren for fifteen to twenty feet, then there was a sheer dropoff. On the left he could see the tops of the cottonwoods growing along the base of the cliff. Somewhere under those trees his horse grazed. The creek flowed. There he could find safety, or at least the hope of safety. Here he didn't have a rusty bucketful of hope.

He waited. Things were quiet across the way . . . too quiet, he thought. Using his field glasses, he scanned the brush. At first he saw no one. Then he got a glimpse of flying black coattails.

Before Kale could make the connection, Holt Rainey dashed from one cover to another, and Kale let loose a string of swearwords. His situation had definitely deteriorated . . . and with it, Ellie's.

Instead of facing two greenhorns, he had a trigger-crazy cowman and a couple of would-be gunfighters on his tail.

And from the looks of things, they had him treed. They could sit back and wait for dark. But would they?

Right now they thought they had him. But if they got to his horse and met him at the bottom of this hill, they would be sure of it, even under the cover of darkness. And Newt Boswell and the man called Saint drew wages to be sure.

Kale took another look around. A thick foliage of grapevines covered the tops of the cottonwoods. He remembered the tart sweetness of Ellie's jelly. The black grapes should be about gone by now, but the vines remained.

Studying the vines through his glasses, an idea began to develop in his mind. The stalks, three or four inches in diameter, appeared firmly attached to the trees. The leaves were large and dense—dense enough to provide cover all the way to the canyon floor.

As he stared at the silver canopy, he recalled swinging on grapevines back home in Tennessee. Could he make it? It would be a move they wouldn't expect, so it might work.

It *must* work, he corrected. Without another thought, he shouldered his rifle bandoleer style and moved out.

One step. Two steps. Four.

Dashing across the hillside, he fixed his eyes on the center of the mass of foliage. He leaped. Shots rang out. One leg took a sudden impact then went numb, a development he refused to consider just then.

He landed in the midst of vines and limbs, grabbing wildly as he fell, branches catching him here and there. The thick vines strained and sagged under the weight of his body. The few remaining grapes crushed beneath his raw hands, shooting his flesh with searing pain.

The vines gave way; his shoulders landed on a large limb. Rolling over, he caught hold and worked his way hand over hand until he could drop to the ground.

The bay lifted his head when Kale threw on the saddle and tightened the cinch. He had taken a bullet in the leg, but there was no time to tend it. He tore a strip from his shirttail and stuffed it into the wound until he could get to a place of safety.

For the next hour he rode among the shadows close to

331

the base of the cliff, keeping limestone boulders between himself and the open canyon where possible.

Night was fast approaching now, and he began to look for a place which would afford a measure of protection and give him a chance to see to his wound.

The bay sensed the rock shelter even before Kale saw it. The entrance was partially obstructed by a small but bushy mesquite tree.

Quickly stripping the bay, he staked him inside the opening of the shelter, where he could feed on mesquite leaves and beans, and where he would warn of visitors.

Then Kale built a small fire and set about tending his wound. He bathed it with hot water and made a poultice using drops of gum he was able to pry from the trunk of the mesquite. He also applied the gum to his palms, feeling immediate relief, and to the gunshot wound on his head.

Before putting out his fire he made some extra slashes around the trunk of the tree. With luck, come morning he would find more teardrops of mesquite gum to dress his wounds. He put out his fire then, not wishing to draw his attackers to him before he was ready.

But when would that be? Tomorrow? His hands wouldn't heal by tomorrow. And his leg would be stiff. But ready or not, tomorrow would be the day. Tomorrow he must find Ellie, and tomorrow he must protect her not only from that madman Costello, but from the gunfighters behind them.

No small task . . . but the most important one he had ever faced.

After leaving the spring at the foot of the cliff,

Armando Costello followed the canyon's curve to the north. The going was rough, but he knew the canyon would soon give way to rolling hills. By traveling hard, he figured they could make the painted cliffs on the banks of the Concho River before dark.

A feeling of triumph gripped his heart; his body quivered with jubilation when he thought of the treasure that was soon to be his . . . *his.* After a lifetime of searching and deprivation . . . *his* . . . to luxuriate in, to squander as he pleased.

The substance of the treasure had never taken form in Costello's unimaginative mind. He had been too concerned with finding it and taking it for himself. Now, however, mental pictures began to dance among the heat waves in the canyon. It had to be gold. The yellow half-moon on the plat indicated that much. And the cross beside it probably meant the treasure had been buried by a man of the cloth. Costello had learned well the symbols used in marking buried treasure.

When a sudden burst of rifle fire erupted from down the canyon, he hurried Ellie beneath some trees while he studied their back trail.

The shots had come from the direction of the spring and sounded to be about that far away.

Panic froze Costello's spine. So they were trying to stop him again . . . they had succeeded before, but this time he would win. This time he *must* win, he told himself, for this was his last chance to possess a part of the treasure bequeathed his grandfather and wrongfully kept from him.

Who *they* were, Armando Costello could have told no one. *They* originated in his mind and were simply the enemy—the forces of evil which prevented him from obtaining what had become the obsession, the passion, the very essence of his life: his treasure.

"I've learned from the past. They won't get me this time." He spoke furtively, under his breath.

"Who is it?" Ellie asked.

Costello turned on her fiercely. Fire flared from his eyes; his breath came in spurts. "Shut up, woman! They'll hear you."

"Who?"

"Silence!" he raged. The point of his drawn Bowie knife struck her throat. I could do it here, he thought . . . kill her now and be done with it. It would be so easy.

Caution prevailed. Not here. She would bleed and they would find the blood. She would scream and they would hear her.

He must get her away from here. Take her to the place he had taken Benjamin. The painted cliffs. There coyotes would find her body and devour it long before human feet ever touched the spot again.

Costello grabbed the reins of Ellie's horse and led it beside him to higher ground. He was consumed with the desire to break and run for his life. Yet at the same time he felt compelled to discover the meaning of the gunfire.

He picketed the horses deeper under the trees and pulled Ellie after him so she could not give warning.

The shots had come from the vicinity of the spring, but the object of the firing could be much closer. It would please him to think someone was hunting. Or that some cowpoke had gotten himself lost and was signaling for help. But he could not allow himself to believe either story. He must find out for sure.

Twenty feet or so up the side of the canyon, he spied a

mass of jumbled boulders. He shoved Ellie down behind them and studied his back trail with field glasses. He took his time, examining everything within range. A man's clothing would blend with the colors of the landscape, so he watched and waited.

Ellie lay huddled against the rocks where Costello pushed her. All day she had remained alert for a chance to escape, for another ravine or draw which would lead quickly out of this canyon and away from Armando Costello, who grew steadily more demented as the day wore on. His sudden swings in mood from joyful to enraged frightened her. She knew he was near a breaking point. When he reached it . . . She shuddered, recalling the Bowie knife at her throat.

She watched him survey the canyon. His knife was sheathed, but his rifle lay on a rock beside him.

She stared at the rifle. This might be her chance. If she could get to that gun and fire it, whoever was back there would know someone was here. Then they might investigate and find her.

Suddenly another round of firing sounded down the canyon. She dived for the gun. Her left hand closed around the stock. It felt smooth and cool under her palm. Her right hand reached for the barrel . . .

Costello turned. His powerful hands grabbed the gun. He pushed her away from him, wrenching the rifle from her and throwing it aside.

"*Puta! Puta!*" he roared. "Whore! Whore!" Then he was on top of her, his face flushed, his eyes aflame, his breathing shallow and quick.

He slapped her face back and forth. He tore at her clothing, ripping a sleeve from her bodice and tearing her riding skirt. He beat his fists into her body.

Finally she managed to roll away from him. He fell forward, hugging his arms to his chest against the cold fear of what might have been, had this whore fired his rifle in warning. Was she to be the end of him? Were his dreams to be crushed beneath the feet of yet another woman?

Armando Costello's hatred for women had begun long ago in Mexico, when he was still a child. There he learned that his mother was not the fine Spanish lady his father had been expected to marry, but instead a mestizo—half Spanish, half Indian. His grandmother told him, explaining why he was not considered a true member of the Costello family. Even after his mother died by her own hand, young Armando was not accepted as an heir to the family fortune, because his veins did not carry pure blood. So his cousin received the plats to treasure mines in Texas and the Indian Territory.

So afraid was Costello's grandmother that he and his father would get their hands on the plats that she spirited his cousin away in the night. He was instructed to stay in hiding until Costello and his father were taken care of.

It was the cousin's misfortune, however, that the grandmother died shortly thereafter. Costello set out to find those plats then, and to this day he had not let up in his search.

Now he was close to the last of the treasures, so close he could taste the wine and feel the pleasure. Now it was almost in his hand, and another woman had stepped in.

But this time would be different, he vowed . . . this time he would win. He would destroy this whore before she got him. He turned his attention back to the trail, away from Ellie's frightened body, crumpled on the rocks at his feet.

The effort of studying the trail calmed his nerves somewhat. His breathing became regular, and he began to think in a more rational way.

He knew he would have to figure on some of those shots being fired by Kale Jarrett. He would like to believe Abe and Martin had done their job, but he dared not rely on hope. If Jarrett had escaped death, he would certainly trail Costello and Ellie.

And the bastard would then lead the Raineys to their trail as well.

Costello felt a chill return to his body. The possibility of the Raineys and Kale Jarrett following him into the canyon alarmed him. He did not want to die in this Godforsaken country. He did not want to die poor as a beggar. He did not want to die mere hours away from riches.

He clamped his jaw against a shudder. He would not die here. They would not get him.

Costello's mood changed suddenly; it occurred to him that the men back there might kill each other—or at least cut down the odds.

Either way, while they were occupied with their own fight, he had time to get to the painted cliffs, kill this whore, and return to the ranch to claim his treasure.

When he turned back to Ellie, the fire was gone from his eyes, replaced by a look as cold and hard as the rocks around them. He was composed now, confident.

By dusk they had found their way out of the canyon and camped in a ravine surrounded by a shin oak thicket.

Although he had not slept in many hours, sleep was now out of the question. His assailants might come in the night. The whore might try to escape. He must be on guard against either.

Sitting back from the fire he kept watch, dreaming his dreams of being rich and famous, able to spit in the face of anyone who dared look down on him again.

He didn't expect to be followed tonight. The men in the canyon would be too busy with each other. Tomorrow the ones who survived would find his trail, but that didn't matter. If they arrived at the painted cliffs before he finished with the whore, so much the better.

There he would have a perfect view from which to shoot them down one by one, before they could cross the river.

A smile curved his lips. Tomorrow he would have his treasure. No one could stop him now.

Kale Jarrett packed up and left the rock shelter before dawn the next morning. He scouted for sign of the Circle R men. Although he found none, he knew they were out there. Matt Rainey didn't pay men to give up. And Holt—well, he was a coyote of a different stripe. A man looking to carve notches on his gun wasn't likely to run off when the quarry got within easy distance.

Half a mile up the canyon he cut sign, all right, but it was not the Rainey crowd. Costello and Ellie had stopped here and taken to the brush. A few feet on he found where the horses had been staked, then up the cliff he found the boulders behind which Costello had studied the trail below.

Kale's knees went weak at sight of the blood, bright and red on the limestone rocks, and the sleeve from a woman's costume, a buff-colored sleeve, the color of Poppy's riding suit, which Lavender had said Ellie wore

338

when she left the Lady Bug.

All thought of the Circle R men fled from Kale's mind. He had to get to Ellie now, and soon, before Costello killed her. The pain from his wounds was as nothing compared to the pain in his heart—the fear he felt for Ellie.

He found their trail and followed it easily. They were traveling faster now. Costello would have ample time to kill Ellie and escape—if he abandoned the treasure.

But after all the man had done to get his hands on that treasure, Kale doubted he'd leave the country without it. He could kill Ellie, then hide out until the fervor died down before taking the treasure, though.

Kale hurried on. The canyon ended and rolling hills began. It had rained good here; the summer grass was dried now and knee-high to the bay. Mesquite and oak trees abounded, with occasional cedars and shin oak thickets along the ravines.

The sun was high overhead when he came upon their camp. From the small footprints around the site, he figured Ellie was mobile. His anxiety over her was relieved somewhat. But time was growing short. Armando Costello was a madman.

Stopping only to water the bay, Kale hurried on. The scraps of Ellie's clothing and the blood on those rocks, even though there were only a couple of spots, worried him. For the first time in his life Kale wanted to kill a man. He could not recall ever wanting to before.

He ached inside, thinking how frightened Ellie must be. Likely she thought him dead, since Costello thought that. She wouldn't have much hope of being rescued.

339

He spurred the bay. Even if she didn't know it, her life depended on him. And he'd be damned if he was going to let her down—neither for her sake, nor his.

As soon as he sent his two hired guns along with Holt after Kale Jarrett and Costello and the girl, Matt Rainey got things rolling. Ira and Till started the cattle moving toward the Jarrett range; by noon, camp had been set up for the hands down by Plum Creek. Cookie had a steer on the spit and beans on the fire.

Rainey established his headquarters inside Ellie Jarrett's house. He'd had a hankerin' to get hold of this place ever since Benjamin Jarrett settled here, and now that he had it, he intended to direct the whole operation.

Before the elder Jarrett arrived, Rainey had assumed ownership of Plum Creek and had planned to stock the ranch one day. As Rainey saw things, land was power, and the man who controlled the most land was the most powerful. Not that he wanted more power, he told himself, but he damned sure didn't want a lot of little people banding together against him.

Ira Wilson approached the porch where Rainey stood surveying his new property. "What'd we do about the Jarrett cattle, sir?"

"Brand 'em," Rainey barked. "Circle R goes on everything."

"But sir, if we're questioned . . . I mean, come sellin' time?" Branding another man's livestock, whether that man was dead or alive, was not an offense Ira Wilson cared to be accused of.

"Judge Cranston from over in Llano County will be out

340

directly; we'll take care of that. You give me an accurate head count, hear?"

"Yes, sir." Ira turned toward the pens.

"Ira," Rainey called after him. "You and Till will be staying on here to look after things. Move your belongings into the house first chance you get."

While waiting for Cranston, Rainey walked out to the pens where the men had started branding Jarrett's cattle. Time was, not long ago, when he'd have been in the thick of things, right in the middle of all the dust and bawling cattle. The acrid smell of fire and flesh burning under the iron still stirred excitement in his blood. It always would, he reckoned. Lately, though, he left the physical work to others.

The activity in the pens also stirred memories within Matt Rainey. Memories of Mary, of their life together starting the Circle R, of their hopes and dreams. There wasn't even an heir to show for their time together. His son had died before he was even born, taking Mary along with him.

Only Holt remained to inherit, and Matt hated the thought. Though he carried the name, Holt was no Rainey. Not in inclination, anyhow, nor in disposition. All Holt was interested in was gaining a "reputation."

Rainey spat furiously to the ground. Where the hell was that judge, anyhow?

As if on cue, a buckboard bounced over the rocks and rolled up to the house. Rainey met the judge with a handshake. "Let's have a look at those papers."

Judge Cranston followed Rainey into the house and spread the papers on Ellie's table.

"This one here is a bill of sale for Benjamin Jarrett's

341

cattle. I've signed his name, copied it from some papers over at the bank."

Rainey grunted. "Where do I sign?"

The judge pointed to a blank space on the document, then another. "Here's where we add the number of cattle."

Rainey signed the bill of sale, set it aside, and studied the other document.

"That's a deed to this property," Cranston said. "It isn't exactly legal, but it'll do until you can get down to Austin and file on the land yourself."

"You sure Jarrett didn't file on this place?"

"If he had, he'd have kept the deed in the bank with all his other papers. I checked with Holcomb."

"Makes me uneasy."

"I know you like the loose ends taken care of, Matt, and they will be. In no time you'll have a deed that'll hold up in court. You're not going to need one sooner."

Rainey grunted again. "Long as my boys take care of Jarrett's brother."

"I've never seen you worry like this. Why, we oughta be having a drink to celebrate."

Rainey agreed. "Come on outside. I'll get the whiskey."

They sat on the porch, enjoying the shade and taking turns at the bottle of rye. Cranston broke the silence. "What about the treasure?"

"Hogwash!"

"The story's intriguing, you'll have to admit."

"If that talk were true, somebody would have found something by this time," Rainey argued.

"I agree that most of those stories don't hold water, Matt, but this one's bound to have some truth in it. Zofie

Wiginton told it to me herself."

Rainey looked surprised. "Why didn't she go after it?"

"She's a lot like you. She doesn't believe in it, either. But I'd lay you odds Benjamin Jarrett found it. Otherwise, why'd he pick this particular piece of land?"

"It's a good place."

"Sure it is, but would you expect a nester like Jarrett to recognize that?"

"Sounds like you have it all figured out."

"Not all, but I'm sure that treasure is here. What it is, I don't know. And I don't know exactly where it is, but there's treasure on this place somewhere. We're sitting on rich land, Matt."

"You're right about that," Rainey agreed. "This soil is as rich as any you're apt to find. The grass it grows will feed cattle for hundreds of years, if it isn't stripped clean. Now, if you cut up the range into little pieces where each man has to overstock in order to make ends meet, you're going to strip the ground of any cover, wash the topsoil clean away, leave nothing except bedrock. But if you run it like I plan to, not overgrazing, moving herds around, the range will reseed itself and we'll have grass forever. Take buffalo, they don't ruin a place. There's a damned sight more of them in a herd than there are cattle, but buffalo move around. Don't make sense to me why people can't learn from nature at least once in a while."

"Well said, Matt. You've done some thinking on this."

"You bet I have, only I usually keep it to myself." Matt took a swig of rye. "I've been giving thought to something else, too."

"What's that?"

"I'm obliged for your help in this matter, Cranston. I asked you to go against the law—hell, even against your

343

own oath of office—and you did it without a whimper."

"We agreed on this thing. Twenty percent of Matt Rainey's profits for the next five years is reward enough."

"Even so, you went out on a limb, and I'm obliged. The treasure's yours."

"What?"

"The treasure. If it's here, it's yours. Don't bother the range or livestock, that's all I ask. Fair enough?"

Judge Cranston's mouth fell open. "You sure about this, Matt?"

"Hell, yes, I'm sure. Let's shake on it and be done."

Chapter Sixteen

When they reached the Concho River, Armando Costello drew rein and pulled Ellie's mount to a halt behind his own.

She sat quietly. They hadn't spoken for several hours, and she had no desire to talk now. Fatigue amplified her hopelessness; it settled over her like a pall. Being led to her death, she found no power to resist.

The small measure of hope she had felt back in the canyon disappeared when they saw no further sign of pursuit. Likely the shooting they heard bore no relation to her frightful state of affairs.

The thought that she had caused Kale's death by sending him away that night at the Lady Bug depressed her, but the impact was lessened by a numbness which gripped her brain.

Without warning, Costello jerked the reins of her horse, pulling the animal alongside his own. When she was within reach, he ripped a scrap of lace from her chemise, which, although she tried to conceal it, still peeked through her torn bodice.

She watched him sight on a boulder on the far cliff, then snag the piece of cloth on a limb within his line of vision.

Ellie's head cleared somewhat with this action. She studied the line Costello marked from the cliff to this spot. A rifleman behind that boulder could . . .

Armando Costello was setting a trap. A trap must have prey. Her heart beat faster than it had since they heard gunshots in the canyon, pumping hope into her, glorious hope. She might have given up being pursued, but obviously Armando had not.

They forded the river to the east and picketed their horses in a thicket. Costello steered her roughly by her upper arm, but she hardly noticed. Neither did she pay attention to the paintings which had always held such interest for her.

The only thing she found of interest at this moment was the person for whom Armando set his trap. Dared she hope it was for Kale? Perhaps not, but she knew she'd better lay plans for that possibility. If Kale was alive, if Armando had set a trap for him, then she would need a very clear head indeed. If Kale took the swatch of her chemise from that limb, she'd have to keep Armando from shooting him.

When they reached a point beneath the boulder Ellie had seen from the opposite bank, she recognized it instantly: the ancient staircase to the cave where Kale found Benjamin's buckle.

She should have expected as much. Stopping abruptly, Costello ordered her to climb. She steeled herself. Desperately she tried to force her brain to work.

Finally, at his repeated prodding, she removed her

boots, placing them close to the wall of the narrow ledge. Kale would find them and know where to look for her.

Her stomach tumbled at the thought of him finding her body. Costello nudged her roughly with the barrel of his rifle.

She began the climb, only to be hampered repeatedly by the hem of her riding skirt. The rocks were warm with the heat of day. Dirt clung to her sweaty palms; her mouth felt cottony and parched. Her nose itched, and she ached to rub it. She was alive. Soon she would feel nothing.

Suddenly, as she felt for a grip on the nearly smooth stone, her fingers slipped. Her heart lurched, as if it had been struck by a falling boulder. She had to get to the top alive. Kale's life depended on it.

Costello caught her leg with an iron clasp and heaved her back toward the cliff, where her flailing hand found a hold.

"I told you not to fall!" he thundered.

Beneath the anger in his voice, fear trembled; she recognized it immediately. If she fell she would knock him off the side of the cliff. Her mind buzzed with the possibility of doing just that, but the fall would kill them both, and she was suddenly struck by how desperately she wanted to live.

Reaching the ledge some fifty feet above the river, she heaved her body up. She considered trying to push him off the cliff before he could gain the top, but he still held her leg in a tight grip, and she knew he could jerk her off balance before she could dislodge him. She dragged herself, pulling him along, to a place of safety and bided her time.

Immediately upon gaining the ledge, Costello let go of her leg and took cover behind the boulder, his rifle trained on the distant trees. After a time he took out his field glasses and surveyed the area. Suddenly he threw them down and jumped from behind the cover of the boulder. He stared intently into the line of trees.

"It's gone!" he cursed. "He took my bait and—" He stepped toward the ledge and peered intently at the bank across the river, and Ellie found her chance.

Stealthily but quickly she moved toward him. One push and he would be gone forever.

Arms outstretched, hands open wide, she started for him. One step . . . one more. Her hands found his back. She lunged forward. She pushed, then pushed again.

He was much faster than she imagined he'd be. Wrenching himself to the side, he grabbed for a hold on the boulder to his left. When his body twisted away from her, she grasped after it with clawing fingers.

"Demon!" she cried. "Monstrous demon!"

Flesh gave way beneath her nails as she raked her fingers down his face. She pulled at his hair, tearing loose a handful. He struggled to get away. She sank her teeth deep into his arm, tasting blood. He howled, flinging her from him.

Her legs flew out from under her, and she screamed as she landed inches from the precipice, teetering on the edge. Rocks clattered to the riverbank fifty feet below.

She struggled to regain her footing. Pain seared up her right leg when she moved it. Pain followed by panic.

Costello could finish her off with one swift shove. Bracing herself against the expected move, she managed to roll away from the edge of the bluff.

She glanced around for Costello and discovered him hovering behind the boulder, frantically searching the opposite shore.

The tiny flicker of hope in her heart leapt into flame at the fear she saw in Armando Costello's eyes. If someone really *was* across the river in those trees, as he seemed to think, there was hope.

"*Help me! Please! Up here! Help!*"

Costello lunged for her. He clapped a hand over her mouth. His eyes shone like black coals.

"I ought to kill you now and get it over with!" He jerked her arm. "Get up, whore!"

"I can't. I think my leg is broken."

He pulled her by the arm then, dragging her back inside the cave. She could see he was agitated.

"Who is following us?" she asked. "You confessed to killing Kale. Who else would bother?" She made no effort to conceal her contempt. She thought only to get his mind off her and onto his plan again.

He had dragged her to the rear of the cave, near the point where Kale had found Benjamin's belt buckle. At her contemptuous tone of voice, he kicked her in the side. She flinched. The pain from her ankle made her dizzy and perspiration beaded her forehead.

"Fool!" he retorted. "I didn't personally kill Jarrett. Abe and Martin were supposed to do it for me—for a sum, of course. Now I fear I shouldn't have trusted those disreputable men. Who but Jarrett would have taken your scrap of lace?"

Who, indeed? she wondered, still holding herself back from complete hopefulness. As Kale had told her weeks ago, this thing was far from over.

349

Without warning, Costello unsheathed his knife and moved toward her slowly, his eyes alive with hatred. A wave of nausea swept over her; she fought to clear her head. If someone really was out there, he wouldn't chance a shot. But she knew he would not hesitate to use his blade, which she had watched him hone to a fearsome edge.

When she spoke again, she didn't recognize her own voice; it sounded hollow, distant, as if it belonged to a stranger. "Someone heard my cries," she told him. "If you kill me, you'll never get away. Whoever took that piece of lace will find my body, and they'll know. They'll hunt you down. You'll never get your treasure."

He stopped. His eyes flashed and he spat his contempt in her face.

She suppressed a shudder. "Kale Jarrett will kill you. If he's alive, he'll avenge my death—and Benjamin's. He and his entire family will come after you. You'll never live to see your treasure."

Costello fingered the Bowie knife while pinning her to the stone floor with his eyes. She held her breath, too exhausted to continue. What more could she say? If she had not convinced him of the foolhardiness of killing her, more words would do no good.

Finally he spoke. "You have not talked yourself out of death, *puta,* only into a respite. While I am gone you may contemplate the pleasures that await you when I return from killing Jarrett."

His smile froze in place; his eyes laughed at her terror. He poised the blade at the base of her throat. "Pleasures which will end with your death."

She lay still, the pain in her ankle dulled by the violent

350

beating of her heart. Surely Kale could hear her heart, she thought. If indeed he was alive and not the figment of this madman's imagination.

Costello tied her hands and then her feet, causing excruciating pain in her ankle.

"He will kill you," she mumbled. "Kale will kill you." But she knew that Kale could well be lying dead back in Summer Valley—or in the canyon.

With a slash of his blade, Costello cut a strip of fabric from the front of her bodice and gagged her with it.

"You had better hope not, *puta*. Then no one would find your body."

She watched him take cover behind the boulder and carefully search the area below before he descended from the cave.

Kale would find her. If he was alive, he would know exactly where to look.

Kale Jarrett adjusted the angle of his hat against the unrelenting sun. Ahead of him the hills rolled forward in waves of faded green and gold. Everything in sight seemed to be dusted with a thin coating of windblown silt.

He drew up at a creek and watered the bay. Travel was easier now; he was making good time. But he knew Costello was, too.

Before leaving the creek, Kale took out his field glasses and studied his back trail. Still no sign of the Circle R outfit. He hadn't seen hide nor hair of them since the encounter back in the canyon, and that worried him.

He moved out, headed due north. The bullet wound in his thigh throbbed with every hoofbeat. Before breaking camp this morning, he had cleaned and dressed the wound again, wrapping the bandage extra tight to staunch any bleeding the trip might bring on.

His head wound was healing nicely, so after dabbing it with a measure of mesquite gum, he left the bandage off. He figured he was beginning to resemble a war casualty and he hadn't even reached the battlefield yet. The wound stood to heal faster in the open air, anyhow.

His hands were stiff and sore, but they were beginning to heal, too. He clenched and unclenched his fists, trying to work the stiffness out before he caught up with Costello.

Five miles gave way to four, then to three. Up ahead a line of trees followed the river. As he approached them, Kale sized up the situation and decided it might be unhealthy to ride directly up to the bank of the river. So he picketed his horse and snaked his way into a position from where he could see the river and the opposite bank of cliffs.

The wide curve he remembered in the Concho was directly in front of him. Across from it he recognized the fractured wall of limestone which was riveted with caves.

He examined the tracks he followed through his glasses. They led to the edge of the river, then disappeared. The opposite bank was mostly rock, with the cliffs rising straight up from the bank. He saw no sign of Costello's horses over there, but he hadn't expected to. Likely they crossed upriver, where Ellie had suggested last time.

Still using his glasses, he scanned the cliffs, searching for the cave where he and Ellie had climbed, searching for any sign of movement. He saw nothing, yet assumed nothing.

Next, he inspected the cliffs with assault in mind. He could either climb up the front of the bluff, as would be expected. Or he could go over the top, an exercise that would be hazardous under the best conditions, and very foolish with a shot-up leg. A natural break appeared to cut the cliffs into two sections. That, too, was an option.

He saw it then, and his heart danced a frantic jig—a scrap of white lace blowing not ten feet ahead of him. It was Ellie's. He'd bank on that. It came from one of her petticoats or something. Had she left it as a sign?

The instant he moved toward it, he stopped himself. Though he didn't have much book learning, he was sure as shootin' educated in the ways of cunning men.

Was Costello even now across the river, his rifle trained on that spot? The thought sent a shudder up Kale's spine. But a second thought warned him that if Ellie had left it as a sign for him, she needed to be reassured that he'd arrived.

Then she might find the strength to hold out until he could get to her. That is, if he could retrieve the swatch of cloth without getting himself shot.

One jump and he had it clutched tightly in his damp palm. But even as he moved deeper into the trees, he was followed by a premonition so black it must surely have been born in the bowels of hell.

He shook his head to clear it, and after a quick glance to his back trail he mounted and rode east, careful to keep good coverage between himself and the river.

A mile upstream he found the crossing he and Ellie had used. One end of the piece of lace fluttered from his breast pocket where he'd stuffed it, reminding him of the need to hurry. If Ellie had left it, she probably knew he was following her.

And if Costello had left it . . . the thought struck Kale with an additional fear. If Armando Costello had taken a piece of lace from Ellie's underclothes, what else had the bastard done to her?

With the greatest of difficulty, he chased these notions from his mind and turned his thoughts toward a cold and desperate plan of action. He must save Ellie from this madman.

He rode north, then cut back west. He must act quickly and carefully. If Costello saw him first, Ellie's life wouldn't be worth two hoots and a holler. Nor would his own.

Holt and Saint followed Newt's lead across Brady Creek. From there they struck out west, skirted Kickapoo Creek, and found themselves in a rolling prairieland of knee-deep buffalo grass.

Wildlife abounded. Had they been hunting camp meat, their choice would have been anything from ground squirrel to white-tailed deer to buffalo.

But they weren't out to bring home the bacon. At least, not in any ordinary sense, Newt thought. That five hundred dollars Matt Rainey had waiting for him and Saint would buy a fair-sized side of bacon, though.

At the Concho River they drew up and let the horses water. Saint got down and started to loosen his cinch, but Newt stopped him.

"No need to rest the horses. We're only a few miles upstream from the cliffs. They'll get plenty of rest and grazing while we tend to business."

Saint started to balk at his air of authority, then thought better. The sooner they got this matter settled, the sooner he'd be shut of Holt Rainey.

"We cross here," Newt continued. "That way they don't hear us. Sound carries across water farther than a body would think."

"The sort of thing Kale Jarrett's likely listening for," Saint added.

"Kale Jarrett," Holt hissed. "I'm plumb fed up with the feats of that mighty warrior. When I get through with Jarrett, you can stuff what's left of him in an ant hole."

Saint sneered. "I'm plumb fed up with something, too. You want to buy chances on what it is?"

Holt turned in his saddle. "You'd better run first chance you get, Saint, 'cause when I finish with Jarrett, I'm comin' after you."

Saint grinned. "I'll be waiting."

Newt leveled his Colt at the two men. "Enough! I'll have no more bickering until this job is done. After that the two of you can kill each other, for all I care. Now get a move on."

They crossed the river and kept north for almost a mile, then Newt led them back east.

"Keep your eyes peeled," he advised. "I figure to be right about this layout, but in case I'm not, we'll have to scatter quicker'n quail to find cover on this prairie." He dismounted. "We lead the horses from here."

Newt Boswell did not enjoy the role of leader. By nature a loner, he had assured Matt Rainey he could handle this Jarrett affair by himself, but the old man brought in Saint, anyhow. Now, to top things off, he was saddled with the boss's trigger-happy brother. Considering it all, he told himself, he'd be damned lucky to get away from here with all the hair on his head. That is, unless he could shake his two sidekicks before the shindig commenced, which was exactly what he determined to do.

No one had ever considered Newt good enough. Now, at last, he had a chance to show them. A notch on his gun for Kale Jarrett would be proof to any man that Newt Boswell measured up.

Soon as he got shut of Saint and Holt, he'd take Jarrett himself. Sometimes events in life seemed to fall into a man's lap, like drawing the right card in a poker hand. That had never happened to Newt before, but this time he knew he held the right card, an ace for sure.

Newt Boswell had been born at Fort Concho to the west of here, the product of an army officer and a whore from the riverfront. He'd run away many times during his early years, and it was the painted cliffs that he always ran to.

There were few people around these parts then, and none to remember the kid who hid out in the hills because he was too ashamed to face folks at the base.

It rankled Newt now and again. Sometimes, when he had a gut full of tequila, he even admitted to hitting the outlaw trail because of a whorin' mother. Mostly, he didn't think about the officer father who never spoke to him on the street.

Newt's drinking was confined to barrooms, however. He never drank on a job, and he never let emotions get in his way. That was the trouble with Saint, he told himself—Saint had a trigger-temper. That's why Newt preferred to work alone.

The men approached the spring with caution. A mockingbird sang from a pecan limb that swayed in the afternoon breeze. Clear water bubbled up through the rocks and fell into a secluded pond. Maidenhair fern, curled and brown from cool autumn nights, grew from holes in the moss-covered limestone.

At Newt's motion they picketed the horses on a good grazing patch back in the trees.

"You boys get a drink and a bite to eat. No fire. I know this area, so I'll scout around a mite."

"What'd you mean, you'll scout around?" Holt challenged. "Jarrett belongs to me. It's my party."

Newt restrained his boss's brother. "Take it easy. I won't spoil your fun. I just want to scout around. Sit tight."

After Newt left them alone, Saint and Holt stared in different directions for a while. Neither dared risk a confrontation this close to the showdown.

Then Saint stepped back into the trees to relieve himself. When he returned, Holt Rainey was gone. Tracks showed where he'd hightailed it around the backside of the cliffs.

Good riddance, Saint thought . . . I hope he gets hisself shot. He moved back against a wall of rocks, settling his saddlegun across his knees.

At that instant a spine-chilling scream rent the natural silence. A woman's scream. And she sounded to be in a heap of trouble. Saint drew deeper into the shadows and wished this place were more protected. Should he stay here as Newt said, or should he move out? That damn fool kid might've drawn them right to him here, and yet . . .

Decisions had always come hard for the man called Saint.

A mile or so north of the river, Kale cut back west. The

357

terrain was rockier now and rising as he climbed to the top of the cliffs. He was worried. He was also tired and irritable—his leg pained him, his hands were stiff, and the wire stubble of his beard scratched. But mostly he was worried.

What had happened to those blamed-fool Circle R men? Kale found it highly unlikely they'd have gone to the trouble of tracking him through the canyon and setting him up for the kill only to let him slip through their fingers.

He rode warily, occasionally studying his back trail, but keeping a keen lookout ahead for any thicket where Costello could have staked his horses.

He wished for Carson, whose knowledge of these cliffs would surely come in handy. A few years back, Carson had been stationed at the ranger camp near Menardville, and Kale recalled stories Carson told of Captain Roberts and his men scouring this country for renegade Comanches who preyed on scattered settlers.

But Carson wasn't here, and Kale fought against the feeling of being hobbled by his own lack of knowledge. At least he'd seen part of the front side of the cliffs. And he knew the cave where Benjamin had probably been killed.

The air was blue with the haze of autumn. Back behind a live oak thicket Kale drew up and studied the area ahead as it sloped gently to the river. This was where he and Ellie had picketed their horses, but Costello's animals weren't here. He momentarily considered starting his search by going directly to the cave he knew. Then he thought better and decided to stick to his original plan of locating that dry wash up ahead. Costello likely expected him to take the known path.

As he nudged the bay forward, a thrill went through

358

Kale's body, not unlike excitement, yet a sensation heavy with negative overtones. He reached down and patted the bay's neck.

"Get ready, old son. We're headin' down the homestretch."

One thing Kale had learned about himself long ago was that if any blessing had been bestowed on him, it was his sixth sense to smell trouble. He recognized the feeling now and his body relaxed. His fine-tuned reactions were alert and ready.

Up ahead the ground dropped off. That must be the break in the cliffs. To the right of the dropoff he spotted a cedar brake which would provide cover for the bay.

Kale nudged his horse toward the cedars. Restlessness welled up inside him at the thought of what lay ahead. His primary concern was to get Ellie safely away from Costello, and he was eager to be done with the task.

But he was hesitating, too, knowing that this time when he faced the gambler, he'd learn the truth about Benjamin's death. He had guessed it, of course. But hearing that his brother had been killed for buried treasure likely would be hard to take.

Fighting to erase all extraneous thoughts from his mind, Kale was suddenly swamped by images of Ellie: at Benjamin's grave, watering the rosebush, wearing that silky green thing that drove him mad with wanting her, and his last sight of her, gussied up like a painted lady. Thinking of her now in that red gown, he wondered how he'd resisted—

The scream was faint, but it pierced his reverie like a clap of thunder. He drew rein and looked around. It was Ellie for sure, but where was she? The cry had come from the cliffs. Was it from the cave they'd visited?

He was surprised to notice how far he had traveled since the scream tore through the silence. He'd passed the cedars and was practically upon the break in the cliff.

Quickly he backtracked, picketed the bay in the cedar brake, and struck out for the dry wash. He made the gully with two oversized steps, his leg throbbing with each jolt. Suddenly, he heard a clattering of rocks below, and he dived behind a clump of prickly pear which was large, though not large enough for cover.

He looked down the gully in time to see the back of a leg disappear to the left along a ledge.

Whoever it was didn't appear to have seen him, but from the brief glimpse, Kale knew he had more company than he'd bargained for. That leg did not belong to Costello, who wore flat-heeled, city-bought boots. Instead, the boot Kale saw was the sturdy, no-nonsense boot of a western man.

So the Circle R made it to the party, he thought. He hadn't doubted they would, but he'd hoped to take on the troops one at a time.

Of course, they might come in handy—if they drew Costello out in the open . . .

Thing was, they could get to Ellie before he did. And there was no doubting where they stood on that score. They might as well be in cahoots with Costello.

Kale let the man get out of earshot, then picked his way amid the jumble of rocks to the next ledge.

Bracing his back against the wall, he peered around the corner to his left. No sign of the Circle R man. He waited a moment before leaning forward to check right. All clear.

Then he moved to step around the corner and his senses were shattered by a sound above his head—the

360

sound of a human laugh.

Kale froze with one foot poised in midair, uncertain what move to make. The laugh, more of an amused snicker, came again from the cliff behind him. So much for his dependable sixth sense.

"Gotcha, Jarrett."

Chapter Seventeen

Holt Rainey's voice was low but unmistakable as it came to Kale from not more than twenty feet away.

"Gotcha, Jarrett. Toss that rifle off and turn around nice an easy-like."

Fury struck Kale like a fist to the gut. If Holt shot him now, Ellie was as good as dead. Even if he missed, which was hardly likely, but say his gun misfired, the shot would call Newt and Saint. And it would alert Costello to their presence.

"Toss off that gun," Holt repeated.

Kale complied, pitching the rifle as gently as possible into a nearby clump of bear grass, hoping the matted stems would absorb some of the noise.

"Now, turn around and face me," Holt commanded. "You don't think I'd shoot a man in the back, do you?"

Kale bit his tongue to keep from replying. He knew full well that Holt Rainey would do anything his pea-sized brain suggested. But shooting Kale Jarrett in the back would play hell with the reputation he hungered after.

And Holt's hunger for a reputation might just save

Kale's life. In this game, emotions were always a liability.

Love . . . hate . . . fear . . . ambition . . . greed . . . any one of them could color a man's outlook and cause him to act illogically. He would act to satisfy the emotional need, often missing whatever opportunity the situation offered.

Holt could have shot him in the back. He certainly was not above such an act. But his need to be a big man took charge of his logic and bought Kale some time to think.

"Face me, Jarrett!"

Kale glanced down briefly to get his bearings, then slowly swung his foot around, pivoting on his bad leg. Pain shot up his side. He braced against it.

That he could take Holt, Kale had little doubt. He might collect some lead himself, but it wouldn't stop him killing the man.

At this particular time, however, he could afford neither to get himself shot up nor the sound of a single gunshot. Up to this point, there was a chance Costello was unaware of their presence. Holt's voice had been low, uncharacteristically low.

But a gunshot was a different matter altogether. A gunshot would echo up and down these cliffs, reaching into every nook and cranny. A gunshot would signal their arrival as surely as a calling card placed in Armando Costello's lily-white hand.

And it would leave Costello too few choices. Gunfire meant more than one person. He'd know his chances of escaping all of them were slim, especially carrying a woman along. He might feel forced to get rid of Ellie and try his luck alone. Kale recalled Ellie's scream, and an image of Costello's Bowie knife flashed through his brain.

He couldn't afford a single shot. But Holt Rainey stood above him itching for a showdown. And Rainey could afford as many shots as his heart desired. Or could he?

Kale suddenly had second thoughts about the man— usually so loud and blustery. Why was he so quiet now? Did it have anything to do with Newt and Saint?

Newt and Saint were being paid to do a job—and paid handsomely, no doubt. But Matt Rainey was a sly old codger. Kale would wager Rainey was holding a good half of their pay until he was satisfied the job had been accomplished.

A couple of missed shots and Kale might hightail it out of here, along with Costello and Ellie. A couple of missed shots and their fighting wages would go flying out the window, blowing away like so many grass seeds. Newt and Saint could be counted on to come down hard on Holt if he missed. Kale wondered if Holt had considered this. Would he risk an unsure shot?

Before Holt had a chance at the sure thing, Kale stepped out and dropped to the ledge directly beneath him. It was only a ten-foot drop, and he landed unsteadily on his one good leg on another ledge not more than three feet wide. Quickly he stabilized himself with his bad leg, tensing against another flash of pain.

He drew his six-shooter and took a moment to get his bearings. He listened for sounds from above; none came.

What about Newt and Saint? He'd give a spotted pony to know the whereabouts of those two right now. After a second he edged his way to the right, knowing only that one of them had disappeared to his left.

He decided Holt likely wouldn't jump down the cliff after him, but he had little hope of escaping them all.

His shot-up leg objected fiercely as he made his way from

365

one foothold to another. In some places he was able only to stand, his back to the cliff, and slide his feet along.

Every now and then he stopped to listen. Once he looked down to the river twenty feet below. The water was a ruddy color. Not far ahead it swirled as it left the bank. Behind this a grove of trees stretched their tops above the cliffs. From what he had seen from the opposite bank, he figured these trees marked the end of the cliffs. A spring must run out of the rocks there and feed into the river current.

He moved steadily toward the grove of trees, came to a dropoff about four feet wide, and prepared to jump across. He was within earshot of the trees now. Their shade spread over the part of the ledge he approached. His tongue touched dry lips at the sound of water trickling over rocks. A cool drink would be mighty satisfying about now.

Grasping the edge of the cliff, he shoved off. The instant he moved, a bullet slugged into the soft limestone where his head had been a second before. He lost his footing, fell to the rocks below, and struggled to get his feet back under him. Limestone splinters stung his eyes. He clawed at them, fearful of facing his enemy blinded.

The shot had come from the trees. He expected another, but it didn't come. When he could see again, he scrambled up the side of the cliff, which at this point was one smooth slope of limestone. An outcropping of smaller size had stopped him from going straight into the Concho River.

He climbed over another boulder and found himself looking down into a shady nook beside the spring.

No sign of movement.

His assailant couldn't have gone far or he'd have heard

366

him. Three horses were staked back in the trees. The spring gurgled from the hill and gently merged with the river.

Suddenly, a trickle of rocks began to fall from the ledge above. He stepped back, saw a gun barrel above him, aimed, and fired.

Saint's shot ricocheted from the rocks at Kale's feet; the hired gunman fell from the ledge and rolled into the river, shot through the center of the forehead.

Kale dropped quickly into the spring area. All was quiet. Saint must have been left to guard this end of the cliffs. When he heard Kale coming, he climbed up on that ledge and took aim. Kale realized he'd been saved more by Saint's clumsiness than by his own quick thinking.

Knowing the shots would bring the others, he hurried to swing up on the ledge, looked around, and started for the opposite end of the cliffs.

He must get to Ellie before the other two got to him. Where was Holt Rainey? Kale had figured on him being at the spring, but since he wasn't, he could pop up anyplace.

Kale traveled warily, his shoulders tensed against the expected impact of a bullet. Moving from rock to rock, he came to a wall, shinnied it, and found himself again near the top of the cliffs. After a while this played out, so he dropped to a lower level and continued.

With all this climbing, his throat was getting dry; he recalled wanting a drink back at the spring. He paused to catch his breath and made a mental note to tell Carson where he could send a telegram the next time he got a hankerin'.

Continuing on, he passed several large rock shelters, all empty. The one where he and Ellie had found

Benjamin's silver buckle was at the far end of the cliffs, to the other side of the cleft where he had evaded Holt Rainey.

All around him were the markings of ancient man. The drawings of buffalo and turkey were obvious, but others he could only guess at. There must be dozens of outlines of various-sized hands—passing humans saying "I was here," each in his own unique way.

He wondered what sign he would leave in this place . . . and Ellie. Already he'd killed one man on these rocks, so his handprint would be bloody. Would he kill again? Would he be killed? Had men before them swarmed over these cliffs with clubs and arrows and knives, intent on extinguishing the lives of fellow men?

Kale shook his head to clear away these unwanted thoughts, forerunners of guilt and emotion. He had come here to save a life, he reminded himself. If evil men died in the process, it was their own doing.

Finally he came to the draw where Holt had surprised him earlier. Making up his mind not to get caught again, he took his time before striking out across it. A little further he rounded the bend in the river. Here he was forced by a wall to lower himself. He picked his way among the rocks at the base of the cliff.

The hairs along his neck fairly prickled. Where were Newt and Holt? And Costello?

Then, not ten yards in front of him, he saw the place he hunted. And she had left him a sign—her boots on the ledge below the rock shelter. He suppressed a shudder, recalling how, when they'd climbed this cliff together, she'd tucked her boots into her backpack and carried them to the cave.

She'd left her boots for him to find, she was depending on him . . . and by everything holy, he would not let her down.

At the point where he stood, the cliff had another break in it, although he couldn't tell how deep it went. He took a couple of steps back, looked up to get his bearings, and was instantly blinded by the afternoon sun, which had now reached the crest of the hill.

Instinctively, he stepped in close to the rocks. In his head he pictured a bead drawn from the top of this cleft to Ellie's boots. His breath caught in his throat.

Someone was up there . . . he hadn't seen sign, yet he knew. The setup was perfect, a surefire trap: bait to draw the victim, the sun to blind him. Even if he got off a shot, it would be neither fast enough nor accurate enough to do any harm.

Someone sat at the top of the hill waiting for him to come along and pick up Ellie's boots, he'd bet his life on it.

He leaned back against the wall, his heart pounding. A close call for sure. Whoever was up there had deliberately set this trap and planned to shoot him on sight . . . in the back. Costello? Newt? He couldn't rule out Holt Rainey, either. Although the man was hunting a showdown, his pride might be so wounded by now that he'd settle for an old-fashioned murder.

Quickly Kale ran through his inventory of possible moves. Only one appeared practical: retrace his steps, climb the cliff at the first opportunity, and try to circle around behind the man on top.

He saw one drawback to this plan: two other men prowled these cliffs, and they were also gunning for him.

Moving as quickly as the terrain would allow, he retraced his steps for fifty yards or so until he came to a place which looked possible—not the cinch he'd like, but possible. He started up, hand over hand, testing every hold before he trusted the weight of his body to it.

Reaching the crest, he chinned himself up and peered around in all directions, half expecting a fusillade of bullets to decapitate him. His climb appeared not to have attracted any unwanted attention.

A second later he had scrambled up and taken cover behind a live oak thicket. Then, moving quietly from cover to cover, he made his way to a position even with the point where he expected the gunman to be waiting.

About this time he wished mightily for his rifle which lay back in that draw. Now he would have to get close enough to use a six-shooter, while his assailant would be able to use a rifle with ease.

The ground dipped, then swelled to the point. Kale crouched behind an agrita bush in the dip. He could barely see the man's hat from here. Cover between them was scarce.

With a quick look around to be sure they were alone, he stepped suddenly into the clearing and called the man's name.

"Newt . . . throw down that gun and turn around. I don't want to have to shoot you."

The man on the hill turned toward the sun, aiming his rifle as he did so, and Kale fired. He stepped to the side and fired again.

Newt's knees buckled and his rifle fell from his hands. "Damn you, Jarrett. I had you dead-to-rights." He pitched face forward to the ground.

Kale thumbed shells into the chamber of his Colt. "I had to do it, Newt. You were too good with the sun at your back." *And wasn't this what you planned for me?*

370

* * *

Ellie lay still on the cold floor of the rock shelter, pain and despair her only companions. The bodice of her riding habit fell tattered and torn across her body, victim to Armando Costello's knife.

She lay quietly near the place where she was convinced Benjamin had been murdered, grief growing inside her like a tumor. "I want to live," she cried through the cloth which gagged her. "I want to live, to live."

As she said the words, a fierce determination to survive began to take hold of her, determination to defeat Costello's evil plan. To get away from these cliffs. To see Armando Costello punished for his evil deeds.

But she knew the will to live was not enough. She couldn't depend on anyone to save her. She would have to do that for herself.

She struggled with the ropes that bound her hands. Every movement brought pain to her ankle, pain so intense that her body became clammy and cold; waves of blackness pulsated through her brain. But her will was strong, and she was determined not to lose consciousness.

Glancing around the shelter, she tried to formulate a plan. Remnants of a rock midden, used by ancient people to cook meat and to warm a shelter during cold months, stood in the center of the space. If she could get loose— *when* she got loose—she would take one of those soot-blackened rocks, she would hide beside the entrance, and she would attack him from the rear as he entered the shelter.

Quickly she looked around again, this time for something to use as a crutch. If worse came to worst, she could prop herself against the wall of the cave. The force of the blow would knock her down, but she would have to fell him with one strike anyway. Armando Costello would hardly give her a second chance.

She rested in her struggle with the ropes, giving in for a moment to the pain in her ankle. Perspiration covered her cold body. She fought to keep her stomach calm and her head from swimming.

By sheer willpower she forced her mind away from the fate Costello had planned for her. Several times his crude threat returned to taunt her, but she shoved it behind a wall in her mind and worked harder. She must keep hope in her heart; she must beat Costello and see him punished.

The gunshot came to her muffled by layers of limestone, but she recognized it nonetheless. Her heart stood still, waiting. Then two more shots echoed almost in unison, as from some distant place.

She struggled frantically with the ropes, but now they seemed even tighter than before, and her fingers could do no good. Her hands had already begun to swell.

Panic swept over her; her trembling turned to shivering, then to deep, soul-wrenching sobs that wracked her body and blackened her mind. Gradually unconsciousness swept her thoughts away.

Sometime later she opened her eyes to find a man standing above her.

"That damned gambler thought he could hide you out up here all for hisself, but I found you, anyhow." Holt Rainey's voice carried a note of triumph. He dangled her boots in front of her.

She squeezed her eyes tight in a futile effort to close out that smirking face. He continued.

"Ain't seen hide nor hair of that gambler, but Saint done got your man."

She gasped. Could he mean Kale?

"An' I got you. Now, ain't you the lucky one?" He looked at her more closely and laughed. "Seems that gambler done started my work for me. All trussed and scored. I ain't never had no woman who was all tied up before."

She knew what he wanted and that he would take it. What could she do to defend herself? And what difference did it make now?

If Holt left her alive, Armando would surely return later and kill her. But she knew what he would do first. She'd seen it in his eyes. His calling her "whore" had stopped hurting days ago.

Tears flowed down her cheeks and spilled to the floor. Why could they not let her die with a measure of dignity?

The echo of two gunshots filled the silent cave.

Holt froze momentarily, then relaxed, apparently having satisfied his warped mind as to the only explanation.

"Well, little lady, sounds like Newt just saved you from the gambler." He leaned forward as he spoke, reaching for her shoulders.

When he touched her, she rolled into his legs, throwing him off balance. He toppled over her, landing on all fours, his body straddling hers.

"Whoa, hoss," he called, "that ain't the way we play this game." He crawled around, trying to position himself over her body while she rocked back and forth beneath him. "You hold still now, so we can get on with our business. They tell me you looked mighty fetchin' in ol' Poppy's dress. Wonder, do you know the same tricks to satisfy my appetite?" The way he accentuated the word *appetite* caused Ellie's skin to crawl.

His knees on either side of her hips, he began to fumble with his own clothing. "I'm gonna give you a ride like that dirt farmer never dreamed of."

They heard the noise outside at the same time—boots scraping against rock, climbing up the wall.

Holt paused in his attempts to undress. "That's ol' Newt. He'll want a piece of this action hisself. He . . ." His words faded; a puzzled look crossed his face. "How'd you reckon he knew where to find me?"

The footsteps came closer.

Holt stared at Ellie's boots lying on the cave floor where he had dropped them. He found this place because her boots were on the ledge. How in hell—? His eyes darted to the mouth of the cave, then back to Ellie.

"Sit tight a minute, darlin'." He struggled up. Tugging at his breeches, he crossed the room and flattened himself against the wall, muttering out loud.

"I'll make sure, that's all. Holt Rainey ain't no fool. I'll make sure."

Kale took a long look at the rock wall in front of him. This had to be the place. But the boots were gone. He passed it twice looking for Ellie's boots, thinking perhaps some other path resembled the one to the cave where he and Ellie had gone that day.

But there was no other place, so he started to climb the cliff, knowing there was only half a chance she was still at the top. Costello had probably gotten her away from here when the shooting heated up. It would take but a minute to look, though, and Kale knew he couldn't strike out on their trail without being sure.

374

He climbed as quietly as possible, anticipating a shot in the back, or even one from above. If Costello was still around, Kale could find himself walking into a hornets' nest.

The whereabouts of Holt Rainey worried him. He'd seen no sign of the man since early afternoon, and he was sure Rainey was smarting from the effects of their last encounter. A man with wounded pride could be as mean as an injured grizzly, given the chance.

At the top of the cliff, Kale pulled himself up and took a moment to catch his breath and flex his fingers. With Newt's saddlegun slung across his back, he unhooked the leather thong on his six-shooter.

Then he stepped around the corner into the cave, and Holt Rainey was waiting for him.

On occasion Kale had given thought to the end of his life—his last moment on earth. And it had always been violent, going out in a blaze of bullets, or whatever those dime novels called it. But in his dreams, the flying bullets had been his own as well as the other fellow's. The other man paid the price along with him.

So here it was, here stood Holt Rainey, ready and able to blow him to kingdom come. Only that's where any resemblance to daydreams stopped.

This time was real—for life or death. And this time Kale found himself hog-tied.

His glance about the cave had taken in Ellie, and he could see she was in trouble. Blind fury surged through him at the sight of her bound and gagged like that. Her wide eyes full of fear, she wormed herself away from behind Holt. Thank God she was alive, but he knew she wouldn't be for long if he cut loose and started shooting.

Slivers of limestone and ricocheting bullets could cut her to doll rags, when he had come to save her life. He'd sooner face Costello's Bowie knife in these close quarters.

Holt's light-colored shirt, the front part running down his middle between the edges of his black coat, glared at Kale against the darkened backdrop of the cave. The man stood straight, fearless, legs braced, arms dangling by his side, loose and ready.

"What took you so long?" Holt demanded.

"Had a couple of matters to take care of," Kale answered, staring at the streak of light down the front of Rainey's body. Three buttons down. Two inches to the left. Holt spoke again.

"Only a couple?" At Ellie's scooting around, Holt sneered. He pierced Kale with cool gray eyes as he addressed her. "Hold on a bit, darlin', while I finish off this dirt farmer. Then I'll come tickle your fanny."

Concentrate, Kale cautioned himself. Go for the body. Let the body absorb the bullets. That way there would be no rock splinters.

"Two down, two to go," Kale replied. He stood still, relaxed, wanting to blow the blustering self-styled cowman to kingdom come, waiting for Holt to make the first move. His arms felt light, his head clear, but his heart was clenched as tight as a fighter's fist.

Holt sneered. "Ain't no lowdown dirt farmer who calls hisself a gunfighter gonna outdraw a Texas cowman."

Holt's shirt glowed in the near darkness. Kale knew he offered a perfect target, standing in the mouth of the cave as he did, silhouetted against the sky.

"A lowdown varmint who calls himself a Texas cowman," Kale challenged quietly. His words seemed somehow detached from his body.

Then Holt moved and Kale came to life.

He felt the Colt buck in his hand. As soon as he shot, he

376

lunged to the right, going down on one knee. His hat flew off. A bullet grazed his left cheek. Rock spit up in his face, throwing dust into his eyes.

He heard choking, a moan, the thud of Holt's body hitting the floor. Then nothing.

Kale kicked away the man's guns and rolled him over. His breathing had already stopped. Kale's had just started.

Then he was by Ellie's side, holding her, soothing her. He felt her tears hot against his cheek. He fumbled with the knot behind her head, finally managing to remove the gag from her mouth.

Her lips trembled. He covered them with his own. Tenderly. Urgently. Desperately. Then he kissed the tears from her cheeks, her eyes.

"Ellie, Ellie . . . God, I was so afraid. So afraid." He ran his fingers through her hair, clasped her head in his palms, pressed her face to his chest, to his beating heart, rejoicing in her life—not mourning her death.

Or his. They were alive.

Finally, he held her back to untie her hands. She sat limp, scarcely breathing. But her body trembled in his grasp. "Here." Quickly he removed his shirt and slipped it over her shredded bodice. "One dirty shirt."

When he tried to untie the ropes on her legs, she winced and he stopped immediately. "What is it, honey?"

"I think my leg is broken."

As gently as possible he finished untying the rope that bound her ankles together. Her flesh was extended, he could tell that by feel. "How did it happen?"

"I fell trying to push Armando off the ledge," she answered in a tired, listless voice.

377

Drawing her near, he wrapped his arms around her in a protective fashion, as though to shield her from desperate memories. "Where is he?"

She stiffened at the question. "I thought—the shots?"

"Newt and Saint."

At his reply, she began to tremble. "I thought—"

"Shhh . . ." He placed a finger on her parched lips, then kissed them softly. "I'll find him."

"No," she pleaded. "No. Please. He'll kill you."

"The others didn't," he responded with a confidence he did not feel. Everyone's luck ran out sometime. And he didn't need a genie to tell him he had used up a bunch of his this afternoon. He prayed his winning streak would hold until he got Ellie home.

Suddenly he was tired. Bone tired. Tired of shooting and being shot at. Tired of killing. He wished Costello would go away. Better yet, he wished the man had never existed.

But that was not the case. He had a job to do. Ellie clung to him.

"He said he would kill you, then he would come back and—" Her voice broke and her trembling increased. He knew the end of that sentence without another word being spoken.

Drawing her close to him again, he spoke softly into her hair. "I'll move you over there behind that boulder, where you can see anyone who climbs onto the ledge before he can see you." He thumbed shells into the two pistols he had taken from Holt's body and handed the guns to Ellie.

"Will you use them?"

She nodded.

"I'll see to your leg when I return. And I'll bring food

and water. How does that sound?"

She nodded again.

Kale scooped her up gently in his arms and carried her to a spot behind the boulder, past Holt's fallen body. "Keep your eyes on the ledge," he told her. "Shoot as soon as you see a head."

He reloaded his own gun then and climbed down the cliff to find the last of their assailants. He hoped his luck held. For at least a few minutes more.

Chapter Eighteen

After leaving Ellie in the rock shelter, Armando Costello went directly to his horse. Their fight and his subsequent near-fall from the cliff had taken its toll. He was physically and emotionally drained.

He drank long from his canteen, then poured the remaining water over his scratched face and torn shoulder.

That whore! He never imagined she would try to harm him. But she had actually intended to kill him, to push him off the cliff. She would pay for that!

First, however, he must find Kale Jarrett—find him and kill him. Costello's thoughts were filled with bitterness. Why must he always fight so hard for what rightfully belonged to him?

He sat in the shade and rolled himself a cigarette, trying to figure out a way to finagle Jarrett into a trap. He told himself he wasn't afraid of the gunfighter. But no one was going to keep him from his treasure. He was too close this time.

Besides, he would save valuable time by drawing

Jarrett into a trap and taking him with his Bowie knife.
Using his knife, the act could be accomplished with the
speed of a bolt of lightning.

Face to face there would be talking, and he recalled
how well Jarrett had handled himself in such con-
frontations. Costello considered himself intellectually
superior to most men, certainly to this unread gunfighter. Still, why take unnecessary chances?

Armando Costello admitted to being less than proficient with handguns. The knife was his weapon. Letting
his cigarette dangle from his lips, he unsheathed his
Bowie knife and felt the edge reassuringly. He took
pleasure in the fine, tempered steel, the highly polished
brass handguard, the stock of carved walnut which felt as
if it had been molded to his own hand.

Costello grinned at the swath his blade had cut across
Texas and Mexico. The graves were unnumbered in his
mind; the method was not. Except in rare instances, the
knife had entered the victims' bodies between the
shoulder blades.

He would set a trap and take Jarrett with his blade. He
wouldn't give the gunfighter a chance to draw on him.
Jarrett was a fair hand with a gun, he'd give him that, but
little good it would do him this time.

Another thing that bothered Costello about Jarrett was
the gunfighter's unlimited self-confidence. Costello
shied away from men with too much self-confidence.
Somehow, they always managed to undermine his own.

Kale Jarrett was not afraid of the devil himself.
Costello saw that the night they searched for the
intruders who returned Benjamin's horse to the ranch.
Jarrett had showed so much enthusiasm then that
Costello had feared Abe and Martin, whom he paid

generously to bring the puddin'-foot to the ranch, would be unable to elude him.

The gunshot shattered his thoughts and shredded his already frayed nerves. He jumped to his feet, ground out the cigarette with the toe of his boot, and looked around him in terror.

That whore! She couldn't have gotten a gun and killed herself. Of course not, she was tied. But Jarrett would hardly kill her, either.

Two more shots rent the air—and Costello's senses.

Then he recalled the shooting back in the canyon. The Circle R men? He hadn't realized the Raineys would go to such lengths to ensure their claim to Jarrett's ranch.

Did Matt and Holt Rainey know about the treasure? Were they even now taking it, while Costello was off on this fool's journey.

It hadn't begun as a fool's trip. He'd planned it well— he'd bring the woman here and kill her where nothing could link him to her death or Benjamin's.

But Abe and Martin were supposed to have taken care of Jarrett. They had failed, it seemed, and his plan began to unravel. Now, the Raineys were after his treasure!

But wait. Were not the Circle R men after Jarrett and the woman, also? Why not let them have at each other? The woman was out of commission, and Jarrett was only one man among several. Certainly the Circle R outfit could take him.

Why not leave Jarrett and the whore to them and head back to the ranch right now? That way he could retrieve his treasure before the Raineys located it.

They could have the ranch and were welcome to it, but he'd be damned if they were going to touch that treasure.

Armando Costello was considerably bolstered by the

way things were shaping up . . . in his favor, just as he always knew they would.

He saddled his horse and made his way around behind the cliffs. He'd find a place to cross the river farther north, where he could get away undetected.

Coming out in the thicket beside the spring, he was startled to see three Circle R horses. He had supposed them to be behind him, nearer where he'd staked his own horses.

A nagging thought took hold of Costello then—the idea that maybe he should hang around and be sure they killed Kale Jarrett. If that gunfighter got away from here, Costello knew he would dog his trail the rest of his life.

So Costello got down and inspected the spring area. He found Saint lying facedown in the mud along the bank of the river. Turning the body over, he stared at the one bullethole in the man's forehead; his mind struggled to sort out the message.

He wiped his hands on the seat of his pants and looked anxiously toward the cliffs. He could not let the Raineys get his treasure, but neither could he afford to have Jarrett after him.

That was crazy, he told himself. There were three Circle R horses, leaving two men out there gunning for Jarrett. The odds were two to one. One of those gunmen would get the gunfighter. Kale Jarrett was not invincible.

But what if they didn't? Costello shook his head to clear the fog. What was he thinking of? He had a plan, and he would use it. Those shots had momentarily confused him, but now he was back on track.

Hadn't he left Ellie's boots where she'd dropped them at the base of the cliff for a purpose? As bait for Jarrett? He hurried along the bottom ledge to a niche he had chosen in his mind.

It was a secluded place etched into the side of the cliff from where he could watch the pathway to the cave; it would afford him one perfect strike at Kale Jarrett's back with his Bowie knife.

Costello paused long enough to roll another cigarette, then hurried on. He could feel apprehension building steadily within himself. What if Jarrett had already found the boots and climbed the cliff? If that had happened he would have lost his chance.

Costello's heart raced as he hastened to the other end of the cliffs. His eyes darted here and there. He must remain alert, yet he found it more and more difficult to concentrate. He had lost valuable time. That shot confused him. There were so many things to consider now.

He stopped abruptly when he came to the place where he and Ellie had climbed the cliff. The boots were gone! Jarrett was already in the cave. His head swirled with dizzy thoughts. His breath came in spurts.

He won't defeat me, he told himself . . . *he won't defeat me.* Costello kept repeating the phrase, and a calming thought came to him. *He can't stay up there forever. When he comes down, I'll get him.*

With that decided, Costello climbed into his hole in the wall to wait.

Sweat stung his eyes. His clothes were stiff with dirt and grime. His hands were raw from climbing the rocks, and his fingernails were ragged and caked with dirt.

Costello had been as filthy many times before, but he had never learned to like it. This time it was especially infuriating, because by rights he should already have the treasure and be on his way to a life of luxury. Instead, here he was on this Godforsaken hillside—

Several shots rang out directly above him. Now, who the hell—? He stared at the path he'd expected Kale Jarrett to descend, at the empty spot where the boots had been.

Who was up there? Was someone else with that whore? Or had Jarrett been there and left?

Costello gripped the handle of his Bowie knife. His palms were wet. He wiped them on his pants, one by one. His hands were trembling; he trembled all over.

A simple fact dawned slowly but with certainty in his brain—he did not want to meet up with Kale Jarrett after the gunfighter saw that whore bound and gagged, her dress torn . . .

Those shots? Perhaps Jarrett was dead already, but what if he wasn't? He'd come back to this cliff, to the woman.

Then Costello entertained another disturbing thought. Suppose Jarrett had never seen those boots—did not know about this place. It'd take him a long time to find the whore without any clues as to where to look.

And what was he to do in the meantime? Stay here and wait for his chance, while the Raineys got closer to his treasure?

Costello dried his shaking hands again and stared at them in disgust. If Jarrett showed up now, how accurate would his aim be with these trembling hands? What were his chances of getting Jarrett now?

Suddenly Costello realized he had no chances to give away. He was playing for the highest stakes of his life. To miss meant certain death at the hands of Kale Jarrett.

Armando Costello did not want to die here in this wilderness. He had places to go, women to have, treasures to spend before his life was done.

He must get away. He must get to the treasure, take it, and be gone.

The decision made, he raced for his horse. He gritted his teeth the whole way, expecting bullets to rip through his body with every step.

He reasoned that this was the only sensible move to make. Let them kill themselves . . . he'd have the treasure and be halfway to Mexico before the survivors, if there were any, could get back to Summer Valley.

If Kale Jarrett managed to survive, he wouldn't leave without that whore. And it'd take him time to locate her, more time to get her down the hill with her injured leg. Costello would have more than enough time to escape.

And if Jarrett tried to track him, the gunfighter would find himself out of luck. Changing a name was a simple matter—hadn't he already changed his name so many times he'd almost forgotten the one blessed by the priest?

His heart still raced within his breast, but his hands were steadying. He reached his horse and knew he'd made the right decision. It was simple, really; let them fight it out among themselves while he retrieved his treasure.

By the time Armando Costello rode away from the painted cliffs on the Concho River, he already felt like a new man—a rich man.

Once Kale located the live oak thicket where Costello staked his horses, he had no trouble reading the sign.

Ellie's horse and the packhorse remained staked, but all the provisions and Costello's Morgan were gone.

To the ranch, Kale surmised, in answer to his own question about the gambler's destination . . . to find the treasure and be long gone before anyone could catch up with him. A nagging thought vied for his attention—the idea that Costello could be lurking about, waiting for darkness, when he could strike unseen at any survivors.

Riding Ellie's horse, Kale tracked Costello past his own mount to where the gambler had crossed the river. He'd watered at the spring, and his tracks in the silt showed where he rolled Saint's body over, likely examining the bullethole in the man's skull.

Kale buried Newt and Saint in the trees back of the creek, because the ground was softer there and he was tired. Holt Rainey he would take home to his brother, expecting no thanks for the trouble.

After watering the Circle R horses and his own, he picketed them in the thicket along with Ellie's horse and the pack animal. It was closer to the cave, and if a wild animal or renegade Indian—or Costello himself—tried to get to them during the night, he'd have a better chance of saving them.

The sun was sinking in the west by the time Kale got together a pack of kindling, grub, and water, and some clothing for himself and Ellie.

They would spend the night in the cave. He knew she would not take readily to the idea after all she'd been through up there, but he would rather not try to get her down that cliff by moonlight. It would be tricky enough come morning.

He called to her, then started up the cliff. When he reached the top, she stared at him with wide eyes and tearstained cheeks.

"Did you find him?"

He shook his head and handed her a canteen of water.

"He'll find us, then," she said. "He'll wait until dark, then he'll come after us."

Kale tried to assure her that her fears were unfounded. He told her about the tracks crossing the river. As he talked, he put together a small fire and made coffee.

"Will he be there when we get home?" she asked.

"I don't know, but I'll find him." Giving her a threadbare shirt he'd intended to use for rags, he took back his dirty one.

"When can we start home?"

"First thing in the morning," he replied. "Now, you sit tight, and I'm going to see to that leg." He handed her a cup of coffee. "Sorry I don't have anything stronger."

"You're safe. That's enough."

He stared at her then, long and tenderly. "I'm right here beside you, Ellie, where I'll always be."

He inspected her ankle. "Take a deep breath and yell as loud as you want," he told her. "I need to feel around a bit."

She clamped her teeth together, but he was gentle. Even through the searing pain when he moved her foot, she felt soothed and secure.

"I don't think it's broken," he said at last. "Likely a bad sprain. Your leg tied up like that didn't help matters. Increased the swelling." He bound her ankle correctly then, using strips he tore from a soft sack in which he sometimes carried food.

"How're you doing?"

She smiled. Fear still beat a bitter dirge through her veins. Hesitantly she ran her fingers along the healing scar on his head. "What happened?"

Kale shrugged. "Ran into a couple of hombres who had

389

it in for me."

Her fingers trembled against his face, and he clasped them in his hand.

"Armando said he paid Abe and Martin to kill you."

Kale winked, recalling all too clearly his meeting with Abe and Martin. "I don't kill easy."

When she sighed, her breath trembled from her lips. "Thank goodness for that."

"Here," he offered, refilling her cup. "Drink this while I take care of a few things." He went about the task of wrapping Rainey's body in a blanket from his bedroll. He rigged up a pulley system using his rope and the boulder on the ledge to lower Holt to the ledge below, climbing down after him.

"I'll be back." He left the body in the thicket with their horses. They wouldn't particularly like the company, but he couldn't leave that body up there where Ellie was going to sleep. He thought about her aversion to violence and knew this day and the days before it had not been easy for her.

With trembling hands he rolled a smoke and stood for a long time in the cool evening breeze, trying to quiet his nerves and get his thoughts off the deeds he had performed this day.

"An eye for an eye," the Good Book said. And weren't these men, whether directly or indirectly, guilty of Benjamin's death, of attempting to kill Ellie and himself? Yet even as he thought on it, he realized that this kind of thinking made of the world a vicious cycle of violence. He felt caught up in it against his will; he wanted desperately to get out, to find peace. At the same time, he knew at least one more act of violence likely awaited him.

Costello was out there someplace, and neither he nor

Ellie could rest easy until that evil man was brought to justice.

When he returned to the cave, Ellie was asleep. After making sure she was covered, he curled up next to her and cradled her in his arms, supporting, comforting, being himself supported and comforted. Holding Ellie he felt like a whole person again. He never wanted her any farther away than she was at this moment. In minutes he was fast asleep.

Next morning they headed out, Holt Rainey strapped across the back of the packhorse. Ellie rode with her leg in a sling he'd rigged up alongside the saddle so blood wouldn't pool in her ankle. She'd have to hold the saddle horn for balance, and he knew it would be a mighty uncomfortable way to ride.

"We'll stop often so you can rest," he assured her.

She shook her head. "I just want to get home."

She had spoken little this morning, and he worried about her. These past few weeks she'd been through more than a grown man could be expected to take. She seemed to be holding up well enough, but he knew she was filled brimful of pain—and fear.

Folks handled such difficulties in different ways. Some ranted and raved and beat their chests, while others kept quiet about it. He guessed that was what she was doing, keeping it to herself.

But that might not be good, either. He'd heard of folks going into shock over a lot less trouble than Ellie had seen. He remembered how his ma had quieted up after Pa had left. She'd never come out of it.

He didn't want that for Ellie, but he didn't know how to prevent it, either, except by treating her gently and getting her home as quick as possible.

They crossed the Concho River and headed southeast. Suddenly he thought of the stage road. If they could get to it, traveling would be a whole lot smoother. He might even be lucky enough to catch up with a stagecoach, which would be easier riding for Ellie.

When they stopped to rest a couple of hours later, he suggested it.

Her eyes widened. "I'm staying with you."

They nooned at Brady Creek. Kale fixed a thick soup of jerked meat, and Ellie ate what he gave her. But she was still awfully quiet, and it worried him.

"There's nothing to fear now, Ellie. It's over—for the most part."

She shook her head. "I'm not afraid for myself. It's just that—" Breaking off, she tried to shake the black feeling that enveloped her. "My life has been nothing but trouble. I brought down Benjamin, and now you. If we stay together, Kale, you're doomed—"

"Ellie, stop such nonsense. There isn't any such thing as a doomed life, especially one as young as yours. And even if it was," he paused to give her a knowing wink, "I'll tell you this right now, honey, you aren't getting rid of me."

Moving beside her, he took her in his arms, soothing, murmuring words, nonwords, humming lightly.

Her tears came then. He held her while she cried, sobbing as if her heart would break. Finally she cried herself to sleep.

He didn't rouse her for an hour or more. What did it matter how long they spent on the trail, if Ellie recovered her strength?

They hit the stage road after that and rode side by side, trailing the other horses. She talked of her life before

392

she met Benjamin, and later moving to the ranch with him. She told Kale about the death of her parents.

"When they were killed, I thought it was punishment for something I'd done wrong. I had that same feeling when you left the rock shelter to find Armando. My whole life came back to me then, and I felt as if I had brought death to Benjamin—and to you."

"That's nonsense, Ellie. You haven't done anything to bring down the wrath of God, far as I can see. Anyhow, He doesn't punish one person by destroying someone else. All of us make mistakes, some consciously, and some because of the cards life deals us, but if we keep plugging away at it, we can leave tracks worth following."

"I'm not sure I can," she said.

"I am, Ellie Jarrett." He turned the name over in his mind—Ellie Jarrett.

"I like the sound of that name," he told her.

She looked at him, saw his tentative smile.

"I like the way I feel when I say it," he added.

She returned his smile and saw his face brighten by degrees. "I like the way I feel when I look at you," she whispered.

He knew then she would be all right. Leaning across the space between their horses, he managed a quick kiss on her lips. "How's that?"

She grinned. "Wonderful."

He caressed her drawn face with his eyes. He could see the want for him return in her expression. "There's more where that came from."

"There'd better be," she teased softly.

By dusk her spirits and stamina had returned in good measure. Leaving the road, he found a campsite in a glade of live oaks where the creek made a wide-angle curve, running fuller over the rocks and around the roots of a cottonwood that grew nearby. The bank was rocky, but, he thought, you couldn't ask for everything.

He helped Ellie down, and while he spread their bedrolls back in the thicket, she hobbled around trying to unpack their gear to fix supper.

"Hold on there. You're my patient," he objected. "Sit on this pallet while I fix supper."

At his mention of her ankle, her eyes went to his leg. "You aren't getting around so well yourself."

"Me?" He feigned surprise.

She sighed. "Here I am, caught up in my own problems, and look at you—you've been limping all this time, and I just realized it. What happened?"

He hemmed and hawed, but in the end he told her the story of getting caught on top of that hill above the spring with no way down. He left out the emotional aspects as best he could.

"Let's just say," he finished, "that I decided to pick you a few grapes for jelly."

She carried the skillet to the fire he'd put together while he talked. "Since we're both stove up, I'll cook."

"I won't let you." He took the skillet from her hand and pecked a kiss to her lips. "Rest yourself, honey. You'll have plenty of chances to spoil me."

She hugged her arms about her chest. A feeling of relief began to seep into the awful void inside her where fear had resided for so many days now. A small whirlwind, like a ghost from the past, ruffled through the trees and stirred the water before setting down on the opposite bank in a dusty swirl.

Water pooled and eddied around roots on one side of the cottonwood tree, inviting, reminding her of how long it had been since she'd had a chance for anything more than to quickly wash her face and hands.

Suddenly she felt as if she couldn't bear it another moment. "If you want to do all the work, fine," she joked, "I'll retire to my chamber for a long, leisurely bath."

Kale glanced from her to the creek and back again. "I doubt it'll be leisurely or long this time of year—in that water. It looks to be about as cold as our creek."

"I know," she called, sticking her head around the trunk of the tree. She'd already begun pulling off her clothing. "I love it cold."

It took Kale about two minutes to make up his mind. Giving her time to settle into the water, he crept up to the other side of the tree, removed his own clothing, and stepped out into the creek.

"I brought you some soap."

She looked up, startled by his presence—his very nude presence. She gasped at the wound, red and ugly, that distorted his thigh. "Oh, Kale."

He knelt quickly. "The cold water'll do it good."

She watched his beloved body move toward her, and suddenly an intense longing caught in her throat—a longing to touch his body, to have him touch hers, to feel their skin each against the other, to feel his lips on hers, his body against her own, inside her own, filling her with pleasure and happiness and . . . life.

She held out her arms as though to a child. "It's warmer once you get all the way in . . ."

He came into her arms, his eyes merrily acknowledging the absolute truth in her statement.

". . . the water," she finished, just as his lips closed over hers.

Cushioned by the buoyancy of the cool spring, they lay on the smooth rocks, with the rough bark of the exposed tree root for a backrest. Water played over their heated skin, swirled gently in and around them as they strove to bring themselves closer and closer still.

Kale cupped her to him with an urgency he tried desperately to control. The cold water temporarily relieved his almost overpowering physical need to make love to her, but it did nothing to slow his racing heart.

Since the last time they made love his desire for her sweetness had grown, until even with their difficulties the last few days, he'd had no peace from the constant need to touch her body, to taste her body, to move into her body and travel that passionate road to glory together with her as one.

Since her experience with those two evil men—Lord knew what Costello and Holt Rainey had actually done to her—he'd hesitated even to touch her. She needed time to straighten things out in her mind, time to get herself back to normal. He'd worried over whether she would resist his intimacies. Now he rejoiced all the more at her eager invitation.

From the moment his lips touched hers, Ellie responded with the fervor born of their long separation, nurtured by the monstrous lie Armando Costello had told—that Kale was dead.

To have him now, alive and in her arms, proved as heady an aphrodisiac as his hands stroking her skin, his lips at her breast, coaxing life and desire from her body, filling her with a spiraling need she knew only he could satisfy. When she pressed herself to him, however, he drew back.

"Oh, your leg."

"My leg is well." He kissed her face. "Be careful of your ankle."

"My ankle's well."

He shook his head, grinning. "You just want me too much to feel the pain right now."

"Since you know so much about what I want," her lips whispered across his, "hurry up and give it to me."

Shifting himself he took up the soap he had left on the tree root. "Let me see," he lathered soap in his hands, ". . . a long, leisurely bath. Isn't that what you said?"

Although she protested that she had changed her mind, he began to bathe her all the same, first her hair, then her body, and his touch ignited them both as oil that had been spilled on water and set afire.

When the last soapsuds floated like fairy clouds down the creek, he set the soap aside and ran his hands over her clean body, pausing only when he came to the curly patch of hair that guarded their path to fulfillment as though it were the richest of mines.

And, indeed, he thought, it was. Loving Ellie and being loved by her in return was a treasure more valuable and real than any gem found beneath the earth or above it.

Uninhibited, her eyes held his, and she knew he could read the pleasure he inflicted upon her with his wanton assault. Merely looking on his face was enough to set her skin to prickling.

The intensity in his eyes disguised none of his own desire. His slightly parted lips invited her own, and when she reached toward him, letting her tongue play around the surface of his lips, she absorbed his wild tremor like a tree struck by lightning.

With her hand she traced his shoulder, then down his chest, letting water spray through her fingers as she reached beneath the surface, conscious only of an inexpressible need to draw him to her, to guide him inside her.

At her touch, her eyes darted to his.

He grinned. "I'm not like you, honey." Instead of withdrawing his own hand, he gripped her as he spoke, as though to emphasize his meaning. "We'll have to get out of this frigid water for me to be able to go on."

"Let's hurry, then," she whispered.

After they had dried themselves and slipped inside the bedroll, after he was buried deep inside her, she hugged him close and felt tears well in her eyes.

"Oh, Kale, this is perfect, the most perfect thing I've ever known in my life."

"Ummm . . ." he mumbled, carrying them to the crest of the mountain, where they experienced fireworks as if from the center of a volcano itself.

Afterward she snuggled against his chest and he held her tightly and had to agree that their lovemaking was as close to perfect as a man could get without dying and going to heaven.

The thought was sobering, for it called to mind the task awaiting him.

Armando Costello.

Kale tightened his arms around her and fell asleep with a new terror gnawing in his gut. He prayed this would not be the last time he made love to Ellie Jarrett.

Chapter Nineteen

They rode into Summer Valley a little after noon the following day. When Kale turned his mount toward the hill crowned by the Lady Bug Pleasure Emporium, Ellie objected.

"Let's go straight home."

He pursed his lips. He had waited until the last possible moment to reveal his plans, telling himself he didn't want to alarm her unnecessarily on the trail.

Another motive, he knew, was that he hadn't wanted to dispel the warmth between them. He figured what he had to say would be sure to provoke an argument.

And he hadn't been wrong, he discovered, when he replied to Ellie's objection. "I'm leaving you with Lavender—"

"What?"

"For a few days," he added quickly. "Your ankle—"

"My ankle is fine, Kale Jarrett."

"But—"

She fixed him with a stare he knew was meant to be stern. Her words distracted from it, however. "My ankle hasn't hampered our—"

His wicked grin stopped her. He winked. "I'll agree with that."

". . . our trip," she finished.

"Nor that, either."

"Then let's go home. Please."

He shook his head, wordlessly spurring his mount up the hill. She kept pace.

"I don't want to stay in town without you."

"And I don't want you to, honey." He drew rein in front of the Lady Bug. "But as things stand—"

"What things?" she interrupted.

He glanced down at her ankle, then shrugged.

"You mean Armando?"

He nodded. "Among others."

"You don't need to take Holt's body to the Circle R," she protested. "Send word for Matt to come fetch him."

"That isn't all." Taking her reins, he flipped them over her horse's head and tied both horses at the rail. After he'd done the same with the packhorses, he raised his arms to her. "Come here like a good girl. Swing your leg over so you won't hurt your ankle."

She glared at him. "Don't patronize me, Kale Jarrett. You may be able to coax me into your bed with syrup in your voice, but right now all you're apt to attract is ants."

He laughed, but the caress in his eyes was anything but a jest. "All right. Put on one of those silky dresses, crawl into bed, and wait for me. When I get back tonight, we'll see what I can coax from you."

She slid from the saddle into his arms, clasped hers about his neck, and covered his lips with her own. He returned her kiss, eager to have her alone, though not at all eager for what lay ahead of him this day.

400

"You think Armando is at the ranch?"

"Maybe so," he mused, quickly changing the topic. "I can't get enough of you." His lips caressed hers.

Suddenly the door to the Lady Bug opened and a group of twittering women descended the steps, breaking the magical silence.

"Ellie, baby, I'm so thankful you're safe. We never should have trusted that damned Costello."

"Is he here?" Kale asked.

Lavender shook her head. "He hasn't been back since he left with Ellie."

"What about his two men?" he asked.

"Haven't seen them since they rode out with you," she told Ellie.

Kale frowned, and Ellie explained. "Armando promised Lavender that Abe and Martin would ride to the cliffs with us. They parted ways at the Celery Creek trail. I was glad—"

Poppy's shriek interrupted her.

"That's Holt. He's dead."

Briefly Kale explained, with Ellie filling in details he omitted which she thought pertinent but he did not—such as how Kale dispatched the two killers Matt Rainey sent after them, then saved her from Holt.

"He was such a handsome man," Poppy sighed.

"And sorry," Lavender added. "Holt Rainey was as sorry as the day is long."

"He's been asking for this for a long time," Snake said.

Lavender sized Kale up, her expression approving. "Guess he asked the wrong man."

Kale had carried Ellie to the porch while they talked. At Lavender's words, he stood her down and squeezed her to his side. His stomach still did flipflops recalling the

401

situation in which Holt Rainey got himself shot, the ugly manner in which the man had treated Ellie. "Guess he asked the wrong way," he muttered.

"We'll leave him at the undertaker's and send word to Matt at the Circle R," Ellie said.

"No need," Lavender replied. Kale and Ellie watched her inhale a deep breath before continuing. "Matt has moved into your house, Ellie. A couple of his men rode into town yesterday for supplies. Rainey's taken over your range."

"That bastard!" Ellie exploded. "I won't allow such a thing. I'm going out there myself and move him off."

In the end Kale won by appealing to her good sense.

"Then you don't go, either," she pleaded. "Kale, I know I've always told you I couldn't leave the ranch. But that's no longer true. Nothing is true, except—except that I couldn't bear to lose you. I don't care where I live, as long as it's with you."

"You'll be with me, honey . . . I guarantee that."

But after he rode away from the Lady Bug, having gained Lavender's assurance that she'd feed Ellie and put her to bed for a day of much-needed rest, he wondered how in the world he intended to get out of this one.

At the bottom of the hill he turned toward the telegraph office, where he picked up his wires and read them on the way to the ranch.

They took his mind off the mechanics of what lay ahead, even though the one relating to Armando Costello came a bit late to be of any use, other than confirming what they had already discovered the hard way. Brady wired that the description of the man fit an unsavory character who went by a number of aliases and was suspected of having been involved in a couple of murders along the waterfront.

"Ride shy of him," Brady advised.

Nothing he'd like better, Kale thought. But from the sound of things, folks had been riding shy of Armando Costello too long already. It was time somebody met him face to face, called his hand. Maybe it would keep someone else from ending up in an early grave.

Briefly Kale allowed himself to wish it were someone else who'd drawn the hole card on this one. Someone else who would have to face down the gambler.

But it wasn't. He had drawn the card, and he would play the hand. No belly-achin'.

Gabe, the telegraph operator, had added his warning to Lavender's concerning Matt Rainey's presence at the ranch. Short-lived presence, Kale thought, what with the telegram proving Benjamin's ownership riding safely in his saddlebags. It'd had quite a journey, that telegram, beginning with the night Ellie had run away to the Lady Bug, the night that had set into motion the nightmare just past.

And the confrontation ahead.

"How many men d'you think he has?" Kale inquired.

Gabe shrugged. "Can't rightly say, of course, but couldn't be many. There ain't many of 'em left. To hear folks tell, Ira and Till are men to ride with. They've been with Matt since the beginning."

Kale knew what that meant. They rode for the brand, and they'd stick by the boss through bad times and good. Mostly, their kind didn't question whether their orders were right or wrong. They depended on the boss to be responsible for the morality of the outfit. But would they go so far as murder?

"He's got some judge from down in Llano County on

his side," Gabe added.

"What's the judge's hand in this draw?" Kale inquired.

"Can't say," Gabe admitted. "I do know he spends as much time in that buckboard of his as he does holding court. Matter of fact," he paused to stroke his grizzled face, then continued, "I seen that jackrabbit headin' out your way not long after you rode into town this morning."

The two men shook hands, and Kale turned to go. Then he called back, "What about Armando Costello?"

"The gambler? Ain't seen him around for days. Figure he finally made enough to take out for Frisco."

One bit of good news along with the other kind was a telegram from Fort Griffin. The soldier was out of the woods and the army had quit making noise about locating the cowpoke who roughed him up.

On his ride to the ranch, Kale turned over in his mind the information he'd gathered so far. He was uncertain what to expect from Rainey, but the telegram from the State should wrap things up.

He wondered how Matt Rainey would see things now, confronted with the death of his own brother. Kale knew how that felt firsthand, and he pondered how to go about breaking the news. How did you tell a man you'd shot down his brother?

To be sure, Matt should have been expecting as much. Any fool could see Holt was likely to wind up on the wrong end of a bullet. But truth was not always an easy thing to see by the man closest to it.

Especially a man like Matt Rainey. Kale didn't want to have to kill Matt, too. He was sick of all this killing, but if push came to shove, he'd be ready.

Sitting atop the hill that overlooked the valley, he felt a wave of sadness envelope him. Greed had robbed his own brother of his life. Contrary to Holt Rainey's chosen path, Benjamin Jarrett had been a decent, law-abiding citizen.

Kale's mind drifted over the showdown he faced below while his eyes took in every inch of the valley. The apparent peace was deceiving, for he knew this valley was a cauldron that could boil over without an instant's warning.

He dreaded what lay ahead, whether it was to be measured in hours or days. And it wouldn't stop with sending Matt Rainey packing back to the Circle R. After that, he had another miscreant to deal with; he had to find and stop Armando Costello.

When the time came to face Costello, Kale knew it would be no-holds-barred, and he dared not let Costello get the upper hand. He must take the fight to the gambler.

Kale nudged the bay and started down the hill, following the path of fresh buckboard tracks. It appeared they had company; recalling his earlier conversation with the telegraph operator, he had a pretty good idea who it was. By now that judge had likely filled Matt in on their return from the painted cliffs, the empty saddles on the horses he led, and the one full one.

Suddenly he spurred his mount and raced down the hill, drawing up abruptly in front of the house. Matt and another man came to stand on the porch. Ellie's porch. Matt Rainey cradled a shotgun in his arms.

"That's far enough, Jarrett," the big man bellowed. "You're trespassing on private property. And if what Judge Cranston here tells me is true, I'm placing you under citizen's arrest for the murder of my brother and

405

two of my employees."

"You're wrong on all counts, Rainey." Kale swung his leg behind his saddle, preparing to dismount.

"Hold it right there," Rainey ordered. "Throw down those handguns, then come around here nice and slow-like."

Kale paused to consider the situation.

"Before you use that shotgun, Rainey, you'd best hear me out. Newt and Saint are buried up at the painted cliffs. I killed them; I buried them." As he spoke, Kale finished dismounting. He stepped around his horse to face Rainey, careful to keep his hands clear of his gun.

"You lost a brother, and I'm sorry for you. I know how that feels. But you know as well as I do that Holt came gunning for me. I shot him while defending myself." He stared frankly into the older man's glowering eyes. "And while protecting my brother's widow."

Rainey cocked the shotgun, and Kale went for his gun. But the judge placed a restraining hand on Matt's arm. Kale froze in mid-action, speaking.

"I don't want to shoot you, Rainey. You've done a lot of good for this country, and there's more to be done. If you get off your high horse, you can help. Right now you're trespassing on my sister-in-law's ranch."

"The hell I am," Rainey sputtered.

With the slowest of motions, Kale removed the telegrams from his pocket and handed one of them to Judge Cranston, who scanned it with a scowl.

"Damn it, Matt, he's right. Jarrett *did* file on this land after all."

Matt raged. His face became scarlet. He huffed and snorted until Kale wouldn't have been surprised to see smoke coming from the man's nostrils. Kale spoke again.

"Mrs. Jarrett will be returning home as soon as she recovers from the ordeal you and others put her through. At that time she will make the decision whether to press criminal charges against both of you."

Rainey continued to rage and fume, but no coherent words came forth. Defeat came swiftly, then, like a sharp instrument puncturing his pride and his dreams of grandeur.

Kale stood perfectly still, awed by the destruction of a human mind which he witnessed before him. When he spoke, he directed his speech to Judge Cranston. Matt Rainey stared vacantly at the body of his brother, apparently unable to comprehend how his world could have crumbled so quickly.

"She will hold Rainey accountable for any destruction of property which occurred during her absence, as well as for any missing livestock."

Cranston nodded wordlessly and led the larger man down the steps. While they made their way to the buckboard, Kale tied the three Circle R horses to its tailgate. One carried the body of Holt Rainey.

After helping Matt onto the seat, the judge flicked the reins and turned the team toward the town road.

Kale removed his hat and wiped his brow with his sleeve. He'd expected something different, he conceded. He wasn't sure what, but different.

He supposed every man had his limits. And Matt Rainey had been tottering on the brink of his for a spell now. No one in the valley had any respect left for him, yet Kale found himself pitying the man. Why, he couldn't say. If the tables were turned, he would certainly receive none, nor would he expect to.

As Rainey and Cranston drove off, Ira and Till came

around the corner of the house from the pens. When Kale explained the situation, they agreed to return and help him with the branded cattle. First, however, they must see to the needs of their boss, for they rode for the Circle R.

In the house Kale found things pretty much the way Ellie had left them. He walked through each room, imagining her here now, longing to have her beside him.

When he reached the spare room, he stared long at the bed they had shared, then turned his attention to the trapdoor beneath it.

Where was Armando Costello? Was he below this floor even now? For an instant Kale wondered whether he might be mistaken about the treasure. He moved the bed and tarp and tugged at the trapdoor.

He stared in disbelief. The entire entrance to the tunnel, which he had crawled through only days earlier, was now filled with fallen rock and debris.

He studied the debris-filled opening. Costello had surely been here, but where was he now?

Whether intentional or not, and Kale was now of the mind that everything Costello did was well thought out, it was a clever idea. Say he closed off access to the tunnel at this end—then he could come and go as he pleased from the other end. With the right timing, any sounds he made extracting the treasure would be covered by the branding and other ranching activities Rainey had going on above ground.

Kale eased the trapdoor back in place. From a rear window he studied the area between the house and creek. Although he could see no indication of it, he knew the opening to the tunnel had to be somewhere near the creek.

Everything he recalled hearing about the tunnel was vague. No one had ever said exactly where it led, only that it had been dug as an escape route from the house in case of Indian attack.

After a cursory search of the creek bottom turned up no clues, Kale decided it would be better for his health if he retreated and planned his attack. No sense sending Costello an engraved invitation to use his back for target practice.

Also, it was getting close to dark, and he had made a promise to Ellie. If he was to get back to her before midnight, he'd best get a move on.

He could look for Costello tomorrow.

Or could he? The man surely wouldn't tarry any longer than necessary. By tomorrow any trail he left could be cold. And neither he nor Ellie would be safe until Costello was apprehended. Now that they could finger him for killing Benjamin, Costello couldn't leave them alive.

Pulled by his promise to Ellie, as well as by his own heightening aversion to this confrontation, Kale walked out on the porch. He wanted nothing more than to climb aboard the bay and head to town—to the Lady Bug and Ellie.

But something equally strong fought against his leaving, compelled him to hang around a bit longer.

Instinct. He recognized it. His old friend. That thing folks called instinct had saved his bacon many a time.

Right now it was telling him to stay put, act natural, and see what fell into place.

From the porch he scanned the valley, the part of it he could see from here, all the while checking the loads in his Colt. His gaze fell on Benjamin's grave.

Benjamin's grave and the rose clipping Ellie had struggled so hard to get started. Since he was here, the least he could do was water it for her.

Drawing water from the well, he walked up the hill. Ellie's presence filled him; her absence . . . her absence was a blessing, he countered, bringing himself back to the present.

The desperate present. Instinct told him to be glad Ellie was well away from this valley tonight.

Instinct, he scoffed, recalling how his sixth sense had deserted him when Holt Rainey confronted him from that cleft in the painted cliffs. Instinct? Or stupidity?

He squatted on his heels beneath the old oak tree. Where was Costello? Pulling a blade of grass, he chewed on it and wondered what the hell to do next.

While he contemplated the situation, he surveyed the valley as though he were searching for the proverbial needle in the haystack, alert to any sign of the tunnel or of the man he was fixing to have to face.

The evening star came out. He rolled a smoke and leaned his head back, watching the fire at the end of the cigarette glow in the deepening dusk. Then an idea came to him.

Same old trick, he thought as he made his way back to the house, watered the bay, and headed out for Summer Valley. Once over the hill, he cut back, passed the cave where Rainey's men had camped, and picketed the bay in a grove of trees on the opposite side of Plum Creek from the house.

If Costello hadn't retrieved the treasure, Kale felt his plan had a fair chance of working. The last time he play-acted leaving the ranch was with the Rainey hands. Likely Costello didn't know about it.

If he didn't, and if he were here—a hell of a lot of ifs for Kale's mind—the gambler might come out in the open and try to finish the job. It was a longshot, but maybe . . .

Kale stationed himself in a thick stand of scrub oak from which he had a good view of the creek and house.

The moon was a mere sliver, a crescent, and the night grew dark. Kale thought he had never seen so many fireflies for this time of year. He was reminded of the game they played as kids, catching fireflies to keep in jars filled with grass.

He yawned. The events of the past few days were fast catching up with him. His body was exhausted, and he became drowsy. Several times he caught his head dropping to his chest, then bobbing back up. Once when he shook himself awake, the lights by the creek seemed to flare up, then as quickly die down.

He came fully awake. What had he seen? Had it been merely more fireflies, seen through eyes only half awake? He waited, scarcely breathing. Not half a minute later, the light flared again across the creek and down a good ways.

This time he knew what he saw: someone was trying to strike sulfur matches. His plan had worked.

The night was pitch dark now, and Kale made his way mostly by sound. He crossed the creek where water gurgled and trickled over rocks above the pond, which itself wasn't more than four or five feet deep this time of year. After a good rain, though, it would run higher, he knew.

In front of him, not thirty yards away, the shape of the house stood out a shade blacker than the night. Off to his left he saw the still smoldering embers and smelled the

411

acrid odor of burning hair and flesh from the branding Matt Rainey had done this day.

He tried to align himself with the house and judge exactly where the tunnel might run.

Fireflies still flitted, and crickets chirped their messages back and forth across the creek. A bullfrog karoomped from a lily pad. Kale thought of Ellie, standing there in that green silk thing, letting it fall to the ground.

Then he knew where to look.

Easing himself into the cold water, he shuddered when it reached his skin. He held his gun above water with one hand and groped his way along the edge of the bank with the other, searching for an opening well above the water level, but still covered by the growth of lilies.

That was the only place he hadn't searched during daylight, and he decided it would be a logical place, allowing the residents of the house to escape to the lower side of the embankment, swim across the creek, and come up in the weeds on the other side.

Logical, but probably wrong, he thought as he searched back and forth in the matted lilies with no luck.

Then, just when he began to wonder whether he'd seen the light at all, he got a whiff of sulfur, and a new sound rang through the night air. It seemed to come from the earth itself. It was followed by several more blows.

Striving to steady his racing emotions, Kale located the tunnel just under the crest of the embankment at the base of the cottonwood tree. The slab of limestone where Ellie had placed his clothes—an event that seemed as if it must have happened years ago instead of only a few weeks—stood white in the surrounding darkness. Something about it looked wrong.

The slab still partially covered the mouth of the tunnel, which was probably as far as Costello had been able to budge it from its place among the exposed roots of the tree. Kale recalled sitting on the slab that wretched night his brothers had decided to draw straws for Ellie. And how many times before and since had he walked past it on his way to bathe? Never had he suspected a thing.

He was still dripping wet from wading through the lilies. Before entering the black hole in the ground, he checked his handgun and wished his shot-up leg wasn't so stiff. With his left hand he grabbed hold of the cottonwood tree to swing himself into the tunnel.

The trunk was oddly cool to his touch. The thin brown bark curled beneath his hand; he felt the smooth trunk beneath, which he knew to be white—alive. Suddenly he felt very tired.

All he wanted was to live in peace with Ellie, but inside this tunnel was a man who would not allow that. Inside this tunnel was the man who had killed his brother, who had badly abused Ellie, both physically and emotionally. And Kale had no doubt that Costello would kill both Ellie and himself unless he were stopped now.

Like it or not, this was one last hurdle he had to overcome before either of them could live in safety again.

Kale gave the tree an affectionate pat, hoping he'd come out of this hole in the ground as alive and well as he'd been going into it, and dropped himself gingerly into the tunnel.

A few feet inside he found standing room. A pinpoint of light showed ahead; the echo of the pick rang clear.

Shadows from a stubby miner's candle danced against the wall. Costello was hard at work. The air was musty, hot. Kale fought the urge to break and run for fresh air.

He made his way carefully. When he was within twenty yards of the light, he saw that Costello had done an enormous amount of work.

The second branch of the tunnel, which he'd found sealed off before, was now dug out for three or four feet, the debris piled against the trap door. Clever . . . it appeared as a cave-in from above and would not be likely to attract anyone's curiosity, unless that person had reason to be suspicious.

Suddenly, as he watched, Costello's shadow dropped to the ground. Kale heard the sound of metal struggling with metal, then Costello's voice, guttural but clear.

"*¡Madre de Dios!* I have found it!"

Kale stopped short. As he did so, his foot struck a loose stone and sent it rolling. He froze where he stood, his gun aimed toward the flickering shadows.

"I'm here to take you in, Costello. Come along peaceable."

Instantly the candle was extinguished. Kale fired twice at the opening. His shots ricocheted off the metal spike where the candle had been secured and thudded into the rock wall.

His thoughts came fast and furious. What did that opening look like? How far back did it go? What chance did he have of hitting Costello in the dark?

He had lost his advantage of surprise. If he fired now he'd only show Costello where to aim that bowie knife.

Kale recalled the story told throughout the West about Jim Bowie's fight in the dark warehouse in New Orleans. Thing was, Bowie's opponent had used a sword which sang through the air, giving away his position. It had been a matter of waiting for the man's patience to wear thin, for his nerves to snap. And Jim Bowie had had his knife.

Here in this dank tunnel, Kale faced a different situation. He had a handgun, and somewhere in the bitter darkness Costello had the Bowie knife.

Kale had used his six-guns so often he hadn't realized how much he depended on them for protection. Now, with the advantage of light removed, he felt naked, vulnerable.

Right then and there, he made up his mind about two things: nerves were not going to get the best of him, and Costello wasn't going to get him in the back.

With that decided, he placed his back squarely against the wall and began to inch his way forward along it. Costello might get him, but it would be face to face. That way, he would get off enough shots to take the gambler with him. He had no intention of leaving the man alive to seek out Ellie.

His ears strained for any sound. He breathed deeply and slowly, trying to still his pounding heart. All his senses were alert for the presence of another body. He knew when the moment came, it would be only a moment, no more. The first man to sense the other would have the edge, however slight. He reckoned it would be plumb foolish to figure on either of them leaving this tunnel untouched.

The flesh along his back quivered as he took yet another step. His movement made some sound, yet Costello would make the same sound.

That was what Kale awaited. A sound, any sound. He would point and fire . . . and keep firing, trying to stop Costello before that knife could be thrown. He wished for

415

two guns—twelve shots. Instead of six, and only four of them remaining.

He had the overwhelming feeling of being entombed. If he was killed here, if Costello escaped—or was killed along with him—this tunnel would become their tomb.

It was impossible for him to judge how far he had moved. The darkness obliterated all sense of distance.

He stopped to listen, then took another step.

The knife struck suddenly. Kale moved forward. His left hand clutched at the handle, at the hand holding the handle, gripping the wrist, pushing it backward.

His right hand shoved the Colt into his opponent; raising the muzzle, he fired through the body which bore down upon him. He fired again and again and again.

He fired until the gun clicked empty. The body fell backward, pulling Kale along. A deep burning in his side raced down his body, and he collapsed on top of the other man.

How long he lay there, he didn't know. When his mind began to function once more, he became aware of something wet and remembered wading in the creek. Hands on the ground to either side of his body, he pushed himself up. The knife was still in his side, and his arms were so weak he had trouble removing it. Once it was out, fresh blood flowed into his hand.

Stuffing his shirttail in the wound, he held a hand over it and tried to stand up, but pressure, as of two giant hands on his shoulders, bore down on him. His legs wobbled; two steps later he fell flat on his face.

When he came to again, his one thought was to get out of this hole in the ground. He must see how badly he was wounded, and he must not die in this tunnel.

But he was so weak he couldn't stand again, so he ended up half crawling, half dragging himself toward the creek.

How many times he collapsed, he couldn't say, but when he finally awoke, his body was draped over the roots of the cottonwood tree. Cool, fresh air filled his lungs and bathed his damp, hot body.

The night was still dark, but it looked much lighter since he'd been inside the tunnel. Kale dragged himself along the bank to a place near the springhouse where the creek bubbled through the rocks, and where he knew, if he passed out, at least he wouldn't be likely to drown.

His wounded side throbbed with every beat of his heart. Finally, while passing back and forth from consciousness to unconsciousness, he managed to remove his shirt and wash his wound.

The slash was wicked, no doubt about it. It started with just a scratch at his heart, then became an ugly gash below that point for a good five inches down his side. He was unable to tell whether anything vital had been damaged. Time would take care of that.

He found some dried grass within reach, which he stuffed into the wound to try to stop the flow of blood. Then he wrapped his shirt around his makeshift bandage and tied it as tightly as he could manage. He had seen enough wounds to know he was in trouble. Unless he got help soon, he wasn't likely to be around come sunup.

He thought of the bay staked across the creek. He couldn't cross the creek, but if he could make it up the hill, he could ride the packhorse to town.

But right now he had to rest. He was so tired . . . in a while, he promised himself, he would crawl up the hill.

Then he would saddle the horse and get to town. After a while. Right now, he had to rest.

When he opened his eyes again, the morning sun shone brightly through bare branches overhead. As he awakened more fully, he became aware of a burning pain which radiated from his wounded side, penetrating all parts of his body.

Then he heard the sound which had awakened him. Footsteps . . . someone was walking down the path to the creek. He listened. Two steps, a pause. Three steps, a pause. Whoever it was was looking for something . . . or for someone.

Vaguely he recalled the previous day: he'd been alone out here except for Armando Costello. Alarm spread through his pain-wracked body when he tried to rise, to reach for his guns. Now both were missing.

He looked around again to get his bearings. He was lying in back of the springhouse on rocks beside the water. As soon as that person rounded the corner, Kale would be in plain sight.

The footsteps came closer and stopped, and then a voice called. "Jarrett? Are you around here someplace? Jarrett?"

The voice sounded vaguely familiar.

"Jarrett?" The man called again.

It wasn't Costello. Maybe it was help. Surely even Matt Rainey wouldn't let a man die in his own blood. He tried to call out, but a wave of blackness engulfed him.

When the voice called again it was closer, and Kale opened his eyes to see Snake's furrowed brow.

"Well, I'll be damned!" Snake gave a low whistle through his teeth. "Miss Ellie! Come a-running." He grinned at Kale through those awful tobacco-stained teeth. Only at this moment, Snake's teeth looked pearly white. "Is the other feller as bad off as you?"

Kale managed a feeble smile. "Worse, I hope."

Snake knelt beside Kale to get a closer look at his wound, while Kale's ears attuned themselves to the trail, listening for footsteps.

For Ellie's footsteps.

"You know womenfolk," Snake was saying. "Nothing would do for Miss Ellie but that we ride out here and have a look-see. And danged if she wasn't right."

Kale smiled again, then he passed out still listening for Ellie's footsteps.

Epilogue

It took three weeks for Kale to recover. He had lost a lot of blood, but as Lavender told Ellie, Costello's Bowie knife hadn't damaged anything necessary to life, limb, or the pursuit of happiness.

When Snake and Ellie found him, Kale was still bleeding, and Ellie had been afraid to move him any farther than the house.

After she spread a clean sheet on the bed in the spare room, she had Snake lay him there. While she cleansed and dressed his wound, then fixed him broth, she sent Snake back to town for Doc Lowell.

Kale passed out again while the doc sewed him up, and it was a week before he realized where he was.

Lavender and Poppy rode out the next day, bringing food and medicines. Although Lavender tried to persuade Ellie to return to Summer Valley with her patient, Ellie refused. She never wanted to leave home again . . . especially not now, with everything settled, with Kale here beside her.

Poppy stayed on to help out until Ellie's ankle healed.

After Lavender drove away in her surrey, Poppy produced the package containing the red costume, complete with net stockings, silk shoes, and a feather for her hair.

When Kale began gradually to come around, Ellie told him the story.

"Snake found Armando," she said. "He followed your trail of blood to the tunnel." Even with Kale recovering, it made her insides go queasy to think back on that horrible morning and the long days after, when she was so afraid he would not live.

She sat in a chair beside his bed, and when he patted the sheet, she hobbled over and sat next to him, holding his hand as she had every day.

"It was so dark, I didn't know whether I'd killed him or not," Kale told her. Ellie's face went pale.

"You killed him, all right," she answered. "Snake buried him in town. I didn't want his body on this place."

Kale dozed off again, and when he came to, she was saying something about the treasure. Then he recalled Costello's last words.

"He found it?" Kale asked.

Ellie nodded. "It was probably a disappointment, not the sort of thing he had in mind all those years, but he could have sold it for a good sum, I suppose."

"What was it?"

"Relics from the old Spanish mission outside town," she explained. "He found a trunk full of religious articles and a pair of iron mission bells. The letter inside the trunk from Father Terreros was dated January 1, 1758. The priest in Summer Valley translated it for us. Father Terreros wrote that he was sending the trunk and the bells to the mission on the Guadalupe River by supply train, under the protection of a man named Lieutenant Juan Galván."

"Why were they buried here?" Kale asked.

Ellie shrugged. "No one in Summer Valley even knew they were missing. The mission was destroyed by a combined force of Comanches and Apaches in March of that year. Father Terreros was murdered, along with almost everyone else. The supply train may have been attacked by Indians, too, and Lieutenant Galván could have buried the treasure."

Kale nodded. "Then he drew up a plat to lead authorities to the site at a safer time. The plat got filed away and was later given to Costello's grandfather, like the story goes. Only that doesn't explain how Galván was fortunate enough to be attacked beside a tunnel."

"Maybe the tunnel came later," Ellie laughed. "We'll never know the truth of it, but I'm glad to have the relics out of our lives."

"What did you do with them?"

"Gave them to the priest in Summer Valley. He'll contact his bishop, who'll decide where they belong."

In the next week Ellie's ankle healed, and Kale's side and leg did the same. He regained his strength bit by bit.

Ira and Till came over and helped with rebranding the Jarrett cattle. Poppy went back to town with Snake, and things settled back into the normal routine.

One afternoon when Kale went to the creek to bathe, Ellie remembered the dress . . . Poppy's flirty red dress.

On impulse she tore into the package, and before she took time to think, she slipped it on, laced it up, and donned the black net stockings and red silk shoes. When the back door squawked she crossed to the doorway of their bedroom, formerly the spare room, holding the feather in her hand.

She recalled how at the Lady Bug she had expected the skimpy bodice of the dress to fall down. This time she was certain that her bosom was about to fall out.

Kale turned from setting aside a bucket of water and saw her. His eyes swept her with such intensity, riveting at length on the bulging mounds of her breasts, that she looked down to be sure.

"By damn!" he whistled, crossing the room in three strides. "You're a sight for sore eyes."

She laughed.

His hands spanned her corseted waist, slipped slowly up her satin-encased rib cage. A groan escaped his lips. His eyes never left hers.

"It feels the way I dreamed," he whispered. His fingers found the black lace ruffle shielding her nipples. "Only better."

She was barely able to stand still when the tips of his fingers dipped below the lace, tantalizing her already aching breasts.

Longingly she ran her hands through his hair, stroked his forehead, whispered her fingers over his cheeks. Their eyes held.

He lowered his lips, meeting hers halfway in a kiss that flooded her with longing . . . intense, sweet longing.

Long denied, Kale's passion had gone from scratch to start in the length of time it took him to cross the room. Now, with her in his arms, pressed to his aching heart, his lips delved into her sweetness with the sure knowledge that his passion was fixing to reach its zenith any minute.

His hands swept up and down her back, pressing her closer to him with every stroke. Wads of silk bunched in his hands as he fumbled to feel her, all of her, close to

424

him, ever closer. When his hands touched bare skin beneath the skirt, he grinned.

"There's something to be said for painted ladies' clothing," he murmured, gripping her buttocks in his palms. "Or lack of it."

The bodice of the red silk gown was actually no more than a corset with black lacings up the front. When Kale pulled her to his chest, the bulge of her breasts pressed seductively against his shirt. Dampness left over from his recent bath seeped through his shirt, enticing her.

Lost in his kisses, in her own heightening passion, she wriggled against him as he began to lift her body against his own, upwards . . . upwards, until finally her breasts worked free of their nest of silk and lace and nuzzled in all their nudity against his chest.

When he realized the soft mounds of her breasts had climbed his chest like roses on a trailing vine, he lifted her once more, until her legs wrapped snugly around his waist, then he dipped his face toward her breasts.

"Your wound," she gasped, feeling his lips close over one breast, reveling in the wave of sheer passion that washed over her.

"My wound is healed," he mumbled against her.

"Not enough."

"More than enough." He turned toward the bedroom, carrying her in the same position. "I may be ready for bed, but for a different reason now."

"Wait."

His face was pressed into the cleft between her breasts. He glanced up at her face without breaking stride. "Wait?"

"I hear something."

He frowned, but listened along with her to sounds

coming from outside the house. It didn't take long to identify them.

"A wagon," she sighed.

"Who the hell . . . ?" His words died away in the babble of female chatter.

"Lavender," Ellie broke in. She slid to her feet and they both retreated to the bedroom. Ellie tucked her bosom back into the scanty bodice. "What could she want?"

"From the sound of things, she's brought her entire household." He clasped Ellie's face in his hands, kissed her quickly on the lips. "Don't suppose you could get rid of them so we could get on with what we started?"

She smiled ruefully. "Not soon. It's a long way out here from town."

Dropping his hands, Kale began to work to rearrange his own clothing. When Ellie saw what he was about, she laughed.

"Go ahead and laugh. You got me into this fix. Think I'll head for the creek and soak in that cold water till they leave."

Ellie reached for one last kiss. "If you go to the creek . . . don't stay *too long*." She blushed at her own words, recalling how on the way back from the painted cliffs he'd said cold water kept him from being able to make love to her.

His teasing eyes told her he remembered as well. "You can bet on it." He didn't let her forget it for the rest of the evening. Every so often, when she least expected it, he'd come up behind her and whisper in her ear.

"I decided not to go to the creek, Ellie."

And she'd blush and turn quickly away, her train of thought temporarily broken.

426

Only once during the long afternoon did he not even think of jesting. That was when the parson Lavender had brought along—who was, of course, her sole reason for coming—pronounced them man and wife in front of the fireplace with Ellie's fancy photograph on the mantel.

"Man and wife, Mr. and Mrs. Jarrett. You may kiss the bride, sir."

Kale took her in his arms, stared long and tenderly into her misty eyes. "Mrs. *Kale* Jarrett," he prompted the parson.

"Mr. and Mrs. Kale Jarrett," the parson corrected.

Whereupon Kale lowered his lips and kissed her with just enough fervor to assure her he hadn't forgotten where they'd left off earlier.

Earlier, before Lavender Sealy had taken things in hand to get them married proper-like.

Later, after the ceremony, after the champagne, after their guests—painted ladies and parson alike—had departed, Kale caught Ellie's hands just as she began to remove that devastating dress.

"Let me," he whispered in a voice too husky to disguise his passion. Taking the black lace in his large fingers, he stared deeply into her eyes. "I've wanted to undo these damned ties ever since that first time I saw you in this getup."

Slowly, seductively, he began to undo the laces. Beneath it lay nothing but bare skin, heated skin that cried for his touch.

"Wonder what in the world Parson James thought about my dress," she mused.

Kale grinned. "If it was half what any other red-blooded hombre would think, I'm glad the sonofabitch is gone."

427

"Kale! You shouldn't call him that. He's a man of the cloth!"

Kale's eyes gleamed, following the silky red dress as it fell to the floor. "And you, Mrs. Kale Jarrett, are now a woman *out* of the cloth."

She stood stock-still except for the rise and fall of her bosom. His mood changed suddenly from playful to serious—serious, and sensual. She could tell by his eyes that he wanted her—wanted to touch her and feel her and taste her and love her.

At length she reached for his shirt. And when he was finally undressed and standing opposite her, she knew he could read the same things in her eyes.

Then she saw the scars—all of them. She had seen them before, but never all at once. At one time on his now healthy body, they told a story of death and betrayal that brought instant tears to her eyes.

She touched the scar on his head where Abe and Martin had tried to kill him; moving her hand, she stroked his newest scar, which ran a good five inches from just below his heart; then she stooped and touched the scar on his leg where Holt Rainey had shot him the day he escaped by throwing himself into the grape vines.

Her heart throbbed with the renewed knowledge that she almost lost him.

Bending, he grasped her shoulders and brought her up to face him. "None of that, honey. We agreed to put it all behind us."

"I know, but—"

He tipped her chin so she looked into his loving eyes. "I almost forgot my wedding gift, Mrs. Kale Jarrett."

"Wedding gift?"

Taking her gently by the hand, he led her across the room, both of them naked as the day they were born, where he opened the trunk and pointed to his guns.

"Had you missed them?" he quizzed.

"I thought you were waiting until your side healed," she whispered.

He shook his head. Then taking a lock from inside the trunk, he closed the lid and locked it. Straightening, he handed her the key. "I've put them up for good, Ellie. Or until together we decide I need to take them out. Lord willing, that day will never come."

She stared at the key resting in the palm of her hand. A tear fell on it.

"You have *two* keys that belong to you alone." He took her hand and placed it over his heart. "The other one fits here." His tone lightened. "Now, can we get back to the business we started several hours ago?"

Much later, when they lay in the dark in each other's arms, he nudged her forehead with his lips to see if she was awake.

"What?" she responded.

"I'm glad Lavender protected you from the seamy side of things around the Lady Bug—for more than just the obvious reasons."

"Why?"

He pulled her close, nuzzled her seductively, and chuckled against her. "You blushed when you mentioned . . . ah, the effect cold water has on me."

"So?"

The room was pitch dark; she could *see* only by feel. When he kissed her lips, she raised her hands and traced his face, kissing him in return. She let her hand drift down his chest, play in the furry hair.

429

He nuzzled her face with his own. "So, I'm glad ther are still some things I can teach you myself."

She held him close, knowing she loved him more tha she had ever dreamed a person could love. She laughe softly. "Are you accusing me of being naive—me, wh was raised in a house of painted ladies?"

He nipped her nose with his lips. "The gunfighter an the floozy . . . look at us now." Suddenly the power o his love for her gripped him with such force it brough moisture to his eyes. He tightened his arms about her.

The gunfighter and the floozy, he mused. Neither one o them had amounted to much after all. They were just cowpoke and his lady; they always had been. And nov she was Mrs. Kale Jarrett. And he was the luckiest man alive.

Author's Note

The painted cliffs of this story are located in Concho County, Texas, near the town of Paint Rock. Although the cliffs are on private property, they may be viewed by arrangement with the owners.

The "old Spanish mission" is in reality the Mission San Sabá, located outside the town of Menard, Texas, my hometown. The mission was destroyed by Indians, as related here, in March, 1758. The religious articles were indeed shipped under the charge of a Lieutenant Galván; they have not been located to this day.

Neither has the Lost Bowie Mine been found, although folks still search diligently for it. Every fall the city of Menard hosts "Jim Bowie Days," a festival honoring James Bowie and the mystique of treasure hunting.

An interesting development occurred in November, 1989, when U.S. Customs agents seized a million-dollar oil painting from a rare-book dealer. This painting, entitled *The Destruction of Mission San Sabá*, was commissioned in 1758 by relatives of the slain Father Terreros to commemorate the massacre in which he lost his life. Based on an eyewitness account, the painting considered by scholars to be the most important Texas historical painting in existence. Until the Customs Service settles the case, the painting is on loan to the Museum of Fine Arts in Houston, Texas, where it can be viewed.

Further information concerning the above-mentioned sites may be obtained from the respective Chambers of Commerce or from the State Department of Highways and Public Transportation, 1101 East Anderson Lane, Austin, TX 78752.

A special note of thanks to my special friend Elaine Raco Chase, for discovering and "giving" to me the true story of the pirates Anne Bonny and Calico Jack. We will meet them again in a later book.

This book is the first of several involving Jarrett family members and friends. The next story will feature Carson Jarrett, Kale's Texas Ranger brother, and Jarrett's friend, Santos Mazón. Santos's sister, Aurelia, gives Carson a run for his money in a spicy story set in the mountains of Northern Mexico during the opulent silver mining days.

All these stories will feature settings which you can visit later, either in person or vicariously through additional reading.